# CAT PURPLE

*in*

## *Grosse Pointe*

to Cristina & José-Luis
with affection
and gratitude

JC.

# CAT PURPLE

*in*

## Grosse Pointe

*J C Di Musto*

*I…am a jealous God*
*visiting the iniquity of the fathers*
*upon the children*
*unto the third and fourth generation.*

EXODUS 20:5

*Cat purple will catch no mice,*
*Cat purple will feed on blood.*

KHA CHILDREN PLAY-SONG

# Copyright © 2005 by J.C. DiMusto

ISBN 0-7414-2517-3

Contact the author at catpurpleingp@aol.com
Editing by James R. Coggins
Book Design by Fiona Raven

**Published by:**

**INFINITY**
PUBLISHING.COM

*1094 New DeHaven Street, Suite 100*
*West Conshohocken, PA 19428-2713*
*Info@buybooksontheweb.com*
*www.buybooksontheweb.com*
*Toll-free (877) BUY BOOK*
*Local Phone (610) 941-9999*
*Fax (610) 941-9959*

*Printed in the United States of America*

*Printed on Recycled Paper*

*Published April 2005*

*This book is dedicated*
*with awesome reverence*
*to all women*
*who ever consented to shelter and feed*
*a stranger inside their bodies*
*for ten lunar months.*

# FACTS

The placenta is a remarkable organ. It takes form, develops into a large, complex structure, engages in intricate biologic processes and becomes senescent in a nine-month period. During that time it serves as a means of interchange of many substances between the fetal and maternal blood streams. It has many activities which are in part comparable to those of the gastrointestinal, respiratory, circulatory and urinary tracts. It is an active biochemical laboratory in which endocrine substances and enzymes are produced.

HUFFMAN,
*Gynecology and Obstetrics*

You, afterbirth, do not say that I do not love you; we love you. Do not tickle the soles of the feet of your little brother and do not pinch his stomach.

TORADJA (CELEBES ISLAND) RITUAL.
ADRIANI AND KRUYT,
*The Bare'e Speaking Toradja*

Several cases of human neonatal graft-versus-host disease have been reported, presenting either with the typical signs of runting or with severe combined immunodeficiency.

IAN L. SARGEANT,
*The Human Placenta,* CHAPTER 6

People of Tikopia, Oceania left the placenta of female babies outdoors overnight. The next morning, certain objects were observed "moving and crawling within the placenta." These objects, "ururu atua," manifestations of Feke—the Octopus Deity—were buried separately.

R. FIRTH, "CEREMONIES FOR
CHILDREN IN TIKOPIA,"
*Oceania*, VOLUME 27

The placenta has enormous genetic endowment, comparable to those of the brain and ovary....Thus, the placenta can be viewed as the third brain, which links the developed (maternal) and developing (fetal) brain.

SAMUEL S.C. YEN,
*Journal of Reproductive Medicine*, 1994

According to population researcher A. Bitties at the University of Michigan, currently at least 10 percent of the world's population, more than 500 million people, are married to close relatives.

*Michigan Medicine*, SEPTEMBER 1990

Anyone can deliver a baby,
but it is the placenta which kills.

A BARIBA MIDWIFE,
QUOTED BY C. SARGEANT,
*Anthropology of Human Birth*

This is a work of fiction. Any resemblance to persons living or dead is purely coincidental.

# Acknowledgments

I owe gratitude to my book designer, Fiona Raven, for her cover artwork and for the visual appeal of the book; to my editor, James R. Coggins, for his meticulous editing job; and to my wife, children, sons-in-law and many friends who gallantly fought the temptation to dissuade me from this senile folly.

## CHAPTER I

# Postpartum

An excerpt from the statement that Sister Mary Redempta, Administrator, read to the Board of Trustees of Our Lady of Lourdes Hospital of Grosse Pointe, Michigan at the emergency meeting convened on 5 February, 1970:

"This country enjoys personal and institutional freedoms and a standard of living unparalleled in the history of humankind. In order to preserve these privileges, certain secret interventions of Federal Agencies must be accepted in situations where, in their judgment, the long-term implications to national security make it inappropriate to share the information with the average citizen.

"Therefore, you should read no criticism in this report, implied or explicit, of the performance of Military Intelligence or their Bestiary Encounter Team as it relates to the incident in Delivery Room Five.

"Those men carried out with impeccable professionalism the instructions given them by a high authority.

"We deeply regret that human lives were lost in the incident.

"We are, of course, very saddened by the loss of our dear co-workers, and our deepest sympathy goes to their families.

"Now you will hear a very detailed chronicle of the actual events that took place early Sunday morning in Delivery Room Five.

"Any questions that you might have—and, you must know, they are not encouraged— should be addressed to the Public Relations Department of the Army USA-TACOM in Warren at 555-3300.

"Thank you for your cooperation."

## CHAPTER II

# The Second Stage of Labor

Leslie, a veteran nurse of the night shift in Labor and Delivery, picked up the telephone on the desk and dialed extension 225.

Dr. Clareby picked up the receiver in the OB sleeping quarters. "Hello," he said in a voice still scratchy from sleep.

"Is Dr. Irving there?" Leslie asked.

"Let me see," laconically but politely Dr. Clareby replied. "Dr. Irving is not here," he added after checking the other beds. His voice reflected the chronic fatigue of years of interrupted sleep.

"We'll be taking his patient to the delivery room soon. D'you know where he might be?"

Dr. Irving's ability to disappear was legendary.

"It's not my week to watch him," Dr. Clareby answered semi-jokingly and hung up. Before his head hit the pillow, he was asleep again.

Leslie shrugged her shoulders. It was all right to wait a while, providing he was in the hospital.

Since Mrs. Truong had been admitted in active labor, Leslie decided to complete the ritual of opening for her a delivery room. The process of "opening a delivery room" was not difficult, but tedious. It involved first checking that the room had been properly cleaned after the previous delivery and then fetching and arranging the instruments, the sterile drapes and all the other paraphernalia that were required for the usual delivery, taking into account the whimsical preferences of each obstetrician.

In full OR attire, scrubs, mask and cap, Leslie unwrapped a large rectangular package and placed it in the center of the instrument table that was stationed to the right of where the obstetrician would sit. She checked that the heat-sensitive tape that sealed the package had turned color, indicating that it had been properly sterilized; she tore the tape and opened the package. Being very careful to touch only the edges with the tips of her fingers, she discarded the fabric and gently set the inner, sterile package on the table. She pulled the corners of the green cloth that wrapped the package and let them hang over the sides of the table; thus, she created a large sterile field, with the tray and its contents in the middle. She then moved to a round package that sat on a stand with wheels, the ring-stand, and rolled it to the foot of the delivery table, to the left of where the doctor would sit. She opened the wrapper of the round package, letting the edges drape the base of the stand and exposing a large stainless steel basin that would later be filled with sterile water. Then she checked a small stand that was by the entrance of the delivery room holding the necessary supplies for the usual delivery: cotton balls, a spray bottle of Betadine paint, cord clamps, a box of DeLee's mucous traps to suck the secretions of the newborn, wax vials that contained the silver nitrate to treat the newborn's eyes, inkpads for the foot-printings and the name bracelets with pockets for the identification labels. She opened the glass door of a built-in cabinet and took out two pairs of sterile surgical gloves, size eight for the doctor and size six-and-a-half for herself, and several packs of sutures. She closed the door and moved to the large table with the rectangular tray. She opened the outer wrapper of the gloves and folded it back, without touching the inner paper wrapper that was sterile; then she tossed them onto the table. After removing the sutures from their sealed envelopes, she did the same with them. From the little stand by the door she had taken an orange plastic bag that contained four test tubes for collecting the blood from the umbilical cord; she dropped that onto the table as well.

She had performed all these tasks in the correct order without thinking, because she had learned how to do them a long time ago; once one learns how to walk, it is not necessary to think which muscle to move next.

Yet, she had also learned to check one more time. She moved her eyes all over the table to be sure that everything that was routinely needed was on it. With the sterile technique that she had painstakingly learned in the operating room, she deftly gloved herself and returned to the delivery table. She began to remove the instruments from the rectangular tray and lay them on the table in the order that Dr. Irving preferred: the two Péan clamps for the umbilical cord by the sterile gloves, the Mayo scissors for cutting the cord and the plastic cord clamps in the left far corner. These self-locking disposable clamps would replace the Péan clamps on the umbilical cord before the newborn was passed to the nurse. The other hardware that was seldom used she laid at the back of the table. The stainless steel container, which was then empty, she set on the other far corner of the table; it would be used for the placenta. Next to it she placed the receiving blanket for wrapping the baby.

Another visual check: Now Leslie was satisfied that the table was ready. She covered it with a sterile sheet to keep away airborne contaminants. Then she removed her gloves and tossed them into the trash bag. As she was leaving the room, she turned on the Ohio Warmer, an automatic electric heater that stood above the bassinet to keep it at the optimal temperature. The last item she checked was the instrument cabinet to make sure that different types of forceps were available, should they be needed.

She walked out of the room. Delivery Room Five was ready and waiting. It would be considered sterile for eight hours; if it was not used in that time, a fresh pack would have to be opened; that was seldom necessary because the staff was very expert at predicting when a delivery would occur.

Leslie walked to the front desk and asked, "Is Dr. Irving coming from home? You'd better call him."

"No, he was here a while ago to check Mrs. Truong. He said to page him when we needed him," answered Lorraine, the unit secretary. "Do you want me to page him now?"

"No. If he's in the hospital, we can wait."

They exchanged mischievous smiles. "At least he will be in a good mood," added the secretary.

Leslie went to check on Mrs. Truong. The woman had received the Grosse Pointe Storks' favorite cocktail—Demerol, Phenergan and scopolamine—and she was in a blissful slumber between contractions. Leslie inspected the fetal monitor. It was properly connected, and the tracing looked fine.

She left the room. As she passed by the desk, she glanced at the board behind it. The "board" was the chalkboard where the status of every patient in the Labor and Delivery Suite was recorded by the nurses and the doctors as it progressed. A quick look at the board could tell the staff what to expect. That night there were three patients in active labor plus two in observation. One of the latter was a woman with twins at thirty-one weeks of gestation who was receiving an intravenous drip of drugs to stop her premature labor.

Leslie treated herself to a well-deserved break that she knew was not going to be a long one. Diane Truong would go any moment. She walked into the staff room and poured herself a cup of coffee. The old armchair moaned as she dropped her overfed body onto it.

A nurse's aid was looking out the window. "It keeps coming down," she sighed. "They say we already got seven inches."

"I heard we're going to get up to a foot before morning," Leslie responded. "They've closed I-75 north of Flint."

Lorraine and Joyce, the head nurse, walked in together and sat down. "There are two more coming up, and one is pretty active I heard," said Joyce.

"We've already had four deliveries tonight, and the Vietnamese girl will go for sure in our shift," said Leslie. "We've earned our money already."

"What's with that Vietnamese woman?" asked Joyce.

"She's doing fine. Why?" answered Leslie with a surprised look on her face.

"Oh, she doesn't know," said Lorraine. "She was on break when Dr. Santoro called."

"What did she call about?" Leslie sounded alarmed.

"Actually, she called about the twins' mother. I told her she's holding fine and that Dr. Irving had seen her," explained Lorraine. She added rather apologetically, "Then, for some reason, I mentioned to her that Mrs. Truong was in and quite active. She screamed in my ear: 'What? She's not due until next month!' She was panting. She sounded like she was in shock, as if I'd told her that her house was on fire. Big deal, I thought, the woman is thirty-six or thirty-seven weeks."

"You know Dr. Santoro; she's high-strung," said Leslie.

"Now tell her the rest," the head nurse urged Lorraine. "Leslie is her nurse. She should know."

"Dr. Santoro asked about Mrs. Truong's fetal heart tones," said Lorraine. "I had her talk to Judy, who was taking care of her then. Judy told her that they were fine, that every so often the rate'd go up. And then she happened to mention that when the resident was doing a pelvic, the FHT shot up off the chart. That's when Dr. Santoro started to scream, 'Oh, my God, oh my God! I'll be right over. Be very, very careful.' And then she hung up."

"You know, she can be very theatrical sometimes," said Leslie. "Be right over, she said, huh? That was an hour ago."

"There's a blizzard, you know," said Joyce.

"She lives less than a mile away."

"Sorry, I didn't tell you," explained Lorraine. "She said that she was in Ann Arbor."

"In Ann Arbor? Really?" Joyce said. Then, looking at Leslie, she asked, "Did you see anything wrong with Mrs. Truong's monitor tracing?"

"Not really," she answered. "There have been no decelerations. Once in a while the rate jumps up. I believe, though, that it only happens when you play with the transducer on the belly or when she changes positions. But accelerations are a good sign, right? That doesn't mean fetal distress, does it?"

Leslie knew quite well that certain drops in the heart rate, called decelerations, could be a sign of possible fetal distress, but accelerations in general were interpreted as signs of healthy nervous and circulatory systems in the baby. She was just seeking reassurance.

"Dr. Santoro sometimes doesn't seem to have both oars in the water," said the nurse's aid, still looking out the window.

"She is a little melodramatic, at times," stated the head nurse.

"That broad could use a good lay," pronounced Lorraine. She was going through that stage when she believed that most problems could be solved by a good lay.

"We got to find her a mate," volunteered the aid.

"The only male that could've boarded that ship was shot by planes at the Empire State Building," said Lorraine. They all laughed.

Dr. Santoro was frequently the butt of jokes, some quite merciless. She was a big woman with some rough edges and a volatile disposition. No one had ever heard her mention an old boyfriend, and apparently she did not date; at least, she never talked about it. She was barely tolerated by her colleagues, and the nurses, in general, disliked her because she was too demanding; everything had to be how she wanted it to be, or else she screamed or became abusive.

"She is going to miss the delivery, that's for sure," said Joyce. "I saw on channel four, half of the cars on I-94 were in the ditch. It'll take her four hours to come from Ann Arbor tonight, if she makes it at all."

Leslie paced up to the window. The grounds of the hospital looked like a vast white blanket, dotted here and there by little bumps—the roofs of the parked cars. The northeast wind was driving the snow against the side of the building. All was still except for an ambulance with flashing red lights; it was gliding slowly and quietly along Jefferson Road towards the Emergency entrance of Our Lady of Lourdes Hospital. It carried the usual, an old man who should have known better than to shovel the snow.

Leslie and Joyce walked out of the staff room together.

"I love a good snowfall," sighed Joyce. "If only I could stay at home by the fireplace with a beer."

"What the hell did she mean by 'be very, very careful'?" said Leslie, still brooding over Dr. Santoro's cryptic warning.

The head nurse shrugged her shoulders.

The entrance doors to the Delivery Suite swung open; the admitting clerk was wheeling in a new patient.

"Third baby. Dr. Broski. Seems to be quite active," said the clerk.

"Take her to Room Four. No, wait. Six is ready. You doing the wheeling tonight?" said Joyce.

"Two orderlies called in."

"Sissies. Thanks, Rosie."

"Don't thank me as yet. I have another one for you downstairs."

"Are you giving away green stamps down there?" she joked.

Leslie went back to Diane Truong's room. She sat on the

side of the bed, put a glove on her left hand and squeezed some KY jelly onto the tip of her index finger. She asked Diane to raise her legs and to separate her knees. The patient obeyed.

"I think the baby coming," said Diane.

The nurse inserted her finger into the rectum and felt all around. She could feel no cervix left; it had opened completely, and the head of the baby had moved down one notch.

"I think you're right, Diane," Leslie said. "Don't push!" She ran out of the room and yelled: "Seven is going back. Get Dr. Irving."

She returned to the room with a gurney. "Move over, Diane. Quick," she commanded as she started to loosen the straps that held the fetal monitoring equipment. She then transferred the IV bottle from the bed pole to the one on the gurney. Diane had already moved onto it.

As Leslie was negotiating the stretcher through the doorway into the corridor, Diane asked, "Is baby all right?"

"Of course," the nurse replied. She had no reasons to think otherwise. Except for that call from Dr. Santoro...

"Please tell husband I am going to have baby," asked Diane.

As they rushed past the front desk, Leslie repeated Diane's request to Lorraine.

"Be a minute," replied the clerk, "Dr. Youssef's patient started to bleed. He wants two more units on top of the two we already have. I'm paging the resident stat, and I'll call the blood bank first."

"That's fine," yelled Leslie. She was laboriously pushing the double-doors of Delivery Room Five with the foot of the gurney. "Did you get Dr. Irving and anesthesia?"

"They're coming," Lorraine yelled back.

Lorraine had already paged Dr. Irving on his beeper, and then she had called the nurse anesthetist in her room. Lorraine knew that the doctor was with her, and although her first inclination, to save time, was to tell her: "You two, get your asses here right away, we're in a pickle," she phrased it in a more polite way: "Sophie, we need you in Room Five pronto; and if you happen to see Dr. Irving in the cafeteria, tell him to hurry up. It's his patient."

"There," she said to herself with pride. "That was tactful."

Sophie came up first. When she passed by the desk, Lorraine said to her: "Room Five. They also need someone in Two. Who's on second call?"

"Brian is," Sophie answered. "I think he's in the ER." She stopped at the desk to put on her surgical cap, tweaking it until she was sure it sat properly and pushing under it a few strands of her blonde hair. "It can't wait until we finish in Five?" she asked Lorraine.

"No way. They think it's an abruptio, and it began to bleed pretty heavy."

"Call him, then," Sophie said. "I don't think they are too busy in the ER."

She scampered away towards Delivery Room Five. The drab, ill-fitting scrubs she was wearing could not hide her youthful, sensuous figure. She walked with a well-rehearsed, elegant sway that started at the hips and spread to the long legs and to the torso, the whole body gyrating as if reacting to some subtle inner rhythm. Sophie was a very attractive young lady, and she knew it.

Two minutes later, properly distanced from Sophie for appearance's sake, Dr. Irving walked by the desk. He gave Lorraine a perfunctory smile. "Which room?" he asked.

The telephone receiver by her ear, Lorraine raised her hand with all her fingers spread out.

When Lorraine finished her urgent chores, she walked to the "Heirport"—that's what Sister Redempta had named the maternity waiting room. Mr. Truong was slouched on a couch in the far corner of the room, snoring softly. Lorraine gently tapped him on the shoulder. "They're taking your wife to the delivery room," she said quietly.

A little startled, the man sprang up. "Diane all right?" he asked.

"She is fine," Lorraine said with a smile. "Would you like a cup of coffee?"

He shook his head. Then he bowed and said "Thank you" many times.

Mr. Truong, Diane's husband, was a thin, short Oriental man about Lorraine's height—five-foot-five, probably. From what she could see, he seemed quite muscular. He was wearing jeans and a white tee-shirt with the GM logo under a light blue jacket. When he smiled at her, he showed a perfect set of white teeth. Lorraine noticed that the smile was mostly a mouth effort; the rest of the face did not contribute. His eyes, although small, were quite vivacious, but they did not join in the smile effort either. One of his eyes had something peculiar, Lorraine noticed, but she could not tell exactly what it was. She smiled back at him. "We'll let you know as soon as the baby is born," she said and rushed back to her station.

Dr. Irving stopped at the double door of Delivery Room Five. A sign on the door read "PUSH—DON'T PUSH—PUSH—DON'T PUSH"—another brainchild of Sister Redempta's. He raised the straps of his face mask and walked in. Sophie was already at the head of the table and had placed the mask on Diane's face; with every contraction, Diane received a welcome dose of nitrous oxide.

"Enough to take off the edge of the pain, not enough to depress the baby," Sophie kept repeating softly in Diane's ear.

The sight of the doctor was the cue for the nurses to coach Diane to "bear down." Leslie and Sophie began to shout as enthusiastically as cheerleaders: "Push, Diane, push!" That's what Diane would have been doing for the last ten minutes if she had not been sternly advised against it.

Dr. Irving returned to the room through the side door, already scrubbed and putting on his gown. Leslie tied him in the back, and he sat silently between the legs of the parturient that hung from the candy cane holders.

It was one forty-five in the morning. "Normal people are in bed sleeping. What was I thinking when I chose this business?" the doctor asked himself, as he had done many times before in that situation at that particular time of the night. "It made the old man happy, I suppose, and I make a decent living," he answered.

"Push!" yelled Leslie.

"Push, push, push," echoed Sophie.

"Now, Diane, push," commanded the doctor.

"Relax. The contraction is over. Save your energy for the next one," instructed Leslie. "You're doing just fine, Diane."

"How much more?" Diane asked in her slumber.

The doctor drove a small needle into her perineum that had been thinned out by the pressure of the baby's head. "Ouuu!" Diane responded. He then injected a generous amount of Xylocaine to anesthetize the area of the episiotomy. As the fetal head retracted after the contraction, he inserted one jaw of the Mayo scissors inside the birth canal between the head of the fetus and the perineum. He closed the jaws in one deliberate motion. The cut was smooth and straight, exactly in the midline; blood spurted from both sides of the incision. He applied pressure with a sponge and swiped away some stool that had trickled out while she was pushing. The next contraction was building up.

"Push more?" said Diane, semi-conscious.

"Yes, this is it. Push, push, push...Take a deep breath and push...Don't you dare let up."

"Go, girl, go. Give it all you got."

In the opening of Diane's vagina, a luscious mat of black hair began to show as a small circle that grew while she pushed. The circle soon turned into an ovoid that shrank and stretched with the flow and ebb of Diane's straining. The black hair was now tinged red with the mother's blood.

Crowning, it is called. In a normal labor, the fetal head is extremely flexed during the descent through the birth canal. When the occiput—the base of the back of the skull—comes to rest under the pubic bone, the head begins to extend, and the forehead appears first through the opening, followed by the nose, then the chin. Diane's delivery, to this point, had followed the book. As soon as the nostrils became visible, the doctor inserted the tip of a rubber syringe and suctioned the baby's secretions to clear the breathing passages. With his other hand fully stretched, he applied pressure on the perineum to protect it from tearing.

"Stop now," he commanded aloud. "Don't push any more."

After the mouth appeared, the chin followed rather quickly. At this point, the accoucheur always tries to avoid an explosive delivery of the head that can cause major tearing of the tissues, but it is very difficult for the parturient to control the reflex urge to push produced by the pressure on the perineum.

Once the head was outside completely, the doctor, his fingers straddling the baby's neck, pushed the head straight down towards the floor to liberate the shoulder from under the pubic bone. The head turned a little, and the anterior shoulder was out. Now the rest of the body came out as smoothly as toothpaste from a tube being squeezed. It slid along the doctor's cradling arm.

"It's a boy!" Leslie yelled. "Congratulations, Diane. You have a beautiful baby boy."

The newborn did not even need the slapping de rigueur. He cried aloud and vigorously without any coaxing.

"A boy?" said Diane. "I have a boy? He all right?" Her speech was slurred, but she broke into a huge, blissful smile when Sophie raised her head so she could see the baby.

"The baby is perfectly all right, and he is beautiful too," Leslie said.

The doctor placed two clamps on the cord and unceremoniously cut it between them. He passed the baby to the nurse, who showed him to the mother one more time.

"Thank you, Doctor. Thank you all," stammered Diane.

The fun part of the delivery party was over. Now came the delivery of the afterbirth and the repair of the damage that is bound to occur every time a large object is forced through a small canal.

The doctor stepped to the bassinet where the baby lay. A perfunctory inspection of the baby reassured him that he did not need a pediatrician. The baby was pink, making fists and crying louder than the doctor welcomed at this time of night. He returned to his place at the foot of the delivery table and sat down, staring at the uterus for a sign of the contraction that would presage the separation of the placenta. He had not assessed yet the damage to the birth canal caused by the delivery, but the bleeding was not excessive, and he decided to await the expulsion of the afterbirth before starting to repair it.

After several minutes, he became a little frustrated with the stubborn placenta that refused to come out. He began to probe the episiotomy incision to keep himself busy, dabbing it with a sponge and picking off the clots that had already formed on it. Diane made a grunting sound and moved her legs so as to close them, but they were tightly strapped to the leg-holders.

"Damn," said the doctor under his breath. "A nasty extension." He inserted his index finger into the patient's anus and saw the tip of it in the vagina.

Leslie turned towards him. "Fourth degree?" she asked. Fourth degree meant that the laceration had extended into the rectum.

"Umpteenth degree," he snarled.

"You need a BANAH set, huh?" she said and headed for the cabinets to get the special pack and the extra sutures necessary for the repair.

Every year the senior residents would tell the new ones that the procedure was named after Professor Banah, an eminent surgeon in Tehran. The innocent rookies were told that the professor had performed that operation on one of the wives of the shah and that the shah had been so pleased with the results that he made Professor Banah a prince. Endless embellishments were added each time to the story, some of them quite obscene. The gullible new doctors were sternly advised to read up on the technique.

They could not find it in any textbook, of course, because "BANAH" was actually an acronym, like FUBAR and SNAFU, that had started as a witty jocular moniker. "BANAH" referred to the surgical procedure used for repairing an episiotomy that had extended into the rectum. Eventually it had lost all its amusing implications and become widely accepted. Even the packages with the instruments for the procedure were labeled "BANAH." The original funny meaning of it was therefore mostly forgotten, and learning the meaning of "BANAH" became a kind of rite of passage for new interns and residents. "BANAH" stood for "Building A New Ass-Hole."

"A good two inches into the rectum," Dr. Irving announced wretchedly. Leslie dropped several chromic catgut sutures onto the table and handed him a fresh pair of gloves. He yanked the contaminated gloves off and threw them angrily into the bucket. He put on the clean ones, and, as he kept waiting for the elusive placenta, he placed a couple of hemostatic clamps on the severed vessels in the incision that were spurting blood.

There is no agreement among obstetricians on what is an acceptable wait for the placenta to separate spontaneously. Ten, twenty minutes, thirty minutes tops. Often all that is needed is a brisk tug on the umbilical cord to initiate the process of expulsion.

A subtle wave extending down the abdominal wall is the welcome sign that the placenta is descending from the strong, muscular vault of the uterine cavity—called the fundus, where it usually resides—to the thin-walled vestibule—the lower uterine segment—and from there to the birth canal proper.

The extent of the waiting time is frequently determined by the urgency of the accoucheur's desire to get out of the delivery room. That's when the Credé maneuver becomes handy. It is a simple maneuver and works mainly when the uterus is good and ready to release the afterbirth. The reasons why the uterus on occasions refuses to let go of its superfluous guest has remained unknown to the medical profession. The adage "Anyone can deliver a baby; the placenta kills" is still reverently invoked.

Dr. Irving tugged resolutely on the Péan clamp that held the cord. The uterus responded with a violent contraction that dragged up the cord a couple of inches so that the tip of the clamp disappeared inside the vagina. He decided to go ahead with the Credé maneuver. He looked at Sophie and gave her the thumbs-down sign.

"How long has she been NPO?" she asked.

The nurse leafed through the chart. NPO was the abbreviation for the Latin words "Nihil per os"—nothing by mouth.

"Last intake...er...wait...hmm...here...a cup of tea at five p.m."

The anesthetist turned the knob clockwise a few notches, and the halothane gas began to flow into Diane's lungs at full rate for a quick induction.

"How long do you think it'll take you, Doc?" she asked.

"To repair the laceration, no more than twenty minutes; then, it'll depend on the pig-headed placenta."

The Credé maneuver and the suturing of the laceration, Dr. Irving knew quite well, did not require deep anesthesia, just enough to keep the patient from feeling pain and prevent her from thrashing about.

"Keep her light," he told Sophie. Then he added, "This is the woman Alfie thought she heard a second heartbeat."

"But the ultrasound showed only one, right?" Sophie asked, alarmed.

"Of course," the doctor rejoined, "and if those clowns in ultrasound missed twins, it'll be the last mistake they make."

"If you think there might be another one inside, you'd better hurry," Sophie admonished him half jokingly. "It's going to be a veeeery relaxed baby, I'm telling you."

"One of those 'like-I-don't-care-maan' babies," he quipped.

"Yeah, he'll be threading beads on a California beach," she retorted, "and you and I will be supporting him and his family for life."

The doctor acknowledged the joke with a nervous laugh.

He tugged at the cord again and again while pressing at the top of the uterus. "The damned thing is not coming," he said under his breath. Then he turned to Leslie. "Give me the version glove, will you?" He added in a gloomy tone, "I'm going for it. Get someone to look after the baby, Leslie. I might need you here."

"Sorry, Doc," Leslie replied. "Everybody is in the Section Room. They are having problems there. Dr Youssef has an abruptio pouring out like hell."

"Like we're having a beach party here," he snapped. A curly strand of hair slid out of his cap and clung to his sweaty forehead. Dr. Jonathan Irving, "Cool Jon" as he was known, was beginning to lose his cool.

"No dice, Doc," Leslie countered. "What you see is what you get. But even if I have to assist you, I'll manage to keep an eye on the baby. He's doing just fine. So, chop, chop, Doc."

"Stop the bitching and get to work, Doc," Sophie weighed in as she winked at him.

The doctor grumbled some profanity probably, but it sounded just like a growl. He put the version glove on his left arm; it extended beyond his elbow. The version glove was originally devised to cover most of the arm as it was inserted deeply into the uterus to turn the baby around from a head first into a breech position—a procedure called "internal version"—so it could be delivered quickly by pulling on the legs. The version glove looked like a thin rubber jacket sleeve with five fingers at the end.

The doctor looked at Sophie and gave her the thumbs-down sign again.

"Deep, real deep," he commanded this time.

Sophie opened up the intravenous drip and turned the knob on the machine clockwise all the way as she kept squeezing and releasing the breathing bag. She opened the patient's eye time and again to look at the pupil's size. It was a trusted gauge of the level of anesthesia.

In a few seconds, Diane's body went completely limp.

CHAPTER III

# The Third Lunar Month

The Grosse Pointe Storks' office was a tribute to Dr. D'Onofrio's vision and keen financial sense. It stood on Mack Avenue, which marked the border between the Pointes and Harper Woods. The building was a remodeled old Georgian colonial home —for the tax incentive—on the Harper Woods side of the road where the taxes were already substantially lower. The black-shingled roof, the red reclaimed brick, the gray trim and the severe columns bespoke of the clientele The Storks intended to attract. The waiting room reinforced the concept of understated elegance so dear to the Grosse Pointers. Mahogany wood coffee tables and armchairs matched the stair banister. The soft old rose walls were dotted with prints of bucolic scenes in hunter green mats and cherry wood frames. Copies of Harper's Bazaar, Town and Country, Vanity Fair and Yachting Magazine were neatly piled on each side table. Kelly green touches on cushions, on the carpet and on the signage completed the Grosse Pointe atmosphere. Pink and kelly green were the unofficial, but unchallenged colors of the Pointes.

A few chairs were occupied by middle-aged ladies who could all have been members of the same band—bob haircuts and tailored earth tone suits over white blouses. The remainder of the group-in-waiting consisted of young women whose most salient feature was their bellies.

In the north corner of the room, gently bathed by the late July sunlight that the louvered shutters had tamed, sat a petite Oriental woman. She was young and smartly dressed in a floral-patterned dark green shift that clung to her shapely body. Her legs, crossed at the calves in a charmingly feminine pose, added a touch of class. High-heeled shoes matched a leather handbag that she held on her lap like a fashion model. Her jet black hair cascaded straight to the middle of her back, swaying voluptuously as she turned her head. She was sitting in the section of the waiting room traditionally occupied by expectant mothers—the area closest to the washrooms. Even though her abdomen was as flat as a ballerina's and she could zip her size two outfit without holding her breath, she was with child.

After a few minutes, the young woman picked up the magazine on top of the pile and opened it at random. She cast her eyes on the open page, but she did not intend to read it. An undeniable feeling of restlessness had been growing in her since she had entered the waiting room. Actually the feeling had started when she had learned that she was expecting a baby.

It was her first doctor's visit for this pregnancy. Her friend Kathy had told her that the Grosse Pointe Storks were the best obstetricians in the area and "probably in the state." The young woman was not worried about liking or not liking the doctors. What she really wanted to hear was what every pregnant woman wanted to hear—she wanted someone to tell her that her baby was all right. More than that, she thought, she wanted to believe it.

When they called her name, Diane Truong returned the magazine to the pile and stood up. Perhaps it was only her own personal fear, she thought, as she straightened her dress. Perhaps every woman who had ever been with child had experienced that same fear, that vague, ever-present premonition

that some unexpurgated major sin or some string of individu-
ally trivial peccadilloes had laid her open to divine retribution.
What will the fruit of my womb be like? It is my baby, but it is
not me. Will it have ten fingers and ten toes? Will it thrive in
that bubble of blood and mysterious fluids that has spawned
inside me which I cannot understand or control? What can I,
what should I do to protect my baby inside of me? Will it survive the countless dangers of the birth process? Will I? Will my
child some day walk, run and play like other children? Will my
baby grow up to call my name some day? In some shrouded,
dark corner of the self of every expectant woman, hidden in
the crevices of the soul between innocent memories of childhood and adolescence, lies guilt—guilt that hides, guilt that is
invisible to other human eyes, but not to God's. For God can
see all, and his justice knows no bounds. Can God fulfill his
divine duty of meting out justice in any more appropriate way
than by marring the child in the sinner's womb?

Diane's mind had been wandering in those dark alleys of
the inner soul while she pretended to read.

"Mrs. Truong," the receptionist repeated aloud.

Reality.

Her usual smile sprang forward as she walked courageously
to the reception desk. The truculent thoughts fell back to the
bottomless pit of the unconscious, where they belonged.

Yet she still carried them in her.

She hurried across the waiting room with tiny steps, as
her dress would allow. She walked in front of many other
pregnant women, all pretending to read.

"Doctors, at least obstetricians," Diane thought, "should
have some training in interior design. The waiting rooms are
so impersonal, so oblivious to a woman's needs. Mirrors. Diane
was becoming conscious of her anxiety. A mirror, Diane wanted
a mirror to see if her face betrayed her gloomy thoughts.

"Hi, Diane." The receptionist greeted her with a fake smile
as required by her job description. Diane followed the recep-

tionist to a small office. A young woman in a pale green scrub suit was sitting behind a desk. The woman stood up to shake Diane's hand and introduced herself as Dr. Palazzo. She was a senior resident in Ob/Gyn at Wayne State University, she said. After a short exchange of pleasantries, she began to take a detailed history—mother's, father's, husband's, sisters' health, the previous pregnancy and delivery, the baby's condition and on and on. The doctor was pleasant but quite down to business. The gathering of the medical history took almost half an hour, and then Diane was led into an examining room where the same doctor carried out a very thorough check-up—weight, height, eyes, lungs, heart, limbs, abdomen—and made lengthy notes. The doctor drew several tubes of blood and then gave her a plastic bottle for the urine specimen and called the nurse to show Diane to the restroom. Dr. Palazzo smiled at Diane and shook her hand again. She told her that she would then be seen by Dr. Rao, an obstetrician, a partner of Dr. Irving's.

As the doctor was about to leave, Diane asked, "Is the baby all right?"

The smile died instantly on the doctor's face. She said, "As of this moment, we have no reasons to believe that the baby is in any type of distress. However, many conditions will not show up until delivery, and sometimes not even until years later."

On that note, Dr. Palazzo left the room.

While waiting, sitting on the examining table, Diane tried to reach back in her memory to her first pregnancy. She could not remember that pervasive feeling of gloom. But then the first pregnancy was so many years ago, and at that time the unforgettable horrors she had witnessed as a child in her native land (now conveniently stored in the subconscious, where they belonged) were excruciatingly fresh in her memory and pre-empted all other thoughts.

Dr. Rao came in with the nurse and introduced himself. The doctor was an affable young man, generous with eye contact and quick to smile; he spoke with a reassuring voice. He performed a pelvic examination and announced to the nurse that the uterus seemed the right size as expected from the last menstrual period; he said that the cervix and the ovaries were normal. When he had finished, he sat on his low stool in front of her and repeated the advice that the previous doctor had given her—take the vitamins everyday, avoid exposure to children with contagious diseases, reduce or avoid alcohol, watch the weight gain and the salt intake.

When he had finished his discourse, he stood up. "Do you have any questions, Mrs. Truong, before I leave?" he asked as he stretched out his hand to her.

Diane smiled back and repeated the question she had asked the resident doctor before: "Is the baby all right?"

Dr. Rao withdrew his hand, and his smile faded away. Very seriously he answered, "As of this moment, we have no reasons to believe that the baby is in any type of distress. However, many conditions will not show up until after the baby is born, and sometimes not even until years later."

"Give Mrs. Truong an appointment in four weeks, with Dr. Irving if possible," he told the nurse. He waved Diane goodbye and performed a measured bow as he left the room.

Diane was quite satisfied with the doctors and with all the staff of The Grosse Pointe Storks. She had learned that her due date was February 15, that she was expected to gain no more than twenty pounds and that she could work until the seventh month if no complications developed.

As soon as she got home, she rushed to the telephone to call Kathy and thank her for referring her to such nice doctors. She told her that she would see her friend, the good-looking doctor, next visit.

## CHAPTER IV

# The Fourth Lunar Month

The majority of people, in developed countries at least, gravitate towards an occupation that they find interesting. Sadly, the joy that the performance of an interesting task should produce is often eclipsed by the repetitiveness required by most remunerated jobs.

Diane Truong had been born and had spent all her childhood years in a poor region of a very poor country. She was always very mindful of how fortunate she was to be able to perform a job that she enjoyed, in a comfortable place, and to be remunerated for it. She considered it a source of personal fulfillment, and she was grateful.

Any job, however, even the most coveted and agreeable, will at times become a dreadful drudgery.

One hot and muggy August evening, while she was driving back home from her office, Diane thought that that day her work, which she usually enjoyed, the job she was so grateful to have, had been no fun at all. Her friend Kathy, she remembered, referred to something of this sort as a "pain in the ass."

"My job today was a pain in the ass," she said aloud, and she giggled.

It was almost seven o'clock when Diane entered her apartment.

"I'm home, Quang," she shouted.

There was no answer. She did not expect one, and somehow she welcomed the lack of it. The window air conditioner was whirring aloud, but the room was still too warm for her liking. She let out a long sigh and plunged herself into the cozy sofa in the living room.

She lay there, immobile, for a long while. She stood up at last, holding up her skirt—she had undone her belt for comfort—and headed for the kitchen for some ice tea, her favorite refreshment. She returned to the living room with a pitcher and a glass. She sat at the table and started to sort the mail: "Ads, ads, bill, bill, ads, bill, bill." She tossed them all onto the table again. "Quang's mail," she said chortling.

She poured herself a tall glass of the cold drink and wobbled back to the sofa. She slumped on it; she rolled up her blouse and pulled down her skirt to let the air dry the perspiration on her abdomen. Clothes were already beginning to feel much like body restraints.

She placed the sweating glass on top of a folded paper napkin on her bare belly. The glass stood steady, and its coolness felt good. Quang's snores from the bedroom felt reassuring to Diane; they were the comforting sound of home.

She took a big gulp of the ice tea and groaned as she swallowed it. She said aloud in her native language something like "Home, sweet home." She replaced the glass on her abdomen and placed her hands, fingers locked, behind her head, and soon she was asleep.

A strong cramp that bordered on the painful awoke her. She opened her eyes in time to see the glass propelled off her abdomen; it landed on the floor, but it did not break.

"My goodness," she yelled. "I know babies can kick, but this hard?"

She smiled. She looked at the glass lying on the carpet in the center of the dark, wet spot that the spilled tea had made.

"It's just tea," she said. "It will leave no stain." Too tired to get up to clean it up, she returned to her idyllic slumber. Images of a very robust boy on a soccer field pervaded her dreams. "Goooooal!" she heard in her reverie. "My baby can kick. He will be a soccer star."

Babies still in the womb can kick a glass down from the mother's abdomen—any woman who was ever pregnant can attest to that.

Diane's baby had hurled the glass two feet away.

At that stage of the gestation, Diane's fetus measured about seven inches.

That she did not know.

CHAPTER V

# The Fifth Lunar Month

Diane was on time for her four o'clock appointment with Dr. Santoro at the hospital office. The doctor was not.

It was past five and the September sun was dropping toward the horizon when the receptionist called her name.

Dr. Santoro's nurse walked into the examining room as soon as Diane had sat on the table. She introduced herself: "Hi, Diane. I'm L'Nore, Dr. Santoro's sidekick." She gave a big smile and apologized for the doctor being late. L'Nore was a vivacious young woman who exuded warmth; her cheerful presence was a welcome boost for Diane's anxiety. L'Nore was wearing a fresh white lab coat over a green scrub suit, accessorized by large silver ear loops and her name pin. The immaculate whiteness of her coat set off her dark skin; she had large hazel eyes, restless and engaging. Her smile lingered on her face as she led Diane to the scale.

"Gained two pounds. That's good," she said while entering it in the record. Then she took Diane's blood pressure, "Couldn't be better," L'Nore said.

"Really?" asked Diane as if surprised.

"One-sixteen over seventy," said L'Nore.

"That's low for me," said Diane.

"It is always lower in the second trimester," L'Nore reassured her. She then became busy dipping the color-sensitive strip in Diane's urine sample.

"Is all right?" questioned Diane. Her anxiety was beginning to show in her voice.

"Glucose negative," L'Nore read aloud. "Protein...negative. Right on target."

L'Nore complimented Diane on her taste in clothes, partly to make her relax, but mainly because it was a fact. Diane always dressed very elegantly. Her petite figure could show off any kind of fashionable outfit, but she chose the conservative look—a rarity in those days.

"Dress for success," said Diane giggling.

They engaged in small talk while they waited for Dr. Santoro. After a while, a subtle vibration of the floor disrupted their conversation. The clip-clap of high heels hitting the tiled floor soon accompanied the vibration, and both the sound and the vibration grew in intensity as the footsteps approached the door of the examining room. The door opened, and some instruments on the treatment cart rattled a little as if heralding a very determined person. Or a very heavy one.

Dr. Santoro was both. At five-foot-eleven-inches and 198 pounds (admitted), with broad shoulders an athlete would brag about and breasts marginally contained by a 38E brassiere, Alfonsina Santoro, MD, cut an intimidating figure. Her hair, a chestnut shade in a nondescript perm, framed a squarish jaw, a prominent thin nose and a large mouth with perfectly delineated lips. And then there were the eyes, Dr. Santoro's *pièce de résistance*. Light blue ("celestial," her mother would have corrected) like a seal pup's under a sunny sky, they often gazed at a faraway point with cool detachment as if she were engaged in some momentous metaphysical quest. At times, they converged past the subject they should be fixed on, and the subject felt pierced by them. That could be frightening, but she did not know it.

Dr. Santoro was wearing a faded rose lab coat that could have benefited from pressing a few weeks back. There were several pens clipped to the chest pocket, and the side pockets bulged from overstuffing. Under the coat, which was totally unbuttoned, she wore a polka-dot navy blue dress with a wide white collar. From her neck dangled a large gold medallion of the Blessed Mother and a stethoscope with purple rubber tubing.

"And how are we today, Diane?" the doctor asked in a tone that could have been described as friendly had it been several decibels lower and an octave higher.

"I am fine. And how are you, Doctor?" said Diane.

The doctor made some guttural sounds for an answer. She stretched an arm towards L'Nore, who handed her the calipers. She placed one tip of the calipers on Diane's pubic bone and the other on top of the uterus, "Seventeen centimeters," she said aloud, and L'Nore recorded it on the chart. Then the doctor turned to the counter, picked up the Fetone and set it on the tray at the head of the examining table. The Fetone was a bit of a status symbol, because it was a rather new instrument and many obstetricians could not afford it. The housing of the machine, which contained the rechargeable batteries, was a wood-veneered box the size of a shoebox, reminiscent of the venerable Kloss table radio of a previous era. A handheld transducer was connected to the box by a long cord. The transducer sent out ultrasonic waves produced by the machine. When it was placed on the skin of the abdomen, any movement inside, such as the baby's heartbeat or a pulsating blood vessel, would reflect the waves. Using the Doppler effect, the machine would translate the movements into audible sounds and transmit them to the speaker in the front of the box.

The doctor smeared Diane's belly with mineral oil; an oily interface was needed in order to transmit the waves properly. She then placed the transducer on Diane's belly and moved it all about the protruding abdomen. Suddenly, a loud lub-dub, lub-dub, lub-dub filled the room. It was the sweetest music to the ears of a mother-to-be: the baby's heartbeat.

Diane's tense face broke into a big smile as she heard the distinct sounds above the background static noises.

Any obstetrician, at this point, would have counted the beats for half a minute and would have recorded their rate and location, and that would have been the end of the prenatal visit. Not Dr. Santoro. Obsessive-compulsive woman that she was, she could not help going always a little farther, turning the next stone. She continued to move the transducer in larger concentric circles, and as she did so, the fetal heart tones faded, and the speaker began to emit intermittent background crackling and gurgling noises. At times there was complete silence; then the cacophonous sounds resurfaced like a radio switching between stations. Dr. Santoro poured more oil on the belly and spread it with her own hand to the very edges of the uterine outline. While she was rubbing the oil on the skin, there was a visible, jerky movement of the whole abdomen.

"Touchy little brat," said L'Nore.

The three women smiled.

The doctor kept probing. When the transducer was a little below and to the left of the navel a beating was heard again. The new beats, amplified by the machine, filled the small room like the previous ones. Although rhythmic too, they were clearly faster, less intense and of a different pitch. The sounds somehow suggested the "whoosh" of cascading water or of a strong wind rushing through trees.

After listening to them for a few seconds, Dr. Santoro slid the transducer back to the area where the first sounds had been heard. The three women heard the distinct lub-dub again, louder, slower and sharper. The doctor shifted the instrument back and forth several times between the two areas. The sounds, even to an uninitiated ear, were clearly distinguishable from one another.

"Not two babies, please!" shouted Diane. "The house too small for two babies."

The doctor ignored her. Without displacing it, she turned the hand that was holding the transducer rather awkwardly to look at her wristwatch. With her other hand, she marked the tempo of the beats at the first site. L'Nore was counting on her watch too.

"One forty," said L'Nore aloud.

Dr. Santoro nodded. Then she moved the transducer back to the second site and counted the rate there. "One fifty-eight," she said.

Two more times they repeated the counts aloud. One-forty remained unchanged. The "whooshy" sounds rose to 162 beats per minute, then to 168, then fell back to 160.

L'Nore and the doctor exchanged glances. They were both reciting under their breaths the old rule for the diagnosis of twins: "A positive diagnosis should not be made unless there is a difference of at least ten beats per minute in the rate of the two hearts after counting the sounds simultaneously for at least a full minute." It said "simultaneously" quite plainly. L'Nore reached into a drawer of the cabinet for a fetoscope.

The fetoscope was the old, dependable tool that had been used to auscultate the fetal heart sounds for decades; it was still widely used, even though the electronic instruments were beginning to replace it. The fetoscope was similar in appearance to the usual stethoscope used for listening to the heart and lungs, except that the bell was conical instead of flat and it had no membrane. The examiner usually pressed the bell against the abdomen with his forehead.

L'Nore gave the fetoscope to the doctor, who attached it to her head and pressed the bell against Diane's belly at the site of the first heart tones. L'Nore kept the transducer of the Fetone on the second area, where the "whoosh" had originated. They counted in silence for two full minutes, for extra accuracy.

"Three hundred twenty-four," announced L'Nore. "That is...162 beats per minute."

"Two seventy-six...138 bpm," said the doctor without any enthusiasm.

The criterion for twin gestation was fully met, no question about it.

"Twins," pronounced L'Nore. Her thick lips framed her white teeth in a big, happy smile. Diane's face betrayed her disappointment.

Then L'Nore looked down at the chart she was holding, and a severe frown soon replaced the happy smile. "She had an ultrasound last visit," she said.

Diane nodded.

L'Nore leafed through the sheets of Diane's obstetrical record. "Here." She read the report to herself. "Oh, no! They missed it," she exclaimed. "It says"—she read aloud now—"fourteen weeks gestation, single fetus, cephalic presentation, placenta in the fundus."

"Single fetus, huh?" echoed the doctor.

Diane's face was growing paler as they talked. "Two babies?" she asked.

Dr. Santoro overruled Diane's question with one of her own. "Who did the ultrasound?"

L'Nore leafed through the sheets again, "Er...here..." She finally found it.

"Dr. Weinstein read it...er...Ken did the scan."

"Ken wouldn't have missed twins at fourteen weeks," the doctor remarked, mostly to herself.

"Is something wrong, Doctor?" Diane interrupted.

"No, Diane. Everything is fine," said the doctor and patted her on the shoulder. "Don't worry." Then she turned to L'Nore. "I want another ultrasound," she added.

"Monday will be all right?" asked L'Nore, although she knew the answer already.

"Not Monday. Now."

"It's Friday, five thirty-five," L'Nore protested, looking at her watch. "They are not going to..." She did not think it was necessary to finish the sentence because Dr. Santoro was already out of earshot.

L'Nore helped Diane to sit up and straighten her clothes. While she was handing her her purse and jacket, the doctor came back into the room pushing a wheelchair.

"Sit here, Diane." She motioned to the chair.

"Where are we going?" asked Diane. Now she was as confused as she was worried.

"We're going for an ultrasound," said the doctor. "Don't worry, Diane. Everything is fine, but I don't want to wait until Monday for it."

"Two babies?" insisted Diane.

"I don't know, but I want to look at the scan myself," Dr. Santoro tried to explain. Then she kept uttering unintelligible words as she pushed the wheelchair along the corridors and hallways at a speed that could not be considered safe in a healthcare facility.

L'Nore was carrying Diane's purse and briefcase. Her legs were a good six inches shorter than the doctor's, so she had to engage in a brisk jog to keep abreast. L'Nore turned her head right and left, offering apologies to the people who had to jump out of the wheelchair's path.

The narrow institutional corridors were flanked on both sides by doors with nameplates. They stopped at the one that read "Ultrasound Department." The doctor tried the handle. It was locked. She parked Diane's chair and motioned to L'Nore to wait there. Dr. Santoro knew that the door of the file room was never locked, so she rushed to the end of the hallway and gained entrance to the department. She followed an inside corridor that wound around the radiologists' offices. The offices were deserted. The weekend had already started.

Dr. Santoro entered the Ultrasound Department through a side door. There was a small reception area, a room furnished with one coffee table and three plastic stackable chairs in one corner. Mangled magazines, soiled coffee cups and candy wrappers covered the table. A stainless steel treatment cart was parked in the opposite corner, stacked three feet high with radiograph folders. A chest-high counter extended almost the entire length of the room, leaving a narrow access at one end closed by a short double swinging door as in a western saloon. The wall behind the counter was lined floor to ceiling with shelves almost completely filled with film jackets filed in some esoteric order. On a radio, perched on one of the shelves, Petula Clark was going downtown when Dr. Santoro entered the room.

A young woman in a white lab coat was standing at one end of the counter, clipping Polaroid pictures. She was handing the pictures one by one to a technician, who pasted them onto the report sheets already typed. They were the pictures of the ultrasounds performed that day; ready to be sent to the doctors who had ordered the tests. Many of the doctors preferred to look at the pictures themselves, and then, of course, all the mothers-to-be always wanted one for the baby's scrapbook. Ken, the technician who was pasting the pictures, thought it was a waste of time. He was convinced that most of the obstetricians could not tell a fetal head from a swollen toe on the prints.

Ken was very opinionated. He was a burly young man, in his late thirties. He had long blonde hair, a beard, an unruly mustache and long sideburns—the works, a furry frame for the face as the current fashion dictated. His eyes were light brown, small, intense and mostly melancholy. He didn't talk much. He liked his job, and he was very good at it. Ken was tough. He had spent five years in Vietnam as a medic with the 3rd Brigade of the 1st Air Cavalry; he was with them when they fought for Hue. He took shit from nobody.

Ken was sitting at a desk behind the counter working on the sheets with the Polaroid pictures. As he finished each sheet, he would place it on top of one of several neat piles on his desk.

Dr. Santoro tapped her heels on the tiled floor as she walked straight up to the counter and stood in front of Ken. "I have a patient outside who needs an Ob ultrasound," she said softly.

The young file clerk at the end of the counter stopped her clipping momentarily; looked at the clock on the wall and said, "Sorry, Doctor, but we are already closed."

"It is an e-m-e-r-g-e-n-c-y," Dr. Santoro explained to the girl. She enunciated "emergency" as if it had nine syllables instead of nine letters.

"Come Friday five p.m., everyone has an emergency," Ken muttered without raising his eyes from the sheets he was working on. It was basically a statement; only the subtlest trace of sarcasm could be discerned in his tone.

As if the remark were the cue the doctor was awaiting, her face flushed beyond purple, the veins in her neck stood out as gun barrels, and her fingers clawed the edge of the counter like a falcon's talons gripping its prey. As she inhaled deeply through her slightly open mouth, her throat made a sound like a faint growl. Then Dr. Santoro leaned forward over the counter, which only reached a bit above her navel. When her face was not farther than two or three inches from the blonde hairy mass of Ken's head—he was still looking down, concentrating on his chore—she burst out, "But this is MY emergency!" Accent on MY. She did not say it very loudly, but in the five words she exhaled all the air that her capacious lungs were holding. As a result, the Polaroid pictures and the sheets on Ken's desk became airborne. They made several pirouettes in mid-air and landed on the floor, on the chairs and between the film jackets on the shelves of the back wall. The young clerk at the end of the counter, startled by the commotion, dropped the scissors and the stack of prints she was holding.

The room became deadly still, except for Jim Croce on the radio, saving time in a bottle. Ken began to raise his head from the now perfectly clear desktop. He was pondering what would be an appropriate response to this insult that would not result in his being fired—actually "court-martialed" came to his mind first. As he raised his eyes ever so slowly, he saw on the other side of the counter the drab pink coat of the doctor. The coat was wide open, exposing the navy blue polka-dot fabric of her dress stretched widely around her hips. Higher up, he saw a wide black patent leather belt with a shiny chrome buckle. Above that he recognized the bell of a stethoscope swinging gently side to side, barely touching the top of the buckle. He then caught sight of the purple tube that connected the bell of the instrument to the earpieces. Further up, the purple tube vanished in the deep valley between Dr. Santoro's colossal bosoms. One on either side of the young man's head, the two massive warheads stood immobile, for Dr. Santoro was not breathing. Whatever sexual connotation women's breasts had ever held for the poor fellow, these definitely had none. They stood as an ironical antithesis of sex appeal.

Ken began to grasp their recondite significance: seminal tools for gender balance in the homo sapiens species. Dr. Santoro, in spite of all her protestations of asexuality, was aware of their value as finely honed weapons for the survival of the female of the species. And, subconsciously perhaps, she used them. Ken, who had had military training, realized that to do battle with an enemy in that state of combat readiness would be sheer folly.

The battle-flags were furl'd. He capitulated before firing a gun, before even attempting to look past her breasts, and it was better for him that he didn't, because her face was just as ferociously menacing as her bust.

The young clerk was picking off the floor the strewn pictures and sheets.

Ken turned towards her and said tersely, "Bring the patient in."

"Thank you," mumbled Dr. Santoro, her rage spent.

They wheeled Diane in through the side door.

L'Nore and the doctor waited for Ken and the girl to ready the ultrasound room for Diane's test.

"Is it possible to miss multiple pregnancies at fourteen weeks?" L'Nore asked. She was leaning on the back of the now vacant wheelchair. Her face was quietly hollering, "My feet are killing me," but she did not think it proper to sit down.

"Sure, and the reverse too," answered the doctor, gazing at some distant point past the room's confine. "You see," she began to explain, "the ultrasound images are not real time. So, while you move the transducer to another area, the part you scanned before, a head for instance, can move, and if you scan it again, you call it twins. And the reverse is just as bad—you can think it's the same head you saw before when actually it's another one, and you miss a twin."

"Maybe," L'Nore protested, "but I don't remember them ever being wrong before."

"I've seen it," said the doctor. "I'll never forget one night when I was covering for Dr. Morgan. I delivered the first baby of this big woman and sat waiting like a damned fool for the second twin to descend into the birth canal. It didn't exist. And she had had two ultrasounds that called it twins."

"Not at Our Lady of Lourdes, though?"

"No, not here." Dr. Santoro shook her head.

"Diane's," L'Nore asked, a glint of preoccupation in her voice, "do you think it is twins, Doc?"

The doctor was still staring at that distant point. L'Nore was staring at the doctor. L'Nore saw her squint. Her baby blue eyes that had been wide open until then shrank to a fine slit.

The look on the doctor's face frightened L'Nore. Dr. Santoro was her hero, and although the doctor admitted to being "a devout worrier," she always seemed in control; no complication was a surprise for her, and she could handle anything that cropped up. They had worked together for over eight years, and L'Nore had never before seen this forlorn expression on her face.

Ken barged into the room through the back door. "Doc, come see for yourself," he said. There was not even a trace of rancor in his voice.

"That's a professional for you," thought Dr. Santoro to herself. A subtle feeling of guilt crept up in her, almost an urge to apologize for her outburst. She chose to ignore them both, the urge and the feeling.

The two women followed Ken to the scanning room. The room was entirely dark but for the gray hue of the ultrasound screen and the light of a low-wattage bulb in a gooseneck lamp aiming at a wall. The reflected light reached Diane's belly; the mineral oil that was smeared over it made it shine like a newborn piglet's.

"Twins?" snickered Ken sarcastically. "Bullshit! I remember her. I did her last time with the student. What's her name?"

"June," said the young clerk.

"June, that's right. Just one fetus. You can bet your bottom dollar on it.

"Now, the placenta…is real big. In fact, I remember June, the student, called it 'the octopus placenta' because it seemed to have tentacles stretching all over the uterus."

Everybody in the room was concentrating on the shadow show.

"See?" Ken pointed with his finger to some blips on the screen. "A humongous placenta."

"Uh-huh," mumbled the doctor.

"That bad?" asked Diane with obvious concern.

"No, it's good." L'Nore touched Diane on the shoulder. She understood her anxiety. "The placenta is what feeds the baby. The bigger the better," she added with her big smile full of pearly teeth.

Dr. Santoro stood up abruptly, "Make sure she sees me next time," she said to L'Nore and dashed out of the room.

L'Nore was cleaning the mineral oil off Diane's abdomen. "I'll take care of it," she shouted, but the doctor was too far away to hear.

"She always like that?" asked Diane.

"Only on her better days." The clerk volunteered the answer. She was tidying up the room, removing the Polaroid pictures from the camera and placing them in an envelope.

"That woman!" exclaimed L'Nore. "She can make coffee nervous."

"Tell me about it." Ken threw in his two bits, shaking his head.

Diane started to giggle. "Make coffee nervous," she repeated.

"Sometimes she can get on my last good nerve," added L'Nore.

"I'm sorry for you," said the clerk with a grin of sympathy. "You have to work with her every day."

"Don't be," L'Nore hurried to reply, somewhat offended. "I wouldn't work with anybody else."

"Really?" exclaimed the girl with genuine disbelief.

"She can be a prickette, I know," answered L'Nore, "but if you have a real problem, you go see her. She'll solve it for you if she has to beat the solution into your head with her fists." There was pride in L'Nore's voice.

"I know," said Ken. "She saved my sister's baby when all the other doctors had given up. For thirty-six hours she sat by her bed." Then he added, sotto voce, "But she's still a bitch."

Ken and the young clerk hurried to finish bagging the refuse generated by Diane's test, and they left the Ultrasound Department at the same time as L'Nore and Diane. The four of them walked down the now deserted corridors, L'Nore and Diane in front, Ken and the file clerk a few steps behind.

Diane kept telling L'Nore how happy she was that it was only one baby. She described her apartment in detail. "Mai complains now. She wants own room when she comes from school," Diane explained. "When husband gets promotion usto loudly.

and raise, soon I think, we'll move to big house with garage, garden, everything." She giggled. "Mai will be very happy."

When they were crossing the Maternity Clinic lobby, L'Nore said goodbye and entered the staff room. The door was wide open. Dr. Santoro was standing by the sink, a steaming mug in her hands, still the vacant gaze on her face.

Diane leaned into the room as she walked by. "Bye-bye, Dr. Santoro," she said giggling, "Thank you. Have a nice weekend."

"You too, Diane," the doctor answered loudly. "See you soon." She almost broke into a smile.

By then, Ken and the file clerk were passing by the door. When they heard Dr. Santoro's voice, as if on cue they both whispered something almost to themselves. "Cop a life," said the girl. "Bitch," said Ken.

The doctor was drinking hot cocoa out of her favorite mug. A birthday gift from her staff, the mug had an inscription on the side: "When I need your opinion, I'll beat it out of you."

"So what's the scoop, Doc?" L'Nore asked.

There was no answer.

"You look worried, Doc," she insisted.

"Listen here, L'Nore." Dr. Santoro was now looking her assistant right in the eye, which she seldom did. "We heard the fetal heart tones, right?"

"Yes, we heard the FHT clearly, no question about it."

"One hundred forty beats per minute, right?"

"Right."

"Then we heard the other ones elsewhere, the 'whooshy' ones, right?"

"Right."

"Now, you were checking the mother's pulse. What was it?"

"Sixty, sixty-six; never higher than seventy, seventy-five per minute."

"So the 'whooshy' sound could not have been the mother's circulation, right?"

"Right," was L'Nore's answer again.

Dr. Santoro's deductive process came to a momentary stop.

L'Nore thought it was time for her to contribute more than "Right" to the conversation. "The other beats, the 'whooshy' ones, sounded to me more like placental sounds...like the blood running through the cord...What is it called?" She paused for a moment. "You know, the sound made by the blood flow in the umbilical cord."

Another longer pause. "The funic souffle!" she exclaimed excitedly.

"Bingo," said the doctor.

After a few seconds of rejoicing at her significant contribution, L'Nore looked perplexed again. She was an assiduous reader of "The Bible"—that was what Dr. Santoro called Williams's Textbook of Obstetrics. The relevant versicle presently came to L'Nore's mind. She recited it almost verbatim: "The funic or umbilical cord souffle is caused by the rush of blood through the umbilical arteries. It's a whistling sound synchronous with the fetal pulse."

"Since the fetal heart propels the blood through the cord," said the doctor, again gazing past L'Nore—and the door, and the waiting room and the windows—"the funic souffle must be at the same rate as the fetal heart."

"Uh-huh," nodded L'Nore.

"That's what 'The Bible' says, right?"

"Right."

"So, then?"

L'Nore thought very hard for a moment. She thought that the doctor was testing her, which she was keen on doing. L'Nore had that intellectual curiosity that the doctor admired. She wanted to know all there was to be known about pregnancy. She absorbed every notion and had a prodigious memory. She would often put interns and residents to shame during rounds. That answer, though, she did not know. "I give," she said at last. "What's the answer?"

"Beats me," the doctor replied.

Her assistant was taken aback. ("Why would she ask me something she herself doesn't know?" she thought.) "Really? Why did you ask me, then?"

"It was just a question, L'Nore. You may know something I don't," the doctor said apologetically. "Remember: The stupidest person can ask questions that the smartest person cannot answer."

"Truly?" L'Nore was incredulous that her boss would not have the answer. "You don't know where the 'whoosh' comes from?"

"I'm afraid not, L'Nore." The doctor tilted the mug upside down and sucked the last drop of the cocoa. "It is indeed very baffling, but we'd better go home now," she said with a tired smile. "Our brain cells are running out of oxygen. Have a nice weekend, L'Nore."

"You too, Alfie. Go out, have some fun."

"You have fun. You're the young one."

As soon as L'Nore had left, Dr. Santoro, letting out a long, loud sigh, dropped her heavy anatomy onto a chair. The chair creaked. She removed her glasses and rubbed her eyes with the back of her wrists. She sat still for a while. Then she yawned and picked up the telephone, dialing a number by heart.

When the voice came on at the other end, she said, "I am sorry, but I don't think I can make it tonight. Too pooped to party."

She listened for a moment. Then she spoke: "Domani? Certo."—Tomorrow? Sure. She added, "Love you too, Mamma," and hung up.

CHAPTER VI

# The Second Lunar Month

At six forty-five exactly, Quang donned the powder blue double-knit polyester jacket of his leisure suit over a florid yellow, blue and lime shirt. Checking his appearance in the mirror in his apartment in Troy, a Detroit suburb, he was confident that in forty minutes he would be sitting in his cubicle at the GM Tech Center.

With a mathematician's brain and an engineer's punctiliousness, he had plotted each leg of the drive to work, and he adjusted the car speed or his stride to maintain the planned schedule. Four minutes to reach his old Corvair in the guest lot, around the building by the dumpster—Diane kept her car in the carport. In three more minutes he would be out of the subdivision and into Big Beaver Road. It normally took him seventeen minutes to reach Van Dyke; there he would turn right, heading south. Nine more minutes to reach the gate of the Tech Center and park the car. In seven minutes, at a leisurely pace, he would cross the parking lot and the main lobby, climb one flight of stairs and zigzag through a maze of cubicles on the second floor to reach his own, in the corner that overlooked the parking lot.

At seven twenty-five, he would be looking at his drawing

board, juggling mathematical equations in his mind. His task at the Tech Center as a junior engineer was to work out a front-end design to minimize the drag coefficient for a concept sports car. If that model ever went into production without major snags, he would see it on the streets of metropolitan Detroit in five to seven years.

Quang performed this routine every morning, five days a week—six or seven when overtime was required.

The quintessence of monotony.

He loved it.

Monotony has been greatly maligned. Its true beauty can only be fully appreciated by those who have lived through war and political turmoil.

On a hot, humid day in late June, Quang's comforting routine was to be broken. The sultry morning was the harbinger of a broiling summer day that in the Midwest was usually referred to as "a scorcher."

That special morning, at six forty-five as always, Quang walked out of the apartment. His first step into the hallway landed his foot on the rim of a wooden bowl, causing it to flip over. The rice that filled the bowl spilled every each way over the carpeted hallway, and some grains rolled down the first steps of the staircase.

"What the..." Quang started to shout. He stopped in mid-sentence. He brought his hands to the sides of his face and squeezed it.

Then he froze into a smile full of teeth.

He was still in this pose when his neighbor, attracted by the unusual noises, appeared at the door on the other side of the hallway. His neighbor was dressed in a yellow business shirt, a wide tie that displayed all the primary colors, brown penny loafers and boxer shorts. He was holding a mug in his hand. He stood at the door watching Quang with a perplexed look.

"Vot is the matter, Quang?" he asked. The neighbor was a

Hungarian doctor who was completing a postgraduate fellow-ship in cardiology at Harper Hospital of Detroit.

Quang was still standing on the same spot, his hands clutching his face, his bulging eyes staring at the spilled rice. He cut an image somewhat reminiscent of "The Scream," except that his expression suggested contentment rather than the horror portrayed in Munch's masterpiece.

It took Quang a few seconds to answer the neighbor's question. The half-clad doctor kept shifting his mystified look back and forth from the spilled rice to Quang's face. At last, Quang lifted his eyes from the floor and looked the neighbor straight in the eye. The cryptic smile still on his face, he blurted out: "Diane is going to have baby!"

The doctor tried in vain to make some sense of the in-congruous situation: rice all over the floor, an upside down wooden bowl, Quang smiling and holding his face, his wife expecting a baby. It was beyond comprehension, he decided. He set his mug on the floor, walked across the hallway and kissed Quang on both cheeks.

"Congratulations!" he shouted.

"Fourteen years no baby," Quang said time and again.

"A baby, how vonderful!" exclaimed the doctor.

The two men, giggling like inebriated adolescents, set themselves to scoop the rice off the carpet with their hands.

Marucha, the doctor's wife, came to the door of their apart-ment. She stood there with an inquisitive look. She stared for a while at the two men kneeling on the floor and giggling

Marucha was a stout woman with an imperious demeanor. Wrapped in a long, red velvety robe, gazing down at the two grotesque characters on their hands and knees, she looked like a diva ready to attack her final aria. Laszlo, the doctor, explained to his wife in their native language that Quang was going to be a father after many years of trying. And that was all she understood of the whole ridiculous scene: that Quang was going to be a father. That was enough for the woman. She walked resolutely up to Quang. He stood up. She was almost a foot taller than he and twice his weight. She lifted him off the floor in a forceful bear hug and planted a sonorous kiss on each cheek.

As she scurried away to her apartment, large tears were running down her own plump cheeks. She was back soon with two mugs of coffee.

The threesome sat on the top step of the stairs. Quang started an attempt at explaining the meaning of all that commotion. Quang's ability to express himself in English beyond the technical jargon of engineers was even less than the Hungarian couple's ability to understand it. It took some time and a lot of repetitions to complete the explanation.

It was a tradition in Quang's culture that when the wife learned that she was pregnant, she would place a bowl of rice outside the house. The original meaning of the ritual, supposedly, was that a new member would join the family table. The husband was expected to save all the rice in a sack and hide it until the baby was born and only then give it back to the wife. The expectant wife should never see the sack before the child was born lest some mishap should befall the mother or the child.

In spite of the repetitions, Marusha and Laszlo missed a good deal of the explanation, but she understood at least that a sack was needed. She ran into her apartment again and returned with a pink silk satchel covered with sequins and lace and with elaborate embroidered tassels in each corner. It had belonged to her mother, she explained.

"All the rice in bag," commanded Quang. "No good for baby if mother sees rice." The three of them set to the task of transferring all the rice grains into the pink satchel.

When the job was finished, Marusha pulled the fine silk cord, rolled it around the neck of the pouch and tied it with extreme care. She gave it to the father-to-be, and she admonished him: "Hide it vell. Ve vant a healthy baby, don't ve?"

Quang looked at his watch. He realized that he would be

very late for work. He ran down the stairs clutching the magical bag and repeating aloud: "Thank you, thank you very much."

Quang was more than an hour late for work. It was the first time he had been late in his five years at the Tech Center.

"What happened, Quang?" asked his boss. "We were beginning to worry."

Quang flashed his mouthful of teeth at him. "I'm going to be father!"

"A baby? When?" asked the boss with feigned enthusiasm, but a little confused.

"I don't know. Nine months?"

The boss was now completely confused, but he knew that asking for clarification would only delay things even more. "Congratulations," he said quite perfunctorily. "There are two memos from Purchasing. You'd better take care of them right away."

He thought about Quang's excuse for being late. Rather lame, he mused; acceptable, though, if he didn't try to use it too often.

Quang did not leave at five o'clock, his normal quitting time. When he walked by his boss's office at almost six-thirty, he opened the door and said, "Pay back hour late."

The boss waved him off; he had no doubts that Quang had put in his day's work, and then some.

On his way home, Quang stopped at Ho Chin, the Chinese restaurant that had stood at the corner of Van Dyke and the Metropolitan Parkway for years and was a bit of an institution for the Asians who worked as engineers at the Tech Center and for the postgraduate students at Wayne State University. Quang stood by the carry-out counter and pointed to the blackboard. He ordered Number Two and Number Five, sweet and sour pork and shrimp fried rice, Diane's favorites.

CHAPTER VII

# In Sorrow Thou Shalt Bring Forth Children

The morning after Diane's appointment, Dr. Santoro was sitting at a table in the staff lounge.She had spread in front of her the The American Journal of Ob/Gyn, an old issue of Time magazine, yesterday's copy of the Toronto Star and an historical novel in Italian. Like a two-fisted drinker, that was the way she read, usually three or four printed items at a time.

From the moment she had learned how to read, reading had become Alfonsina's main source of solace. She would read books, magazines, leaflets, cereal boxes and postage stamps. She surpassed the label of avid reader and developed a dependency on the printed word; she turned into a readaholic. As a child, her favorite readings were stories of knights and damsels, dragons and fairies; she would wander into those unreal worlds and become lost in them. Fueled by those fantasies, her imagination would fabricate, often at the wrong times, the assuaging images of things desired: of having her father again, of going on a family vacation, of hosting a dress-up party at her house, of being petite and popular. Her reveries, discouraged by her pragmatic teachers, had resulted in many after-school detentions and fueled her mother's rage. These memories of her grade school years were often revisited as she strove to absorb the substance of printed words.

When L'Nore entered the room, Dr. Santoro was still at the table by herself in front of the magazines. She was, unsurprisingly, in a somber mood. She put down her cocoa mug and wiped her mouth. "Did you notice that Diane seemed worried yesterday?" she said, looking up at her assistant.

"What do you mean?" asked L'Nore.

"What part of the sentence didn't you understand?" said the doctor sarcastically.

"You said she seemed worried," answered the nurse while pouring some coffee into her mug.

"I'm impressed. Your comprehension of spoken English is improving."

"And your understanding of pregnant women is not," L'Nore snapped back. "Of course, Diane is worried. She should be."

"Why?" The doctor sounded surprised.

"Why?" L'Nore's eyes popped. "She is pregnant."

"She should be worried because she's pregnant?"

"She will be having a baby." L'Nore added emphatically, "She'll have to go through labor, and through delivery."

"You mean Diane is worried because labor and delivery hurt?"

"No, Alfie," said L'Nore, as if explaining to a child. "If you burn your arm on a hot frying pan, it hurts. If you slam the car door on your finger, that hurts. Delivering a baby is entirely different."

"How so?" asked the doctor rather teasingly now. "I've never had a baby. Please do explain."

"Well, let me think," said L'Nore hesitantly, as if searching for the most descriptive image. "How can I describe it to you graphically? It is like shitting a pumpkin."

The doctor shook her head and laughed loudly. "I asked for it," she said.

L'Nore laughed too. So did two other nurses at another table who had overheard the exchange.

That was not what the doctor had meant when she had said Diane seemed worried, but she could not entirely discard L'Nore's explanation.

"Let's go to work, smart-ass," the doctor said, and the two of them walked out of the room chuckling.

CHAPTER VIII

# Your Young Men Shall See Visions, and Your Old Men Shall Dream Dreams

When Quang walked into his apartment with the delicacies on the day he learned that he was going to be a father again, Diane was sitting at the kitchen table, statements and receipts that she had brought from the office spread in front of her. She was dressed in a red kimono. The light from a ceiling lamp splashed subtly on her face and highlighted her perfect almond-shaped eyes and her unblemished cinnamon skin. She could have set standards for Oriental beauty. Her lush, thick, jet black hair fell almost to her waist. Her breasts were perfectly proportioned for her thin body and her narrow boyish hips.

She looked up at Quang standing next to her. The frank smile still on his face confirmed that he had gotten the message. She gave him her warmest smile in return. A happy and loving couple they had been from the day they married, and, as happily married couples usually do, they tended to look more like each other as time passed.

"Sexy mamma," he said in English and planted a loud kiss on her forehead. He laid the food on the table and brought two cans of Stroh's beer from the refrigerator for the celebration.

Soon they reverted to their native tongue, for they both spoke the same dialect.

They ate, and they drank. But mostly they reminisced.

They had met by the Kong River.

"When I was pedaling the water wheel for Thu'a Cụ," he said, "you brought me a glass of fresh buffalo milk. It was still warm."

"No, silly." Diane giggled. "I had set my eyes on you two or three months before that, when you were bathing in the river after your shift at the wheel."

"You naughty girl," he scolded her. "That doesn't count."

She kept giggling. "You gave me four pink poppies."

"But the first time we touched was in Mr. Kompur's jeep," he said.

Two more Stroh's. They kept reminiscing. Their story, not much different from that of all their friends and relatives who lived to tell it, could give goose pimples to most Americans.

Quang knew nothing at all about his parents. As far back as his memory could reach, he was living among Theravada Buddhist monks from the highlands who ran a monastery by the Kong River. He learned the monks' language, although he kept using his native dialect with other novices at the monastery. His primary job was to tend to the monastery's vegetable garden, but often he had to go with the Sangha mendicant monks on their early morning door-to-door begging. The monks depended on food donations from the villagers for their daily sustenance because whatever they made out of the crops of the garden was used for the upkeep of the temple. The other boys enjoyed the street; Quang had preferred to work in the garden.

Quang was the tallest boy in the monastery. That sunrise-to-sunset laboring had given him a strong, muscular body that had helped him to command a good deal of respect from the other boys.

He was about ten or eleven years old when Thu'a Cụ paid a visit to the monks looking for a few farmhands for his rice fields. Thu'a Cụ was treated with the outmost courtesy, almost reverence, by the monks because he would give them generous contributions from time to time. Thu'a Cụ had a good eye for workers; he picked out Quang first, the most muscular. The monks liked Quang and would have preferred to keep him as well as the other boys, but they had their own problems, and a few less mouths to feed was a proposition they couldn't afford to decline. They sent Quang, along with a sack full of fresh vegetables and fruits, a spade and 1500 kips—about five dollars.

No one knew Thu'a Cụ's real age; he could have been eighty or ninety or perhaps a hundred years old. For many years he had run a large rice plantation on the Kong River, and he owned many buffaloes, chickens and pigs. The Kong River originates in the Annamite Cordillera in Vietnam, runs southwest for seventy-five miles through Laos by the Boloven Plateau and flows into the Mekong River by the city of Pakxe in Cambodia. Thu'a Cụ's farm extended for several miles on the right bank of the Kong River, north of Pakxe.

No one knew the old man's real name either; they all referred to him as Thu'a Cụ—Old Man—in the accepted respectful sense of the word "old." There were always a couple of dozen boys and girls working at Thu'a Cụ's farm. From the beginning, Quang's assignment, because he was strongly built, was to pedal the water wheel ten to twelve hours a day.

Water wheels were like stationary bicycles used to scoop water from the river and route it to the rice paddies. Thu'a Cụ owned five of them, but only four worked; one had been broken for years. Soon after arriving at the farm, Quang fixed it with some parts he removed from a military truck that had been abandoned by the riverbank a few miles up the road. Thu'a Cụ was very pleased; from that day he began to call him "Clever Boy."

Xang, Thu'a Cụ's granddaughter or great-granddaughter— she did not know which—was in charge of the workers. Xang was about twenty years old and rather heavy-set. She had a deep scar on her forehead that she covered by tilting her hat in a rather coquettish way. She was not able to work in the fields because she needed a crutch to walk; she had lost a leg and several fingers in the land mine explosion that had also caused the scar on her face. Handicap notwithstanding, Xang earned her keep. She cooked for Thu'a Cụ and for all the workers. Thu'a Cụ spent most of his time sitting on an old wicker arm-chair on the verandah, looking over the fields, smoking a long bamboo pipe. When Thu'a Cụ tapped his cane twice, Xang would hurry with his tea. Three taps of the cane meant that he needed his pipe refilled with "the stuff." Thu'a Cụ kept "the stuff" next to him day and night in a discolored tote bag on which one could still discern the word "Miami" over a faded outline of the city skyline. To light up the pipe was also Xang's job; she did it quite willingly because she had made it a habit to inhale several puffs before passing it to the old man. "The stuff" made her feel very good.

Xang admired the old man. She was very proud of him. She enjoyed telling the workers how powerful Thu'a Cụ was and how he could get anything he wanted because he had so many friends. "Thu'a Cụ has no enemies," she would say as an introduction to her favorite story. "He had some enemies once. Many years ago, three boys came to ask him to lend them some money. Thu'a Cụ did not like them, and he turned them away. They shouted insults and kicked dirt towards him as they were leaving. Thu'a Cụ was upset. The next morning, a buffalo and a pig were missing. Now Thu'a Cụ was very angry. He called a friend from the mountain people to help him find the three boys. A few days later, the friend came back with the buffalo; the pig he never found." Xang would then lean forward towards her audience and lower her voice to a whisper. "The buffalo was wearing a necklace," she would say very slowly, "a wire ring with six human ears." At this point, she would break into loud laughter. "Now Thu'a Cụ has no more enemies, you see."

Diane was probably born in 1938, the Chinese year of the tiger, because at times she was teased about still having the big cat in her. She was probably born in Laos, but was given a Vietnamese name: Dáo. The borders of Cochin China, Funan, Laos, Cambodia, Vietnam—they are all conventional partitions, unrealistic, unsustainable boundaries, the results of gerrymandering on a grand scale wrought in Paris, London, Berlin, Washington. They change every other decade.

All Diane learned about her father was that he had left the village before she was born, heading for the rubber plantations that were hiring at that time. She heard from the neighbors that she had three older brothers and two older sisters. When she was only a few months old, an uncle—or cousin—took her mother to Bangkok in Thailand, where he said he had friends that could find work for her as a waitress. Diane's mother left her in the care of a relative until she was settled in Bangkok and could save enough money to send for her. Diane's mother and the cousin, or uncle, who took her away were never heard of again.

The year Diane was probably born, there was a war in her country. When her mother had been born, there had been another war in her country. Diane had heard stories of families split at checkpoints by the different armies or guerrillas; some were allowed through, and some were detained, and they would never be reunited.

Although Diane's family always moved only within a radius of a few miles, they never lived in the same village more than three or four years at a time. One army or another would move in, kill or draft most of the men, violate the women and take many of the children away. There had always been a market for the children. Some were sold in the next village. Some were dragged to big cities such as Vientiane or Bangkok. Those who survived the journey were sold there or left to survive on the streets as best they could.

The relative who raised Diane when her mother left for

Bangkok was several years older than Diane and had no children of her own. She was related to her, probably a cousin or aunt. Diane called her Me nuôi, which meant "Mother Substitute." She was as kind to her as a mother could be.

Every so often, a rumor would spread in the village that an army was coming, and the younger men, the women and the children would run away from the village to hide until the soldiers left. One night, when soldiers were expected to go through the village where they were then living, Diane and Me nuôi and a few neighbors hid under a rope bridge spanning a rice paddy, crouching in the stagnant waters as a platoon of soldiers was crossing the bridge single file. They had to breathe very quietly, their nostrils barely above the surface of the still water.

When the soldiers were out of sight and they could talk again, Me nuôi told Diane, "It's too late for me now"—she was about twenty-five years old—"but you are still young. Run away. Try to go to America."

"If they catch me, I'll be shot," Diane protested.

"Yes," Me nuôi answered, "and the entire you will be dead in one minute. If you stay here, a little piece of you will die each day."

Diane never forgot that.

Me nuôi had heard of Thu'a Cụ's farm. She had learned that it was a safe place where the workers never went without food. Even though it stood right in the middle of the guerrillas' supply line, the farm was never attacked. The Ho Chi Minh trail, as it was later named, meandered around the farm. It was murmured in the villages that Thu'a Cụ was a personal friend of Ho Chi Minh.

It was towards the end of the rainy season, when Diane was almost twelve years old. Rumor was growing that troops were about to move into the village. Me nuôi woke Diane up one morning earlier than usual, made her dress in a hurry and walked her to the center of the village. She gave Diane some money for the bus fare and a tote bag with her few belongings. Ignoring Diane's protests, she pushed her into a crowded bus and told the driver to drop her at Thu'a Cụ's farm. Me nuôi held Diane's head so she could not turn around, kissed the back of her head and said firmly: "Go. There's nothing for you here." Then Me nuôi turned around and bolted away before the bus started.

Diane followed her with her eyes and waved. Me nuôi never looked back.

Thu'a Cụ was good enough to accept her at the farm.

Diane's recollections of her days at Thu'a Cụ's farm—she stayed there for four or five years—were mostly happy ones. The work was hard, from sunrise to sunset, except for the rainy season, but she was always fed and seldom punished. It was traditional at the farm to eat some chicken every weekend, and all-you-can-eat roast pork for the full moon celebrations. After every full moon feast, those who remained awake gathered in the verandah around Thu'a Cụ. Xang would tell stories of the people of the highlands, the workers would exchange gossip, and Thu'a Cụ would fall asleep, his long pipe dangling from his lips. Sometimes he just pretended to be asleep, and he would mete out swift and painful justice with his cane to those who ventured naughty remarks.

The sight of the full moon rising over the majestic Nui Ba Den—Black Lady Mountain—the purring of the Kong River and the flat, smooth rice paddies remained engraved as cherished memories of their youth for Diane and Quang.

In the afterglow of one of those roast pork parties, which usually included some rice wine, Quang gathered the courage to ask Thu'a Cụ a very personal question. "Do you have dreams, Thu'a Cụ?" he asked, trying to sound as nonchalant as he could.

It was one of those quiet evenings in late April, a rain halo encircled the moon over Nui Ba Den, but there was no rain yet. The winds were gathering some force, and the swelling of the Mekong River was beginning to push the purling waters of the Kong River above its banks and into the countless rivulets that festooned the edges of the farmland. It was the prelude of the monsoon season.

"Do you ever dream, Thu'a Cụ?" Quang repeated after waiting for an answer for quite some time. The original question was disrespectful. Repeating it after Thu'a Cụ declined to answer the first time could have been considered outright insolent and could have cost Quang several whacks of Thu'a Cụ's stick.

The old man, however, remained unperturbed. He nodded at last. It encouraged Quang to pursue the point.

"What do you dream of, Thu'a Cụ?"

The old man puffed on his pipe three or four times before he answered. His head did not move. His eyes remained totally closed, or minimally open, as they were most of the time.

"When I dream," at long last he answered, his lips barely moving, "I dream that I am sitting in front of my house, gazing at a full moon over Nui Ba Den, smoking 'the stuff' and listening to the Kong swell."

The full moon makes people dream. Many of the youths that were gathered around Thu'a Cụ could not help pondering what there really was to dream about.

Thu'a Cụ broke the silence. "And what do you dream of, Clever Boy?"

As if he had been waiting for the question, Quang's answer rang out loud and firm: "I dream of going to America."

America, he said; of course, he meant the image of America. In his mind, it was not any clearer than that of heaven, or hell for that matter. It was just a new world beyond an unpleasant one.

If the answer surprised anyone, no one acknowledged it. Just a muffled voice from afar uttered, "Me, too." It sounded much like a church congregation responding "Amen" after each general intercession. Diane said it. She was lying on a straw mat inside the house.

Thu'a Cụ did not look at Quang or Diane; perhaps he never really heard her. The old man just brought the tip of his index finger to his lips. Shush, it meant. "A dream can kill a man," he said very softly, under his breath.

Another silence followed, longer yet than the previous one. Thu'a Cụ seemed to have fallen into a slumber. Then, suddenly, as if talking in his sleep, he said in a hushed tone: "A dream can keep a man alive, too."

The full moon can make even wise men say foolish things.

Nothing else was said after that. One after another, they all fell asleep. The total quietness was broken now and again by gun reports in the distance, not loud enough to wake anybody.

Some days later, before the next full moon, a Thai businessman came to see Thu'a Cụ. He was a short and very thin man in his late fifties perhaps. His name was Mr. Kompur. He was dressed in camouflage fatigues and carried a large, black umbrella and a brown box briefcase. He wore round gold-rimmed glasses, and his mouth showed some dark spaces where teeth should be, which made his smile comical rather than businesslike as it was intended to be. He bowed very deeply to Thu'a Cụ, who countered with a faint nod. Xang brought tea to them. They both smoked their long bamboo pipes and talked for a long time. Every now and then, they exchanged small packages.

Thu'a Cụ filled a large box with "the stuff" from his beach bag and gave it to Mr. Kompur. When the visit came to an end and Mr. Kompur stood up, Thu'a Cụ tapped his cane on the railing, and Xang came at once to the verandah. He motioned to her to summon a young boy who was feeding water buffaloes near the house. The boy came running, bowed ceremoniously to Thu'a Cụ and listened attentively to him. A few times, the boy cupped one ear with his hand, because the old man spoke very softly. The boy nodded, bowed again and ran to the fields. Soon he returned at a fast pace with

Diane on his heels. Then the boy ran again, in the opposite direction, towards the riverbank.

Diane was left standing in silence facing the two men and wondering, "What am I going to be punished for?" She had done all she had been ordered to do, she had not quarreled with any of the other workers, she had kept her sleeping mat tidy, she had not said anything that could have...

A faint recollection began to push its way to the forefront of her mind, subtly at first, then more forcefully as she tried to ignore it. She finally yielded to it, and it came to the forefront. There was no denying. She had said it. It was true. Now she was sorry she had said it. Fear was beginning to well up in her; she was familiar with the feeling.

When she saw the boy coming from the river with Clever Boy, fear turned into paralyzing terror.

"That's what Mr. Kompur is here for." She reached that terrifying conclusion. Both she and Clever Boy had revealed their sinful wishes. Now he would turn them both over to torture and execution as they deserved. They would be brought to the town square for a trial. An expressed wish to leave the homeland was unquestionably treason. They would be taunted and scorned by the populace, tortured by the soldiers and shot as a warning to other potential traitors to the land. That was what Thu'a Cụ had meant when he had said that a dream could kill a man.

She could read the same fear on Clever Boy's face as he stood motionless next to her. Xang told Diane and Clever Boy to pack up their things. She helped them to fill two wicker bags, and she threw the bags onto the passenger seat of the jeep. Mr. Kompur motioned to Quang and Diane to get into the back seat; they obeyed. He exchanged a few more words with Thu'a Cụ in Thai and placed the boxes and bags the old man had given him under the front passenger seat.

Thu'a Cụ, without opening his eyes, told them: "Do as my friend tells you."

Mr. Kompur jumped in behind the wheel, and they were off. Thu'a Cụ never turned to look at them. It was almost noon; the sun hung straight up in the middle of the sky. The heat caused a thick steam to rise from the rice paddies.

The last glimpse Quang and Diane had of Thu'a Cụ was to remain in their memories as a surreal tableau—his profile cut against the distant undefined hills as that of a very old man on a wicker chair with a long pipe in his mouth and his chin propped on his cane. The silhouette seemed to be float-ing in the mist above the rice paddies; once that silhouette had eventually dissolved in the mist, Thu'a Cụ's very existence would forever after have an aura of marginal reality for Diane and Quang.

In the back of the jeep, still terror-stricken and bouncing at every bump and hole in the dirt road, Diane and Quang, did not talk to each other. Once in a while they would exchange inquisitive looks, feeding each other's terror regarding the fate that awaited them.

After an hour of riding, they came to a checkpoint. Mr. Kompur talked to the guards in a language Quang and Diane could not understand. Then he reached into the tray under the dashboard, took an envelope and handed it to the guards. A pistol that was under the envelope was exposed. The guards at the crossing smiled at Mr. Kompur and motioned at him to go on. The gun remained visible for the rest of the journey as a disturbing reminder for the couple.

When Quang had gathered enough courage, he leaned forward and asked the driver in Vietnamese, "Where are we going?"

Mr. Kompur turned around and beamed on them both a mischievous toothless smile. He answered in Thai, "It is a surprise." The tone, however, was somehow reassuring.

In mid-afternoon they stopped at a restaurant in a big town they had never heard of. Mr. Kompur ordered fried rice and chicken and Coca-Cola for the three of them. Quang explained that they had no money. Mr. Kompur gave them the same quizzical smile and motioned to them to hurry up and eat. "It's Thu'a Cụ's treat," he added.

When they had traveled for a couple more hours, Diane felt confident enough to ask the driver with her sweetest smile, "Is it going to be a nice surprise?"

Mr. Kompur answered in Thai, "A surprise," without turning around. Again the tone allayed their apprehension a little. The two exchanged hopeful glances.

They reached the Thai border at Poipet. Mr. Kompur stepped out of the car at the checkpoint. He argued with the border guards for a good while. Then he produced some papers from his briefcase and pointed at Diane and Quang in the back seat. The guards checked under the seats, inside the glove compartment and under the chassis. They ignored the gun. At last, Mr. Kompur gave the guards several small envelopes and shook hands with all of them. They went on into Thailand.

When they entered the city of Aranyapratet in Thailand, Diane and Quang breathed with relief; their fears vanished almost completely. They knew it was a much safer land than Cambodia or Vietnam. Quang smiled at Diane, and she reached for his hand.

"Very greedy people, the Thai," Mr. Kompur said to them in Vietnamese.

By sunset they were in Bangkok. Mr. Kompur drove the jeep into the courtyard of a rather large inn. Two young men in business suits and an older woman in fashionable Western clothes were obviously awaiting them. They greeted Mr. Kompur ceremoniously, and he introduced Quang and Diane to the group. There was a young Thai girl in tight jeans and a low-cut white blouse sitting at a table smoking a cigarette in a long holder. She came running towards the group; she smiled at everyone and exchanged some lighthearted bantering with the young men. Quang and Diane's command of Thai was not sufficient to understand the subtleties of the conversation, but they laughed too and kept up with the jovial mood of the assembly. One of the young men called aloud to a waitress from the restaurant to bring beers for all. Quang placed his arm around Diane's shoulder and held her close to him for the rest of the night. The young girl with the long cigarette holder grabbed Mr. Kompur's arm and pulled him away from the group. She led him to the stairs at the back of the court-yard. As they were climbing the stairs to the upper floor, Mr. Kompur turned towards Quang and Diane and said to them in French: *"Bonne chance."*

*"Merci, merci, merci beaucoup,"* they shouted back. *"Au revoir, Monsieur Kompur."*

The girl with the long cigarette holder pulled Mr. Kompur by the arm, laughing aloud; they disappeared forever from Quang and Diane's lives, into the twilight of the second floor rooms.

Many years later, when it was resurrected by Diane and Quang in an apartment in Troy, Michigan, that image of Mr. Kompur, like that of Thu'a Cụ, still carried the ethereal qual-ity of questionable reality. In Western culture, perhaps, the two characters would have been referred to as "angels."

That warm Bangkok night, Quang and Diane were jubi-lant. What was going to happen to them they did not know. As they stood under that starry sky, holding on to each other, it did not seem to matter much.

Later that night, one of the men in business suits led Diane and Quang to a room on the ground floor of the inn. The other man brought their bags from the jeep. Then the two men sat down on the bed and started to spread papers over the bed as they pulled them from a large manila folder. They handed to Quang and Diane passports from the Republic of Thailand (the pictures resembled them enough), US permanent resident visas, Northwest Orient airline tickets to Los Angeles, five hundred Thai bhats for food at the airport and one hundred US dollars.

Quang's sense of humor had returned. He placed the passport with his picture next to his face. "Looks like me?" he asked Diane, smiling.

"No," she protested. "You're much more handsome."

"Not to worry," said one of the men in suits. "To Americans, all people from Southeast Asia look the same." They all laughed aloud.

They spent the night together in the small hotel room. They were going to America! Diane and Quang bounced back and forth from laughter to weeping, like children. Their first and only night in Bangkok, their union was consummated. Fifteen years later, their unspoken promises of fidelity remained unbroken.

Almost as an afterthought, they asked a monk to bless their union the next morning. A few days later, another monk married them again in Los Angeles in the Theravada Buddhist tradition, and, for good measure, a Baptist minister insisted on marrying them once more in Georgia. That's when Dáo—"Peach in Blossom" in Vietnamese—quite willingly became "Diane." Quang preferred to remain Quang.

"Me and Diane very married!" Quang would often say jokingly.

As they descended into the big city of Los Angeles, they peeked out the window, gazing at the lights in awe. They had never before seen so many bright and colorful lights. They squeezed each other's hand to remind each other that they were indeed awake, in America.

When the plane touched down, Quang whispered in Diane's ear in their native tongue, "See? Thu'a Cụ believed in dreams after all."

CHAPTER IX

# The Sixth Lunar Month

ven though Diane's mysterious "whoosh" had remained vivid in Doctor Santoro's mind, in the month that followed she had had little time to dwell on it. Unusual occurrences, bizarre as they may be, do not remain long in the forefront in the busyness of real life. New occurrences replace them continuously. In the time-constrained environment of a busy obstetrical service, afterthoughts, second guessings and recaps are not affordable commodities. Boldly and unannounced, challenges, complications and near-catastrophes sprouted every day. Since Diane's last visit, Dr. Santoro had attended to two placenta previas, three fetuses in distress that demanded emergency caesarean sections, one abruptio placentae (premature separation of the placenta from the uterine wall) complicated by the dreaded disseminated intravascular coagulation and kidney shutdown, and a handful of hemorrhages.

Clinical practice—the firing line, as Dr. Santoro called it—does not allow its practitioners to indulge in the luxury of in-depth research of unusual phenomena. The intellectual elucidation of out-of-the-norm occurrences are the domain of researchers in large medical centers. Dr. Santoro resented that the exciting cases—those that challenged the routine of the

craft beyond a certain point, usually measured in time—had
to be farmed out. Much to her chagrin, Dr. Santoro had to
send to University Hospital quadruplets, a choriocarcinoma,
an invasive cervical cancer and an advanced ovarian cancer.
She had been adequately trained, and she felt quite capable
of handling all of them, but Dr. D'Onofrio would hear none
of it.

"You don't have the time. They don't pay you for it," Dr.
D'Onofrio would bellow. "Send her downtown."

Dr. D'Onofrio specialized in uneventful pregnancies, easy
deliveries or easy caesarean sections, routine hysterectomies.
He was good at it. He was a skilled craftsman. "They are your
bread and butter," he often said. They were. He himself generated more revenue than any of the other doctors. And he was
revered in Grosse Pointe.

Dr. Santoro grew up with Dr. Kildare and Ben Casey, the
glamorous medical practices. Dr. D'Onofrio had grown up in
the Depression.

"I'll tell you why Dr. Kildare and Ben Casey are so loved
and so successful with their patients," Dr. D'Onofrio lectured
her one day. "Because they only take care of one patient per
week. That's why." Perhaps glamorous medicine had influ-
enced Dr. Santoro's choice of careers.

As a child, Alfonsina Santoro was quite shy and given to
daydreaming; as a result, her school performance was less than
average. In grade school, she marginally succeeded in passing
each year. Her lack of concentration had brought upon her
severe reprimands. Her mother was used to hearing rather
disturbing reports about Alfonsina's academic abilities at most
parent/teacher conferences.

At one of those meetings, the fourth grade teacher, seeing
that Mrs. Santoro was quite distraught at Alfonsina's performance, tried to cheer her. "You mustn't worry, Mrs. Santoro,"
she said touching the mother's hand patronizingly. "I'm certain
that, with a little assistance, Alfonsina will, in time, be able to

learn some skilled, or semi-skilled, job. We will place her in a special school which is not demanding academically or socially threatening. We will help you."

Mrs. Santoro stood up, uttered a terse "Thanks" to the teacher and walked away, Alfie lumbering behind. Just a few steps away from the teacher's desk, without turning to her daughter, she said under her breath: *"E una scema"*—she is stupid.

Alfonsina's father was an Italian immigrant to Canada. Although quite bright, he never learned English well enough to advance beyond a press operator job at the Ford Motor Company in Windsor, Ontario, just across the river from Detroit. A secure job it was, with a low but dependable income that sufficed to sustain the family if luxuries were avoided. With only the most basic education, Gelsumino Santoro had the ability to analyze and find solutions to difficult algebra problems, those with multiple variables that can daunt a mathematician; and when it came to practical wisdom, he was a master.

One day he was called to the school by the teacher because Fabio, Alfonsina's older brother, had punched the nose of a classmate, causing it to bleed. "Why did you do it, son?" he asked the boy when he returned home from the conference.

"He was saying bad things about me again and again. I warned him first."

"What was he saying about you?" Father asked.

"You wouldn't understand," the boy answered.

"Would your mother understand?"

"No," Fabio replied, tears welling up in his eyes.

"And your sister, can she understand it?"

Fabio shook his head, holding back his tears.

"But you still think you did the right thing?"

Fabio nodded.

"And only you know it was the right thing?"

The boy nodded again; the tears began to roll down. *"Mi spiace, Babbo"*—I'm sorry, Daddy—he kept repeating.

Then Father patted him on the shoulder and said, *"Sta bene"*—It's all right. Then Gelsumino Santoro said, partly in Italian, partly in English, something that Alfonsina, about seven or eight years old, thought was exceptionally wise. She translated it fully into English and jotted it down inside the back cover of the book she was then reading, *Rebecca of Sunnybrook Farm.*

While Father was alive, the Santoros lived a rather drab but satisfactory existence, without luxuries but without lacking any basic necessities.

One Sunday morning in early December when Alfonsina was nine years old, after finishing breakfast with the whole family, her father complained of a headache and went back to bed. That was not entirely unusual because he suffered from migraines. That day, though, he did not come down for supper. That was unusual. Sunday supper with the uncles, aunts, cousins and *La Nonna* was as important an event as ever took place at the Santoros' house. Father had never missed it before.

Father Collucci said at the funeral that Gelsumino Santoro was a devoted family man, a good Christian and the hardest working man he had ever known and that, even after his death, he should remain a living example for his children. Alfonsina then turned to her brother and mother; they were both crying. She assumed that crying was the right thing to do to stop pain, and she cried too. It did not make her feel any better, so she never cried again until the night when Diane Truong had her baby.

Gelsumino Santoro, besides his two children, left few mementoes of his passing through this world. No memoirs, no recorded voice, just a black-and-white photograph of his wedding and a few snapshots taken at parties. Whenever Alfonsina felt a need of something tangible to remember her father by, she would go to the back cover of *Rebecca* for inspiration.

The Italian community of Windsor was very supportive of the Santoros. Some cousin or aunt or *comare*—a friend— would visit daily with the family for many weeks after Father's death. Eventually the dust settled, the tears dried up, and Mrs. Santoro mustered enough courage to tell her children that the Santoros were flat busted. A minimal life insurance policy barely covered the funeral expenses, and the pension from the Ford Motor Company was not even sufficient to pay the mortgage and taxes on the house.

Mother, who had occasionally done some sewing for friends, took a full-time job as a seamstress at a clothing store on Ouellette Avenue in the center of Windsor. The shop's clientele consisted mostly of rich women from Detroit's suburbs. The pay was good, and with lots of overtime she was able to put Fabio and later Alfonsina through school.

Fabio was twelve years old when Father died. He started working as a stock boy at an Italian grocery store on Erie Street. When school was out, he would move to Leamington, a few miles away, to work on the tomato farms, which offered better pay.

Uncle Vito, Gelsumino's brother, got Alfonsina her first job when she was twelve, in a produce store at Windsor's Farmers' Market. It was a catastrophe. The owner, Signor Damiani, was her uncle's friend, a popular figure at the market, one of its founders. He was affectionately known as "The Watermelon King." He was a short, heavy-set man, past middle age, with grayish hair, bushy eyebrows and a bushy mustache. He was quite a colorful feature in the market. All summer, he dressed in an impeccably pressed white sport jacket and wore a red carnation boutonniere. Signor Damiani was a well respected man, very powerful in the large Italian community of Essex County. He had only two weaknesses, and they were benevolently ignored because he was a generous and very kindly person: He gambled to excess, and he liked to pat young girls' butts.

Signor Damiani could not overlook Alfonsina's butt. "Cute ass," he said with his warm smile as he grabbed it in the back room of the store.

"That's not nice," she fired at him with a murderous gaze.

He chuckled and blew her a kiss.

Alfonsina's ass at twelve, cute perhaps, was not her trump card, though. Her breasts were; they had blossomed far beyond any girl's that age and stood defiantly with all the firmness of adolescence. "The Watermelon King" could not miss them either. The following week, when she was arranging some cans on the top shelves, he came up to her from behind. *"Bellissima!"*—Beautiful!—he said and cupped her breasts in both his hands.

Signor Damiani was standing with his back to what was known as the watermelon mound. The mound was the center display of the store; it consisted of dozens of the largest and freshest gourds piled ceiling-high in the shape of a pyramid. "The Watermelon King" was still holding her breasts when she turned around and stared down at him—she was almost a foot taller than he. He gave her a childish guffaw as on the time before. Alfonsina closed her left hand into a fist (she was left-handed) and delivered a half-strength jab into Signor Damiani's solar plexus. Then, very calmly, she undid her apron, dropped it on the floor and walked towards the exit.

Her punch had caused "The Watermelon King" to lose his footing and fall backwards into the pyramid, upsetting its precarious balance. Alfie was by the exit door when she began to hear the deafening roar of the rolling watermelons. Once outside the door, she turned around and saw the melons running wild in all directions over the floor, knocking down other displays. Some burst when they hit the floor, and the expanding red puddle gave the scene a rather macabre hue. "The King" was partially buried by the melons, his white sport coat smeared by the fruits' blood. He was waving his arms out of the heap into the air, as a drowning man would, and vociferating something like, "You'll never work in this city again."

Alfonsina walked the five miles to her home and told her mother she did not intend to work there anymore—without giving her any reasons. "The King," understandably, was not in need of the kind of publicity such an incident could generate, so he did not pursue the issue. Mrs. Santoro was wise enough not to ask any questions and never knew the whole story until many years later. She had always suspected, though, that Alfonsina had something to do with the incident at the produce store that required summoning the fire department to wash the sticky juices off the floors. The local newspaper called it a "Watermelon Stampede."

Alfonsina did find another job—in the Laboratory at Hotel Dieu Hospital. She started as an aid on the midnight shift, cleaning the counters and sorting the samples; by the time she moved to Toronto to attend medical school, she was the supervisor of the Laboratory, in charge of mostly everything.

Out of ignorance—or pride perhaps—Alfonsina never thought of applying for a scholarship. When she finished her residency training at Wayne State University in Detroit, she was so deeply in debt that she had to decline offers to remain in that institution and become a member of the faculty. Instead, she joined The Grosse Pointe Storks, a prosperous group of obstetricians started in the fifties by Dr. D'Onofrio in a suburb of Detroit. Dr. Santoro was little more than an indentured slave but with a substantial salary that enabled her to start paying off her debts and to help support her mother.

~ ~ ~

The day of Diane's next visit, Dr. Santoro and L'Nore were alone at the table in the Ob/Gyn staff room. The other employees had their lunches in the cafeteria, and most other doctors would usually eat at Aldo's, The Golden Lion, The Bronze Door or whatever Grosse Pointe restaurant was fashionable at the time.

When the two of them were alone, L'Nore would often ask the doctor, as if inviting reassurance, "Alfie, do you really think

I'll ever make it to medical school?" In private, she called Dr. Santoro Alfie, as almost everybody else did.

"I know people on the admissions committee. We'll get you in. Don't worry," the doctor always replied. "Not that you will need any help. You are still four-point-zero, aren't you?"

"You bet. But then, med school is so expensive."

"Listen here," Alfie admonished her, half jokingly. "You're a woman."

"No question about it."

"You're a single parent."

"Don't remind me."

"And you are black."

"No, I just dyed my skin to get into the country club," L'Nore quipped.

"The scholarship fairies will be beating a path to your door."

There was, perhaps, a tinge of resentment in the doctor's heart because a scholarship would have been such a blessing for her and her mother in her college years.

L'Nore felt reassured enough. "And some day I'll be an Ob/Gyn and join The Grosse Pointe Storks," she mused.

Alfie nodded.

"And some day I'll be making the big bucks, just like you."

"Yes, and you will also be dealing with the fucking-lawyers."

Dr. Santoro, as physicians go, was not much prone to use profanities. In her vocabulary, however, "fucking-lawyer" was a compound word. She just could not think of the second half of the word without the first, and almost never used the first half alone.

It was so much a habit to prefix the word "lawyer" with the expletive that once she uttered the compound word in front of her mother at supper. Bad enough. The fact that Father Collucci—now Monsignor Collucci—happened to be a guest at the table aggravated the offense immensely. Mother was speechless. Alfie reddened to the roots of her hair. "Er…excuse me, Father," she stuttered.

Father Collucci broached the subject with his usual tact. "We, in the church," he said, "as a rule, decry the use of profanity. Yet, in this case, within the context it was used, I believe it is excusable." Everyone at the table laughed. The bishop, it seemed, had had his share of legal problems.

L'Nore was not thinking that the lawyers would be much of a preoccupation for her. "Don't worry, Alfie. I think I'll be able to handle the bastards," she said, making a gesture as if holding a baseball and squeezing it.

"You'll make an excellent doctor, L'Nore." Alfie continued the pep talk. "It'd be nice if all the candidates entered medical school with the same commitment as you."

"Thanks," said L'Nore.

"But you're still a smart-ass."

By then, they had finished their salads and crackers. The doctor's mind wandered a little. It searched. It reached the conclusion that L'Nore was her best friend and her only confidant. Then her brain returned to what she had named years back "the anxiety du jour." This time it was that damned "whoosh."

~ ~ ~

At one-thirty on the dot, they were seeing their first patient of the afternoon. Somehow, they always managed to fall behind later on.

"Move it, you two," Dr. D'Onofrio would scold them once in a while. "You talk too much with your patients."

When, towards the end of the afternoon, L'Nore led Diane into the examination room, Dr. Santoro was already there, perusing Diane's medical record.

"Here she is, the enigmatic patient," said L'Nore cheerfully. The preliminaries—weight, blood pressure, measurement and palpation of the uterus, and the urine tests—were carried out in a perfunctory manner. It was clear that the three women were anxiously awaiting the main event: the heartbeat show. Dr. Santoro, in preparation for it, had brought in an extra Fetone machine, in case she had to listen to the two different tones simultaneously.

At eighteen weeks, the fetal heart tones are always clearly audible even with the old-fashioned fetoscope. The first set of beats had moved up, above and to the right of the umbilicus, but they were easily found and recognizable without any effort. They had remained mostly unchanged from the previous visit—sharp and loud—and the rate showed little variation, still 144 beats per minute. The doctor looked at Diane and nodded; L'Nore made the "thumbs-up" sign.

Next came the hunt for the other sounds, the puzzling ones. They would not show up this time. Not in the area where they were heard before. The doctor tried that area for some time, then different areas all over the uterus, which had grown considerably since the last visit. The three women often exchanged quizzical looks during this exercise.

"If you hadn't heard them, too, last time, I'd say I had been hearing things," said the doctor with a worried voice.

"I never heard them," retorted L'Nore with an impish smirk, as she winked at Diane.

"Very funny," said the doctor without raising her eyes from Diane's abdomen. All of a sudden, a "whoosh" came out of the speaker. The next moment it was gone. A few seconds later, the "whoosh" seemed to surface again in the background of the loud fetal heart tones. L'Nore's eyes and the doctor's locked on each other for a brief moment. The sound soon faded.

"Let me try this, Diane," said the doctor gently. "Will you roll over onto your right side?"

Diane obliged.

"I thought that, perhaps, from the side, the beam could reach the back part of the uterus," she explained.

L'Nore squirted some more mineral oil on the head of the transducer and handed it to Dr. Santoro. Their nonchalant dialogue belied their grave concern, which they tried to conceal from each other and from Diane especially.

Diane could not quite ignore their downplayed anxiety, "What's wrong?" she asked.

"Nothing serious," answered the doctor. "It's that the baby is now upside down, in a breech position, and that sometimes makes the transmission of the heartbeats quite unpredictable." That was the first lame explanation that came to Dr. Santoro's mind. Without being an outright lie (although she did not believe it), it might help allay Diane's fears.

"It means caesarean delivery?" asked Diane, just as anxiously.

"Not necessarily. Besides, the baby can change positions many times before labor."

Before Dr. Santoro could place the transducer on Diane's abdomen, the silence of the room was broken by a deafening roar that startled the women. It was followed by a loud voice.

"Dr. Santoro there?"

"Oh, my God," yelled L'Nore. "It scared me." She walked to the intercom on the wall and pressed the "Talk" button.

"Yes," she said. "What is it?"

"They need her right away in Delivery."

"What's happening?" asked the doctor aloud.

They heard her at the other end. The intercom blurted: "Six let go."

L'Nore and the doctor exchanged glances. "Dammit," said one of them. They both understood the cryptic message. Six—Labor Room Six, it meant—was a woman at thirty-one weeks of pregnancy with a placenta previa. A first pregnancy after a long infertility, it was what was referred to in the business, always with some hesitation, as a "premium baby." Someone would always counter: "All babies are premium."

Placenta previa meant that the afterbirth was lying in front of the baby—previous to it—rather than behind it, at the top of the uterus, where it should be. The placenta previa often lies over the cervical opening, and when the cervix starts to dilate, it pulls on the placental tissue, causing its blood vessels to tear; bleeding ensues. As the placenta is basically a very large sponge filled with blood, the hemorrhage can be life-threatening for the baby and sometimes even for the mother. An emergency caesarean section is usually the only solution.

"Sorry, Diane. Got to go," said the doctor in her usual loud voice, made more strident by the adrenalin rush. She laid the transducer on the instrument table, and she was already out of the room when L'Nore shouted at the doctor to encourage her, "Thirty-one weeks—it'll make it."

"Have Diane come see us next week," the doctor shouted back.

L'Nore came back into the examining room. Diane was still lying on her side. "Let me see," she said. "Sometimes the headphones are more sensitive than the speaker." She reached into a drawer and removed a set of headphones; she plugged it into the back of the Fetone cabinet and placed the earpieces carefully in her ears. She then applied the transducer high on the left side of Diane's abdomen, right underneath the ribs, aiming the ultrasound beam way back, almost to the mother's spine. A loud, roaring "whoosh" filled her ears with violent clarity and strength. She looked at her watch discreetly and counted the beats for fifteen seconds: thirty-nine beats, 156 per minute. She pressed on the transducer and noticed that the rate increased. She counted again: forty-four beats in fifteen seconds, 176 bpm. Trying to erase the worried look from her face, she shut off the machine and removed the earphones.

L'Nore's satisfaction at finding the mysterious sounds was short-lived. Besides the fact that Dr. Santoro could not explain their origin, there was something weird and unsettling about the sounds: their instantaneous and violent response to outside stimuli. At the slightest increase in the pressure on the abdomen, the rate would shoot up to over 180 bpm, and the sound itself would acquire a maelstrom-like pitch. L'Nore likened it in her mind to the crescendo growl of a feline ready to leap on its prey.

"Did you hear anything?" asked Diane.

L'Nore turned away from Diane to answer. "Just the baby's heartbeats, I think," she said, blushing.

Diane stood up and began to arrange her clothes. "You know, L'Nore," she whispered—perhaps the ill-concealed worried look on L'Nore's face invited the confiding—"I am a little worried about this pregnancy, about the baby too."

"Tell you something, Diane. Every expectant mother is worried about her baby," L'Nore answered. "That apprehension is normal. I was pregnant once. I know."

"I was not worried like this in first pregnancy. Also, something happened this pregnancy. I never told anybody because they will think I am crazy."

"What happened? You can tell me." L'Nore leaned towards her to listen.

"You see, I have this old friend; her name Kathy. Kathy and me are best friends…"

The intercom blasted even louder than the first time: "L'Nore, come scrub in. They need help right away in OR Four."

The nurse looked at Diane with a forlorn expression on her usually happy face. "So sorry, Diane. I got to go too," she said.

"Don't worry. Go ahead," said Diane.

L'Nore helped Diane off the examining table. "You'll tell me the story next time, won't you? Don't forget to make the appointment," she shouted from down the corridor.

"My God," Diane said aloud, although she was alone in the room. "Like every day is April 15 in this place." She worked in an accounting firm. She knew April 15, tax deadline day.

The frustration at being abandoned twice in the same visit brought with it a rather comforting thought—Diane understood that it could have been her emergency and that, if it was, L'Nore and the doctor would drop everything to be by her side.

Diane straightened out her dress and her hair, picked up her handbag and briefcase and headed for the front desk to schedule her next appointment.

CHAPTER X

# Facts are Facts

When L'Nore saw Dr. Santoro the morning after Diane's visit, before she even said, "Good morning," she looked the doctor straight in the eye and blurted: "I heard 'em."

She did not need to explain what she was referring to.

"Are you sure?" the doctor challenged her with a full-blown scowl.

"You can bet your sweet bippy," L'Nore responded, pointing to the doctor's buttocks.

Dr. Santoro rested her head on her wrists, elbows propped on the counter; she remained in that pensive attitude for a long while.

"I've been thinking about that *maledetto* 'whoosh' more often than I have cared to," the doctor said with spontaneous intensity. *Maledetto* was Italian for "damned." She always reverted to her first language when under undue stress. "Where did you hear it?" she went on.

"Way, way back, almost by the mother's spine," said L'Nore pointing to her own abdomen. "I heard them loud and clear."

"Did Diane hear it?" the doctor asked. Her face suddenly showed serious concern.

"No," L'Nore hurried to answer. "I used the headphones."

"You're a smart cookie, L'Nore," said the doctor as her apprehension dissipated and a smile almost broke on her face. "Why didn't I think of the headphones? What about the rate?"

"All over the place," said the nurse gesticulating." Sometimes they shot up to 180 easy. And you know what?"

"Is there more?" The doctor squinted and shrugged her shoulders as if preparing for a solid punch.

"I got them to speed up by pressing hard with the transducer."

The doctor withdrew to her somber musing again, and her gaze floated away from the confines of the room.

"Perhaps we are seeing things that do not exist," said Alfie. "Maybe we are going mad. But facts…"

L'Nore joined in—she had heard that adage many times before.

"…are very stubborn things," they said in unison.

"Do I have surgery Tuesday morning?" asked the doctor.

The nurse opened the surgery book and leafed through it. "Tuesday…Only Mrs. Taormina's section, and she delivered last week. You're free."

"Great!" said Alfie.

"What is your little brain scheming?"

"I'm going to talk to Carruthers, see what he thinks about this."

"Professor Peacock?"

"Yes," Alfie answered with a smile. "Next Tuesday, he is giving his famous introductory lecture in Embryology."

"Peacock" described pretty accurately Professor Carruthers's attitude and demeanor, and it was one of the most benevolent of the epithets that were applied to him.

"Professor Trevor Carruthers," announced L'Nore stretching herself tall, crossing her arms on her chest and extending her head in a regal pose, "a legend in his own mind."

"But he knows his stuff," said Alfie. "Maybe he has heard of something like this or he can suggest something."

"Don't forget your waders," said L'Nore. She had attended the professor's performances. "He's full of it."

## CHAPTER XI

# A Cat Named Yul

The story Diane meant to tell L'Nore perhaps would have encouraged Dr. Santoro to share with her colleagues her outrageous suspicions about the mysterious sounds.

Then again, she probably would have been laughed out of the room by her colleagues all the same.

At that time at least, before the major events took place, attempting to attribute to Yul's incident any significance beyond a sudden reversion to instinctive aggressiveness of a cat that had been subjected to genetic abuse, would have been dismissed as pure superstition.

Without doubt, Diane's strange story reeked of provincial old wives tales. Yet, it was obvious that the scars left in Diane's mind by the incident had outlived those on her belly.

When Diane arrived in Michigan from Georgia, Kathy was the first acquaintance she made, and it was friendship at first sight. Kathy was to a great extent a mentor to Diane. She encouraged Diane to register at college and coached her in the use of the English language and in American customs. She gave her advice on how to dress, how to converse and how to entertain. Kathy also cheerfully volunteered to babysit Mai when needed.

The two young ladies were very clever, besides being astute

observers. They soon realized that life in a big city can be a maelstrom that devours the socially undisciplined. Woe to those who believe that a friendship between career women can be cultivated in spare time. So they made an explicit pact early in their relationship to meet once a month no matter what, even if for only a very short while. In the many years of their relationship, they had only failed to meet their objective twice, both times because Kathy was called out of the country for business. In both cases, they made up for the lapse by meeting twice the following month. Their trysts were often at their homes, sometimes at a restaurant, occasionally for a shopping expedition. Many times Diane brought Mai along to help her get to know "Aunt Kathy" better.

At the time of Diane's second pregnancy, they had been friends for over ten years. Kathy Mestra was about Diane's age, happily divorced after an ill-fated trial at the connubial business; her work as a graphic artist at a major advertising agency afforded her all the emotional fulfillment she coveted, on an ongoing basis at least. Kathy and Diane were best friends.

Kathy could have been the poster child for ailurophiles. She had shared her house with cats all her life. She had lived with shorthairs, longhairs, calicoes, tailless cats, crossed-eyed cats, one-eyed and three-legged cats, straight-eared and folded-eared cats, friendly felines and short-tempered cats. She doted upon all of them, in an indiscriminate manner.

Shortly before Kathy moved into her new upscale apartment in Birmingham, her Himalayan, named Attila, had died rather unexpectedly, and Kathy was left in what she referred to as an "interregnum." About that time, she read in a magazine about a new breed of hairless cats that had been developed in Ontario, Canada, and had been recently accepted by the Crown Cat Fanciers' Association.

This curious feline had an unglamorous background; it was a descendant of an unfortunate kitten who had been born bald. With some mating maneuvering, after a few generations, it bred true. Often called the "Canadian Hairless," the official designation of the breed was "Sphynx." The ideal Sphynx cat is expected to have a longish body with a delicate skeleton and strong muscles and a long, thin tail, at the end of which a bunch of languid hairs is acceptable. The skin is to hug the body without wrinkles, and a velvety short pile on the face, which feels like wet moss to the touch, is also acceptable. A Sphynx cat often assumes an arrogant stance and moves with a calculated, precise gait. The piercing look from its slanted, golden eyes contributed to its name and to the widespread legends, undoubtedly fostered by breeders, that Sphynx cats can see through things and can forecast gathering storms hundreds of miles away. Unquestionably, they elicit an unsettling, eerie reaction from people when they walk regally into a room.

Kathy had never shared her house with a hairless cat. As she reread the article time and again, she decided that she simply must have one of these arguably beautiful but definitely unique creatures move in with her. When referring to a cat, Kathy never used the word "own" because she thought it was patronizing to the cat, as well as totally inaccurate.

She drafted Diane for the expedition to Kingston, Ontario. The breeder had five six-week-old Sphynx kittens. Kathy found it difficult to take only one—two cats can entertain each other, she reasoned—but the price was a deterrent. So, after some haggling, for the hefty sum of four hundred Canadian dollars, Kathy and Diane returned to Michigan with just one kitten, but it was the pick of the litter. To avoid unnecessary hassles at the border, the Hairless Canadian entered the USA surreptitiously, sleeping in a kitty carrier, hidden under jackets, in the back seat of Kathy's Camaro.

Before they reached Kathy's apartment, the illegal immigrant already had been named "Yul" after the most famous hairless human. Yul was one of the most congenial cats Kathy had shared her house with. He was gentle, quiet and an exemplary host. A scrawny, hairless cat is not a very appealing sight, and a sinister streak is often evoked in people who meet one for the first time. Yul always managed to overcome that barrier of unfounded prejudice. He would always come to the front door to greet a visitor, and, after a perfunctory inspection of the newcomer to exercise his own prejudices, Yul would gently rub the side of his face on the stranger's legs and softly meow some platitude until the first reaction of repulsion was overcome. He would then make a regal retreat to the bedroom, tail straight up, head straight forward. As a rule, he would return later a few times, so as not to be judged unsociable. His behavior was always quite civil, and if he ever committed the *faux pas* of climbing onto a guest's lap, he was seldom rejected because he was always impeccably groomed—and, since he had no hair, he didn't shed.

Yul was particularly fond of Diane. Probably sharing a small car with her for four or five hours as a kitten had imprinted her image on his tender brain. Whenever Diane came to visit, Yul would give her some extended nose-rubbing greetings, acquiesce to her picking him up and contentedly settle on her lap for most of her visit, purring now and again to acknowledge her thoughtfulness.

The second Tuesday of June, Diane went to Kathy's apartment, as planned, for tea, cake, free-flowing conversation and lots of giggling. When she entered the apartment, Yul ran up to her as usual and rubbed the side of his face on her long skirt a few times. But then he retreated. He sat a couple of feet away from her and began to sniff, moving his head up and down and side to side. His upper lips curled, and he inhaled in short breaths. Then he turned about and scurried away into the bedroom.

"What's with Yul today?" asked Diane.

"Who knows?" replied Kathy. "Cats are funny people."

"He's always so nice to me," protested Diane.

"It's unusual, really. Were you in contact with a dog or another cat or pet today?" Kathy asked. "Are you on the rag? They can sense it."

Diane shook her head. "No, I'm not, and I don't touch any pet recently, or even close to one."

"Go figure." Kathy closed the issue.

Yul's behaviour was forgotten as soon as they moved to the living room and began to pour out their stories of the last weeks. Kathy had reasons to believe that she had met Mr. Right, again; Diane discovered a sixty-five-thousand-dollar overpayment by her company, and they rewarded her with a handsome bonus; Quang was in line for a promotion; Mai had a three-point-eight grade point average at the private boarding school she attended; and on and on.

Yul never came out of the bedroom until after Diane had left.

~ ~ ~

In July, they met again at Farrell's, a fashionable ice cream parlor by the Oakland Mall. After a long wait, they were seated and ordered their banana splits; Diane whispered something in the waitress's ear. When the sinful dishes finally arrived, Diane's sported a gherkin pickle on the edge of the dish. When Kathy saw it, she motioned to the waitress to remove it. Then she looked at Diane inquisitively. Diane shrugged her shoulders and started to giggle. Kathy shouted aloud, "For real?" When Diane nodded, they both held hands, and Kathy cried. It was a tradition at Farrell's to adorn the ice cream of an expectant mother with a pickle.

The rest of the afternoon, they only talked about maternity clothes, baby's names, the Lamaze method and obstetricians.

"You must see Dr. Irving," Kathy commanded. "He is great, he's gentle—and he's handsome too," she added enthusiastically.

"Kathy," replied Diane, "I'm married. I don't need good-looking doctor."

"Can't hurt," Kathy insisted.

"That's right," Diane giggled. "Actually I was going to ask you for one."

"Great! He'll be perfect for you. I'll make the appointment for you. I don't think he's taking new patients, but he knows me well. I'll tell them you're my best friend."

Diane looked Kathy straight in the eye with a conspiratorial look. "How well do you know this doctor?" she asked.

Kathy laughed aloud. "Not that well!" she replied, acknowledging the message. "I think he is still married—and to a rich bitch to boot."

~ ~ ~

Yul's unsettling behavior during the June visit was not the story Diane intended to tell L'Nore. When Diane talked about it to Kathy before the next incident, she would always explain it by saying that Yul had smelled her pregnant state. Kathy did not believe that was the reason, because Yul had been around Heidi, the housekeeper, throughout her pregnancy and had never acted "goofy" like that.

"Maybe I'm special to Yul, and he was jealous," Diane would close the argument in a joking tone.

The next incident was what Diane had meant to tell L'Nore, and for that one they had no explanation.

The August rendezvous was at Kathy's apartment. The much-touted fare to feed mom and baby included homemade scones with peaches and raisins, orange comfitures and tea with rum. They both looked forward to that respite in their hectic lives.

When Diane rang the bell, Yul came to the door with Kathy, as would be expected of a proper host. He recognized Diane and advanced towards her, tail up, its tip tilted. He stopped a few steps from her and lifted his head with his mouth slightly open and his upper lip curled. He breathed in and seemed to flick the smell back with his tongue. Small cats use this process, called flehmening, to direct the smell towards the Jacobsen's organ. It is not a gesture of displeasure or aggressiveness, but rather of concentrated analysis of a particular smell. After repeating the exercise for some time, always at a distance, Yul backed away and, uttering low-pitched sounds under his breath, withdrew to the bedroom. The two women, busy hugging and exchanging pleasantries, scarcely noticed the cat's antics.

It was after the tea and scones that Yul returned to the dining room on the way to the kitchen for his food. He crossed the dining room unobtrusively, hugging the walls, ogling Diane from the corner of his eyes. At that moment, Diane was proudly showing off her swollen belly to her friend. She had lifted her blouse and lowered the waist of her skirt to expose her protrusion.

"It looks so cute," Kathy said while patting it.

Yul, still hugging the wall, stopped in his tracks, his gaze fixed on the prominent abdomen. He crouched then. His tail dropped to the floor, and he began to sweep it from side to side. His upper lip curled up, and, repeating the flehmening with more intensity than before, he let out a low but steady tremolo. From the front, his rather wide chest, his bowed legs and his glowing metallic pupils gave the cat a ferocious look, something like an albino panther on the prowl.

The two women, exchanging jokes and giggling, were oblivious to the cat's presence and kept rubbing the belly to stir the baby's kicks. The baby obliged, responding to the stimuli with jerky movements that showed like ripples on the abdomen, much to the women's delight.

Yul's gold eyes were now transfixed on the bloated belly. His growl grew louder and louder until it reached a level that could no longer be ignored. The two women turned simultaneously towards him.

That's when suddenly, hissing loudly and spitting, the cat sprang. His hind legs propelled him into the air across the five or six feet that separated the wall from the chair where Diane was sitting. The women could not react fast enough to guard the belly. Yul landed on all fours on it. His back arched, and his lips retracted, showing ferocious canines, as saliva ran out the sides of his mouth. His front paws began to dig viciously at Diane's skin as if burrowing for dear life. He drew the paws over the belly again and again with beastly furor, and, although he had been declawed, the remaining quick sufficed to scarify Diane's belly in long, parallel tracks in multiple directions.

"Yul, stop it, stop it!" shouted Kathy.

"He gone mad," moaned Diane. "Get him away from me."

Yul persevered in his frantic digging until Kathy pulled him up by the scruff of his neck and threw him into the bedroom. He was still hissing and salivating when she closed the door after him.

Fresh blood covered Diane's belly. Kathy ran to the bathroom for peroxide and cotton balls. "I think we'd better go to the emergency room," she said.

"It's not that bad," protested Diane. "It will be all right."

"I'll take him to the vet," mumbled Kathy, cleansing Diane's scratches.

"Ouch! It burns," shouted Diane.

"There's a disease from cat's scratches; I have to find out if he has it. Do you have your tetanus immunizations up to date? If the vet cannot find what's wrong with Yul, I might have to put him to sleep."

"Oh, no!" protested Diane as she fanned her belly. "He probably was jealous because you rubbed my belly instead of his."

"That's not an acceptable behavior, no matter what," insisted Kathy. "I've had cats all my life, and not one has behaved like this. It is not acceptable. Look what he's done to your belly! The monster. He had no reason to do it." She continued caring for her friend's abdomen while talking non-stop, as was her habit when she was much stressed.

## CHAPTER XII

# Professor Peacock

**P**rofessor Trevor Carruthers walked with calculated precision to the front of the auditorium, the hem of his lab coat only a few inches above his spit-polished wing-tip shoes. A solid navy bowtie, bent just so at the wide ends, rested on his starched white shirt. He stood tall in front of a large print on a piece of oilcloth. It showed ten drawings of an embryo and fetus at each of the ten lunar months of intrauterine development. At some time during his lecture, he would say that this print was eighty years old and it had flown over the North and South Atlantic oceans. Words such as "foetus" and "arteriae" on it reminded the audience that it had come from the Old World.

After a protracted silence to build up the audience's concentration, the professor leaned on the lectern and pronounced his dramatic opening statement: "To consider a fetus anything but an intruder that is merely tolerated, never welcomed, by the host is melodramatic, sentimental rubbish, soap-opera fodder, devoid of any scientific value."

The professor's voice reverberated off the walls of the Kellog Auditorium and, as was intended, bored deeply into the malleable minds of the freshman medical students. His statements would remain indelibly recorded in their brains, partly because of their scientific content but mainly because of the punch that the professor's voice delivered.

Before entering medical school in Manchester, the professor had had a rather long stint in a dramatic arts school in his native Pretoria, South Africa. His ability to project his voice, his fashionable British accent and his penchant for controversial and powerful statements, delivered with theatrical knock-out zest, had worked just fine for Professor Carruthers. His opening lecture in freshman Embryology—the department in which he was an associate professor—had become by far the best attended lecture in the whole medical school. It had displaced the department chair's presentation many years back, and, in order to accommodate the growing audience, it had been moved from its original site, the anatomy laboratory, to the department classroom and eventually to the Kellog Auditorium. Still Professor Carruthers was able to fill the room with his commanding voice and with med students, interns, residents and postgraduate fellows.

His self-touted "teleological approach" to the science of embryology had been widely publicized in the School journals, the local press and a few international publications.

The development of organ transplants, particularly the grafting of skin onto burned surfaces, had been a welcome shot in the arm for Professor Carruthers's curriculum. He was then able to compare the situation of the placenta to the host-graft system and the study of donor-recipient compatibility that was beginning to be developed on scientific grounds.

A mutual acquaintance had introduced Alfie to Professor Carruthers at a party for the medical staff at Wayne State University.

"How do you do, Mrs. Santoro," he said when he met her, giving her an imperceptible nod and a condescending smile. "Is your husband a doctor?"

"I've no husband. I am Doctor Santoro," she answered.

"Doctor Santoro. I'm quite familiar with that surname. We had a greengrocer back home in Pretoria by that name." He turned to his wife, who was standing behind him, and added, "Didn't we, Margie?"

"Not Santoro, darling," she replied. "San-ti-no."

"Close enough, I suppose," he chuckled. "Nice to meet you, Miss Santoro. Pardon me now. I must say hello to Mrs. Berger." And away he sailed, cocktail in hand, to greet the dean's wife with his broadest smile.

Marge and Alfie, who had not been introduced to each other, exchanged glances. Alfie stretched her hand to the woman.

"Pleased to meet you, Doctor," said the woman.

"I love the professor's lectures," said Alfie for lack of a more intelligent remark.

Marge smiled.

To meet a Santoro or Santino, and a female doctor to boot, at an upper crust social affair was more than a little disconcerting for the professor. Santoro—or Santino—evoked vegetables in his mind. The professor had very pragmatic, simple ideas for social stratification and was absolutely convinced that Planet Earth would be a more organized place of business if everybody adhered to his tenets. His scheme for ethnic interaction was quite simple: Italians were to sell foodstuff, gathered by Latinos, to Greeks and Orientals, who would cook them and pass them to French waiters, who would serve them at the clubs and restaurants where important people would congregate to discuss the handling of the not-so-important people. The women—the wives of the important men—would busy themselves in another room with gossip and harmless discussions of inconsequential matters. Professor Carruthers found it very irritating that this simple and practical design would be so often upset by people unaware of their position.

The less-than-pleasant impression that the professor made on their first meeting would have deterred Alfie from seeking his assistance, had it not been by the fact that a patient's welfare might depend on his advice.

When the professor had finished his presentation, wrapped in loud applause, Alfie waited until most of the audience had left and then marched to the front of the room.

"Doctor Santino!" he exclaimed when she approached him, quite pleased to have remembered her name. She chose not to correct him.

"Do you know why I remember your name, Doctor Santino?"

She did, but she preferred to let him tell the story of the greengrocer.

His secretary was standing by him, and she smiled as if in awe of his prodigious memory. She also found the greengrocer story quite amusing.

"And what brings Doctor Santino to a freshman's lecture?" he asked quite affably.

"I have this patient," Alfie started, and she bit her lip. "Bad opening line," she chided herself, "a cliché for small town doctors when consulting with academia."

She went on, nonetheless, to describe the maledetto "whoosh" and how it seemed to respond to stimuli. She stressed the fact that the rate was independent of the fetal heartbeat. Finally, she threw in all the pertinent information that she could include in one long, concluding sentence.

The professor listened with feigned interest, and when he thought that it would not be intolerably impolite to interrupt, he did. "Pardon me, Doctor, but it seems to me that this is a clinical problem and you'd be better off asking advice from clinicians."

"Well..." She hesitated for a second. "The reason I decided to ask for your input is that, embryology being your area of expertise..."

Now she was coming to the hard part of the business. After several false starts, she decided it was best to get to the point.

"Have you ever heard, in any species, of a placenta that grew beyond its boundaries and sort of developed into some primitive, autonomous…life form?"

The professor bent his head and looked Alfie intently in the eyes over his lunettes. At last, he said with hostile gravity, "You are joking, Doctor, are you not?"

"Not entirely. I must confess I don't know what else to think," she answered with some vacillation.

Still focused on her eyes, as if trying to uncover the gag, he said, "You mean, like a placenta gone wild and starting an independent life of its own?"

Alfie's heart went pit-a-pat. ("At least he got the idea," she said to herself.) She nodded.

Professor Carruthers looked up toward the ceiling. He seemed to be concentrating, as if searching in his mental archives. Then, he lowered his head again, and his eyes pointed at hers inquisitively over the double barrel of his lenses. After he had gazed at her for a while, at last he burst out, "No, I'm afraid not. Now, if you will excuse me, Doctor, I must be off."

"But…but…" Alfie stammered, "you've heard stories about…er…placentas gone wild."

"Yes, doctor, I have," he replied with a condescending smile, "and you've heard stories about Dracula and the Tooth Fairy. Do you believe in them?"

She could find no intelligent rejoinder.

"Thanks for your time, Professor," she babbled.

He began to move away in a hurry. Suddenly, he stalled for a short moment and turned his head. "You ought to discuss this with Dr. D'Onofrio," he said.

Then he dashed off with his secretary on his tail.

Alfie walked towards her car nursing a severely bruised ego. To her joyous surprise, however, she noticed that the clinometer was reading plus five. The angle that the base of her nose made with the horizontal when she walked had always been a very dependable indicator of her moods. She had named it "the clinometer" after the instrument that measures the listing in a vessel. Minus twenty to thirty were frequent readings, and she had survived minus ninety. Any reading above minus ten could qualify as "hunky-dory" status. Professor Peacock's derision had not caused her any serious injury; actually, she had found his admission that he had heard about placentas gone wild quite uplifting.

Nose-lifting at least.

CHAPTER XIII

# A Good Consultant
# is Hard to Find

**W**hat did Professor Peacock say?" L'Nore asked the doctor as soon as she had returned from her meeting with Professor Carruthers.

"Nothing good. Tell you later."

"What did he say?" L'Nore asked again.

"Tell you later," Alfie almost shouted. "Any calls to return?"

"I returned all the routine calls, seventeen of them. Mrs. Woodruff called in a frenzy, again. She was all worked up because she read somewhere that the Bendectin she is taking can cause birth defects."

"Tell her to stop it if she is afraid to take it. The pea brain is worried about the medication, and she burns thirty L & Ms and downs a pint of Cutty Sark every day."

"She wants to talk to you. She wants to know if there is something else that is safe if she starts puking again."

"I'll call her when I have time. Let her barf her guts out."

"What did the professor say?"

"He thinks I'm nuts. Who else called?"

"Oh, another VIP, Mrs. Kaufman. She wants to know if she can continue riding her horse in the second trimester."

"Pace yes, not trot or gallop."

"I told her, but she wants you to call her."

"Tell her to call Jon; he is her friend." She was referring to Dr. Jonathan Irving.

"I suggested it. She said she left several messages for him. Belinda answered them, but she wants to talk to a big kahuna."

"I'll talk to her."

"Want me to get her on the line?"

"Later."

"She'll pester you all afternoon," L'Nore warned her. "Now, I've got some good news. Fateema called. Her period is late, and her boobs are sore."

"Tell her to come in tomorrow and get an HCG." That was the name of the pregnancy test that measured the "Human Chorionic Gonadotropins" level, the hormone that increased immediately after conception.

"I told her, but she is in a tiff. Maybe you should talk to her."

"Get her on the line, please."

"Remember what you promised if she got pregnant."

"I remember, and I'll do it too," the doctor answered with faked uneasiness.

"You'd better."

L'Nore got Fateema on the line. The doctor talked to her for a good while. When she had finished, she turned to L'Nore and asked, "Is that all?"

"Uh-huh. And now is later. What did Professor Carruthers say?"

"He thinks we are nuts. And he wasn't even nice about it. When I asked about the possibility of some overgrown placenta capable of propelling its own blood, he looked me straight in the eye and said: 'You're not serious, are you?'"

"He didn't buy it, huh? What did you say?"

"I sort of backed out. 'I don't know what else to think,' I said with an idiotic sneer. You know the professor and Dr. D'Onofrio see each other at the Maternal Mortality Committee, and I didn't want him asking the old guy if he thinks I'm losing it. Probably they would agree I'm going bananas."

"What now?" asked L'Nore.

"I was thinking of discussing it with Dr. Lee. He's good at reading fetal tracings, but you know what he'll say…"

"Altifact, altifact, altifact…" said L'Nore, squinting and waving her arms. She was mocking Dr. Lee. They laughed.

"What about Dr. Shah? She is our perinatologist, after all," suggested L'Nore rather hesitantly. Perinatologist was a nascent subspecialty of obstetrics that dealt with the care of the fetus in the uterus and at delivery time.

"I thought about her, too," said the doctor, "but she won't help any, you know. She never does. She'll say: 'One mustn't rush in this business; one must wait and see.' And she'll talk about her experiences at Chicago Lying-in and how she single-handedly saved all the newborns in Cook County from a fate worse than death."

"True. She usually is not much help."

"So, what can we do? What's the right thing to do in a situation like this?" the doctor asked.

Her assistant shrugged her shoulders.

"Really, now, is there a right thing to do?" The doctor answered her own question pensively, "Perhaps I'm pussyfooting because I'm afraid to share our suspicions with someone else."

"I've been thinking about it," said L'Nore. "Probably the best thing to do is to be prepared just in case it turns out that we are right. Because, if all hell broke loose and we didn't warn anybody about our suspicions, they'll crucify us. And even our consciences will punish us."

"Maybe we should try to get the National Guard to stand by. A wild animal in a delivery room. It could get pretty messy," added the doctor, tongue-in-cheek.

L'Nore did not see the humor in the remark. "When the moment comes, we might not find it funny at all," she said.

"I was trying to make light of it," Dr. Santoro said apologetically. "See, L'Nore, the problem as I see it is: How does one prepare for something if no one has ever seen it, its modus operandi is unknown, and only two persons on this planet seem to believe in its existence—and neither one of them certifiably sane?"

They remained silent for a long while.

"What if we call someone else just to listen in?" L'Nore broke the silence.

"For instance…?" said the doctor.

L'Nore was quiet, thinking in earnest.

After some time, the doctor repeated the question: "Good idea. Whom shall we call?"

L'Nore hesitated for a while. She then threw her arms up as in surrender.

"See what I mean?" said the doctor. "If we call someone in, it will be considered a consultation, and we should discuss it first with Dr. D'Onofrio. Now, if we call Dr. D'Onofrio, you know what he will say: either, 'You're nuts. It sounds quite normal to me' or—"

"Send 'er downtown. They don't pay us for this," L'Nore said in a deep voice, thrusting her abdomen out, mimicking the old doctor.

"Well, if she goes downtown, she won't be our headache any longer," Alfie pondered. Her conscience vetoed that option. "She'll be lost in the shuffle. They'll do nothing. Her baby will be in kindergarten before she sees someone with any experience. We might just as well do nothing here." She added, "But if I call outside consultants without letting Dr. D'Onofrio know, my ass will be grass."

"Wait, wait," said L'Nore, quite excited. "Dr. D'Onofrio will be going on vacation soon. Then we can call anyone we want."

"No such luck. I checked already. His next vacation will be in January."

They stared at each other and sulked for some time

A large group of residents, interns and medical students in the midst of a lively exchange of witty remarks and jokes marched into the staff room where Alfie and L'Nore were brooding over their narrow range of choices. The group paid no attention to them; they were headed for the doughnut box.

Dr. Santoro and her assistant left the room inconspicuously, heading for the outpatient clinics. The maledetto "whoosh" retreated to the back of their minds for the time being.

The next morning, when Dr. Santoro entered her office, the first thing that she saw was a tall can of red spray paint. A note attached to it read: "Hope it is enough to cover the whole surface."

She laughed loudly. It was great news. Fateema's pregnancy test was positive, it meant. Fateema had been Dr. Santoro's most difficult infertility patient. She had worked with her—and her over-anxious Lebanese family—for over two years. She had tried every trick in the book, and then some. A few months back, in a fit of desperation, she had yelled in front of L'Nore: "If I ever get this woman pregnant, I'll paint my ass red and parade it downtown."

L'Nore did not forget it. Alfie just hoped that she did not insist on her making good the second part of the promise.

CHAPTER XIV

# Visiting the Storks

athy had made Diane's first appointment with The Grosse Pointe Storks. She mentioned that she was a friend of Dr. Irving's and asked if Diane could see him on her first visit. The receptionist transferred her to Belinda, Dr. Irving's nurse. After much negotiating on dates and times, the first visit was arranged for a Friday at four o'clock. Kathy thought that was acceptable; it would only require that Diane leave work an hour earlier than usual.

A few days before the appointment, Diane received a call from Belinda, apologizing for having to change it because the doctor would be out of town. She had arranged for Diane to see Dr. Rao, who had an opening that day.

"I'm soooo sorry, luv," said Belinda with a British accent too thick for anyone who had spent more than a few months in the Midwest. "Kothy said the niiiicest things abut you, and, of course, we're dying to meet you. But, you see, luv, Dr. Irving got an unexpected call for a consultation in Texas. An old patient of his, a VIP just like you, is to have surgery in Dallas, and she won't unless Dr. Irving agrees with the diagnosis and the operation. One can understand that, I suppose."

"Then I meet Dr. Irwin…"

"Ir-ving," corrected Belinda.

"Some other time." Diane finished her sentence.

Belinda did not think Diane sounded disappointed enough. "You will loooove Dr. Rao. He is such a daaaar-ling," she added, "and I personally will arrange for you an appointment with Dr, Irving. Bye, luv, and thanks for being soooo understanding."

Diane usually set her appointments late on Fridays, and that was precisely when Dr. Irving was heading for his weekend golf trips. So, she saw Dr. Rao on her first visit, Dr. D'Onofrio on her second visit, and Dr. Santoro on her third visit. They were all quite pleasant; Diane liked them all.

She wished, though, that someone would tell her that her baby was going to be all right.

CHAPTER XV

# Five Exclusive
# Residential Communities

In the southeast corner of the state, at the base of the thumb of the Michigan mitten, rubbing elbows with blue-collar Detroit, stand a cluster of very unique communities: the Grosse Pointes.

The Pointes, on the marshy shores of Lake St. Clair, were settled by French farmers in the eighteenth century. The names of the first families have remained, anglicized, alas, in their pronunciation: Dubois (pronounced Doo-boy), Cadieux (pronounced Ca'-jew), Charlevoix (pronounced Charl'-voi).

The Encyclopedia Britannica describes Grosse Pointe as "five exclusive residential communities on the southwest shores of Lake St. Clair; it is there that in 1712 the French defeated the Fox and Sauk Indians." The name, Grosse Pointe, would not go unrecognized in Rome, London or the French Riviera. Oddly, in America it became famous, infamous rather, mainly through the much publicized and absurd "Point System." The brainchild of some obtuse real estate agents, it saw the light of day in 1960. Potential house buyers in the Pointes were rated on a point scale; points were accorded based on the applicant's nationality, occupation and degree of swarthiness. It was one of the examples cited in the Civil Rights Act of 1964, which abolished this type of discrimination. It probably never had much impact on local demographics, but the story continued to make interesting after dinner conversation for many years.

Many believed that the "Point System," in a less elitist version, had remained in effect; only the points were granted in accordance with the number of dollar signs in the candidate's coat of arms. The authenticity of the heraldic claim was put to the test by the candidate's ability to pony up the loot that the property demanded.

The Pointes consisted of four cities, the Park, the City, the Farms and the Woods, and one village, the Shores. The latter was the original settlement and the core that reached out to gentrify all the other Pointes.

The Shores harbored a singularity of its own: Lake Township, which included the Ford estate and twenty-some homes, all located on just two roads that ran from Jefferson Road (called Lake Shore Drive there) to Lake St. Clair. Lake Township never had more than three hundred residents. The registered voters of the Township cast their votes at the gatehouse of an English Cotswold mansion designed by Albert Khan and landscaped by "prairie school" landscaper Jens Jensen. The magnificent stone house, the abode of Edsel and Eleanor Ford, was built in the center of the estate, invisible from the lake or from the public roads; on its grounds stood the famous child-size Tudor playhouse built by Edsel for his granddaughter, Josephine.

Lake Township straddled the county lines; fourteen of its lots were split between Macomb and Wayne counties, and their taxes were prorated accordingly. As for the school district to which the children belonged…well, that was mainly determined by where the child's bedroom was located. This was not of much consequence because the Township—as one of its supervisors stated—was inhabited by auto executives richer than hell. Quiet, discreet Lake Township, Michigan, had had a per capita income at times higher than that of Beverly Hills,

California and Palm Beach, Florida, so it is extremely unlikely that the children of the Township would ever ride the yellow school buses of either district.

Residents of the Pointes could fill the Who's Who in corporate America. George Hendrie, the legendary Scottish railroad magnate, summered at Willow Bank. Delphine Dodge, Horace's indomitable daughter, was a car and boat racer, an accomplished pianist and owner of Catherine the Great's pearl necklace. U.S. Senator McMillan and Congressman John Newberry, founders of the Michigan Car Works, and Alfred E. Brush used to commute by yacht from their homes in the Pointes to their offices in downtown Detroit.

The local lore had it that many years ago the Pointes had considered seceding from the Union, and some old-timers still referred to them mockingly as the United States of Grosse Pointe.

As they became the stomping grounds of the automobile barons and their entourage, the Pointes grew into some sort of urban oddity, the social hub of an elusive society. In the summer, the exalted gentry would migrate en bloc to Harbor Springs and Wequetonsing on Lake Michigan. In the winter, a bona fide Grosse Pointer would not be caught dead in his homestead in the Pointes; it was all Palm Beach, Carmel—and Europe, of course.

The automobile moguls moved in along Lake Shore Drive at the beginning of the century. The lake side of the road, the even numbers, was reserved for the high brass, the Dodges, the "automobile Fords," the less conspicuous "chemical Fords"—of the Michigan Alkali and the Pittsburgh Plate Glass Companies. The other side of the road, the proletarian side as it were, with the odd numbers, was populated by junior executives and the owners of the booming "nuts and bolts" shops. Provencal Road, gated and guarded, at the edge of the Country Club of Detroit, became the grounds of the more discreet, golf-loving magnates and some nouveaux riches. Any address on Provencal Road and any even numbered address on Lake Shore Drive acquired a ring capable of drawing the attention of the not-easily-impressed Grosse Pointe citizenry.

That demographic set constituted the target market of Our Lady of Lourdes Hospital, and the women of this cadre made up most of the Grosse Pointe Storks' clientele.

Peculiar people the Grosse Pointers—geepeers, as they were known by other Michiganders. The men tended to shun socks; they favored silly trousers with single-animal prints all over them—or cute colorful patchworks—and shirts with alligators. The women sported bob haircuts and dressed in nothing but earth tones over white blouses. Kelly green and pink were the institutional colors, and preppyhood was some sort of a rite of passage in the Pointes. The black squirrel, indigenous to the Pointes, was the local mascot, and legend had it that there will be a Grosse Pointe as long as there are black squirrels.

A genuine Grosse Pointer would think nothing of queuing up for hours in rain or snow on Sunday mornings on Mack Road, in front of The Pancake Palace, to be seated unceremoniously in a crowded, smoke-filled room in order to enjoy the best griddle cakes and crepes this side of the big puddle. Then, after church service, they would recover their exalted status and be greeted by their surnames, with reverent bows, and be escorted to their waiting tables at the Yacht Club, the Little Club or Lochmoor Country Club.

The Edsel Ford Expressway ran parallel to the Pointes for several miles, in some places less than a block away from them. Curiously, perhaps as a concession to the overgrown sense of propriety of its residents, no sign on the freeway had ever mentioned the names of any of the Pointes. The geepeers welcomed that deference to their longed-for privacy.

The city of Detroit was planned along concentric thoroughfares a mile apart, with their center in the heart of the city at the foot of Woodward Avenue on the Detroit River. Interstate

94, the Edsel Ford Freeway, as it ran parallel to the shore of
Lake St. Clair from Detroit to Port Huron, intersected each
of the "mile roads." So, if one were to drive eastward on the
freeway, one would see exits at seven mile (Moross Road),
eight mile (Vernier Road), Nine Mile, Ten Mile, Eleven Mile
and so on.

With one exception.

Between seven and eight mile, a humble exit named Allard
Avenue led off eastwards towards the lake.

It was generally acknowledged that Allard Avenue exit on
the Edsel Ford Freeway was Sister Redempta's labor of love.
How Sister Redempta managed to sway the Road Commission to build that exit that led so conveniently to "her" hospital
had been the subject of much political conjecture, innuendo
and plain old gossip. The road was for some time referred
to, tongue-in-cheek of course, as Sister Redempta's Highway,
and the scuttlebutt was that the daughter of one of the road
commissioners had been the pampered guest of the nun at the
original facility, before it became a general hospital.

Because, originally, Our Lady of Lourdes was conceived as a
circumspect home where girls from prominent families of the
Midwest could quietly retire for a nine-month "tour of Europe."
The Home had been bequeathed to Sister Redempta's religious
order of Les Ursulines de Reims by a French-Canadian lumber
baron who, it was generally believed, lost a daughter as a result
of a botched abortion.

There was a maternity service conveniently located adjacent
to the home. The maternity was equipped with all the latest
technical gadgetries available and some deluxe amenities as
well—such as a telephone in each delivery room so the new
mother could call her family as soon as the ordeal was over.

The maternity was served by resident physicians and fellows in training at various teaching programs in Detroit; they
were supervised by some of the most prestigious obstetricians
in the area.

The records of the expectant mothers contained only their first names and the initial of their surnames. The legal address for all of them was: Our Lady of Lourdes Home, 115 Allard Avenue, Grosse Pointe, Michigan. The girls were officially referred to as "residents," but colloquially they were called "hummers" because the cover of their medical records was stamped "HUM" (Home for Unwed Mothers). They were under the supervision of a housemother, and there was one chaperone for every two residents, assigned to escort them to the clinic for their prenatal visits, to the chapel and to any outside activities, such as visits to the Fisher Theater and shopping trips to Hudson's in the newly opened Eastland Mall.

The young women were delivered invariably under general anesthesia, to prevent them from seeing their babies, lest they should become attached to them and renege on the adoption deal. The arrangements for the adoption of the babies to very good families were made beforehand by the Home itself. Special care was taken never to include the names of the biological mother and the adoptive parents on the same sheet or in the same record; their identities remained forever untraceable.

A few weeks after the arguably happy event, the girls would return home from their "tour of Europe". They resumed their busy social activities, and the disturbing incident was forever expunged from their documented lives.

Sister Redempta's fame extended all over the Midwest, plus Ontario and Quebec; her private telephone number was in the address book of every prominent household with a teenage girl. The fact that most of the residents in the HUM were from wealthy and well-known families was really no expression of snobbery; it was rather due to the fact that premature pregnancies were more tolerated in the less affluent social sets. Actually, the nun extended her assistance generously to whoever requested it, regardless of religion or financial or social status. In return, though, whenever she needed help with her pious ventures, she demanded repayment of the favor unabashedly and unremittingly, and she had no qualms about it. This fact helped give credence to the story about the origin of the Allard Avenue exit.

The transition of the Home for Unwed Mothers into a general hospital was as discreet as its existence had always been. When health care insurance plans started to reimburse hospitals for deliveries, the maternity at the HUM started to accept outside patients. Soon thereafter, an operating room was built, and then wards for medical and surgical patients. The changes took place gradually, in an almost unnoticeable fashion, and, even though Sister Redempta probably never foresaw the changes, she was well pleased with them. They turned out to be a saving grace for the institution because when the wild and shameless sixties rolled in, society became more tolerant of out-of-wedlock pregnancies, and the single mothers-to-be paraded their puffed-up bellies defiantly in their own communities without scornful looks being cast upon them.

The need for the "tour of Europe" for the prematurely pregnant waned; the number of "residents" at the Home for Unwed Mothers rapidly declined, and the facility soon became an anachronism. It collapsed as silently and discreetly as it was born, burying in the rubble its cache of truncated maternal dreams and disgraceful secrets.

At the inauguration gala for the new General Hospital, held at the Grosse Pointe War Memorial when Our Lady of Lourdes attained full recognition by the Joint Commission on Accreditation of Hospitals, Sister Redempta quoted in her speech the City of Detroit's motto, "Speramus Melliora Resurrecit Cineribus," as an auspicious portent: "We hope that a better institution will be resurrected from the ashes of the Home for Unwed Mothers."

As expected, Sister Redempta became the first administrator of Our Lady of Lourdes Hospital. She adapted all too quickly to her new position as administrator of a general hospital. One of her functions was to procure funds for the charity patients, for the teaching programs and for the clinical research projects that were beginning to blossom in the new facility. The nun performed as an astute businesswoman because she had been made a businesswoman by The Provincial. She would have been just as efficient as a missionary in Africa or as an envoy to the Holy See if she had been given that job.

First of all, however, Sister Redempta was a woman of the cloth. No worldly event—and she had been in Algeria during the war for independence—had ever kept her from observing the canonical hours. At first when she became a general hospital administrator, she arranged her meetings around the matins and the vespers, until she realized that it was impossible to run a busy hospital and pray seven times a day. That time constraint imposed by her administrative duties spawned a novel idea in her entrepreneurial mind. The Breviary was very vague on the issue of outsiders joining for prayers at the canonical hours, so she began to invite prominent women of the community to the matins and the vespers. In a short time, being asked to "the vespers" by Sister Redempta became a mark of social distinction akin to an invitation to join the Little Club.

The grand dames of the automobile fortunes felt no remorse about canceling a trip to Harbor Spring or to Palm Beach to attend "Sister Redempta's vespers"—"Tea and petits fours will be served after the canons," promised the elegant invitation—and they bragged about it at social functions. From a financial standpoint, "the vespers" turned into a bonanza for the hospital. The expenses were limited to some coffee cakes, usually donated by Sander's, and some cookies baked by the convent housekeeper. Without exception, every guest dropped a four-digit cheque into the hospital's coffers.

One of the most celebrated "vespers" events was the one in the summer of 1965, which was attended by the heiress of the Albertson's Department Stores. "Albert's" as it was known in The Pointes—as in "going Albertsing"—was an upscale national chain of haberdashery and women's fashions that started in Grosse Pointe. That particular session of praying achieved local prominence not because Mrs. Albertson was the richest or the most distinguished guest to recite the rosary with the sisters, nor because she made the largest contribution to the hospital, but rather due to the fact that she was Jewish.

Sister Redempta was not quite five feet tall. It was said that the world looks daunting from that vantage point because all major events seem to take place a foot above one's head. That did not deter her from carrying out her duties as she saw fit. One evening, Sister Redempta, acting on a tip, waited for Dr. O'Leary in the emergency room. When she saw him coming up the ramp, she approached him quite discreetly. She told him that he could not enter the operating room in his condition. Dr. O'Leary was the chief of surgery, he stood six-foot-four tall, his brother was a U.S. congressman, his voice could reduce nurses, residents and even colleagues to submission, and his fits of rage were legendary. Ignoring his protestations and threats of reprisal, Sister Redempta walked him to his car. She took the keys from the ignition and an empty pint of scotch from the back seat. She then called Mrs. O'Leary to come and pick up her husband since he was unable to drive in his condition..

"I've saved more lives in the OR in this 'condition' than those punks have when sold…er…cold sober," the doctor had protested.

"Still, it does not make it right," replied the nun. She knew that what he had said, unfortunately, was true. Doctor O'Leary had been blessed with two gifts seldom bestowed upon the same surgeon: superb manual dexterity and excellent clinical judgment.

The Operating Room supervisor once had approached the chief of staff to report that Doctor O'Leary had been performing surgery while under the influence of alcohol.

"Did he botch up a case?" he asked, somewhat alarmed.

"No, but…"

"When he does, you let me know," he interrupted her.

Then he added the famous Lincolnian quip: "In the meantime, find out what brand he drinks and send a case to each of the surgeons."

Doctor O'Leary's propensity to drink to excess was no secret in the hospital. Or in the town—he had gotten lost in his neighborhood many times and the police had had to take him home.

"Next time you call me to get the punks out of a jam, Sister," said the doctor, "I'll tell you I can't come because I'm in that 'condition'."

That threat did not worry the nun. She knew he would never do that. He loved to fix train wrecks.

And then there was the time when someone brought to Sister's attention the unusual number of patients that came to the Emergency Room bleeding heavily, straight from Dr. Edelman's office. She confronted him at the risk of losing his business, as he was the busiest Gyn surgeon in the hospital. Sister Redempta told him that he could not bring any more incomplete abortions to Our Lady of Lourdes.

"You know, Sister," he answered, "that I'll take them elsewhere."

"I can't do anything about that," she responded. "That's between you and your conscience."

Dr. Edelman never brought another incomplete abortion in need of an emergency D and C to Our Lady of Lourdes Hospital or, oddly, to any other hospital either.

Our Lady of Lourdes was Sister Redempta's hospital, and she ran it the way she believed a Catholic hospital should be run.

That was the hospital where the group of obstetricians who called themselves The Grosse Pointe Storks delivered their patients. They had also rented a small office space on the hospital grounds. Dr. Santoro and Dr. Rao usually saw patients in the hospital office, while Dr. D'Onofrio and Dr. Irving, the senior partners, preferred the main office on Mack Avenue.

Dr. Santoro liked the hospital office because it was close to the delivery rooms, to the Ultrasound Department and to the Laboratory. That was the office where she met Diane Truong, and it was in Delivery Room Five of Our Lady of Lourdes Hospital where Diane delivered her baby.

After Diane Truong's delivery, Sister Redempta found it necessary to call a press conference for the next morning to explain the incidents that had taken place in Delivery Room Five and to try to quell the rumors that had grown out of control during the night. She knew the television cameras would be there, and she thought about what decor would be an appropriate setting for the matter with which she had to deal. Since it was not used on Sunday mornings, she decided to hold the conference in the waiting room of the Maternity Clinic. As soon as she had decided this, she called Housekeeping to ready it for the conference.

As it turned out, she never had to hold the conference.

CHAPTER XVI

# The Seventh Lunar Month

ednesdays and Saturdays were "mental health days" for Alfonsina Santoro MD. By carefully reworking her schedule, she managed most of the time to have a few free hours in the mornings.

She got up before dawn and donned a very large burgundy jogging suit over the vest of a wet suit. The vest she had purposely purchased a couple of sizes too small; zipping it was an athletic feat in itself. She exhaled all the air from her lungs, held in her stomach and pulled up on the zipper with all the determination and force of a samurai committing hara-kiri. Then, dropping her electronic pager, her watch and her wallet with ritualistic flair on the kitchen counter, she dashed out the door.

She turned to face the rising sun and began the run for her life. By the time she passed Grosse Pointe High School, she had reached full stride. The hospital was exactly one-and-a-half miles from her house; as her timing was quite dependable and her gait, as well as her attire, unmistakable, it was common for some employees of the hospital to gather by the windows of the cafeteria to watch her. Some cruel and witty observer had coined a name for her: "The Twin Pines Express." Twin

Pines was a well-known dairy delivery company. Even though the very tight vest had much curtailed the visual appeal of her running, the nickname endured. Alfie did not find it amusing; it offended her modesty, but that was a woman's fate, she thought, and she accepted it with Christian resignation.

As she jogged in front of the opulent estates on Lake Shore Drive, Alfie would think to herself: "That's what money can buy you." To wake up every morning and glance at the sun crawling above the familiar landmarks on the Canadian shore across the lake; to chart its migration along it, northbound in winter and spring, southbound in summer and fall. To gawk at the cantankerous Canada geese parading on your front lawn sloping down to the lake. To swoon with fascination at the sight of the winter moon over the white expanse of the frozen lake. And then to marvel at the might of its waters when the winds stirred them and catapulted them past the shoreline onto the road. When they offered these extravagant spectacles, why were these palaces always deserted and lifeless? Alfie wondered.

The row of waterfront castles ended at the bend; north of there only a narrow strip of grass separated the seawall from the road. Alfie's heavy footsteps would spook a goose now and then, but mostly the geese gazed haughtily at her as if questioning who the trespasser was. She would usually stop for her second wind when she reached the bend. The next mile was the highlight of her journey; she could enjoy the same views as the residents of the grand mansions, and, unintentionally, she would slow her pace to prolong the thrill.

Each time, when she passed Tonnancour Place, she stared in awe at the spot where a pious maiden, by the power of her prayers, petrified—literally—a rejected suitor turned were-wolf in his attempt to kidnap her. That century-old legend was the closest Alfie had been to the site of a dragon slaying by do-good knights. On misty mornings, she almost saw in the distance the ghostly outline of the long-gone shrine and the carved stone werewolf that a later owner of the land had built on the shore.

Run, Alfie, run.

The unobstructed view of Lake St. Clair ended at Eight Mile Road, by the Grosse Pointe Yacht Club. North of it, other houses on the water restricted the view again; these houses, in general, were smaller, newer and less pretentious than those in the previous strip.

Alfie seldom ran past the Yacht Club. Usually she would rest for a while on the cement slabs that formed the seawall, then head back home at just as fast a pace as she had come. On her way back, she would frequently turn off Lake Shore Drive at Seven Mile Road, and more often than not she would make a second stop at the tiny, anonymous graveyard on the corner of Country Club Drive.

Cemeteries, in general, had always had an appeal for Alfie; she thought of them as manmade stations placed here and there to help restore the everyday preoccupations to their proper perspective.

This one, Alfie thought, was an exemplary one—flat, circumspect, unassuming, just a handful of graves in a small fenced tract abutting two fancy homes. Several of the crosses were slightly bent as an incipient sign of surrender to eternity. The tombstones were wide open to the scorching sun in the summer and laden with the merciless snow in the winter, with never a fresh flower on them. Those graves were visited more frequently by the neighborhood dogs than by humans, yet Alfie knew that, like all graves, they were filled with irreplaceable people.

Run, Alfie, run.

Running, though, did not entirely preempt Alfie's mind; she could never quite outpace her demons, what she had named years back "the worry du jour."

During the fall of 1969, the maledetto "whoosh" occupied center stage in Alfie's mind. Not that there were no other burning issues competing for attention. Lori McHugh's pre-eclampsia upstaged the "whoosh" once or twice in her jogging jaunts. But she had been able to discuss it with her partners, an early caesarean section—ten days too early in her view—was decided on, and it resulted in a term baby in good health. And then there was an intrauterine fetal death, which solved itself as Alfie was conjuring up images of the Dead Baby Syndrome and unstoppable hemorrhage. The year before, there had been another impending crisis, now forgotten, feeding the worry-monster in her mind.

For most of the fall of 1969, however, Diane's pregnancy was the uncontested object of her paranoid cerebration.

"All right," she would say to herself. "You call D'Onofrio to come and listen to the 'whoosh'. If you are lucky and the beat comes through, he'll say: 'Nah, it's the fetus's heartbeat; you know the rate changes constantly. And that damned machine, it can go crazy. Give me the good old fetoscope.'" Then he would beam at Diane with that big, frank, uplifting smile of his and he would tell her, "Young doctors get spooked too easily."

All of her musings ended the same: "It's your call, Alfie." Imagine the irony of it; she had always resented when others wanted to interfere with her decisions.

Run, Alfie, run.

It was during one of those treks that she was finally forced to acknowledge that it would be ridiculous, even criminal, to keep ignoring Diane's case. On the return leg of her jog, she decided she must act on her hunch and she must act immediately.

She sneaked into the hospital through the back door to avoid being seen in that comical outfit. She called L'Nore and told her to meet her at the doctor's lounge in the Delivery Unit. She quickly changed into a scrub suit. Removing the vest was a most gratifying experience, like the proverbial relief of kicking off a shoe two sizes too small.

"We've got to talk, my friend," she said to L'Nore as soon as she walked in.

The girl was standing looking at the doctor with genuine concern.

"We're trying to deny it, L'Nore," said the doctor, "but there is something funny going on in Diane's belly."

She sat at the table and motioned L'Nore to the other chair.

"Let's see if we can deal with this mystery in a semi-scientific way. We will include nothing but the facts. Later we'll try to analyze them."

There was a small chalkboard on the wall used for detailing the schedule for defrosting the fridge and the assignments to buy coffee and sugar. The doctor stood up and walked noisily to the board.

"All right, kiddo," she said, chalk in hand. "If two deranged, eccentric, sex-deprived broads came to you with this scheme, what would you say?"

"Facts. The facts only, ma'am," said L'Nore.

Dr. Santoro wrote: "FACT 1. Another beat (heartbeat?)." She named it the "whoosh."

L'Nore nodded.

"FACT 2. The 'whoosh' has a different pitch, different rate, different location than the fetal heart tones."

"No question about it," said the nurse.

"FACT 3. Outside stimuli caused the 'whoosh' to accelerate more strikingly than average..." She erased "average" with her hand and wrote, "any heartbeat would."

Those were the facts.

Anything beyond this was pure conjecture.

"Now," she said, "let's draw all the scenarios that could possibly explain the facts."

"I give you Scenario One," said L'Nore. "Changes of the fetal heart rate, or even the mother's heart rate, that coincide with the changes of the auscultation sites..."

Dr. Santoro jotted down on the board: "Sc 1. Rate change coincidences."

"Next time we'll listen to them simultaneously. Let's get two Fetones, or we can use one Fetone and one fetoscope at the same time," said Dr. Santoro. "I can give you Scenario Two. Ultrasound scanning basically picks up the head of the fetus; small parts can be easily missed. So, if there were another fetus with a functioning heart but without a cranium..."

"An anencephalic fetus!" said L'Nore. "It is possible." Her jaw dropped.

"Or one with a very small head, a microcephalic fetus—the ultrasound would not pick it up."

The doctor chalked "Sc 2. Micro/anencepahalus."

"That's a good possibility. A radiograph would rule it out," said L'Nore.

"Yes, let's get a picture next visit, but I don't believe it. Anencephalic fetuses are notorious for having an extremely even rate; they don't respond to any stimulus."

"I got another one," said L'Nore. "A recurrent anomaly of the machine." These phenomena, called "artifacts," had consumed many hours of research. They were, indeed, such common occurrences that experts used to say that their most difficult task was to differentiate real blips from artifactual ones.

Alfie wrote down: "Sc 3. Artifacts."

They agreed that it was almost impossible to assume that the changes could be coincidental every time, but maybe the angulation in the transducer would produce it. They would recheck it carefully; they would search for the "whooosh" with the old fetoscope.

L'Nore raised her hand. "Hey, Doc," she said. "We can't ignore the *folie à deux*."

"I thought about that too," said the doctor. "It is a possibility; but I doubt it very much."

She scrawled on the board: "Sc 4. *Folie à deux*."

When two independent observers fed and fueled each other the perception of something that did not exist, it was called *folie à deux*—two-people-madness.

"Now we are getting to the difficult part," said the doctor. "Remember Diane's placenta was described as 'humongous'? The 'octopus placenta', the student had named it."

"But that's not a fact," interjected the nurse. "Actually it is not even mentioned in the final report."

"All right, I grant you that—but I saw it, and it was a damned big placenta."

Dr. Santoro sat down and began to scratch her head; her gaze projected to a faraway point.

After a moment, she started, "The placenta, you know, contains muscle fibers, nerve cells"—she was searching with the utmost care for words to introduce to her assistant her ideas without alarming her more than was necessary—"hormone-producing cells and more blood supply than any part of the body. And, perhaps most important, it contains those embryonic cells capable of developing into any type of specialized tissue. Now, is it entirely unthinkable that a placenta, under certain circumstances, could develop beyond its normal boundaries and start propelling its own blood and build some rudimentary nervous system and a reflex circuit that responded to stimuli?"

Speaking of folies à deux: The doctor's reasoning fueled L'Nore's imagination, and she too joined in the deductive process. "Well," she said, "the afterbirth is an invader of the mother's body. It is really a graft that has to be rejected at the proper time."

"It is indeed," asserted the doctor. "It is a foreign body. It has different genes than the mother, because half of them are contributed by the father."

"Tell you what I think, L'Nore." An indefinable, eerie sensation ran down the doctor's spine. She leaned towards her assistant and lowered the tone of her voice as if preparing to share a deep secret. "I know the idea is wild, but I've been thinking about it a lot, and every other interpretation of the 'whoosh' I entertained I had to discard, and I always had to revert to this absurd one."

She stopped for a moment as if hesitating to divulge this odd idea. "What if," she said at long last, "what if the natural forces that limit the growth of the placenta, the forces that command its rejection, for some reason fail to do so?"

She stood up and with an unsteady hand jotted down on the blackboard: "Sc 5. Placenta gone wild." Oddly, the mere sharing of her disturbing suspicions with her nurse gave her an immense sense of relief.

"You mean, like a placenta growing unchecked, like a runaway placenta?" said L'Nore, trying to wrap up in a few words the elusive concept.

Dr. Santoro erased "Placenta gone wild" on the board with the palm of her hand and replaced it with L'Nore's term: "Runaway placenta." Then she asked timidly, "You don't believe that, do you?"

After a very long silence, the girl replied in a serious tone, "Alfie, if they heard us talk like this, they'd send us to Pontiac Psych Hospital for a long vacation." Curiously, the same tingling in the spine ran through L'Nore when she added, "But I've been thinking a lot about it, and I believe that, at least, Diane's placenta can sense pressure and respond to it independent of the baby."

"Thank you," said Alfie. "It is very important to me that you more or less agree with my interpretation of these…happenings. Truly, L'Nore, at times I think I'm losing it."

They stared at each other for a long while.

"What are we going to do, Alfie?"

"What are we going to do?" echoed the doctor from the throes of her commonsensical quagmire. Then she added, "Perhaps we are seeing monsters, but there are facts also. And facts are very stubborn things."

CHAPTER XVII

# Grosse Pointe to Ann Arbor

One sunny November afternoon, Dr. Santoro left her apartment on St. Paul Street and drove along Allard Avenue. She entered westbound Interstate 94 heading for Ann Arbor. She was driving "Old Faithful," the twelve-year-old powder blue Checker Marathon that her uncle had bought for her during her internship; he had had it repainted in that odious color, but it still sported the checkered strip. Hardly the set of wheels that one would associate with a single young woman with a sizeable income, but, with over 120,000 miles under the hood, "Old Faithful," who had always slept in the street, started every morning and brought her home every night.

Before she made up her mind to go to see Professor Belanger at the University of Michigan, Alfie did some serious soul-searching. She exonerated herself from the charge of having self-serving motives. She asked herself time and again: If it had been someone else at the U of M who was the authority on the placenta, would she have traveled the sixty miles for a consultation? She answered herself yes every time. Even if the expert had been Professor Lamar, a pompous, boorish man, she would have seen him and would have tolerated his clumsy sexual overtures and his tactless jokes about her "bodacious tatas." If she believed it could have helped Diane or her baby, yes, she would have done that. The inner jury acquitted her on that charge.

The fact that she would enjoy seeing Professor Gaston Belanger again, and would have an opportunity to catch up on the academic rumor mill and find out about his present status, probably had some influence on her decision. How else could she explain her urgent appointment at Roma's Beauty Salon and the extra aspersions of Shalimar?

It was too good an afternoon to waste on the concrete canyon of I-94. As soon as she passed the western suburbs of Detroit, she exited the expressway and followed the country roads that traveled through slumbering towns consisting of two or three intersections each, with mysterious names ignored on most road maps.

The scenery more than compensated for the extra time that the back roads added to her journey. The fall colors were nearly peaking. On either side of the road, glorious crimson and yellow maples, birches of still whiteness and the multi-shaded greenery of oaks, aspens and other trees she did not recognize provided a majestic solemnity to the serene landscape. Every now and again the silhouette of a dilapidated barn interrupted the deep blue sky, and lazy cattle stood motionless here and there. As there was little traffic on those roads, she could tarry to take in the scene, a nostalgia-soaked tableau of the days before Ford's horseless carriage, when farming was the charm and the backbone of the Midwest.

The heady smell of burning leaves and the cozy silence of the deserted roads produced in Alfie a cheery and invigorating feeling that at times dispelled the grave purpose of her visit to the university campus.

There was a melancholy excitement in her anticipation of seeing Professor Belanger again. A warm spot in her heart was still reserved for him,

Had it not been, she thought at times, for...

Had it not been—God!—for a thousand different reasons.

But then, of course, it made no difference now.

They had met in Toronto. She was a medical student, and he was an assistant professor of anatomy. They shared many common interests, mostly sports and the *bel canto;* they had gone together to rugby games, curling tournaments and the opera; and a few times they had danced in the jazz bars on the Esplanade. Once he had come to her house in Windsor in his red Citroen to take her to one of his rugby games in Kitchener. He met her mother that day. The professor was quite affable, slightly shy and extremely handsome. His Parisian accent and his debonair civility, like kissing Mother's hand when he met her, contributed to his gracious charm. By that time, Mrs. Santoro had broadened the scope of her expectations for Alfie and was ready to accept a non-Italian suitor. Mother loved him at first sight, and every so often she would still reproach her daughter for letting him "get away". Of course, her mother never knew that his family would have fiercely opposed any serious commitment on his part—his family being his wife and his little daughter in Montreal.

Alfie's relationship with Dr. Gaston Belanger was the closest she had ever come to an affair. Fraternization between faculty and students, although a common occurrence, was frowned upon by the university. Their trysts were carefully planned to reduce the chances of being seen by other students. The other students, of course, knew of their relationship, and they pictured it as far more romantic than it actually was. Really, they did not care. Alfie and Gaston referred to their relationship as a "quasi-romantic sportive affinity." Sportive affinity definitely existed, but how far the "quasi-romantic" entanglement went was unclear even to them. Now, so many years later, blurred by the haze of time, it had acquired a spectral romantic patina; they themselves were no longer certain of the extent to which it had once reached in reality.

Dr. Belanger was seven years older than Alfie. He was born

in Trois Rivières, Quebec, and grew up near Montreal. He was, more than anything else, a sportsman. He had delved into rowing, boxing, tennis and, of course, hockey. His real passion, though, was rugby. He was scrum-half of the Canadian team the year it made the finals at the Commonwealth Games.

Alfie's sports achievements were less momentous. She made varsity in basketball and went to the provincial finals on the curling team. Her promising career in curling was truncated by an unfortunate incident. She never admitted any responsibility for the referee's ankle fracture, and she steadfastly refused to apologize. To this day, she insists that the referee lost his balance on the ice when he backed away from her fist and that it never made contact with him. Charges were eventually dropped when she acceded to banishment for life from the sport. She began then to call curling "a game of sissies" and never touched a stone again.

These were some of the old memories that resurfaced as she anticipated her meeting with the professor. Even the meeting place, which he chose, rekindled cherished memories. The Pretzel Bell, a landmark on Liberty Street, was sacred soil for Wolverines' fans, which is to say half of Michigan's population. It was the place where the Beta Tau fraternity boys used to gather until they moved to their own clubhouse. Saturday nights, The Pretzel Bell was center stage for the after-game recapping, the postmortem examination of the game. Each play was displayed, dissected, discussed, analyzed ad absurdum and replayed time and again. Wolverine victories were celebrated there the loudest, the room filled wall-to-wall with boisterous crowds inclined to indiscriminate and excessive imbibing. And there, too, defeats were drowned in a funereal atmosphere of frosty mugs of hops.

Alfie entered The Pretzel Bell at the exact appointed time. Professor Belanger was sitting at the bar being ogled by the barflies—the undergrad cuties—and obviously enjoying it. He stood up when he saw Alfie, still clutching his Martini.

He called aloud: "Sina!" That was what he always called her, Sina (short for Alfonsina), with the stress on the last syllable. Nostalgia time. It brought back to her the cordiality of the good old times. It was indeed a cruel irony, she thought, that good old times could only be appreciated when they were past their prime. Alfie walked up to him. They squared off a couple of feet from each other and exchanged their elaborate alma mater salute; this time, though, they capped it with the local buzzword: "Go Blue."

Then they hugged for a long time.

It felt so good.

"You look great!" Alfie exclaimed. He did. Impeccable posture, flat belly, the muscular body showing through the smart three-piece suit. Several silver strands had insinuated themselves into his jet black hair at the temples.

"So do you," he lied. She did not look good. Her hair could have used a more fashionable style, her glasses were outdated, and their thick, heavy lenses hid her seal-pup blue eyes. She was wearing a plain gray skirt and a dowdy, ruffle-collared white blouse under a good quality but definitely nondescript navy jacket.

They moved to a table in a quiet corner far from the bar. The sun was beginning to set, and the rays that entered the room reflected on the glasses and bottles on the bar and threw distorted shadows on the tables. The after five crowd would be rushing in at any moment now.

Alfie and the professor exchanged the necessary pleasantries and talked about their jobs, the business of medicine, some academic politics, the Vietnam War, sports and vacations. They tactfully avoided any mention of their family situations as long as they civilly could.

He finally broached the subject, "Getting married soon?"

"Not a chance," she hurried to reply.

"If you are ever going to do it, you should start thinking about it." He motioned to the waitress for another round.

"I'm not losing any sleep over it," she answered, trying to make it sound blasé. "Is your family here?" she dared ask, somewhat fearful of the answer.

"No," he said. A frown insinuated itself on his brow. "My wife refused to learn English, and I refused to commute to Quebec every weekend. So she moved back to live with her family in Trois Rivières. Annette went with her. She will be starting college soon."

"You are divorced, then?"

As soon as she said it, she realized it was a faux pas.

"We are working at it"—he shrugged his shoulders— "slowly."

"You must miss Annette."

"Terribly."

"Will she be coming to U of M?"

"I hope so," he said. For the first time since the conversation had turned to their families, a faint smile broke the serious countenance of the professor.

"But tell me, Sina, you said you had something you needed help with." They both felt relieved to leave the family matters aside.

"Yes, and if someone can help me, it is you. I know you've been doing a great deal of research on the placenta. Actually, one can hardly say the word placenta anywhere without your name popping up."

"Oh, yes, I'm the placenta man," he joked. "When it comes to placenta, I'm world famous—in Ann Arbor."

"Gaston! Don't tell me you're becoming humble in your old age."

"If you want to remain on my good side, do not mention the 'O' word."

The waitress returned and replaced the transparent chalice in front of the professor with a fresh one, carefully wiping off the condensation at the base and properly positioning the toothpick that supported two colossal olives.

He looked at her. "*Merci*, Laura," he said, placing the stress on the last syllable of Laura. "Tell Jeff he still makes the best martinis this side of the border."

"Thank you, Doctor. I will," Laura replied. She placed the frosty beer mug in front of Alfie without lifting her eyes from him.

"I could swear Laura was drooling," she teased him.

"So, what is the problem that brought you to visit with me?" The professor chose to ignore her naughty remark.

"The placenta is a very peculiar organ." Alfie decided to start her story with this bland remark, which would be very much like telling Caruso that high C is a difficult note to reach. Then she stopped, in an attempt to state her case in some kind of order.

"You came all the way to Ann Arbor to tell me that?" he quipped.

"You haven't changed much, Gaston. You are still too handsome for your own good, you still drink martinis, and you're still a smart-ass."

"No more compliments, please, Sina."

They both chortled and sipped their drinks to buy time. They were loosening up. It was beginning to resemble the good old days, and it would have been enjoyable for Alfie if she had not had Diane's maledetto "whoosh" in the back of her mind.

Once she had explained the object of her visit, the professor proceeded to assume his professorial stance. His voice turned deep and resonant, like that of a well-rehearsed actor. Talking about the placenta, his statements could fairly be compared to statements from the pope speaking ex cathedra.

"The placenta is indeed a fascinating organ, unique in all of biology," he proclaimed. "It can best be described as a foreign body temporarily accommodated by the host—hostess, rather. In humans, it has a ten-lunar-month contract; once the lease expires, out goes the guest, evicted, as it were, by the hostess. The supply of blood ceases; its lifeline is cut off. Whatever little oxygen the fetus contributes when it is still attached to the placenta, ends when the newborn shifts to its own circulation system as the cord is clamped."

"What do placentas die of?" the professor asked. He was staring intently at Alfie.

She did not answer. He did not expect an answer, either; it was a rhetorical question. "No blood, no oxygen. Placentas die of asphyxiation, Sina."

He went on to explain how, most recently, the placenta was being considered a graft, to which the laws of graft-versus-host interaction applied. As the principles of transplantation immunity were being formulated, scientists were baffled by the ability of the fetus (called an "allograft") to remain unharmed throughout the pregnancy. A graft of tissue with all identical genes was called a "homograft." The fetus was an allograft because half of its genes derive from a stranger, the father.

"Actually, researchers say, the placenta, not the fetus, is the 'allograft'," he went on, "because the fetus and the mother, under normal circumstances, have no direct contact. The placenta, through some biological subterfuges, avoids recognition and destruction by the mother's immune system for ten lunar months."

Recent research had found that the placenta had a marked reduction in transplantation antigens. Professor Belanger then explained that there was evidence being gathered to suggest that recurrent miscarriages, pre-eclampsia and "runting" in humans, and neonatal graft-versus-host disease (GVF) were beginning to be considered the result of an alteration in the delicate balance between graft and host.

Dr. Santoro thought it was a propitious time to interject. "I'm aware of them. Those are obviously the result of an imbalance in favor of the host."

"That is correct," he agreed.

Now she began gently to bring forward her hypothesis.

"What if the balance were altered in the opposite direction, in favor of the guest, the graft?"

She related to him the statement of a researcher from the University of Washington that she had heard at a conference on genetics: Two people, randomly selected from anywhere in the planet, differ at just one DNA base per thousand. "That means, *mon ami*," she added, pointing her finger at him, "that you and me, you and a Bedouin, me and a Mongolian or me and an Aztec are 99.9% genetically identical."

"I've heard that, of course, and it's probably true."

"Now, add to that a few generations of inbreeding, *et voilà*, the host will find it difficult to recognize a graft growing under her own skin."

"You have seen enough of that, Sina," he answered, "when the mother is unable to keep a check on the placental growth."

"Trophoblastic disease—choriocarcinoma," she said under her breath.

He nodded.

Choriocarcinoma was one of the most malignant cancers known. Some placental cells—the trophoblasts—would grow out of control, invade the mother's circulation system and quickly spread to the lungs, the liver and the brain in a vicious, savage onslaught. Before the advent of chemotherapy, these tumors were invariably fatal.

The discussion was now moving in the direction Dr. Santoro had wished.

"Now, *mon ami*, listen, and don't make fun of me," she said quite seriously. "What if…"

"You haven't outgrown the 'what if' developmental stage yet."

"You must promise not to make fun of me."

He raised his right hand. "I solemnly promise…" he uttered. The waitress saw his raised hand and pointed inquisitively to the empty glasses. He nodded.

"What I mean is…" She was searching for the right words, those that would not trigger the generic answers that he meted out to his students. She needed to lead him into an intellectual digression, beyond the routine explanations. She wanted to ignite some kind of scientific polemic. "If, in a given case, for any hypothetical reason," she began, "the placenta were not recognized by the mother's immune system as an alien and it continued to grow"—she searched carefully for the words—"out of control, as it were…"

"It is possible, I suppose," he replied evasively.

"Can you give me a 'for instance'?" She pressed on.

"Oo la la! Let me think."

He hooked his thumbnail to his upper front teeth; he was thinking in earnest. The new round arrived. It was always easier to think in front of a fresh drink.

"It could happen, I suppose, in a case of major genetic similarity."

She liked that answer.

"As in the case of consanguineous marriage, like first cousins?"

"No, no," he said.

He was really concentrating; she could tell because he was now snapping his nail on his teeth. "That wouldn't be enough, I'm sure."

"Brother-sister mating, maybe?" She said that without looking at him. She was gazing above his head; her eyes converged on a point far outside the confines of the Pretzel Bell.

"I don't think even that would be enough. The genetic complement has to be extremely similar, like identical twins, perhaps."

"Big help you are, mister," she complained. "Identical twins are always of the same sex and can't reproduce."

"I'm sorry," he answered. "I didn't make the rules."

"What if it were more than one generation of consanguineous mating?"

He hummed while staring at his drink. "Maybe. The gene pool in that case would be very similar in both mother and father." He nodded.

Silence followed.

"But you know, Sina, that that combination always results in non-viable fetuses. Those fetuses are aborted."

"Wait, wait," she interjected, trying to put her own thoughts in order. "Suppose, just suppose, that those conditions existed and that for some reason the pregnancy went on. What then?"

"What then? What then?" He mocked her. He shrugged his shoulders. "Suppose you rolled out of bed one morning and you fell up instead of down. What then? I don't know. It's an entirely new ball game."

"Just answer my question, Professor Belanger. What if the host, for any reason, were not capable of doing its job of controlling the placental growth?"

"You want me to say that the placenta would keep growing."

"Wouldn't it?"

"I suppose."

Her eyes were still converging on the distant point, while her hands busily illustrated her ideas. Dr. Santoro, talking to herself rather than to the professor, but clearly awaiting his answer, recited: "Now listen. The placenta has nerves and muscles."

The professor nodded.

"And it definitely has plenty of blood."

He nodded again.

"And remnants of toti-potential cells, those embryonic cells that can evolve into any kind of tissue."

Another nod.

"So it would not be entirely impossible..."

She looked at him. He was beginning to roll his eyes.

"Uh-uh. Hear me out." She pressed on. "It would not be entirely impossible for the placenta to grow on and to develop from all those muscle fibers a heart capable of propelling its own blood, and to develop nerves that could feel touch, that could hear, smell, whatever. And perhaps even limbs capable of moving the whole…" She vacillated on how to refer to it. "The whole thing," she said finally.

She felt a strong sense of relief mixed with embarrassment as she made a clean breast of the preoccupation that had been eating her up for weeks.

Contrary to what she had expected, the professor did not dismiss her with the recommendation that she take a long vacation or get a boyfriend. He responded with genuine interest. Far-fetched as it sounded, her friend did not think that her theory clamored for a psychiatric evaluation. He did not think it was utterly laughable.

That was all she needed at the time. Dr. Santoro proceeded to relate, with all the details, her most dreaded prospect.

Again, he surprised her by not laughing aloud at her preposterous hypothesis. She was even more amazed when he related to her that legends of that type abound in many cultures. He had heard stories from remote regions of Asia and South America of placentas attacking small animals and even children. Of course, from a scientific standpoint, they were inconceivable, and they were always rejected as mere superstitions, plain folk tales.

He brought his thumbnail again to his teeth, a sign that his brain was engaged and toiling.

"What are you thinking?" she asked. "C'mon, tell me. Do I need psychiatric help?"

"Years ago, we had a fellow in pathology here at U of M. Manuel Santos was his name. He came from a prominent family in Bolivia. A good researcher too. He owned his own plane, a Cessna. We used to fly up north together on weekends. We had two close calls at the Petoskey airport, and I stopped flying with him."

"Manuel was very interested in placenta physiology and pathology," the professor went on. "After completing his fellowship at the University of Michigan, he went to the Sorbonne in Paris for a few more years of research and then went back to Sucre, Bolivia, to chair the Department of Pathology at St. Francis Xavier University. From there, he wrote to me several letters about his project at the time. He had heard that the natives of the Altiplano—the high plateaus of Peru and Bolivia—had a legend about a "Gato Violeta," an animal that was much feared because they believed that it fed on the blood of small animals and even children. The local people, aborigines mostly, claimed that the Gato Violeta—the Cat Purple—only appeared after the delivery of a baby. Besides the killing and maiming it caused, there was also a stigma associated with it because the Cat Purple only appeared when the baby was a result of a relationship that was considered taboo by the tribe.

"On one of his vacations, Dr. Santos decided to gather first-hand information on this legend. He flew into an isolated area at the foot of the Andes and spent a month with the local people. When he returned to Sucre, he wrote to us a long letter. He said that, based on his findings, he had come to the conclusion that the Gato Violeta was not all superstition. He was particularly impressed by the fact that some of the witnesses described the Cat Purple in such detail that he had to admit that it was impossible for those simple people to fabricate it. He also pointed out that they all agreed that the creature was far more aggressive when it followed the delivery of a male baby. Manuel had had a considerable amount of training in immunology here at U of M, besides at the Sorbonne and in his own country. In one of his letters, he advanced an explanation based on immunology. He hypothesized that the high degree of inbreeding existent among the natives of that area could have resulted in placentas that were genetically so similar to the mother that they could go unrecognized as intruders. Consequently, the growth of these placentas was not checked, and they were permitted to develop into some sort of self-sufficient, low life form that, he postulated, required a constant supply of blood for its sustenance."

Alfie's jaw had dropped, and she listened spellbound to his tale.

"Interestingly enough," he continued, "Dr. Santos did not try to claim ownership of that theory. During his research in the library of a Jesuit monastery in that area, he came across a manuscript written by an abbot before the turn of the century proposing a rather similar theory, minus the immunologic explanation, of course. Probably, Dr. Santos suggested, the abbot's intention was to add some scientific basis to his struggle against the prevalent practice of incest among the natives."

"So, I'm not alone," Alfie said with a deep sigh of relief. "Maybe I'm not mad after all."

"Logically speaking, all you can say, Sina, is that you are not alone in your madness."

"This is a major thing, and you have known about it for so long. Why didn't you report it?"

"Because I believed it was hogwash. And I still do."

Now she felt comfortable enough to relate Diane's story, describing her background and how, coming from a wartorn region, she could have been separated from close relatives and never have been aware of their true relationships. Although this possibility had entered her mind, this was the first time she had actually spelled it out.

When she finished, he said, "Maybe it is not all hogwash, but I am not convinced yet."

"But there is at least one independent observer," she protested.

When the next round of drinks arrived, Professor Belanger added with a quizzical smile, "Yes, and that is not the only story."

"There is more? Are you bullshitting me?" Alfie asked as if in a trance. "Go ahead. Tell me," she said after a pause.

"There was a Thai or Cambodian or Laotian professor. Ta Huynh was his name. He was a professor of comparative anatomy at the University of Bangkok, who also lectured in the Saigon Medical School. He was also conducting studies on this matter. He corresponded with us for a while until he was captured by the Khmer Rouge or some other guerrillas."

"And what did Dr. Ta Huynh have to say?" Alfie almost jumped off her chair. "Go ahead. Tell me more."

Dr. Ta Huynh had learned about Professor Belanger's work on placental pathology, and he had written to him, in very basic French, it seemed, attempting to explain his own research. Since his writing was almost incomprehensible, Professor Belanger wrote back advising him to feel free to use his native language in his letters. From then on, all the correspondence was in Thai, which was readily translated by one of the several medical students and residents from Thailand.

Professor Belanger thought it fit at this time to make a disclaimer. He told Alfie that when he asked one of his Vietnamese physicians in training if she had ever heard of a Professor Ta Huynh, she responded by placing her index finger by her temple and moving it in circles.

The study Professor Ta Huynh was conducting involved the Kha people, a very closely-knit ethnic group, part of the Hmong that have inhabited the mountains of Laos and other Southeast Asian countries. The existence of an animal, purported to be birthed by a human female, "Con Mēo Tím"—the Cat Purple—as it was known by the Vietnamese people, was uncontested; the story had been around with minimal variations for untold generations. Strangely enough, there it was also linked to some tribal sexual practices, and it was known to bring shame to the whole clan. The appearance of the Cat Purple usually resulted in banishment and, at times, even death for the mother.

"Professor Ta Huynh became deeply involved in this research," said Professor Belanger to close his story. "In the last letter he wrote, he said that he was going to try to gather more information from the Kha people themselves. Since his expedition involved crossing regions under the control of the Khmer Rouge, he said that there was a risk that they might stop him. Apparently, he was captured before he made it to his destination, I heard that he died in jail a few years later."

"It seems that Dr. Ta Huynh will not be able to contribute much to my theory anymore," Dr. Santoro said sadly. "Maybe I can contact that Bolivian doctor—what's his name?" she added enthusiastically.

"You will need a medium for that," replied the professor with a naughty smile.

"He, too?" She sighed.

The professor nodded. "Manuel was an excellent pathologist, but a lousy pilot. He scared me to death every time we came in for a landing. During an approach to an airport in Paraguay, he missed the runway, by a country mile, I heard. He and his fiancé were killed."

"Perhaps there is a curse on this research, like the one on the Egyptian mummies," Dr. Santoro mused.

"Wouldn't be a bad idea to give it up, Sina."

"You know I can't. These stories are fascinating, but there are real people involved in my side of it—my patient and her baby. If the story of the Purple Cat proved to be true, they could be at grave risk."

She paused for a breath. Then she added, "Is anybody else involved in this research that you know of—preferably still on this side of the grass?"

He smiled and shook his head.

A period of silent reflection followed.

"Was it always compared to a cat?" she asked with genuine curiosity.

"Not at all," he answered. "Good old Professor Ta Huynh mentioned folk legends in which the thing was compared to a lizard or a turtle. People heard it neigh, oink and even bleat. And in Bolivia, according to Manuel, it was at times called the *nuna mala,* the bad nuna. *Nuna* is the name the locals use for baby alpacas or llamas."

Alfie's mind seemed to be moving in another dimension, but the professor knew she had heard him because when he finished, she lifted her eyes from the pretzel bowl.

"Nuna? Cute, huh?" she said with a silly smile.

Their eyes met. "Bah, ah, ah, ah," the professor bleated. They laughed loudly.

"Imagine me telling Dr. D'Onofrio that I need time off to do research on a killer llama," she said.

They chuckled for a while.

The length and intensity of their laughter was unquestionably out of proportion to the humor of the remarks. Five drinks on an empty stomach are known to trigger such a phenomenon.

The professor was leaning a little over the table, his hands stretching forward, middle and ring fingers together making slow circular motions as he elaborated on each item. His well-rehearsed voice projected slightly louder than was customary in a bar.

"Here we go," Alfie thought. "He'll give me an academic lecture."

She was trying hard to concentrate both on the contents of his "lecture" and his style. She realized that her ability to concentrate had been significantly reduced by the beers, so she leaned towards him and grabbed his right hand with both of hers.

"Big paw," she said. "You'll grow up to be a big doggie."

He was taken aback. His speech, serious as it was intended, was done for. He remembered the "big paws" remark; it was Alfie's favorite tease. She had used that routine many times before, always at the most inopportune time, to break away from a topic she didn't feel comfortable with.

She held his hand as they kept gazing at each other. Their thoughts journeyed back to happier, if not easier, days.

"Want to do it, Sina?" he said with a conspiratorial smile.

"Here?" she asked, quite alarmed.

He looked all around. All the tables close to theirs were empty, and the lighting in that corner was faint enough.

He nodded.

"Are you sure? They don't know me here, but you're coming back. You're a regular here, I know."

"Let's do it," he said.

"Fine with me," she said, "but, you know the rule: We have to do it twice."

"Fine. Both right and left, and no rubber," he said. "And no screaming!"

She agreed. He stood up, took off his jacket and moved the glasses, the candle and the pretzel bowl to the next table.

She removed her coat and threw it onto the next table. She sat down and fidgeted with the chair until she felt comfortable. She tucked the medal of the Blessed Mother inside her blouse and pulled her skirt up to mid-thigh in order to separate her legs. She placed her left elbow on the edge of the table and rearranged the chair several times. Then she made a tight fist and twirled it around for a while.

He sat opposite her, placed his right elbow on the table and twirled his wrist too.

"Left hand first," she said.

"Why?" he protested.

"Because I said it first."

He mumbled something and changed arms. He kept exercising his fist for a while.

"Enough already," she said. "Let's go."

They locked hands. They tested each other's stance and support points. The forearms leaned a few degrees one way, then the other. The table creaked. Gaston tried to use his deltoids advantage to twist her arm, as her forearm did not budge.

An instant of neglect of his wrist was all Alfie needed. She gave her hand all her strength; his wrist leaned laterally towards the ulnar side. He grunted. Once his forearm was pushed beyond the midline with his wrist cocked, it was all over. She held the position for a few seconds for dramatic effect. Then she slammed his hand on the table with a loud thud.

"You cheated!" he yelled.

"Weakling!" she retorted.

"You leaned your body!"

"Did not!"

"Did too!"

They were perspiring and out of breath. They laughed as they rested, preparing for the rematch.

The right hand wrestle was no real match. It lasted just as long as Gaston thought appropriate to spare her total humiliation.

"A tie again," she proclaimed, "and there'll be no rubber."

He headed for the bar for more drinks. Their antics had gone quite unnoticed by the other patrons.

When he returned with the beer and the martini, Alfie was again totally concentrating her attention on the pretzel bowl. She was silent and oblivious to the surroundings. He could not tell if she was awake or asleep, but an almost empty pretzel bowl could not have merited all that attention.

"I must...do...something," she slurred at last.

"Yes," he replied. "You must go to sleep."

"Of course, of course. I must...go home. We'll solve...the puzzle some...other day." She attempted to stand up a few times.

He watched her, amused. "C'mon, Sina. I'll take you home."

He helped her up and guided her by the arm along the long bar, past the few patrons left. Gaston exchanged greetings with some of them. Alfie stared at them with an idiotic smile. They stared back likewise. It was closing time.

"You are going...to drive fi-fi-fifty miles to Grosse Pointe... and back? Are you...insane, Gaston?"

"Yes to both."

They were on the sidewalk, standing by his car.

"And I thought…professors were underpaid," she said mischievously, pointing at the shiny Mercedes roadster.

"I drive a taxi on weekends," he retorted.

Even though their brains were not working at full capacity, they realized that the idea of her driving home by herself did not make much sense. He knew that she could not safely drive fifty miles in her condition. She knew he could not drive a hundred miles in his.

He opened the passenger door, and she fell heavily into the seat.

"I would invite you to stay at my place but…" he said after a little hesitation.

"I accept." She interrupted him and slammed the door shut.

"I was afraid," he faltered for a while after he had slid into the driver's seat, "that you would construe it as a sexual overture."

"I should…be that lucky," she stammered, and she was out cold.

She was out cold when he parked in his driveway. He opened the front door of the house and propped it open with his briefcase. Then he returned to the car and gently shook her. He shook her again, less gently, again and again. There was no response. He gave up.

It would take a big and strong man to extricate Alfie from the car and carry her to the house. Fortunately, the professor—six-foot-four and 260 pounds, mostly muscle—was both. He was panting when he finally placed her head on his shoulder; he carried her across the flagstone path with visible effort.

If the neighbors saw him, he thought, they would imagine he got lucky at the church fair and came home with an enormous stuffed panda bear.

He was definitely short of breath when he dropped her unceremoniously across his large bed. She never opened her eyes. He lay on the couch in the living room, and he too was dead in seconds.

At six o'clock, the loud alarm went off. The clock was a few inches from Alfie's ears, but she did not move.

CHAPTER XVIII

# The Handsome Stork

he day before one of Diane's scheduled appointments with Dr. Santoro, Belinda called Diane at work. "Diane," she said, all excited, "I didn't forget my promise. Dr. Irving had a cancellation for tomorrow, and since I know you'll be coming in, I did some juggling, and I managed to squeeze you in at four. Yours will be his last appointment; then he'll be off to South Carolina for a tournament at Pinehurst."

"Thank you," said Diane.

"So we'll see you tomorrow," Belinda said. She had gone through some inconvenience to arrange the change; she had expected more from Diane than a perfunctory "Thank you."

The next afternoon, Diane met Dr. Irving.

First, of course, she had to meet Belinda, who was sitting at the reception desk. Belinda seemed to be in her mid-forties. A light even tan contrasted with her too-blonde-to-be-true long hair, which was pulled straight back into a ponytail held by a black scrunchie and then flowed down to her shoulders. Large, wraparound eyeglasses succeeded in their job of hiding the crow's feet at her temples. Belinda had a figure that would beg a second look from middle-aged men.

When Diane reached the reception counter, Belinda said, "You must be Diane Truong." Diane nodded. Belinda stood to her feet for an affectionate handshake. She stood as tall and straight as a Hussar officer. Diane looked up, feeling a little threatened, at the woman's gleaming green eyes a foot above hers. Belinda's ample hips were almost at the level of Diane's breasts.

"Come on in, Diane," Belinda commanded with an almost comical solemnity, as if she were about to lead a visitor through the grand tour of a mansion. "Dr. Irving has been asking about you," she said. She led Diane to an examining room and instructed her to put on a white gown. Then, with an endearing smile, she left the room.

She returned in a few minutes and announced pompously: "The doctor will see you now." She held the door open for his grand entrance.

Dr. Jonathan Irving entered the examining room smiling and shook Diane's hand as if he had known her forever. "Kathy's friend!" he exclaimed. "As beautiful as she said you were."

He was all he was cracked up to be and then some—tall, broad-shouldered, with light brown hair, a perennial tan and the legendary dreamy pearl gray eyes.

Dr. Jonathan Irving, it was rumored, was very fond of golf, the wines of Bordeaux and tall, blonde women with long legs—the order changed according to season, time of day and hormonal status. His father, John Ethan Irving, was an obstetrician who had practiced in the Pointes for twenty years, and Jonathan did not find it hard to follow in his footsteps. By and large, he was satisfied with his profession, although he often referred to it as his B movies, because, if not glamorous, at least it generated the income necessary to pursue his primary vocation, golf, without ever having had the need to dip into his wife's dowry. He had married a beautiful local girl, tall, blonde and long-legged, an heiress to one of the auto fortunes. While he was on call or on the fairways, she had busied herself with fundraisers for the Michigan Opera Theater and other social functions at their home on Provencal Road, and spent many of her lonesome afternoons riding at the Grosse Pointe Hunt Club. The Irvings' parties were always in the grandiose style, and both the doctor and his wife had performed their hosting duties with a zeal bordering on the theatrical. Jonathan had enough golf and travel stories to keep the not-easily-impressed company interested. He could always drop the name of a heavy-duty golf amateur or pro to keep at bay most attempts at one-up-manship. His wife was pretty and witty, able to hold her own even among the most eminent guests. She was immensely popular in all the circles they frequented. She had other graces, which she had bestowed rather generously upon the socially prominent men of her acquaintance; that undoubtedly had contributed to her popularity. The accidental discovery by the doctor of this disagreeable behavioral pattern had led to a protracted and scandalous divorce that even shocked the Pointes' gentry, who were quite accustomed to scandalous divorces. The doctor's untimely death would end the legal strife that had contributed significantly to the financial welfare of several attorneys.

"And how are we today?" Dr. Irving asked Diane as he reviewed meticulously every page of her record. His examination was unquestionably thorough. He measured the size of the uterus himself, and in his first try he placed the transducer on the abdomen at the precise point where the fetal heart tones were clearly audible. He listened for a full minute and said aloud: "One forty-eight," Belinda wrote it down in the record.

"No more sounds? Only one baby?" asked Diane.

"Only one," he stated a little hesitantly.

He went back to the table and flipped the pages of her record. "Of course, only one. You had an ultrasound which showed just one healthy baby." He added, "Why did you ask?"

"One time, Dr. Santoro found another beat. She was worried."

Dr. Irving turned towards Belinda. They smiled at each other.

"Only one baby, my dear," he said, patting her shoulder kindheartedly. "No reason for you or Dr. Santoro to worry."

"Dr. Santoro is a little...er...excitable," interjected Belinda. "You mustn't take everything she says seriously."

"It was a real pleasure meeting you, Diane," Dr. Irving said, shaking her hand. He placed his other hand on top of hers. "If you see Kathy, give her my regards and thank her for referring to us a patient as lovely as you."

Before Diane had a chance to respond to his elaborate compliment, he left the room, still sporting the charismatic smile.

Belinda stayed with Diane to give some medical advice and instructions on how to prepare for the labor. As Belinda was about to leave the room, Diane asked her in a confidential tone, "Is it true that his wife is expecting a baby?"

"Good gracious me!" exclaimed the woman, blushing a little. "Certainly not! He has two beautiful children, a boy and a girl, both already out of grammar school. That's plenty. Wherever did you hear that wild story?"

"They were talking in the waiting room," Diane replied. It was the first explanation that crossed her mind.

"Oh," sighed Belinda as if relieved. "They were talking about Dr. Rao. His wife is expecting their first child."

When Diane talked to Kathy on the telephone and mentioned what she had asked Belinda, Kathy exclaimed, "Of course not! They are going through a divorce. Besides, his wife would not even think of losing her figure. She is a tight-ass who would refuse to be impregnated by the last man on the planet if it meant the end of humankind."

"I did not know that," said Diane giggling.

"Where did you hear that gossip?"

"I made it up. I think Dr. Irving and Belinda...you know..." She kept giggling.

"Even so. Whatever possessed you to make up such a dumb question?"

"The devil made me do it," Diane answered between chuckles. It was Flip Wilson's line.

CHAPTER XIX

# The Eighth Lunar Month

iane was supposed to be here today," Dr. Santoro said in her usual strident voice as the receptionist escorted into the examining room the last patient of the afternoon.

"She was in," answered L'Nore timidly. "I found out she saw Dr. Irving."

"Why?" bellowed the doctor. "She had an appointment with us. I wanted to see her."

"What happened…" started L'Nore slowly, bracing herself for the anticipated outburst of temper, "is that Dr. Irving had a cancellation and Belinda had promised Diane she'd get her to meet him. It seems she had been recommended to Dr. Irving by an old friend of his and she had never got to meet him before."

"That Belinda shouldn't have changed her appointment without checking with us first," shouted the doctor. "That idiot! I'll give her a piece of my mind."

"I suppose not," L'Nore quickly agreed. She could see the gathering storm and was relieved that she was not on the receiving end of it. "I told Anita at the front desk to make sure Diane's next appointment is with you."

"It pisses me off. That conceited mouse fart should have

known better than that. She gets away with murder around here." Dr. Santoro stomped the floor to release her anger. "When is her next appointment?"

"In two weeks."

"Make sure she sees us next time."

"I'll try."

L'Nore was looking forward to being there when the doctor released her wrath on Belinda. There was a general dislike in the department for the British ex-beauty queen. She over-dressed for her position for one thing, and her accent had long ago peaked the charm hill and was now far down the slope of comical affectation. She was suspected of having an affair with Dr. Irving—purely for business reasons on his part because, her classy accent and hoity-toity demeanor notwithstanding, she had been born too early for the doctor's standards and her oft-mentioned crown at the Gloucestershire beauty pageant was becoming quite rusty and ill-fitting.

~ ~ ~

Two weeks later, Dr. Santoro asked if Diane was coming that day.

"At four o'clock," L'Nore answered with relief. "By the way, did you ever talk to Belinda about her changing the appointment?"

"No, I talked with Jon," said the doctor. "I told him that I understood that he wanted to meet Diane and that was fine with me, but if Belinda was going to change the appointment, the civil thing to do was to let us know. He apologized, perfunctorily, as he usually does."

"Is that all you told Dr. Irving?"

"Well…no," she mumbled with a blameworthy smile.

Jonathan Irving, Cool Jon, undoubtedly had some behavioral problems, and Alfie had locked horns with him a few times—but, in spite of his patronizing attitude, she could not help liking him. He was the one who had introduced her into the practice, and into the community as well. "Welcome to the Pointes," he had said to her when they met. Probably he had been assigned by the Old Man to show her around. "The Pointes," Jon had said to Alfie at the start of the initiation exercise, "are the Hamptons of the Midwest—minus the intelligentsia, of course." She smiled congenially in reply although she only had the vaguest of ideas of what the Hamptons were.

When she was ready to move to the area, Alfie had looked up a small rental on the East Side, just a few miles from the offices and the hospital. "Alfie," Jon had told her when he had learned about her choice, "if you are going to work in Grosse Pointe, you must live in Grosse Pointe." He had steered her to an elegant apartment on St. Paul Street in the Village. It was definitely "nicer" than what she had chosen, but twice as large as she needed, and the rent was four times as high. She had taken it; she felt that that was her first Grosse Pointey decision.

When Jon first saw her car, he started a little conversation with her about it.

"That will be next," Alfie had said, without meaning it. "One doesn't become a Grosse-Pointer in one fell swoop."

On occasions, Dr. Irving would give her box-seat tickets for her and her mother to the Michigan Opera Theater, and all in all he and his wife had been quite civil to her.

Alfie could never decide whether the Irvings' behavior was frivolous snobbery or the natural result of having been born to the manner. Worse yet, deep in her heart, she was not sure whether she despised or envied it.

Whatever she felt towards Cool Jon, it did not prevent her from conveying to him her thoughts about his nurse, Her Royal Pain, Belinda.

L'Nore started to giggle. "C'mon, tell me. What else did you tell him?"

The doctor hesitated.

"Don't you think I should know?" charged L'Nore. She was dying to hear it.

"Well, if you must," said Dr. Santoro. "I told Jon to tell Her Majesty that if she ever does something like that to us again, I personally will kick her ass so hard that she'll spit up her hemorrhoids."

"Did you really?" They both laughed heartily. "That'll teach them that we are no pushovers."

"I don't think we've ever been accused of that."

~ ~ ~

Diane signed in at four-thirty that day; she knew that Dr. Santoro was always behind schedule. She was led into the examining room at five-twenty.

Diane reported that the baby was quite active. She complained of lack of sleep because when her husband did not wake her up with his snoring, the baby would wake her with hard kicks.

"He will be football player," joked Diane. "He kicks very hard."

"How do you know he's kicking? Maybe he's punching and he'll be the next Joe Louis," quipped the doctor. "And how do you know it's a 'he'?"

"Oh, I know it is a 'he'," she giggled.

The check-up was going as expected: Her blood pressure was quite normal, her urine was clear of sugar and protein, and her uterus had grown normally.

"All is well," pronounced Dr. Santoro.

Then the fetal heart sounds came through loud and clear, 144 beats per minute, on the speaker of the Fetone.

The doctor shut off the machine.

"Only one heart?" asked Diane.

"Seems that way," mumbled the doctor in reply. Then she added, trying to sound nonchalant, "Can you stay here a couple of hours, Diane?"

"I suppose I can," Diane answered, "if I can call Quang not to worry. Why do I have to stay? What we are going to do?"

"I'd like an activity test on the baby," said the doctor.

"Great idea," L'Nore thought. She said, "Let me call Labor and Delivery to make sure they have a monitor available."

"Oh, we'll find one for Diane," said the doctor.

L'Nore knew the doctor would get one, but she preferred to avoid the kicking and screaming.

She picked up the receiver, "Do you have a monitor available? We're bringing an NST."

They had one available. L'Nore felt relieved that the test would be carried out without any bloodletting.

Dr. Santoro was explaining to Diane what an NST was. The "non-stress test" consisted of monitoring the fetal heart rate for some time, paying special attention to the variations in the rate. Changes in the tempo of the beat, the so-called "beat-to-beat variability," were considered a sign of fetal well-being. For a "stress test," contractions of the uterus were induced with drugs in order to see how the fetus responded to them; uterine contractions were known to be a stressing factor for the mother-fetus system, as they reduced the supply of oxygen by squeezing the vessels of the placenta. For either test, pressure cups were placed on the mother's abdomen and held by straps; the heartbeats and the contractions were picked up by transducers and graphically recorded by a stylus on a running paper strip. A fetal electrocardiogram could also be obtained through the abdominal walls, but filtering out the maternal heartbeat was terribly cumbersome.

Diane was hooked up to the machine, her belly again smeared with the unctuous jell, and doctors, nurses and residents came every so often to look at the tracings and tinker with the transducers and the straps that held them against the abdomen. The tracings became illegible several times, the cups were realigned time and again, and the transducers were changed twice. The room devoted to this type of testing was at the end of the Labor Suite, and the patients for non-stress tests were at the bottom of the priority list for the staff of the Labor and Delivery Unit. There was always more excitement going on elsewhere provided by the women in active labor.

Since the faces of the multiple observers did not show any signs of alarm, Diane dozed off many times in spite of her concern about the baby's condition. She heard the cleaning crew mopping the corridors, and she smelled the disinfectants. She heard the screeching of the stretchers being wheeled back and forth, the PA system calling this and the other doctor, and the laughter and the modulated voices of people talking in the hallways.

Dr. Santoro sat by Diane's side for a long while. She also played with the transducers and the straps and complained about how temperamental these gadgets were. The doctor patiently explained to her what the test meant. She reassured her that she had seen nothing to worry her, but that she would go over the tracings afterwards. They talked about Diane's job, and Diane bragged about finding a sixty-five-thousand-dollar overcharge. She told the doctor about Mai, her daughter, who played violin and was on a music scholarship at the Interlochen School, and about their plans to move to a larger home in the spring.

Diane fell asleep finally. Dr. Santoro tiptoed out of the room and went to the front desk. She sat next to the secretary and made the few telephone calls she had left.

The harsh sound of metal hitting the tiled floor disrupted the doctor's concentration. The orderly had knocked a bedpan from a cart in front of Diane's room. Dr. Santoro hurried to the room to apologize, but Diane was still sleeping, undisturbed by the commotion. "She must be really tired not to have heard that racket," the doctor thought and returned to the desk.

After a few more calls, she looked at her watch. It was past nine o'clock. "I think that's enough," said the doctor. She went back to Diane's room and woke her up gently. She tore off the paper strip and rolled it carefully. The time, the patient's position and her vital signs were scrawled at different points on the back of the strip, which was a couple of yards long.

"I'll have you disconnected from these contraptions," she told Diane. "I'll go over the tracings tonight or tomorrow. They look fine, but if there's something to worry about, I'll call you. If not, just keep your next appointment."

Diane thanked her and began to dress.

"Baby going to be all right?" she asked.

Dr. Santoro dropped her eyes to the paper strip, and her face flushed a little when she answered. "As of this moment, we have no reasons to believe that the baby is in any type of distress. However, many conditions will not show up until after the baby is born, and sometimes not even until years later."

Then she mumbled something like "Goodbye" and left the room in a hurry.

CHAPTER XX

# A Disclaimer is Born

There was a yellow legal pad on the dinner table. Dr. D'Onofrio pushed the pad towards the man with the tip of the steak knife. "Write it down," said Dr. D'Onofrio to the man dressed in a dark pin-stripe suit.

"This will not necessarily keep you out of trouble, Doctor," said Mr. Paloutis.

"Write it down," repeated Dr. D'Onofrio a little louder.

The man looked up at the doctor. Normally rubicund, the doctor's face was then reaching a deep purple hue. Mr. Paloutis feared for the doctor because he seemed on the verge of apoplexy, but he worried a great deal more about his own safety.

Mr. Paloutis started to write.

Dr. D'Onofrio had just come out of the courtroom at Wayne County Circuit Court, and the lawyer could still remember clearly what had happened there.

"What did you answer, Doctor, when my client asked if the baby was going to be all right?" the plaintiff's attorney had asked Dr. D'Onofrio on the stand.

"I tried to reassure her. Peace of mind is very important for…" Dr. D'Onofrio started to reply.

"That was not my question, Doctor," interrupted the lawyer.

"Suppose a patient asks me before surgery if the operation is going to go well…" the doctor interjected.

"Doctor, please answer the question. Is it not true, Doctor, that you told my client that the baby was going to be all right? Yes or no."

"Answer Mr. Barnard's question, Doctor," commanded the judge.

"It is true, but the reason that…"

"Thank you, Doctor. No more questions, Your Honor," said Mr. Barnard.

Later that same afternoon, Mr. Barnard had asked Dr. D'Onofrio, "Is it possible that a doctor might tell his patient that everything is all right so the patient will not seek a second opinion and so he will not run the risk of losing her business?"

"That's a fat lie," screamed the doctor.

"Doctor, just answer my question," the man belched just a few inches from Dr. D'Onofrio's face. "Is it or is it not possible?"

The judge intervened again.

"Of course, it is possible."

"Thank you, Doctor. No more questions."

After the session, the doctor had gone to his lawyer's office in the Penobscot Building.

"I'm sorry, Mr Paloutis is not in at this moment," said the receptionist. "Do you care to leave a message for him?"

Dr. D'Onofrio shook his head and walked out of the office. He knew where to find him.

He told the maitre d' at the Savoyard Club that Mr. Paloutis was expecting him. Actually, the doctor was the last person Mr. Paloutis expected or wished to see as he consumed his steak tartar. The man, however, stood up, shook the doctor's hand courteously and motioned for him to sit down.

"Do you care to join me for dinner, Doctor?" he asked quite politely. Dr. D'Onofrio shook his head and sat down. Then he asked point-blank, "Was it a mistake to tell the patient that the baby was going to be all right?"

"It did not help any," answered the man after some hesitation. He realized at once that disparaging the doctor's statement was not an intelligent thing to do under these circumstances.

"I said it to make her feel well, and there had been nothing, nothing, wrong with the pregnancy," protested the doctor.

"I know," said the lawyer sympathetically.

"What should I say the next time a patient asks me if her baby is going to be all right?"

"Well," mumbled Mr. Paloutis, "maybe something more vague…for instance, something like, 'Nothing worrisome has come up so far…'"

Dr. D'Onofrio stood up; he was still holding the steak knife.

"No for instances," said the doctor, now pointing the knife at the lawyer. "I'm paying you for your legal advice. Write down what I should say to the next patient who asks me if her baby is going to be all right."

The next day, the few lines that Mr. Nicholas Paloutis Esq. wrote on the legal pad were printed and circulated among the staff of The Grosse Pointe Storks. The memorandum said:

*To the Staff of the Grosse Pointe Storks:*

*Effective immediately.*

*Answer to a FAQ ("Is my baby going to be all right?"):*

*"As of this moment, we have no reasons to believe that the baby is in any type of distress. However, many conditions will not show up until after the baby is born, and sometimes not even until years later."*

*Any other answer to this question will result in immediate dismissal.*

*Dr. A. D'Onofrio.*

## CHAPTER XXI

# The First-Born Child

Toting her well-worn leather attaché case, still in scrubs and bloodstained shoes, Alfie entered her office in the Ob/Gyn Department of Our Lady of Lourdes Hospital. She was returning from a peaceful dinner at home. A very peaceful dinner. Solo. After the meal, she had had time to do some of the housekeeping chores that she detested, such as placing the dirty dishes in the dishwasher, returning the leftovers to the fridge, washing some clothes and paying the bills. She was on call that night, and even though she had no patients in labor or in the Emergency Ward, she thought it would be a good idea to stay in the hospital rather than having to rush from home in the middle of the night for an impending delivery.

If all remained quiet, she planned to review the tracings of Diane's NST. As she entered the office, her thoughts were with the maledetto "whoosh," just as they had been when she had been gobbling down her dinner, dropping the bed linen into the washer and stuffing envelopes with checks. The maledetto "whoosh" had been a permanent, attention-hogging guest in her brain for over a month. The origin of the "whoosh" was enough of a conundrum, yet more troublesome for her was the decision on what her obligation was to Diane as her doctor, suspecting that a major, even life-threatening complication could be in store for her. She experienced an immediate, overwhelming sense of responsibility to share her preoccupation with the patient; but she could not ignore the other side, of course, the danger of having alarmed her unnecessarily if the risk did not materialize.

Legally, she was pretty certain that she was standing on safe ground. She had rechecked with another ultrasound that had corroborated a single fetus. A radiograph had further confirmed it and ruled out the possibility of another fetus with a small or absent cranium. She had made very detailed notes of her findings, and, underlined in red for her associates not to miss, she had penned, "Another heartbeat?"

No, her main concern was not her legal exposure; the sword of Damocles hung over her conscience rather than her head. Her consuming fear was that, if her theory—far-fetched and laughable as it was—proved correct, she had not done all that she could to protect her patient. The ethical implications of the issue agitated Alfie. Among the recondite nuances of the issue, a particular item stood out: Why hadn't she come forward to tell Dr. D'Onofrio or the other partners, "I think there is something odd going on, and I want all of you to look into it?"

That's when self-recrimination stepped in. She kept telling herself that the reason she had not followed that option was that she was completely certain that they would brush off the crazy idea without going in-depth into the issue. It was not that they were insensitive people. They were very busy people without the time or the intellectual inclination to delve into a notion that was elusive and, yes, probably senseless.

Alfie had learned as a child to be quite candid with herself. Her conscience did not allow excuses even for self-protection. Unpleasant incidents that she had attempted to hide had always come back to the fore, to castigate her. The "Chancroid Charlotte" incident was such an item. Was her fear of exposure to ridicule what held her back from doing what could possibly be the right and honest thing to do? She was convinced that the fear of facing public embarrassment was definitely not the only reason, probably not the main reason either, but, frankly, she could not entirely deny that it weighed in her decision.

In this downcast mood of guilt and uncertainty, Alfie sat at the desk of her small office and pulled from her briefcase Diane's medical chart.

As was her habit when she reviewed a chart, Alfie read and re-read every syllable written on it. She learned that Diane's real name was Dáo and that she had been born in Laos (question mark) in 1938 (question mark). The actual day was listed as "unknown" although a note was added: "The passport says August 10." The family history entry had a difficult-to-decipher note that said "unknown" perhaps, with "adopted" written underneath in parentheses. The husband's medical history read: "Engineer at GM, healthy, family history unknown."

The chart continued: "Gravida II, Para I, Ab 0, uneventful vaginal delivery, Georgia 1955, term female, birth weight unknown."

The resident who had taken the history had been quite thorough, especially in the physical examination. She had examined her throat ("tonsils normal size, sl. injected"), her spine ("very minor left scoliosis, < 10 degrees") and her skin ("hyperpigmented, benign looking, quarter-inch mole at the posterior base of neck, right side"). There was a note in the EENT section about a "minute iris coloboma at seven o'clock in the right eye," and in the heart section a note about a questionable systolic heart murmur in the mitral area ("discussed with Dr. Rao") had been underlined.

Alfie went over the entries for each subsequent office visit. Weight, blood pressure and urine tests had always been within normal limits. The fetal activity column on two occasions contained a note saying, "Very active," highlighted.

Alfie found nothing that could be helpful to her quest.

When she was satisfied that she had checked the obstetrical record thoroughly, she set it on the floor and pulled from her attaché case several rolls of paper. The rolls consisted of two-inch ribbons of white paper with the record of the fetal heart activity for the three-and-a-half hours that Diane had been connected to the monitor. The tracing on this strip was made by a hot stylus on heat-sensitive paper that moved at a constant speed. Vertical bars at about one-inch intervals marked the time in minutes. A few hours of monitoring resulted in yards of tracings. Any movement of the mother or the fetus or the transducer, or the drying of the jelly used for interfacing, or electric interference, or malfunction of the transducer resulted in distortions, called "artifacts."

Dr. Santoro, in general, used fetal monitoring less than her colleagues. Her reasoning was: "I have to be damned convinced that it will make a difference in the management of a pregnancy before I subject the baby to hours of bombardment by ultrasound waves." When her colleagues protested that ultrasound was safe for fetuses, she countered contentiously, "All you can say is that harmful effects have not been identified so far. For all we know, in a few generations half of the country could be born deaf."

Fetal monitoring was in its infancy; of that she was sure. A "reactive" test gave the obstetrician a little reassurance but guaranteed nothing. The interpretation of the enigmatic tracings, sadly, was left to the imagination of the "experts"—usually self-proclaimed. Dr. Santoro had pointed out to them all too often that the final conclusion, reactive or non-reactive, was little more than an educated guess.

Alfie started to unroll the tracings of Diane's test, itself not an easy job, as the paper strips stubbornly refused to be straightened. Inch by inch, she reviewed the lines, interrupted now and again and fluctuating between more or less legible markings and an incomprehensible jumbled clutter of jagged lines and scattered ink spots. She advanced a few feet in the tracings and then had to rewind to compare. She did the job with disgust. Imprecations such as "goddamned"—and worse—in both English and Italian sprouted every so often.

During the monitoring, the transducer had been aimed at the fetal heart, so most of the time it had picked up the fetus's heartbeat. On occasion, when Diane had moved, or when Alfie had purposely shifted the beam, another beat, quite different from that of the fetus, was recorded in the tracing. So, Alfie could at best detect the extra beat occasionally and usually for a short time because she did not want to draw attention to it. She found the extraneous rate on the strip always faster than the fetal rate and with startling variability. By then, Alfie had little doubt of the existence of the "other" beat. Yet, she knew that if she showed the strip to her colleagues, they would all cry: "Artifact."

Towards the end of the tracings, she noticed something more astonishing yet: The line of the "other" beat shot clear out of the top of the strip, a rate probably over two hundred. That, she had never seen before. Almost a half-minute elapsed before the line descended again to within the range of the tape. The rate remained for some time above 180 beats per minute. "That's no artifact," she said aloud. The rate hovered above 160 bpm for a good while. Then there was a hiatus in the tracing. When the line reappeared, its rate settled at about 144, and it remained there with only minor variations; this one was the fetal heart, no question about it.

The wild one, the one that shot out of the range of the strip, any expert would have called "an artifact." Alfie, though, was convinced that that one was the "whoosh," the beat that was neither the maternal nor the fetal circulation.

She rewound the roll and reexamined the wild tracings several times.

"Judas priest!" she thought. "How can I claim I didn't notice it?"

Every time that the extra rate registered, it was faster than the fetal tones, and it had a high degree of what was called "beat-to-beat variability." That she could understand, even though she did not know the origin, but the violent upsurge that shot the tracing out of the strip was entirely out of her comprehension.

It was past one o'clock in the morning. Staring at the tracing, Alfie had dozed off a few times. Each time she opened her eyes, she saw the enigmatic leap. "Wait a minute!" she shouted in silence as she woke up. She scanned the roll back and forth again and again, hoping that some mundane explanation would materialize. She did wish that all the time and worry that she had invested in the matter were for naught.

An entry on the strip, made by the nurse, about two to three feet before the big leap said: "Eight thirty-five." She counted the bars that separated the time entry from the event—about fifty bars, or fifty minutes. That would place the event at about nine-thirty.

At nine-thirty she was sitting at the front desk making telephone calls; she was quite certain of that.

"Oh, God, no," she said aloud. Something frightful had popped into her mind. It was just a suspicion, but the matter was serious enough. She thought that she had to know for sure, and she had to know then and there.

At two-ten in the morning.

She called the operator and asked to be connected with Housekeeping. She knew they kept a log of the janitors' chores and times. A sleepy voice answered. When she identified herself, the voice became fully awake.

"At what time did the janitor do the floors of Labor and Delivery last?" she asked.

"He's still there," the woman replied.

"No, I mean in the evening shift," the doctor insisted.

"Excuse me, Doctor," the woman said. "I'll have to look in the log."

While she awaited the answer, Alfie's thoughts were

spinning at full speed. That had to be it. She remembered that she was sitting at the desk when she had seen the janitor carrying his cleaning supplies. As he was rushing to leave the unit, he had knocked a bedpan from a table right in front of Diane's room, and it had made a deafening clatter as it hit the tile floor. She had rushed into Diane's room to explain the row, but Diane was still profoundly asleep.

"David went to the Labor Unit at eight forty-five," the voice returned, "and he checked into the ER at nine-forty; so he must of left Labor and Delivery at about nine-thirty. Was there a problem, Doctor?"

"No, not at all," she responded. "I just wanted to know. Thank you."

The doctor hung up the receiver and grabbed her head. Diane had not heard the noise; she was sure of that.

She ran the strip a dozen times back and forth. The awful rise of the rate that propelled the stylus out of the tape had coincided with the loud noise. The record challenged any skepticism.

"God almighty," she said aloud. "The damned thing can hear."

When the stylus dropped into the strip again, there were several minutes of nonsensical lines and dots, and eventually the transducer picked up again the fetal heartbeats at a congenial rate.

"It's not in your head," she said wretchedly. "I wish it were."

She was convinced now that there was an extra heartbeat that operated independently from the fetal heart, that responded in an inordinate fashion to external stimuli and that originated in an area of the uterus where the placenta had been located by the ultrasound images.

"There' s a lot of work to do after the sun rises," she told herself.

A hard day indeed was ahead of her if she insisted on pursuing her search.

"Alfie, you think that there is an extra beat?"

"It is hard to deny, sir."

"And it reacts to loud noises!"

"One cannot ignore facts, sir."

"You are positive, aren't you?"

"Of course not. I'm not positive."

"So, what will you tell the mother?"

"I should, shouldn't I?"

"You might succeed in alarming Diane unnecessarily."

"But we must, at least, be prepared."

There was laughter in the background. And there was panting.

"Nobody else seems to be concerned."

"There are lives at risk, though…We must follow through, sir…They are facts, not artifacts, sir…Yes, sir, human lives at risk, mother, baby, and heaven knows who else."

Dreams, in the fuzzy boundary of nightmares. Dreams that at times spawn solutions, but more often feed imaginary monsters.

The laughing in the background ceased, but the labored breathing did not. It stood apart from all the other sensations in her dream state. At this moment, her eyes burst open, and all of a sudden she was fully awake.

"Dreaming of the maledetto 'whoosh' again," she reproached herself.

No. She was wide, wide awake now. It was no dream. The "whoosh" was still there, and it was real. She propped herself up on her elbows. The rhythmic panting came from the far wall of the room, and the wall itself seemed to vibrate in rhythm with the inflections of the sound.

To her trained ears, it resembled the embarrassed but rhythmic breathing of an asthma attack. After a while, the tempo began to increase. Soon it increased more rapidly. Then the rate of increase increased, as if heading for a violent culmination.

She sat on the edge of the couch, in the dark, choosing not to switch on the light. She conjured the image of a seething creature, crouching, gazing at her neck, inhaling and exhaling rapidly to gather strength for the jump. She reached over and grabbed the letter opener from the desk and held it in her fist as if it were a dagger.

"The rate could not increase much more," she sensed. "The climax should be coming, now."

"There," she mumbled when the climax arrived.

A climax it was, and it came from the next room—loud, boisterous, exuberant, enviable. Giggles and soft-spoken words followed.

"How ridiculous can one get?" she yelled at herself in silence. "Look at you, Alfonsina Santoro!"

She was still sitting at the edge of the couch holding her weapon. Her fear spent, she laughed at herself. She rocked herself for a while. Then she tiptoed to the door of the office, opened it very quietly and peeked out into the softly lit hallway.

The next room was a blood drawing station. A lab technician was treading softly out of the next room, a young intern holding her hand. They both appeared conspicuously contented.

"God, my nerves are shot," the doctor said to herself as she waited to settle down from the unforeseen fright and the belittling mortification.

She returned to the couch and took a few sips of her lukewarm Coke. For a moment, she wished she had been the lab tech.

~ ~ ~

It was past six o'clock; it would be ridiculous to try to resume sleeping. She went to the bathroom, took a quick shower, brushed her teeth and attempted to do something with her obstinate hair.

"Fine, Alfie. You look almost presentable now," she said to herself.

A new day.

"It now seems that there might be some truth to your suspicions," she thought. "Great. What do you do now?" She thought that she had somehow painted herself into a corner. "Which way do I go from here?"

Her mother's advice rang loud inside her head: "*Figlia mia, usa il cervello,*"—use your brain, my child. "If you take the same road, you'll always arrive at the same place."

Look at it from another angle, it meant. And she did. "All right, suppose my theory is correct. Suppose some inbreeding took place and as a result of it a wild placenta developed."

She hit her forehead. "Why didn't I think of it before, *scema?*" she said aloud. The genetic composition of this baby had to be the same as the previous one, since the mother and the father were the same. She knew that Diane had had a normal pregnancy and a normal baby. Mai seemed to be a normal child. So much for her theory.

Well, maybe it did not have to occur in all pregnancies.

Then, she reasoned, "The child is normal, but do we know for a fact that Diane's first pregnancy was normal?"

She looked at the clock on the wall. It was a quarter past seven. Diane's telephone number was on her chart. She answered on the fifth ring.

"Hi, Diane," said the doctor, trying hard not to sound too excited, "This is Dr. Santoro."

"Something wrong?" asked Diane.

"No, no." In her rush to call her, she had not thought of an excuse for the untimely call. "We are…reviewing…patients' records, and we found that we…have no results of… your first baby's…blood work." It sounded credible enough, she thought.

"What you need?"

"First, where was your first baby born?"

"Mai born in Georgia," said Diane.

"Where in Georgia?"

"I…don't remember. Wait, please," after a short exchange with her husband in their tongue, she returned to the telephone. "A place called Elwin Town, close to Macon."

The doctor jotted down: Elwin Town, Georgia. "Did you live in Elwin Town?"

"No, we lived in Maclay, fifty miles away."

"Maclay?" asked the doctor.

"Maclay," Diane repeated.

"How do you spell it?"

A longer exchange with the husband. "No, we don't remember," she giggled.

"If you remember the name of the hospital in Elwin Town, we can get the records." She was getting the knack of creative fibbing.

Another aside consultation. "Miller Hospital, but the hospital is no more."

"It closed?" asked Alfie.

"Hospital closed when Dr. Miller died."

("Use your brain, Alfonsina," she admonished herself.) "Diane, maybe you remember your address in Maclay."

"I do," she said enthusiastically. "315 Georgia Street, Maclay, Georgia 31055."

Alfie jotted down the zip code. Easy as pie to find the place. Alfie smiled for the first time that morning. "Thank you so much, Diane. I'll let you go," she said.

"Why you ask about birth of Mai, Doctor?"

"Well…you see, Diane. It's this thing about blood type and Rh, you know. We have to be very careful nowadays."

To that day, Alfie had believed that liars were born. It took her forty-three years to realize that lying, like any other skill, could be learned and that it improved with practice.

"Oh, Lh," Diane answered. "I know about Lh."

"Now, tell me, Diane, did anything unusual happen during your first pregnancy?"

"I got too fat. Mai kicked a lot. This baby too."

"They do kick," said the doctor. "What about the delivery, anything unusual happen?"

"No. Easy delivery. I was sleeping when Mai born."

"Well, then..."

The doctor started to close the conversation when Diane added: "Oh, something unusual happened. We did not pay for delivery."

"They did not charge you? Why?"

"Don't know. The nurse said if we go out quick, we owed nothing. So we got out real quick with the baby." Diane chuckled.

"They did not charge you? Do you know why?"

"Don't know. There was big trouble in hospital. Dr. Miller died. He was drunk, they say. He fell and died."

"When did the doctor die?"

"The same night Mai was born."

"But you told me that Dr. Miller delivered Mai."

"Yes, he delivered Mai, and he died."

There was a long pause on Alfie's side. The gears were turning full speed in her head. "Well, that was something unusual," she said, for want of some intelligent remark.

"Yes, the police came. All the people in town know the doctor. Many articles in the newspapers. People talked a lot about it."

"And the hospital closed?"

"Yes, the next day."

Alfie thanked Diane and ended the conversation. She was more puzzled now than when she had called, but the information she had just acquired warranted some field research.

It was Saturday. She had no office that day but had a few minor surgeries scheduled. No time to do much this weekend, but next weekend...

~ ~ ~

On Monday, she finished her appointments just after three—a record for her—and left the hospital immediately. Dr. Santoro had a full agenda. She headed for the post office. There were several small towns listed under the 31055 zip code. It took her a while to find Maclay, because the book had the name spelled the American way: McRae.

From the post office, she drove to the Grosse Pointe Public Library. On a large map of Georgia, she searched for Elwin Town. She knew that it had to be about fifty miles from McRae, and, using the clue she had discovered in the post office, in a few minutes she zeroed in on the town where Miller Hospital had stood. The atlas also spelled Elwin Town in the vernacular way: Irwinton.

Dr. Santoro's next stop was Trapani's Travel Agency. She walked to it because it was in the next block. She walked out of it with an Eastern Airline round trip ticket to Atlanta, Georgia, leaving Friday at ten a.m. and returning Sunday at seven p.m. She learned that Macon was about seventy miles from Atlanta. The travel agent suggested that she ask for directions to Irwinton when she got to Macon. As for McRae, it was not even on the map in the travel agency.

It gave the doctor some relief to actually do something in the search for an explanation of the maledetto "whoosh."

## CHAPTER XXII

# Fact-Finding in Macon

n Oldsmobile Cutlass was the most economical car Avis had available in the Atlanta Airport. Dr Santoro took it. She just hoped that the light switch and the windshield wiper switch were in the same place as in her Checker.

She asked for directions to Irwinton. After a few "Pardon me's," she asked for a map. The young man at the counter courteously pointed to Riverdale Road that led into Interstate 85 and then merged with Interstate 75.

"When you get to Macon, you ax again," he said.

Macon was an easy hour-and-a-quarter drive on a smooth road flanked by evergreens and multicolored wildflowers. It was a welcome sight; the flowers had long ago died in Michigan. She exited I-75 straight into downtown Macon and stopped at the Greyhound Depot to ask for directions.

"Take Riverside Road, hang a right. That'll run into Eastbound 57." Fifty-seven would take her to Irwinton, seat of Wilmington County, in half an hour. "'Bout thirty miles. Can't miss it," he said.

Just in case, she asked him if he had ever heard of the Miller Hospital around Irwinton.

"I reckon I haven't, ma'am," he answered apologetically, "but you can ax when you get there."

She mumbled something like "Thanks," and darted for the car. She sped off the parking lot into the road. After driving a couple of hundred yards, she suddenly pumped the brakes and pulled to the shoulder. She had remembered the promise she had made her mother. She opened her purse and searched by feeling, eventually digging out the old crystal rosary from the purse and hanging it from the rearview mirror.

"You need all the help you can get when you drive, Alfonsina," Mother had said.

There was little traffic on the roads; she was in Irwinton in less than half an hour. She parked in front of the county building, a small colonial frame house which also housed the courthouse. "Closed at noon on Fridays," read the sign taped to the door.

"Wouldn't you know it?" It was one-thirty. "Use your brain, Alfie. Who would know about a doctor or a hospital?"

She decided to drive around looking for the drugstore. It seemed easier than asking for directions. She found it at the second turn, on Oak Street. She walked in and asked the girl at the counter for the pharmacist.

"Mr. Owen is outta lunch," she said, showing the chewing gum in her mouth. "I don't reckon he be back today."

"Second choice," she thought to herself tongue-in-cheek, "the funeral parlor."

But where? She went back into the drugstore.

"Funeral parlor?" she said.

The girl shrugged her shoulders.

"Bar open now?" Alfie asked. She was getting the hang of economical syntax.

"'Course," said the girl. "The juke joints don' never close 'round here. Maybe Mister Owen be there too."

"Where's the bar?"

"Right cross th' street." She pointed out the front door

The bar was easy to miss. The entrance was a narrow brown door with a cutout little glass pane and a faded sign that read "Alibi Bar". A barred tiny window, below eye level from the sidewalk, provided the only light in the room. It was dark inside, but Dr. Santoro descended the three creaking steps right into the saloon without any fear or worry. An advantage to being big, she thought—and there were not many for a woman—is that it gave one self-confidence.

Three men sitting at the bar turned to look at her as she stepped resolutely towards them, purposely tapping her heels on the squeaky slats. The girl tending the bar was a young Southern beauty; even in the squalid light Alfie could discern the perfect features of the young woman's clean, pristine face.

"This girl is too young to know anything about Dr. Miller's hospital," she mulled over, "but the patrons at the bar seem more than old enough to have at least heard of it."

She sat next to them and ordered a Coke.

"I reckon you ain't from this neck of the woods," said one of them, a thin old man in a dark overall and an undershirt.

"Of course not," she said, flashing a contrived smile of helplessness. "Perhaps you can help me. I'm looking for a Dr. Miller's clinic or hospital or something. Ever heard of it?"

"Sure did," one of them answered at once.

A short bald fellow nodded in agreement, clutching his bottle of Budweiser.

"Know anybody who worked there?" she went on.

"Been long gone, ma'am," the man in the overalls said. "When old Doctor Miller died, it closed. Been a long time." He turned towards the quiet one holding the beer bottle. "Jack Fallow used to work there?"

"Yeah, but Jack's dead, though."

"Laura Grey's daughter useta work in the kitchen there," said the one in the dark overall.

"But she picked up and headed out west soon as it closed."

"Been too long, aw right."

Dr. Santoro thought she did not have much choice but to sit and listen to the three men, who kept bringing up names and inconsequential stories associated with them.

"Wait, wait," said the thin one, scratching his head. "Remember what's 'er name? The fat woman used to drive the old hearse. The nurse. She worked there. What's 'er name?"

"Miss Louise her name. She's dead now," said the man with the beer.

"Nope. Her name ain't Louise, and she ain't dead neither. That's Miss Lilly, Jimbo's mo'. She's staying at the home yet." He shook his head and smiled, "Put nye dead, I reckon."

"That's her name, but she ain't no Jimbo's mo'. She raised Jimbo. Miss Lilly is black, Jimbo was white, you nitwit."

"Was not."

"Was too. Jimbo's folks was Turks."

"Hell no. They was I-talians," interjected the bald one. "I knew 'em."

"Whatever."

She heard all the details of how Miss Lilly took Jimbo in when he was a toddler after he lost all his family in a fire at his house. Jimbo began racing cars when he was very young and died in a car crash.

Time was an abundant commodity in Irwinton. The stories were told in great detail, and the details were discussed at length since each of the men had a different version that he could swear was "the gospel truth."

"Miss Lilly worked there when the doc died. The police quizzed 'er, 'member?" said the man in the overall. He was drinking from a small tumbler in little sips.

"The doc was bumped off."

"Hell, no. He was always drunker than Cooter Brown. He drank hisself to the grave."

"You don't die if'n you fall on your face."

"You die if your liver is shot. A dingy cut, an' you bleed dry."

"Uh-uh," insisted the fellow still holding his Bud. "They all clammed up to the police. They was hiding som'n."

"Interesting," thought Alfie. "What would they be hiding?" she asked.

That started another lively exchange about foul play, a fight, a bobcat in the delivery room and a Chinaman beating the doctor for botching the delivery of his baby. Alfie could gather nothing useful beyond the scuttlebutt about something going awry at the hospital between the delivery of the baby and Dr. Miller's death.

Her interest in the matter was bound to arouse some suspicion.

"You a cop?" asked the man in the overall.

"No," she said rather loud, fearing that they too might "clam up." "I'm a doctor from Michigan. I'm taking care of that Oriental woman that Dr. Miller delivered. She might have a very serious condition that could be treated if we find out what it is. It would help us a lot if we could see the record of her first pregnancy. It seems that Miss Lilly is my best bet for getting some information on the Miller Hospital." The doctor sighed.

"Don't you bet all your bread on it," said the man in the dark overall, and they all laughed. "Miss Lilly's brain is all dried up, I heard."

"I'd like to talk to Miss Lilly if I could. Any little information might help," she said as she paid for the Coke. "How do I get to that nursing home?"

After hearing several versions of the best way to get to the home and the landmarks to use, she left the bar with the directions written on a paper towel.

The Golden Years Convalescent Home stood, as she was told it did, on Route 29 between the crossings of state routes 57 from Macon and 96 from Jeffersonville. It was next to a

Sinclair gasoline station, a few yards recessed from the road. Next to the driveway that led into the parking area, a fruit stand manned by a sleeping dog advertised tree-ripened peaches at fifty cents a basket. A large sign proclaimed the name of the home, and there was a parking area with a few cars in it. A narrow brick path led to the small structure with a glass front that purported to be the "Lobby."

Dr. Santoro parked her car and stepped into a muddy gravel soil. She looked all around and then, gazing at the sign, pondered the cruel irony of such a name being bestowed upon this squalid structure. She walked with resignation to the "Lobby," avoiding the puddles that filled the spots where bricks were missing.

The door was open. She pulled at the screen door, which yielded after a little resistance. A television set with a rabbit-ears antenna, a mug and a dish with pieces of cornbread and fruit peels lay on a desk. Behind it sat a heavy-set middle-aged woman with a bored expression on her face. She had very pale skin, fire-engine red lips and ill-spread rouge on her cheeks. The original grayish brown showed at the base of her platinum-blond hair.

Dr. Santoro approached the woman and said "Good afternoon" with her friendliest smile.

The woman did not return the greeting but mumbled, "Can I do fer you?" without moving her eye from the screen. An unlit cigarette was dangling from her lower lip.

"I understand that Miss Lilly is a..." Alfie hesitated for a moment, looking around at the jail-like surroundings. "Inmate" was the first word that came to her mind "Er...a resident here," she finished.

The woman nodded.

"I would like to see Miss Lilly. I'm sorry I don't know her last name."

"What you wanna see 'er 'bout?" said the woman, raising her head to look at Alfie.

She had not expected this questioning. "Well, really, I'm not related to her, but I need to talk to her about some mutual...acquaintances."

The woman turned towards an old black man who was sprawled on a reclining chair in the shaded corner of the office. They both laughed.

The doctor suddenly remembered one of the guys at the bar had said that Miss Lilly was black.

"Miss Lilly don't wanna see nobody," the woman replied curtly.

"I know she'd be interested in talking to me. It's sort of...an emergency."

"Uh-uh," the fat woman growled.

They stared at each other for a while. The doctor opened her purse, pulled out a ten-dollar bill and laid it on the counter.

The fat woman shook her head.

The doctor reached inside her purse again, pulled out another ten-dollar bill and placed it on top of the first one.

The woman shook her head again.

The doctor's face was beginning to acquire a purple hue. She took a five-dollar bill this time and placed it on top of the other bills.

"What kin' o' emergency?" asked the woman.

The doctor took a deep breath and grabbed the edge of the desk. She exhaled on the woman's head. The fake-blonde bouffant quivered as she said in a rather soft tone: "It's MY emergency!" She stressed "MY" and stretched the word "emergency" so as to enunciate every letter in every syllable. Then she picked up the three bills, placed them on the woman's palm and, using more force than was necessary, bent the woman's fingers over the money as she whispered in her ear: "And it's none of your fucking business."

She let go of the hand.

The woman stuffed the money in her chest, inside her bra,

turned to the old man on the recliner and said to him in a commanding tone: "Show the lady to Miss Lilly's room."

"Yassum," said the man.

"It worked!" the doctor said to herself with a clandestine smile. She remembered the advice from the chief resident at Woman's Hospital when she was a prim intern: "Used sparingly and at the right times, an expletive can work wonders."

The old man, performing some acrobatics, managed to raise himself from the chair. He walked slowly and with a bit of a stoop. He faced the fat woman at the desk and stretched his hand, palm up.

"When you come back," she said.

The man shook his head. The woman whispered something and pulled a dollar bill from under the desk. He shook his head again. The fat woman reached inside her blouse. She picked up the dollar from the desktop and handed him a five-dollar bill.

He said, "Thank you, Miss Mary Jo," and led the way towards Miss Lilly's room.

The rooms in The Golden Years Convalescent Home were laid out in a U-shape surrounding a center court. There were several metal chairs strewn at random on the brown grass of the court. Two very old men were sitting on chairs under the shade of a large sycamore tree. They were facing away from each other, silently gazing at the sky.

Miss Lilly's room was the last one on the eastern arm of the U. At that moment, the room stood in the crosshairs of the murderous mid-afternoon rays of a surprisingly hot late fall sun.

As the old man knocked on the door, Alfie stood back. "Miss Lilly!" he yelled.

"Carson, that you?" a crackly voice came from the room.

"Uh-huh."

"You bringing lunch?"

"You 'ready had lunch. I got a visitant fer you."

"Come in," the voice replied quickly.

He opened the door and waved to the doctor to go in.

"Thanks, Carson," she said and put two dollars in his hand.

"Thank you, ma'am," he said raising his hat, "but I ain't Carson. Carson been dead for two years." They smiled at each other.

Coming from the blazing sunlight, the room appeared as dark as a catacomb to the doctor. She could barely discern a large shadow on an easy chair by the far wall. She walked up to the figure and, assuming it was Miss Lilly, stretched out her hand to her.

"How do you do, Miss Lilly. I'm Alfie Santoro," she said.

The temperature in the room felt like one hundred degrees, and it was as humid as a rainforest. Alfie was suffocating. Three thoughts came to her mind almost simultaneously: Humans can get accustomed to almost anything; I grew up without air conditioning, so what's the big deal?; and I'd rather shovel snow in Michigan.

"Will it be all right if I leave the door open?" she asked.

"Whatever your li'l heart desires, sugar. Got any smokes?"

"I'm afraid not."

"You kin get 'em up front."

Alfie made the "wait" sign with her hand and retraced her steps to the front office. The fat woman with the platinum blonde hair was still there, filing her fingernails. Her eyes were still fixed on the little screen.

"Where can I get cigarettes?" the doctor asked.

"What brand?"

"What brand does Miss Lilly smoke?"

"Anything she can mooch."

"Have a preference?"

"L & Ms," the woman said. She reached under the desk and threw one pack onto it.

"Got more?" asked Alfie.

She threw five more packs. "All I got," she said.

Alfie gave the woman a five-dollar bill and waited for the change.

"It'll be five bucks," the woman said.

"Thank you," said Alfie. She knew that vending machines would sell them for thirty-five cents a pack, but she chose to accept the abuse.

As she returned to the room, she was careful to squint most of the way so as to be able to see inside. She handed one pack of the L & Ms to Miss Lilly.

"Thank you, sugar," said the woman.

Now Alfie was able to see Miss Lilly. The woman seemed very old and extremely obese. Her breasts were enormous and spread sideways to rest on her large belly. She sat with her legs open to accommodate the apron of fat between them. She was wearing a baseball hat with a faded logo, a mustard-colored smock with the top unbuttoned and well-worn pink slippers with cross slits over the bunions.

The room had just a few more amenities than a prison cell, and it was only twice as large. It contained a twin bed, a metal nightstand, a dresser and one bench besides the easy chair that overflowed with Miss Lilly's anatomy. A coat rack by the door held several blouses and smocks. In the corner by the window there was a small shelf with a crucifix and a small vase holding a few fresh daises on it. A print of some saint with a golden halo and photographs of Martin Luther King Jr. and Elvis were pinned on the wall above the shelf. From where Alfie was standing, she could see the bathroom with a narrow shower stall in the corner. It was obvious that Miss Lilly would find it difficult to negotiate the bathroom door, let alone enter the shower stall. Curiously, the woman—and the whole room for that matter—smelled clean and rather pleasant, like a mixture of pine and lavender.

Miss Lilly was on the last puff of her first cigarette when she said, "You ain't from 'round here."

"No, ma'am, I'm from Detroit," said Alfie.

Miss Lilly giggled. "Have two cuzzins there, work at the Buick plant. You know it?"

"I do. It's in Flint."

"That's right. That's where they be. Making a bundle." She laughed. Her teeth were slightly yellow but all there.

"You oughtta been here Sunday. Guess who come to visit Miss Lilly?"

Alfie could not hear because there was a preacher spitting fire and brimstone over the radio; she cupped an ear with her hand.

"That's Reverend Fohsome," said Miss Lilly. "He's so messed up he don't know daylight from dark." She motioned to Alfie to turn the radio off.

"Last Sunday, Reverend Martin hisself and his deacon, a peach of a girl, come to see me," she went on. "The reverend, a big dude, he be wearing gold chain thick as ma' finger, gold rings both hands. Reverend Martin drives a big white Ca'llac."

"How nice," was all Alfie could think of saying.

"His deacon do. The reverend can't see shit no more. Yeah, the three of us hold hands and wo'shipped the Lord together. Yeah, we did done that."

Miss Lilly never interrupted her puffing for talking and vice versa. She stopped every so often to cough and sometimes to just catch her breath. Alfie heard the story of the Blessed Mother visiting the Home. According to Miss Lilly, the Virgin Mother left quite upset at the things she saw were taking place at the Home.

"The Blessed Mother be soppin' mad," said Miss Lilly. "You see, sugar, this here Home been a motel years back." She looked all around, and then she lowered her voice to a whisper. "Mary Jo used to shack up here with the mayor e'ry Monday. And she screwed the sheriff too. You know Mary Jo."

The doctor shook her head.

"The slut up front, with the big ass. All the balm in Gilead can't save 'er. She's just downright sorry."

Alfie nodded. She screwed me too, she thought, out of thirty bucks.

"Now tell me, Miss Lilly,"—she tried to steer the conversation to the business that had brought her there—"you used to work at the Miller Hospital, didn't you?"

The woman's eyes opened wide. "You bet. 'Bout eigh' years straight."

"I heard that Dr. Miller died the same night that an Oriental girl had her baby boy." The doctor spoke very slowly. "Were you working there that night?"

"Nope." She shook her head for a while. "Nope. The night Dr. Miller died, a Chinagirl had a young'un aw'right, but it be no boy, it be a girl."

"Oh, I'm sorry. That's what I meant, a girl." (She had been testing the woman. "Chalk one up Alfie," she congratulated herself.) "What do you remember about that night, Miss Lilly?"

"I 'member e'rything. Got any smokes?"

The doctor gave her two more packs.

"Got whiskey?" The old woman realized she was standing on a good foot for bargaining.

"Sorry, didn't bring my flask today," joked Alfie.

"They sell a good 'un up front. You just go on up there, sugar, an' buy Miss Lilly a couple good shots, an' she tell you all 'bout the Chinese girl and her young'un."

By now, Alfie had learned how to haggle. She got a bottle of bourbon for three dollars, down from five. She hurried back to the room and half filled Miss Lilly's tumbler.

The woman took a hearty sip, "Mmmm...gooder'n grits," she whispered. "Bless you, sugar." She downed in one gulp the rest of the glass. "Now I'm near 'bout ready to tell you 'bout the Chinese girl..."

It took Miss Lilly over an hour, but probably she told the doctor all she remembered about the night the Oriental young woman had her baby. The husband had driven the woman to the front of the hospital about seven in the evening. She was having good contractions, and she was leaking water.

"I did a rectal 'xam, an' she was near 'bout four. You see, you got to go to ten 'fore you can push. So I d'rectly go an' give 'er the special." She looked at the doctor and winked at her. "I give her the three H's enema. Know what I mean?"

Alfie knew what she meant. "High, hot and a hell of a lot," said Alfie. Miss Lilly had been in the business all right.

The old woman opened her eyes as big as her droopy eyelids permitted. "You a nurse?" she asked.

Alfie nodded. A white lie, she thought.

"Well, sheeew, in two or three hours she be ready to birth."

Then the old woman went into a tirade on false labor, dry labor and the effects on labor of walking, jumping, sex and the moon phases.

The doctor took it stoically. "Did she deliver at your place, finally?" she asked.

"Darn right. And good ol' Dr. Miller was there aw'right." Miss Lilly's head dropped. The slanting rays of the sun made the sweat on her multiple chins stand out as the strands of a shiny necklace.

The doctor waited for a good while for her to go on. She asked at last, "What happened then?" She heard a loud snore. She repeated the question aloud.

Miss Lilly woke up, startled. "When, when?" she asked.

"After the China girl delivered."

"Why you ax?"

"Because I heard something unusual happened then."

"You bet. An' I ax'd Reverend Martin, an' he hisself say I can tell the story now, 'cause Yellow Fallow be dead, rest in peace."

She began to explain what had happened that night and why she had not talked about it for many years. She had made a pact with Yellow Fallow to keep it a secret, and she never mentioned it even to the detective who came to question her after the doctor's death.

Jack Fallow was a chronic patient at Dr. Miller's Hospital. He suffered from cirrhosis of the liver, and the jaundiced skin got him the name of "Yellow Fallow." Dr. Miller kept him in the hospital for free, and Jack did small chores to repay him. He had been an in-patient for over three years, and he and the doctor would often down a few in his office at night. After Yellow Fallow died, Miss Lilly asked the preacher if it was all right to tell the story now. The preacher said that since the other party to the pact was no longer in this world, there was, really, no pact left.

This digression took the woman quite a long time. Dr. Santoro noticed that it was extremely painful for her to talk about that incident, but it was also obvious that the woman wanted to make a clean breast of it. At times she stammered and could not find the words she needed. When her chins fell on her chest, the doctor thought she was again asleep, but the woman reached for the tumbler and took a big gulp. "See, sugar, that be when the blue cat come in," she said at last.

"A blue cat?" Alfie cried out. (*Madonna mia!* Was she hearing things?) "A blue cat," she repeated. "Where did it come from? Were the delivery room doors open?"

"Doors be closed aw'right. Dr. Miller chew you a new asshole if'n you leave a door open when a woman's birthing."

Miss Lilly closed her eyes and was silent for some time. When she finally opened her eyes, she looked all about and gave Alfie a big, friendly smile, as if they had known each other for years. She coughed a few times to clear her throat. She pointed to the tumbler that Alfie had moved away from her, smiled at her again and pointed to the bottle of whiskey. Alfie poured a shot of the liquor into the glass. The woman rolled her forefinger, pointed at the glass and kept rolling her finger until the glass was almost full. "Thank you, sugar," she said and took a good gulp.

Miss Lilly turned her head to the left as if someone had entered the room from the bathroom side. She then turned in the opposite direction. A deep resonant voice filled the room: "How's the wee one doing?"

Alfie looked about, all over the small room. As she could see no one else, she realized that it was Miss Lilly who had said that. Alfie's eyes widened with incredulous amazement. She took off her glasses and leaned forward in her seat.

The old woman's voice was unrecognizable—deeper, raspy and somewhat tremulous, not unlike the trained voice of an actor, with an accent that couldn't be further from her Southern one. Her diction had assumed an unmistakable brogue; it sounded like that of an educated Irishman.

Miss Lilly's head then turned quickly to the left, and, as if replying to an invisible interlocutor, in her usual voice she said firmly: "The girl be just fine."

Again she turned to the right, and her mellifluous voice acquired once more the deep pitch and inflection of the one that had asked about the child. "The poor dear must be dead, or worse, I know."

"The chile be just fine," she answered, curtly.

"I wish she were, Miss Lilly," countered the raspy voice, "but the child was born with the cowl, ye know."

"The cowl don't mean no bad luck, you mushbrain," replied Miss Lilly irately.

"There's no need to be rude, Miss Lilly."

Alfie followed the exchange with interest, and with growing concern about her own sanity at spending an afternoon in a sweltering room with a paranoid schizophrenic who could assume two confronting personalities out of a clear blue sky.

"Wait, Fallow. We know soon 'nough."

Miss Lilly placed the morose dialogue on hold. She wiped her brow and neck and then turned to the doctor. Pointing at the imaginary visitor, she said, "Please, sugar, tell Mr. Fallow here how the chinagirl young'un be doing now."

"The child's name is Mai, she is now a young lady, and she is in a private school doing quite well—heading for college on a music scholarship." Suddenly, Alfie blushed, embarrassed by the thought that she was talking to an empty space.

Miss Lilly let out a loud guffaw. "Fallow, sounds like there's gin down there," she said turning to her imaginary guest.

"'Twas trouble written entirely over the wee one's face. I'm sorry," he replied.

"Hush up, Fallow," Miss Lilly shouted angrily. She turned to Alfie. "Don't listen to Fallow," she said. "The man ain't got a lick o' sense. Never did."

"'Tis regrettable, but 'tis the cowl, and ye know it, Miss Lilly."

"Go 'way, Fallow," she yelled.

"I forgave ye for breaking the pact. Now, the cowl…there is nothing I can do about it. 'Tis trouble, trouble, trouble for the poor darling…A child born with the cowl is destined to a tormented existence."

Miss Lilly reached for a cushion on her bed and threw it in the direction of the invisible guest. She now sounded quite short of breath. She paused for a moment. "Fallow not a bad folk, but too much juice ate his brain," she said.

"Was Mai actually born with the cowl?" asked Alfie after the woman finished lighting another cigarette.

"I din't see no cowl, I reckon," the woman said, "but I be busy passing the gas, you know, to keep the woman sleep. Fallow hollered, 'The cowl, the baby's got the cowl!', and the doc nodded."

"So, probably Mr. Fallow was correct. Mai was born with the cowl."

When, at the time of delivery, the head of the fetus pushed the placental sac without tearing it, then the transparent membranes enveloped the fetal head. In the past, this was referred to as "the cowl." In theory, the newborn could be asphyxiated, but in practice it had little risk because the membranes could easily be torn to free the head.

Being born with the cowl, however, in all cultures was interpreted as a portent—of good or bad—but in all cases, it implied that the child was somehow special.

Miss Lilly reached for her glass. She nodded as she downed the rest of the tumbler. "But, you see, sugar," she said, "some folk 'round here thinks the cowl mean good fortune for the young'un."

The doctor waited as the woman followed Mr. Fallow's ghost with her eyes as it left.

It was clear that Miss Lilly would not last much longer as a raconteur. Alfie had to decide whether to return the next day or to try to squeeze from her the last drop of useful information now. The woman would release her information only if bribed. "Tomorrow," Alfie thought, "I'd be a day later and a few dollars shorter."

Miss Lilly dropped her head again, but she did not seem to be sleeping this time. She raised her head after a few moments and said, "Miss Lilly's now veery thirs'y."

"Wait," Alfie said. She stood up. "I'll get you some cold water from the front desk."

"Old Dr. Miller, God rest 'is soul," Miss Lilly snickered, "say water alone'll rust your pipes."

"You'd like some whiskey in it?"

The woman raised her eyes, and when they met the doctor's, she broke into an angelical smile. "Bless you, sugar," she said.

"Would you like some ice?"

She shook her head. "Ice be fo' the city folk."

The doctor returned with a plastic pitcher filled with water and a few ice cubes. She poured a couple of jiggers of the bourbon into the tumbler and then began to add the cold water. Miss Lilly soon held her hand up. "That's plen'y, sugar. We don wanna drown the good spirits."

Alfie chose to push a few more questions now.

"And what happened to the Oriental girl, after all?"

"She be peachy. A' give 'er the young'un later and say, 'If

you get out of here quick, you don owe a penny.' She an' her man shot out like a bat outta...you know."

Miss Lilly dozed off again.

"Why did you do that, Miss Lilly?" the doctor said aloud to get her attention.

"'Cause the doc was dead. I know the police be coming." The woman went on as if the conversation had never been interrupted.

"You didn't kill the doctor. Why were you afraid of the police?"

"'Cause we don' have no license fo' birthing, and a' be no anes'thist either."

"What did the cat look like?"

"It be no kitty cat. Maybe it be no cat neither. It be giving us a mean look. And a' mean mean."

"What did the cat do?"

"Sat on the crib, looking mean."

"Did it try to attack the baby?"

"No, a' reckon it didn't, but we din' wanna take no chance. A' tole Fallow: 'A' don care what color, no cat be going to hurt my young'uns.'"

She told Alfie that Yellow Fallow came in with a burlap sack and sneaked up to the cat from behind while Miss Lilly diverted its attention.

"The cat had the meanest eyes a' seen in ma' life," Miss Lilly said, and she covered her eyes.

Fallow managed to get the cat into the bag, though it fought him all the way. Fallow asked Miss Lilly what he should do with it, and she told him to put it in the freezer with the placentas.

"Why in the freezer?" Alfie asked, surprised.

"We put all the afterbirths in the freezer," she said, shrugging her shoulders.

"Why did you put the placentas in the freezer?"

"'Cause La France pay the doc five dollar apiece."

Alfie had never heard that name. "What is La France?" she asked.

"A lab'tory. They make face creams an' potions from the afterbirths."

That was news to the doctor.

"So you thought the cat was the placenta?"

"No, sister, it be no placenta. The afterbirth be a piece of dead meat. You a nurse, you know."

"Of course," Alfie said. "What did the cat look like?"

"Sorry, sugar. It moved too fast, an' the doc on the floor an' me keeping the mom sleep, a' couldn't look at no cat. Don know. The color be som'n like a afterbirth," Miss Lilly said between sips, "an' the eyes look'd real mean. So a' say the freezer be a good place for it. It had a big tooth, sharp as a razor, that it did. It bit through the sack, almost slashed Fallow's wrist. An' he had to sit on the lid for a while to keep it shut. The cat be pushing the lid."

"Where was the cat when you first saw it, Miss Lilly?"

The woman explained that when she heard the doctor hit the floor cursing, she looked and saw a dark blue or purple thing jump on top of the crib where the baby was. The animal had a long, knobby tail "like a knotted rope," she said, and it swung side to side. And a streak of blood followed it, she remembered.

She said she couldn't go to help the doctor because she was passing the gas to the mother. She began to yell for Fallow. That's when Dr. Miller stood up and stumbled out of the room holding his face.

"Miss Lilly," said the doctor. "Miss Lilly," she repeated, almost shouting.

The woman opened her eyes minimally.

"Have you told this story to anyone else?"

"Jus' the count, a couple years back. The Polish dude, you know."

Alfie did not know, but this time Miss Lilly was out for the full count. No amount of shaking could wake her.

Dr. Santoro left Miss Lilly's room and headed straight for

the front office. She pulled a twenty-dollar bill from her purse and had it ready to buy the information about the count.

The fat woman gave it to her for free.

"Is he really a count?" Alfie asked.

The woman shrugged her shoulders.

"Could I speak to him now?"

"I s'ppose."

The woman leafed through a notebook, dialed a number and gave the receiver to the doctor. Alfie introduced herself, and the count did not seem surprised at all by the call. He said he would be happy to meet with her, and the next afternoon would be all right.

"Where?" she asked.

"The Orgy Pea Café," the count said.

"The Orgy Pea?" she asked doubtfully.

"On Spring Street. You can't miss it."

She left the twenty dollars with the woman. "Give ten to Carson," she said.

The old man, who really was not Carson, was sprawled on the same chair, sound asleep. He opened his eyes when he heard her say, "Give ten to Carson."

It was quite dark when Dr. Santoro left the Golden Years Convalescent Home, but she found her way back to Macon without any problem. So far, her trip had been worthwhile.

### CHAPTER XXIII

# The Professor's Dilemma

**F**riends don't let friends run into brick walls. That cannot be argued. But when a friend sees a friend picking up speed heading straight for the cement wall, what is the right thing to do to prevent the disaster?

That's how Professor Belanger viewed his position in the "wild placenta" affair. He remembered all too well "Chancroid Charlotte" and how it had hurt Alfie. Compared to this new affair, he thought, the Charlotte incident was a trifle.

He summoned in his mind, very graphically, the different ways he could intervene to avert this forthcoming calamity; or, at least, minimize its impact. The brick wall he could not move; at best, he could place a cushion between it and the head. He could try to lure the runner away from the wall. He could always trip the runner and somehow soften the fall. Dissuading the runner from running full speed towards the wall, the most obvious choice, he knew was not possible.

Looking the other way or remaining out of the picture was definitely not the right thing to do. Nor was adding fuel to the runner's motivation; he was quite sure of that. Telling Alfie about the existence of the drawing that the Vietnamese professor had sent him would be like fanning a pyre. But, then, keeping its existence a secret would be deceiving her.

What do they call it? "The rock and the hard place," Gaston Belanger said aloud. He had been there before.

His intentions were good; he also knew that the road to hell was paved with good intentions. It was a judgment call, and he made it. He just hoped that it was the right call; but, more than that, he hoped that Alfie would never find out.

He knew Alfie all too well. She had a heart of gold. Sadly, it was surrounded by an unyielding will and pulled down by a heavy ballast of inherited narrow-mindedness about right and wrong, black and white—and, to top it all off, an overgrown sense of professional responsibility. Her self-criticism could benevolently be judged as perfectionism; more often, it was interpreted as an impertinent claim of infallibility.

CHAPTER XXIV

# An Absinthe-Minded Aristocrat

Che "Orgy Pea Café" stood on the north side of Spring Street, in an unpretentious locale a few yards from the Greyhound Depot. The café sported a glass front that was half covered by a white fabric curtain hanging on wooden rings from a sagging brass rod. As she approached it, Dr. Santoro understood the proper spelling of the name of the café—"The orgi pea"—and also the origin of the peculiar name. On the sign on the front window, the faded outline of the missing letters G, E, A, C and H betrayed its more mundane title: "The Georgia Peach Café."

The poorly lit lounge smelled of tobacco and stale coffee. There were a dozen tables with Formica tops and chrome edges, each surrounded by chrome chairs upholstered in vinyl with flower designs. A long bar stretched along most of the side wall. A man and a young girl behind it kept busy polishing mugs and glasses and setting them on the countertop. They turned towards the doctor when she entered the room and gave her an inquisitive look: You sure you're in the right place, woman?

Since there were no other patrons, she guessed that the count was the man sitting at the table closest to the glass front. He was a very thin, middle-aged man. The top of his head was bald, and a mat of long, bushy blond hair covered both sides of his head and extended in the back to just above his shirt collar. His deep-set eyes and the very pale skin that clung to every cranny and salience of his facial bones gave him a cadaverous look. Thick lenses hid his droopy eyelids and only suggested large, light blue pupils. He was wearing a gray plaid sport jacket that seemed one or two sizes too large for his chest, solid charcoal gray trousers with a perfect crease and spotless shiny black shoes. A white shirt unbuttoned at the top framed a burgundy ascot.

The man stood up when Dr. Santoro entered the café. Because he was so thin, he appeared at first quite tall, but as she approached him, she noticed that he was shorter than she was.

He extended a bony hand. "I'm Count Stanislaw Poniatowski," he said rather loudly. He bowed deeply and gave her an anemic handshake.

"How do you do?" She smiled at him. "I'm Alfie Santoro. I'm an obstetrician from Michigan. Thank you for seeing me."

"Pleased to meet you, Dr. Santoro," he said coldly. "We could talk here, I suppose, but I think we would have more privacy in my flat." He spoke impeccable English with the slightest insinuation of a British accent.

"Makes no difference to me," she replied, and she meant it.

He placed a dollar bill under the coffee cup and waved at the two people behind the counter.

"I live a few blocks from here. We can walk," he said as they went out into the sun-beaten deserted street.

Fall had not registered yet in southern Georgia. It was late afternoon, but the sultry air was still hanging on. The walk made Alfie start to perspire.

The count could not ignore that she was uncomfortable, and he apologized for the oppressive heat. "The humidity is the villain," he said. "I bet it's not more than seventy-five degrees."

She ignored the unnecessary apology. "I wish to thank you

for your kindness to meet on such short notice, Mr. Poniatowski," said Alfie.

He turned towards her abruptly. "Please, Dr. Santoro. If you don't mind," said the count, "I prefer to be addressed as 'Milord'."

He said it with such a comical gravity that Alfie did not know how to take it. She looked at him to see if he was really joking.

He saw the nonplused look on her face and hurried to justify his misunderstood demand. "I am aware that you Americans find this type of salutation odd, even amusing. Perhaps you even resent it, but…"

"I don't resent it at all. And I'm not American." She interrupted him and, expecting that it would make her more acceptable to the count, added, "I'm Canadian."

"Oh! Pardon me. Since you have a queen, perhaps you may find it easier to use this form of salutation," he said with a cold smile. "You see, when they saw fit, the board of regents of your medical school bestowed upon you the title of 'Doctor'. Now, years after you have seen your last patient, even if your license were revoked, even after you no longer remember on which side the appendix is, you will still be addressed as 'doctor'—until you die."

She nodded. She didn't question his logic. She just wondered if all this was relevant to the business that had brought her to Georgia. So, she said, "Fine with me," to close the issue and move on.

It did not deter the count; he was determined to deliver his story. "In 1647," he continued, "Wladyslaw the Fourth, of the House of Vasa, King of Poland, saw fit to bestow upon one of my ancestors, for reasons that are not relevant this day, the title of 'count' to 'perpetuity'. This day, in Georgia, U.S.A., without an estate to call my own, without a retinue of vassals and servants, in a humble second floor flat, I'm still a Polish count and entitled to be addressed as such."

Although he sounded in earnest, Alfie could not help steal-
ing a look from the corner of her eyes, expecting to find the
count laughing at his joke. The count was serious as a judge.

"Fine with me," she repeated.

They walked down Spring Street. At the corner of Mul-
berry Street, he pointed out to her the Cannonball House; he
told her about the cannonball fired during the Federal attack
on Macon which was still in the house. On Georgia Avenue,
he stopped in front of an opulent Italian Renaissance villa,
the Hay House, once owned by P. L. Hay. It was one of the
first houses in the country to sport indoor plumbing with
cold and hot water, he told her. The count pointed to the
cupola. "On misty days, some people claim they can see Mary
Ellen's ghost pacing in the enclosure," said the count. "See,
Mary Ellen Johnson was the daughter of the man who built
the house. She never wanted to leave it." On High Street, he
showed Alfie an elegant cottage, the birthplace of the poet
Sidney Clopton Lanier, and recited a few lines of his poetry.
The count obviously knew a great deal of American history,
and he seemed proud of his city.

They kept walking past elegant homes, a couple of Gothic
style churches and an impressive antebellum mansion. The
count gave her a description of each of them with the re-
hearsed ease of a seasoned tour guide. The count lived on
College Street, a location more distant than the few blocks
he had mentioned, but with his vivid descriptions, sprinkled
with cute anecdotes, he made the stroll enjoyable in spite of
the temperature.

The count's residence was a far cry from the manors
one usually associates with the aristocracy. Actually, his flat
was the second story of a now vacant movie theater. They
climbed the narrow enclosed stairway, which was stuffy and
hot enough to make Alfie long for the temperature of the
streets. They walked into a small parlor furnished in the Vic-
torian style with an abundance of knickknacks over all the

surfaces. A large Polish flag with the imperial eagle encased in a glass frame covered most of one wall. In one corner of the room stood a four-foot-tall statue, which Alfie recognized immediately as that of the Black Madonna of Czestochowa. Two votive candles were lit at the feet of it. He looked at it and said with obvious pride: "From Jasna Gora." He then led her to an elaborate wingchair in the Chippendale style and motioned for her to sit.

As soon as she sat down, she decided to broach the business that had brought her there. She had prepared herself for the count's reaction to her odd story.

"The reason," she started hesitantly, "Milord,"—there; she had said it—"The reason I'm here—"

He interrupted her almost brusquely. "Pardon me, but I know why you're here, Dr. Santoro."

"You do?" she asked, obviously taken aback.

"I do," he stated rather theatrically. "You're here to learn more about the delivery of the Vietnamese woman and about Dr. Miller's death."

Dr. Santoro was visibly surprised. "How did you come to know that?" she asked.

"Elementary, Santoro." He laughed. "Oh, pardon me. Sometimes I think of myself as a jester. You see, there aren't many reasons why an obstetrician would travel all the way from Michigan to see me."

"I didn't come all this way to see you," she said. "I didn't know about you until I went to see Miss Lilly yesterday and she mentioned she had talked to you."

"Ah," he said, "I thought, since you are from Michigan, that maybe Professor Belanger had told you about me."

"Gaston! You know Gaston?"

The count shook his head. "I'm acquainted with Professor Belanger and with his work on placenta physiology and pathology," he said, "but I would not say that we are more than acquaintances. We have met only once or twice."

Alfie's brain was working at full speed, trying to understand the connections that she seemed to be missing.

"Professor Belanger is a scholar, a brilliant man, but he would not acknowledge a fact if it hit him in the face, unless that particular fact fitted into his narrow scientific mold," said the count. The doctor detected a subtle rancor in his voice. "He always refused to take one of my hypotheses seriously, I suppose because I don't have a PhD after my name. I understand, though. He couldn't publicly accept my ideas even if he knew for a fact that they were one hundred percent correct. He's a mainline scientist, you see, and he couldn't approve of any notion outside of the mainstream, anything that lies beyond a common, natural explanation. He is like a lieutenant who would rather send his company to certain doom than publicly declare that his commander's battle plan is a crock of *merde*."

"Oh, pardon me, Doctor," he added quickly. She knew what merde meant; they teach French in Canadian schools.

"In all honesty, Milord,"—she thought it prudent to warn him about her own prejudices—"I must tell you that I am not much of a believer in anything that is…"—she searched for the right word—"supernatural." Then she thought it would be proper to qualify her blanket statement. "At least as far as medical phenomena are concerned."

"You needn't apologize, Doctor," he hurried to respond. "Yours is the natural stance for a medical doctor. Now I'd like to ask you this question, if I may—as a doctor, you must know the answer—When do cancer patients turn to unorthodox quote unquote medicine"—he made the quotation sign in the air with his fingers—"to supposed healing techniques outside of classic medicine?"

He paused. She remained silent, expecting that eventually he would answer his own question.

"When does that happen, Doctor? Tell me."

She felt as if she were about to betray her profession. She held back as long as she could, but he didn't let up.

"You know it, Doctor. You've seen it. When do cancer patients start seeking alternative treatments?" He was obviously enjoying the winning hand he was holding. Used to being in control of virtually every situation, Alfie was shocked to find herself on the defensive before this little man with the subtly dominating personality. She finally capitulated: "I suppose when the doctors tell them there's nothing else they can do."

"That's right." The count nodded with a triumphant smile. "And that's the main reason why alternative medicine has such a poor track record. It only gets terminal patients."

Dr. Santoro did not close her ears to his statement. As she listened, the count began to appear less of a bizarre character.

"You're here today, Dr. Santoro," the count went on, "because you ran into an occurrence which you cannot explain with all your knowledge of physiology, chemistry, physics and pathology."

She nodded almost imperceptibly.

"Is it not true, Doctor..." He kept pounding.

"Judas priest!" She thought. "The son of a bitch is beginning to sound more and more like a fucking-lawyer."

The idea of excusing herself and running to her car crossed her mind. Then she thought of Diane and her baby and dismissed the inclination. She decided to endure this opprobrious third degree, hoping that somehow this deranged, pathetic, has-been aristocrat could help to solve the maledetto mystery and that, perhaps, that might even save the baby's life or Diane's. She made up her mind to face her predicament as a personal challenge, as a dare, as a double dog dare. It had worked in the past. She kept listening to the count's tirade against mainstream science and orthodox scientists.

"Let me tell you, Doctor, what supernatural is," he continued. "Supernatural is whatever lies beyond the explanation of conventional science. Like leaving port eastbound and returning from the west when the earth was flat. St. Elmo's fire was supernatural. A pregnant woman convulsing until her eyes popped out of the orbits, that was supernatural."

Dr. Santoro was beginning to think in earnest about what the count was saying. It was true that in college, as a medical student, an intern and a resident, she was never encouraged— nor could she afford the luxury—to think outside of her day-to-day, subject-to-subject curriculum. Maybe the count was right; maybe she did indeed think only inside the box. She found herself off balance with this man, uncharacteristically unsure of her ideas.

The count walked across the room to a serving cart. Elegantly placed on the cart was a tray with two bottles of liquor; four ornate, tall, gold-rimmed crystal glasses; a pitcher with water and ice cubes, still well formed; a china sugar bowl; and a metal spoon of an unusual shape. He picked up the spoon, the bowl of which was deep and angled rather like that of a ladle. He lifted the lid of the china sugar bowl, removed one lump of sugar from it with a pair of delicate tongs and placed it into the bowl of the spoon. Then he twisted off the cap of a bottle that contained a vivid green liquid and poured the equivalent of a generous shot into one of the glasses. When he rested the bottle on the cart, Alfie could read the large letters on the label. "La Fée," it said. The count picked up the pitcher of water, placed the spoon above the glass and very slowly dripped water over the sugar cube and into the glass. The liquid in the glass began to turn cloudy, with a green opalescence. The glass was three-quarters full when he flipped the spoon to empty its syrupy contents into the glass. At last, he dropped the spoon into the glass.

The count walked back very slowly to his chair holding the glass high. "Sorry, I'm not offering you a glass," he said. "Drinking absinthe requires some training, and, regrettably, I have no other liquor in the house."

"Not at all. I seldom drink wine, let alone absinthe," she replied.

"Wormwood has got an undeserved bad reputation. Taken in moderation, it is not any worse than other liquors."

The doctor couldn't help commenting, "The mixture has the most beautiful color."

"It's called the *louche*," he said. "Good absinthes form louches the color of the peridot, a chrysolite, a rare gemstone." He took a small sip of the iridescent drink and, after a short pause to savor it, asked, "Have you ever heard, Dr. Santoro, of the mysterious properties of pyramids in harmonic balance, of their ability to concentrate energy in their geometric center?"

She shook her head, although she had read about some esoteric experiments involving pyramids.

"Did you know, Doctor, that a fellow by the name of Antoine Bovis succeeded in mummifying eggs and meat inside a harmonic pyramid?"

She began to wonder if she was wasting her time with an unbalanced host. She shook her head again.

"Do you know what prana is, doctor?"

Prana? Fakirs, levitation, snake charmers. She had read something about it. For the sake of expedience, she preferred to shake her head.

"It is the life-force that allows living beings to move—and sometimes also to move other objects. Now, Doctor, if you would be so kind as to follow me." The count stood up and walked towards another room connected to the parlor by an archway.

The next room was quite large and squarish in shape. All of its walls were lined with file cabinets and shelves replete with books—some new, some old, some in elegant leather bindings, some bound as paperbacks—and piles upon piles of magazines and newspapers. Also on the shelves sat framed sepia photographs of old men with mustaches and beards and women with severe scowls.

As they entered the room, the count motioned her towards a table that stood by a partially open casement window. It was an octagonal-shaped table, the standard height of a dining table. Its only unusual features were that it only had three legs, evenly placed, and that, according to the count, no metal nails or screws but only wooden pegs and dowels held the parts together.

A gentle breeze filtered through the window, barely stirring a pair of yellowed macramé curtains. An enormous, three-tiered crystal chandelier hung incongruously in the center of the unkempt room. As the count flipped the switch, all its pretend-candle light bulbs—two dozen of them—lit up and illuminated a massive mahogany dining table where a well-polished epergne held some fake fruits.

Upon the three-legged-table by the window rested a square-based pyramid formed by fine bamboo sticks, the sort used to build kites; it had no walls. In the geometrical center of the pyramid, a square platform of heavy cardboard stood supported by several similar bamboo sticks. The pyramid itself was centered on the table. Outside the pyramid, a good number of small printed figurines were strewn all over the table. The figurines were cutouts of thick glossy paper representing angels, saints and monks, plus one figure of Satan in red—horns, tail and all—and one of an asp standing on its tail, fangs protruding. The base of each figurine was set in a slot in a tiny rectangle of balsa wood.

The count told Alfie to place all the figurines on the platform at the center of the pyramid. She looked at him inquisitively. He remained impassive, staring at the pyramid. She wondered what the game was about, but the option to refuse to play it did not cross her mind. She began to stand each paper figure on its base on the platform at the center of the pyramid. There were about a dozen of them.

The waft from the window made the little figurines flutter. The count noticed it, walked to the window and slammed it shut. The figurines became immobile.

"Now, Doctor, please knock them all down on their sides," he commanded.

She obliged. She was becoming a little more interested in the game and a great deal more concerned with the count's sanity.

"I want you to watch very carefully. I will concentrate on building my prana and focusing it on the subjects. Please remain silent."

The count then removed his thick glasses and walked towards the bookcases. He took a small box from a shelf and rested it on the table. The doctor recognized it as a Moroccan cigarette case with inlays of different woods and mother-of-pearl. The count opened it and removed two small purple-colored glossy-paper dots. He removed their backings, used his forefingers to trace diagonals on the backs of his hands and pasted each of the dots carefully at the place where the diagonals intersected.

He then removed his jacket and walked to the window. The slanted rays of the setting sun took an indefinable orange hue as they lay on the count's hands. He raised his hands slowly to the level of his face, his fingers tightly gathered together, each hand slightly cupped, palms towards the sun. There he held them steady as he fixed his eyes on the purple dots. He inhaled deeply and remained motionless, resembling an arcane statue of a high priest recently excavated.

Since time is mainly a function of motion, and since every object in the room was stone-like, the doctor could never figure out with certainty how much time had passed; but, whenever she told this story, she insisted that fifteen or twenty minutes elapsed before the count exhaled.

The count finally moved. He walked with short, calculated steps as his hands turned about, now with the palms towards him. His gaze locked on the palms of his hands; Alfie's eyes stared at the purple dots on the back of them. He approached the three-legged table and moved around it to the side opposite to where the doctor was standing. With careful motions, he aligned his body directly behind the pyramid and stretched his arms out until his hands were parallel to the opposite side of the pyramid. He extended his head backwards until his long, pointed, almost fleshless nose aimed straight at the zenith. He began to lower his hands, ever so slowly, along the sides of the pyramid.

Then it began to happen.

One of the paper figurines in the center of the pyramid started to tremble. Then another and another figurine joined in the trembling, as if in some infernal San Vito's fit. Next, the tops of some of the paper figurines, still quivering, began to rise from the platform. They wobbled at first as if teased by a faint breeze. Some fell down and rose again. At last, one rose high enough to stand on its balsa wood base. The figure remained upright, still shaking. Eventually almost all of the figurines stood up on their bases; the quavering lingered for some time. The asp and Satan moved very little during the whole performance and never stood up or even rose from the table.

The doctor then turned to look at the count. There was a steady stream of sweat running down his cheeks to his neck, soaking his burgundy ascot. Only then did she notice that she herself was perspiring just as profusely.

The count bent his head down and looked at the figurines in the pyramid with a faint sigh of exhaustion. He seemed quite pleased to see most of them standing. "I can never get those two to stand up," he said apologetically, pointing to the serpent and Satan. "Perhaps, some day they, too, will stand up. So Papini believes."

Since the doctor at that time was not familiar with Papini's hypothesis that God will eventually forgive the devil, the count's philosophical statement lost all of the impact it was intended to have.

The count pulled a handkerchief from his trousers pocket and began to meticulously wipe his face and neck. Then he slid the window all the way up. The air that rushed in was not much cooler than that filling the room, but it was nonetheless

welcome. He then led his guest back into the parlor and motioned to her to sit down again. Walking to the cart, he picked
up and rang a small crystal bell, then returned to his chair and
sat down.

"Can you explain that occurrence, Doctor?" he asked after
a while.

"No," she answered. "Not now, at least."

"A superb answer, Doctor!" he exclaimed. "That's what
'supernatural' means, what cannot be scientifically explained
at a given time."

"But I am sure there is a mundane explanation for it," she
insisted.

"Perhaps," he replied, "but the moment it is scientifically
explained, it won't be supernatural any longer, will it? And
then"—he smiled—"it wouldn't be worth all this perspiring."

She smiled, too, because she was presently wiping her
face with a paper napkin from her handbag. When she had
finished, the napkin was soaked. As she looked up, she saw a
stranger in the room, a little figure dressed all in black. She
was markedly hunched and had a frail body that she moved
slowly, wobbling her hips like a duck and dragging her feet.
A black babushka extended down to her stooped shoulders,
and her feet were hidden under a long black skirt. She was
carrying a small silver tray with a bucket of fresh ice.

"*Dziękuje*," said the count. The woman curtsied, and then
she turned to the doctor. She looked very old, and, like the
count, she seemed fleshless; but her pale skin hung loosely
over her bones rather than clinging to them. The doctor
smiled at her; the old woman kept staring unmoved. By the
way she gazed and moved, the doctor assumed that she was
almost totally blind.

"Would you care for something to drink, Doctor?" asked
the count.

"Thank you. Some ice tea perhaps."

The count translated her request into Polish to the old

woman, and she wobbled out of the room holding on to the furniture.

"Do you have an explanation for that phenomenon, besides the force of pyramids and the prana?" asked Dr. Santoro. As soon as she said it, she realized how naïve a question it was. Whatever trick he had used, she reasoned, if he had used a trick—"Here I go again," she recriminated herself. "Of course, it was a trick—, but he would never divulge it."

"You are a Catholic, I see," said the count after a rather long silence, pointing to the medal of the Blessed Mother which dangled from the doctor's neck chain.

She nodded. It was some sort of a relief for her to hear this statement, because she had noticed that the count had been staring at her bosom longer than would otherwise be considered proper.

"You believe in the Virgin Birth of our Lord, I presume?"

"I do," she replied. ("What an impertinence!" she thought.)

"And in Transubstantiation, as well?" he asked matter-of-factly.

"Of course, I do." Her tone was a bit defiant now.

"How do you explain those bizarre notions?"

She thought she detected a touch of sarcasm this time.

"I don't even try. I just…believe them," she said proudly, as she had done many times before when confronting pedantic nonbelievers.

"Let me tell you something, Doctor," he went on. "For many centuries, we Catholics had to tolerate scorn from others, even from fellow Christians, for those beliefs. Today, we can say with confidence that virginal conception is not a scientific impossibility, an absurdity, as was claimed. Artificial insemination is a routine procedure in infertility clinics. It takes place daily and, to my knowledge, without any divine intervention."

Dr. Santoro began to entertain the idea that, perhaps, the count was not entirely insane. He was well informed, at least.

"And as far as Transubstantiation is concerned," he proceeded, "it is almost a certainty that in the next few decades scientists will be able to build the whole original individual from a couple of molecules of his DNA, because, as you very well know, one molecule of human DNA can carry all the traits of an individual."

She liked what she heard, but she could not help playing the devil's advocate. "Then, as you said before, Milord," she whispered, as if only thinking aloud, "once one can explain those mysteries within the realm of science, they will lose their preternatural implications."

"True, but then," said the count with a simpering smile, "explaining how His DNA enters the host at the time of consecration will take a few more centuries, or might never be explained before Apocalypse time."

The old woman had returned in the meantime with the ice tea and placed it discreetly on a table near the doctor without interrupting their conversation. She curtsied when she passed in front of her master on her way in and on her way out.

Even though Dr. Santoro had found this philosophical discussion quite engaging and stimulating, it was absorbing more time than she could afford to spare. So she took a deep breath and charged ahead with her business, describing in broad strokes and as objectively as she could the incidents that she considered inexplicable.

When she had finished her story, the count was silent for a good while, visibly concentrated, analyzing the events she had just related. That pleased her a great deal.

At last he asked, "Can you really rule out a recurring artifact from the Doppler machine, produced by certain angulations of the transducer or something of that sort?"

She had thought of it, and her explanation seemed to satisfy him.

"Did you listen to both sounds simultaneously?" asked the count as he crossed his arms on his chest.

"Yes, of course," she replied with assurance.

"Now, in order to listen simultaneously to two different sources, don't you need two persons?"

"That's correct."

"Who was the other person?"

She gave the count a short description of her assistant, emphasizing how intelligent and dependable she was.

"Have you shared with…Miss L'Nore your suspicion of this being a paranormal phenomenon?"

"Yes, I have, but only recently," she responded a little defensively. She could follow the man's train of thought, and her respect for his intelligence and astuteness grew.

"But, from what you told me before," he said, "it seems that she was aware from the very beginning of your concern for that unusual…'whoosh', as you called it."

He was cross-examining her. She nodded in assent.

He remained silent. Then he started speaking again in a soft, somewhat patronizing tone. "You're aware, Doctor, I'm sure, that when two people who work together, especially when they've been doing it for a long time, can…"

"I know what you're driving at, Milord." Curiously, she noticed how much easier it was becoming for her to use this silly title. "When L'Nore and I discussed the matter in depth, we considered that scenario too. We analyzed it as objectively as was humanly possible, and we concluded that the *folie à deux*—that's the name of what you're insinuating—would be an extremely unlikely possibility."

Dr. Santoro was impressed by the count's ability to lay out all the likely possibilities in a few minutes when it had taken her and L'Nore hours of intense analytical thinking.

"And then you flew to Georgia." Now the count sounded clearly sarcastic, almost cruel. "And you talked to Miss Lilly, who fueled your folly."

Looking down at the carpet, she nodded. "I learned of Miss Lilly just by chance, and she knew nothing of my reasons for being here."

"You know, Doctor, that Miss Lilly is a chronic alcoholic with advanced cirrhosis of the liver. She has been diagnosed with senile dementia. I'm sure you could tell that. She suffers from delusions, hallucinations and paranoia. Most of her stories sound bizarre even to me, and, remember, I am quite comfortable dealing with the paranormal."

Now she thought that she was losing the count as a possible ally in her quest, so she took a deep breath and bared it all. She told him in all the embarrassing details the Scenario Five that she and L'Nore had contrived.

When she had concluded, the count recapped her hypothesis with merciless objectivity. "So, Dr. Santoro," he charged," you want me to believe that there is a placenta somewhere in Michigan that is growing out of control inside one of your patients, and that it is similar to another placenta from the same patient that many years ago attacked and killed old Dr. Miller?"

Alfie nodded.

The count continued in his cruel, mordant tone. "You know that Dr. Miller's death certificate states quite plainly that he died from injuries sustained when he fell in the back of his hospital. I read the certificate. The deceased, it said, was obviously intoxicated, as corroborated by a blood alcohol analysis. We must assume that the coroner, although somewhat related to Dr. Miller—and everybody is related to everybody else here in Wilmington County—made an objective assessment of the facts because he stood to gain nothing from the doctor's death, however it could have happened. And, actually, he never claimed anything from the doctor's estate."

She looked at him, ready to try to refute some of his statements, but he went on. "Furthermore, there was an inquiry, and three eyewitnesses testified under oath that the doctor had been drinking heavily—as was his habit—the night of his demise."

"Were Miss Lilly and Mr. Fallow also deposed?" she asked. ("My God," she thought. "Me, too. I'm beginning to talk like a fucking-lawyer!")

"Not deposed, but both Miss Lilly and Mr. Fallow were questioned by the police, and they both testified that the doctor left the delivery room immediately after delivering the Oriental young woman. He lumbered out of the room and left the building through a side door that led to the backyard. They found him soon afterwards, just outside that door, in a prone position in the middle of a puddle of blood, with several deep lacerations in the face and neck."

"That's not what Miss Lilly told me last night," Alfie protested.

"I believe it, but regardless of how much recollection of the event she had soon after it happened, she was definitely much more credible then than she is now."

"I suppose," she admitted wretchedly.

"Now, my dear Santoro," said the count as he got up, walked over to the serving cart and repeated his ceremony with the ice and the sugar cube and the Green Fairy. "Would you please go back to Michigan and abandon this idle and expensive wild goose chase."

Alfie tried to buy some time by removing her glasses, folding them carefully and putting them into her purse. She rubbed her eyes with the back of her wrists like a sleepy infant. Then she propped her head on her hands and rested her elbows on her lap, staring at the well-worn Bokhara carpet that lay under the chairs for as long as it took the count to finish his ritual with the absinthe.

"I don't think I will, Milord," she said, standing up in one deliberate motion. "I do not think so," she repeated for good measure. She stretched her hand to him. "Thanks anyway, Milord, for your time."

The count, who could not tolerate being seated when a lady was standing, sprang to his feet as deliberately as she did, but he did not shake her hand.

"You will not give up the pursuit of this ludicrous fabrication!" He said it aloud, locking his eyes on hers.

"I'm afraid not, Milord, because, preposterous as my hypothesis may be, if it turned out to be correct, my patient and her baby would be heading for a catastrophe that I could have prevented."

"Doctor, you are obstinate and reckless," the count said with feigned annoyance, still looking her straight in the eyes. "I like that," he added. "You passed the test. Now we can work together."

Alfie was dumbfounded. She could not think of an appropriate rejoinder.

"I'm sorry, but I had to subject you to that test," the count continued. "I could never consider associating myself for any task with anyone who can give up at the first obstacle."

Alfie was still sorting out what she had just heard, and aggravated by the count's ruse. "And I don't believe I could work with anyone who needs to resort to tricks to test potential working partners."

"But you will forgive me, won't you?" the count replied with a strained smile that sat awkwardly on his stern countenance. "We Christians are especially trained for forgiving."

The doctor flashed at him a feigned scowl.

"Besides," he added, "I possess a wealth of raw, unsorted information, some of which you will find quite apropos for your task. Now, come look at this."

He led her back into the square room connected to the parlor. He opened a drawer in one of the filing cabinets, extracted a thick folder from the drawer and leafed through sheaves of yellowed newspaper clippings, discolored photographs and handwritten notebook pages. Finally he removed with extreme care a full newspaper page, as yellow and brittle as the others. He was about to hand it to her but stopped in the middle of the motion and asked her, "Did Miss Lilly tell you what they did with the placentas at Dr. Miller's hospital?"

"She said they kept them frozen," Alfie answered, "and they sold them to a laboratory for five dollars apiece."

"That's correct," said the count. "I was able to corroborate that fact. Now, look at this." He handed her the yellow newspaper page.

In the center of the page there was a short article highlighted by a yellow circle. Dr. Santoro went over it quietly.

## FATAL ACCIDENT ON ROUTE 57

The courier for La France Laboratories of New Jersey was killed last night when his van apparently went out of control and hit a utility pole.

The accident occurred west of the intersection of R57 with route 18, near Gordon. The driver was thrown some fifty feet from the vehicle, which was totally destroyed by a fire. The driver's body was found in the morning by a local farmer and pronounced dead at the scene by the sheriff's deputy. The body showed marks of having been attacked by predators.

The Sheriff's Department is investigating the gruesome accident. The name of the victim is being withheld pending notification of his family.

She turned towards the count and looked at him inquisitively.

"Look at the top," he commanded.

She read it aloud: "The Macon Mercury, September 1, 1955, page 3."

"Does the date ring a bell?" he asked her.

She thought for a couple of seconds. It did. "That's the day after Mai's birth!" she said aloud.

"Two days after," he corrected her. "August has thirty-one days."

They sat quietly for a long while.

The doctor was trying to put into perspective this new piece of information. She looked outside. The daylight was gone, but her business had only begun. She looked at her watch. Even though she was capable of going on all night, she thought it prudent to leave.

"This is all extremely interesting to me, but it is late," she said.

"I move we adjourn to a date certain," said the count raising his hand.

"I second the motion," she said, "and propose an amendment to it: that we reconvene tomorrow at half-past one at a restaurant to be determined by the chair. My treat."

The count clapped. "The motion carries, by acclamation," he proclaimed standing up.

"I hope it will not inconvenience you much. I must catch a plane tomorrow evening. I have to go back. Do you mind working on Sundays?"

"On this puzzle?"

She nodded.

"This is not work; it is fun. This is what I call 'mind maneuvers'," he said.

"As in preparing the troops for a 'mind war'?"

"Precisely!" the count said in a firm tone.

He walked her to her car. As if by some implicit covenant, any mention of placentas, purple cats or the Miller Hospital was carefully avoided. They walked at a leisurely pace, talking about barbecued ribs, spiedini, shishka, Georgia peaches, golomki and bagna cauda.

On Spring Street, they passed several groups of youths, mostly blacks, gathered about sports cars, motorcycles or boom boxes playing loud rock 'n' roll.

Alfie had lived and worked in Detroit many years, she was used to street corner groups, but, being in a strange city, she tensed up as they walked by.

At least two youths in each of the groups greeted the count.

"How goes it, my man?"

"'Sup, Count?"

"Hi, Milord. Nice chick you got."

The count nodded, smiled and waved at them. Alfie smiled and waved too.

"I'm impressed, Milord," said Alfie. "You sure know how to deal with the street kids."

"Best kids in the world," he said, "but one must be on the level with them. They can spot an impostor a mile off."

He opened her car door and shook her hand. "Until tomorrow," he said as he closed the door.

As she drove the few blocks to the Holiday Inn, she chided herself on her fickle judgment. In six hours' time, the count had metamorphosed in her mind from a pompous, contentious, resentful, has-been aristocrat into a respectable man of wisdom and principles. Thinking about it, she realized she felt for him the respect that one dominating personality holds for another.

## CHAPTER XXV

# A Rude Awakening

iane woke up holding her breath. A sharp, sudden pain at the base of her chest prevented her from exhaling.

"Ouuu." She held the scream under her breath so as not to wake up Quang.

The attack lasted less than a second, but a dull but noticeable ache that could not be ignored persisted long after Diane dared to let the air out of her lungs. She propped herself on her elbows and waited in fear for a second wave.

Stock-still, breathing ever so slightly in order not to trigger the beastly stabbing again, she waited. At last, she gathered the courage to slide a hand to the top of her belly, where the pain had been. She began to massage the area with a circular motion. The womb was quite soft and relaxed, but the skin over the area felt as if it were bruised when she touched it.

It was not a labor pain that woke her up; that she knew for sure.

As she reached back in her memory to her first pregnancy, she could only remember a few pains of such intensity, and only in the last week, when labor was about to begin. She repeated to herself the trite saying that women who had had several babies had for centuries delivered haughtily to one-child mothers: "Each pregnancy is different."

She also remembered that she had paid little attention to the contractions beyond the respect that the actual cramp commanded and that even that was forgotten as soon as the womb relaxed.

Now, pains, hiccups, nausea, cramps and any minor event would trigger in her intense fear and anxiety that lingered for days, and she construed them often as premonitions of doom.

Each pregnancy is different.

But, then, there were the worried looks on Dr. Santoro's face and the complicit glances she had exchanged with L'Nore.

Dr. Santoro had a propensity to histrionics and would tend to make mountains out of molehills, she argued. That's what Dr. Irving and Belinda had said.

"But what about Yul's antics?" the devil's advocate rebutted.

"Nonsense. Cats are very funny people," she countered, quoting Kathy.

She had to admit that she, too, could be theatrical and that, at times, her vivid imagination would blow things out of all proportion. Think of the panic that Mr. Kompur's visit to Thu'a Cụ's farm had caused her. Even now, almost twenty years later, the mere recollection of that event made her heart race wildly. And think of the outcome of that visit: probably the best thing that had ever happened to her and Quang.

Diane played that thought in her mind again and again. "Silly girl! You build your own dragons and tremble looking at them," she chided herself. "Maybe you even relish the fear they generate, as children enjoy scary stories."

She rehashed that thought. She found it comforting, and she built on it. There was that time when she harbored for weeks the fear that the bill for Mai's delivery would eat up all their savings. It had kept her awake numerous nights. And what was the outcome? They hadn't had to pay a dime. They never learned why; and, of course, they never asked. She dwelled on those examples of pleasing outcomes to her unfounded worries, trying to transplant them to the present situation.

Diane turned on the light on the nightstand and, half-sitting, stared at her naked abdomen as she listened to her husband's cacophonous snore. Smooth, pale cinnamon skin stretched taut and unwrinkled over the protuberant belly—a perfect vault with just a subtle dimple in the center. She looked at her umbilicus and said with a tinge of conceit. An inny. Diane had learned that Kathy's sister's belly button had become an outty during her second pregnancy.

The exercise in positive thinking was beginning to work. She kept gazing at her perfect abdomen, crowned by a perfect navel in perfect stillness, and the soothing thoughts led her into a trance-like slumber.

A modicum of reassurance can often stave off the most insidious fears.

She could not tell for how long she had dozed. When she opened her eyes, the smooth dome of her pregnant belly still gleamed like a lakeside dune on a night with a full moon. But now she could sense more clearly than before the ache on the spot where the pain had struck. She resumed the massaging with circular motions, like a single ripple spiraling out in a still pond. She could still recognize the center of the ripples because the soreness on that spot had not diminished. Like the crater left by a meteor surrounded by an unperturbed landscape, the spot was surrounded by soft, smooth, pliable flesh.

Diane found that massaging the spot relieved the discomfort, so she worked on it for some time, a little harder each time. She then pushed her middle and forefinger into the yielding tissues and the ache vanished almost completely. Gently and slowly she had dug the two fingers almost entirely below the surface of the surrounding skin.

Suddenly, the skin on both sides of the fingers rose abruptly like the claws of a sea creature grabbing its prey; they tightened and squeezed the fingers so strongly that she could not lift them away. She cringed in pain, pulling with all her strength to withdraw her fingers buried in her own abdomen.

Diane gave a loud shriek, and with a violent pull she succeeded in releasing her fingers. Her abdomen then became dreadfully animated, the perfectly smooth dome gyrating in wild contortions. The base of the dome arose, as wave after wave of contractions disfigured the elegant surface until it looked like a bag full of mad cats.

Quang, without waking, responded to her scream with some soothing words.

Diane leaped out of the bed and dashed into the bathroom, where she knelt down, hugged the commode and vomited like she had never done before. She kept retching and gagging and brought up green, fetid stuff, the sight and stench of which caused her to retch and vomit more, in a vicious circle that it seemed would never end. But the end came at last. Diane collapsed, semi-conscious, on the cold tile, her gown and her skin stained by the vile humors that had come out of her body.

She shook uncontrollably and cried without tears, the nauseating smell still clinging to her gown and her flesh. Her energy spent, she lay on the floor for some time. She eventually was able to reach the toilet handle and flush some of the vomit, and the air became a little more breathable. Still on the floor, she yanked her clothes off and threw them into the tub. She reached for the towel, wet it in the tub and rubbed off the larger globs of the emesis that was beginning to crust on her skin. She pulled down a robe that was hanging on the door, covered herself with it and collapsed again between the tub and the commode.

Later, much later, she stood up. She went back into the bedroom, sat on the edge of the bed and woke up Quang. She described to him, part in English and part in their native tongue, what had happened. She held back the tears as she pointed out to her husband where it had all started, afraid to actually touch that point on her abdomen, which was now fully hurting, lest it should provoke another round of that horrible experience.

Quang listened to her with his eyes barely open. Before she finished the story, he said, "Bad dream, Mamma," and kissed her on the cheek.

"It was not a dream. It did happen," she protested.

"Bad dream," he repeated.

"It was not a dream," she said aloud. "Look at the bruises." She pointed at her belly.

Even if her husband had been still awake, he would not have been very impressed. There was only a small area of faint bluish discoloration where the original jab had hit. As if on guard for the next strike, Diane kept looking in terror at the site without touching it. She kept sobbing until sleep overcame her.

## CHAPTER XXVI

# A Basilisk, Milord?

Dr. Santoro's brain, like those of most men and women trained in the sciences, could be graphically described as multiple rows of drawers where every item, from abstract concepts to physical phenomena to fellow human beings, was expected to fit somehow. Frequently, of course, the item had to be compressed and distorted or parts of it would hang out of the pigeonhole due to lack of space or the object's unconventional shape. This violent manipulation was an acceptable price to pay in order to maintain the semblance of order the system provided.

Dr. Santoro propped herself on the large, soft bed of her hotel room wondering about where the count would fit in the "world according to Alfie." The credibility of his ideas and stories depended to a great extent on where he would be placed, as well as her decision on whether to spend with him the limited time she had left in Macon. The doctor had to capitulate at last. There was no drawer capable of accommodating this peculiar character. It was therefore with regret that the doctor found it necessary to create a new pigeonhole for the count. She had to craft a new order in which the European cynicism and superciliousness of having seen it all combined with the Southern, tolerant, laid-back attitude bordering on indolence. Continental formality rubbing shoulders with Southern casualness. A Polish count of refined tastes having to make do in a rustic Georgia town. And then add in his penchant for the paranormal.

So, she resigned herself to listening to his outlandish tales of poltergeists, telekinesis and mythical beasts in exchange for the chance of obtaining some information that might help her in her decision about the maledetto "whoosh."

That grave preoccupation notwithstanding, in the large, comfortable bed of her hotel room, Alfie's brain shut off, and she slept like a baby. She could sleep on a hard floor, on a table, on two chairs side-by-side, standing up, leaning against a wall or cradling her head in her arms. "I can sleep hanging from a chandelier," she would often brag. Actually, that talent was common to all obstetricians and other professionals in sleep-depriving occupations.

She woke up at six o'clock, though, as her inner clock was set, somewhat upset by the unfamiliar surroundings. Once those surroundings registered on her brain, she smiled. "It's Sunday," she said to herself and returned to a blissful slumber. It was past eleven when she came back to life. There was barely time to shower, dress and be at church for the twelve o'clock mass.

Although she had already inquired the night before, she stopped at the bell captain's desk on her way out and asked again for directions to St. Joseph's Cathedral.

The man had to repeat the instructions three times while Alfie cocked her head trying not to miss a single syllable. "It's English too," she said to herself. "I suppose my accent irritates him as much as his irritates me."

The young man gave her the tourist bureau pitch about the church's architectural grandeur, its Bavarian stained glass and its Romanesque neo-Gothic 200-foot spires. It did not register; all she needed to know was where it was. She finally

understood that the church was only a few blocks away, and
the bell captain's instructions were accurate enough to deliver
her to mass on time.

It was the last mass of the day, and the church was quite
crowded.

Since Alfie had never been in Macon before, she only
knew the handful of people she had met the day before.
She was surprised and amused at the coincidence of seeing
someone she knew just a few pews away. Down on his knees
and engrossed in his praying was Carson—actually Carson's
successor, whose name she had forgotten—from The Golden
Years Convalescent Home.

The pleasant surprise was short-lived.

"Coincidence, my ass," she said to herself. Alfie had read
more than her share of detective novels and seen countless
mystery movies. "I'm being followed."

"Don't panic, Alfie. Think logically," she admonished
herself. No one, not even herself, knew she would be in this
church until she asked for directions from the bell captain.
Obviously, he must have called The Golden Years Convalescent Home after she had left the hotel and sicced Carson, or
whatever his name was, on her.

Unless…unless the old man had been in the lobby or
watching the hotel entrance and followed her in the street.
Yet, she was quite certain he had not walked into the church
after her; she would have recognized him as he walked to the
pew. Of that, she was one hundred percent sure. Well, ninety-
five percent, she conceded; he could have come in the side
door and entered the pew by a lateral aisle.

Alfie was engrossed in what she thought was a logical and
realistic assessment of her risks and options when into her
field of vision moved another familiar face to further fuel her
paranoia.

Down the central aisle from the main altar, moving with
slow, rhythmic steps, dressed in a navy blazer a bit too large for

his chest, a white shirt and a red bowtie, marched the count, carrying the collection basket at the end of a telescopic stretching handle. When he reached her pew, he stopped and gazed at her. The colored light from the stained glass windows gave his sallow face a sardonic expression, and the thin nose seemed almost transparent. He placed the basket in front of her and waited while she pulled a ten-dollar bill from her purse.

"Thank you, Doctor," he said with the insinuation of a nod as she dropped it into the half-full basket. She smiled; he moved on.

She turned to look at Carson. The old man was now sitting. His eyes remained downcast until he stood up and followed the line to the altar. She joined the line when the turn for her pew came. There were at least a dozen people between her and Carson. He took communion and returned to his seat, never looking up.

Her concentration on the liturgy was totally disrupted. She kept shifting her eyes from old Carson to the count, and every now and again looked all about for some other suspicious character.

The count was the last of the ushers to take communion. Alfie rushed out of the church before the final blessings. She crossed the street and stood half-hidden behind a massive maple tree waiting for Carson or the count to leave the church.

Carson came out in the thick of the congregation. He was now wearing a baseball cap. She mixed with the crowd and followed him, with some trepidation.

"What the hell are you doing, Alfie?" she kept asking herself. "You're losing it."

The old man moved at a leisurely pace. He shook hands with some of the people, turned into New Street and stopped to light up a cigarette. As the crowd began to disperse, Alfie's cover thinned, and she thought the old man might recognize her. She turned around and pretended to read a tourist map. Less than half a block away, Carson got into an old, battered

Ford pick-up truck and pulled out at the same speed as he walked. As the truck passed in front of her, Alfie tried to read the number on the license plate, but she did not try very hard because she was beginning to feel embarrassed. She stood still there, as inconspicuously as she could, and watched the truck as it rumbled past her. It turned into Pine Street and vanished.

Freud's quip came to the doctor's mind: "Sometimes a cigar is just a cigar." She shrugged her shoulders. "Sometimes a coincidence is just a coincidence," she said to herself. "What the hell are you doing in the middle of Macon, Georgia, trailing a poor old man?"

She felt very stupid.

She walked slowly to the hotel, wondering what made normal people do stupid things. She freshened up and changed her clothes. She called her mother and told her she was doing some research related to her work; it was true. She had plenty of time to walk down the three floors to the restaurant in the basement at a leisure pace and was seated at a table just after one-thirty. She was on her second coffee when the count entered the room.

"Sorry I'm late," said the count contritely. "Ushers must stay after mass is ended to count the collection monies."

"It's perfectly all right," she said. "Besides, I knew where you were."

She pointed to her cup of coffee. "I started without you."

"I was a bit surprised to see you in church. You're a good Catholic, I see. It is not usual for doctors to be practicing Catholics, or to be devoted to any religion for that matter."

"Not really. That was the previous generation, when they thought that science had all the answers."

"I believe," said the count with the insinuation of a smile, "that even atheists should be compelled to stand up for one hour in one place once a week, doing nothing. They would be obligated to listen to their hearts' questions and exercise their brains by trying to answer them."

"I agree with you," she said with conviction. "Silence is a very precious commodity these days. Our senses are constantly inundated by outside stimuli."

"Unfortunately, or perhaps fortunately," the count said, "a time will come soon enough when all of us will have to turn to God for immediate help."

Strangely, the count's I-know-something-you-don't attitude did not elicit in Alfie the negative reaction that such a pedantic way of thinking usually did.

"I hope you don't think it presumptuous, my not being a scientist, but I must tell you something, Doctor, about science," the count went on after they had ordered their meals. "Science has created its own sophisms. Scientists have defined 'normalcy', and anything that does not fit into that framework they call 'abnormal' or 'paranormal', which for scientists are euphemisms for 'sick' and 'superstitious' respectively."

"You've, heard the word 'poltergeist', right?" the man continued. "Well, the first more or less coherent description of that phenomenon, the report that coined that name—German for "noisy ghost"—was about an incident that took place in the Castle of Slawensik in Upper Silesia. It went like this: Councilor Hahn, who was in the service of Prince Hohenlohe, was sent by the prince to investigate the mysterious happenings at the castle. My father knew Prince Hohenlohe—as a matter of fact, I met the prince myself—and my father talked to Councilor Hahn at length about the strange occurrences at the castle. The councilor was not a lunatic or a simpleton, my father confided to me; he was well educated and also a man of the faith. He described to my father in great detail what he himself had witnessed at the castle, and my father kept a detailed dairy of what he learned.

"My father and Councilor Hahn were the last visitors at Slawensik Castle. A few weeks after their visit, the castle was struck by lightning and burned to the ground. A skeleton was later found in the cemetery attached to the castle, outside its coffin, the cranium split and a sword lying beside it."

The doctor thought it was time for her to say something. "Amazing!" she exclaimed for lack of any more intelligent comment.

"My father's diary is still in my possession, I've read it many times, and that's why, since then, I've never looked at the paranormal with the same superciliousness as mainline scientists do. It is a pity that the organizations that engage in research of these phenomena have fallen into the hands of charlatans and publicity-seeking weirdoes. Take the circles in the fields in England—a hoax, a cheap hoax. And then you have the animal mutilations, probably true, but they go unresearched."

Although Dr. Santoro was not familiar with most of the "occurrences" the count was referring to, he was a skillful raconteur and managed to keep her interest. In fact, she never thought of discarding the bizarre stories as products of a deranged intellectual dilettante. After all, the reason that brought her to Macon in the first place was not your everyday happening. But she was a busy doctor. She admitted to herself that had it not been for the fact that she needed the count's assistance in sorting out her own set of bizarre events, she would never have sat still long enough to listen to the man's stories.

Their meals came, and still the count continued to talk. She eventually became fidgety, and at a certain moment she glanced furtively at her watch.

The count noticed it. "I'm digressing," he said apologetically. "Pardon me."

"I was wondering," Alfie started, thinking it would be an appropriate transition. "How did you first become involved with this Purple Cat...er..."—she searched for the right word—"er...affair?"

"Interesting question," said the count. "You heard of a Mr. Fallow, didn't you?"

"Yellow Fallow, Miss Lilly called him," she assented.

"They called him that because of his jaundice. Yet, in spite of his advanced cirrhosis, he outlived Dr. Miller by quite a few years. He died, eventually, of liver failure at University Hospital in Macon. Mr. Fallow was born in County Galway, Ireland. A good Catholic he was."

Miss Lilly's brogue reverberated in Alfie's ears when she heard that Yellow Fallow was an Irishman.

"Mr. Fallow had left detailed instructions for his final arrangements," the count went on. "His funeral services were held at St. Joseph's Church, the one you visited today. And, one must admit, nobody can throw a wake like an Irishman. At the wake, there were far more red eyes than wet ones. As is customary at this type of social event, stories about the deceased were exchanged. I was listening to Mr. Fallow's cousin spinning tales the deceased had related to him. The man, a car salesman in Atlanta, related to us one of the stories that his cousin had told many times. Mr. Fallow was convinced that Dr. Miller, the owner of the hospital in Irwinton where he was a patient, did not die of a fall in the back of the building as the coroner finally ruled, but that the doctor was mauled by some kind of beast that Fallow believed had fed on the afterbirth of a woman who had just delivered a baby—a Vietnamese girl, he said."

The count stopped to sip his tea. He continued, "I found that story quite engaging, so, after the funeral, I approached the gentleman to ask for more details. He was quite willing to relate to me what he had heard many times from his cousin. Mr. Fallow claimed that he had seen the animal that had attacked the doctor. He said it looked like a medium-sized opossum, mostly bald, with a dark bluish skin. Mr. Fallow believed that the animal had been in the delivery room for a long time because all the time while the woman was in there, the doors were closed. He believed that the creature had been feeding on the just delivered afterbirth when, suddenly, it lunged for the doctor's face. The doctor grabbed his face and ran out of the room screaming in pain. Mr. Fallow's cousin insisted that neither he nor his wife believed that weird story, because poor Jack, he said, had been a heavy drinker—a juicer, he called him—all of his life, and the alcohol had obviously begun to eat up his brain. But then the man threw in a disclaimer, as it were. He said that Jack had told many cock-and-bull stories, but this was the only one he repeated time and again, unchanged. 'Poor Jack, he was losing it,' was the last thing the man said."

The count stopped. He took another sip of tea and a bite of his grits. He studied Alfie's reaction. Then he continued, "I remember replying: 'Maybe not.' The man seemed surprised by my statement. 'Strange things do happen,' I added. Then we shook hands, and we parted."

The count interrupted his speech. He sliced a very small piece of sausage, upon which he carefully loaded some scrambled egg, then brought the fork to his mouth. He dabbed the corners of his mouth with the serviette and took another sip of the tea. Alfie was very impressed by the count's manners—which, she reasoned, were to be expected from an aristocrat—but even more by the extremely small amount of food he consumed. Towards the end of the meal, more than half of his food was still on the plate, and the buns and jams he had never touched.

"That intriguing story stuck in my mind," he went on, "and the more I thought about it, the more interested I became."

There was a short intermission, during which the doctor finished her three-egg omelet, four rashers of bacon and a cup of fruit. The count finished one sausage and half of a sparingly buttered piece of toast topped with a dab of strawberry jam.

"I must tell you certain things I think you should know about me," the count said, looking at her with a picaresque smile. "I will also tell you other things just because I enjoy telling them."

It is difficult to dislike a man who is willing to advance this fair warning.

"My father was one of the last of the nobility to leave Warsaw before the Nazis destroyed it. Besides the clothes he was wearing, he took two things with him: the flag you saw in my parlor that had flown over the Uniwesytet Warszawski; my father himself had hoisted it down. He also took the statue of Our Lady of Czestochowa that you saw there too. My father took that relic from the chapel where his parents and grandparents used to pray. He wrapped the flag around the statue and put them in a suitcase. He set out towards his hometown, Braniewo. A German patrol stopped him before he left Warsaw. They looked into the suitcase. 'Looting!' the corporal shouted at the soldiers. He was arrested and taken to the nearest military headquarters. My father knew all too well what the punishment for looting was. The commanding officer at the post said to him in German, 'Let's see what you are willing to give up your life for,' and he looked into the suitcase. He then examined my father's papers carefully. 'Herr Poniatowski. I know that name. You are a duke,' he said. 'A count,' my father replied. The officer, a young lieutenant, waved to the two guards to leave the room. My father stood at attention; the officer seemed to sink into deep thoughts. 'My grandmother,' he said finally in Kashub, which my father spoke quite well, 'prayed to the Madonna every day.' The officer kept looking at the statue absorbedly, almost in a trance, my father said; he then touched the feet of the Madonna with the tip of his fingers and crossed himself. 'Where are you heading to?' he asked my father. 'Braniewo,' he said. The officer sat down and wrote a safe conduct and affixed several stamps to it. He handed the paper and the suitcase to my father. 'Go with God,' he said. My father thanked him in German, in Polish and in Kashub as he was leaving, escorted by the guards. The lieutenant did not answer; he never heard him; he was in deep prayer. That's why I believe in miracles and in other occurrences capable of temporarily suspending the laws of nature."

The count replaced his eyeglasses, which he had removed during his story, and went on. "One afternoon, when I had some free time, I decided to pay a visit to the Macon Police Department archives to learn more about Dr. Miller's death. Imagine my surprise when I found that a laboratory courier had been killed in an accident the very next night. Now, I realize that two accidental deaths in such close proximity do not amount to much in Detroit, but here in Wilmington County, Georgia, it is an extremely rare occurrence. To further incense my interest, I realized that the two accidents shared something in common: The courier for La France Laboratories was carrying in his van the placenta that Mr. Fallow had forcefully stuffed into the freezer. I reviewed the coroner's report on Dr. Miller; it was quite terse and entirely irrelevant. Then I read the autopsy report on the courier. That one was very thorough and meticulous. It described multiple lesions on the victim's body involving loss of tissue—the result of bites from raccoons and crows and other predators, the examiner proposed. But the finding he thought most striking—and he mentioned it twice in his report—was the almost complete absence of blood found in the corpse. There was not even enough blood to run the usual tests. You can see that report too, if you wish."

He went on, "And even though the body was found lying on a large boulder, there were no blood stains on it or on any rock in the vicinity. The coroner proposed that perhaps the body had been dragged to this place from where it had been originally thrown.

"Then the report described a large tear on the man's shirt by the left shoulder, which coincided with a stab wound in his supraclavicular fossa that severed the subclavian artery. It was a deep, gnawing wound as if made by a hook. Now, the description of the blood and the dirt stains on the shirt was quite prolix. The clerk of the crime laboratory of the Georgia State Police, a Mr. Art Nichols, who wrote the scene of crime report, was a very smart young man. He went on to become district attorney and is now in Washington working for the Department of Justice. I talked to him a few years after the accident, when he was still district attorney. He never forgot that case, especially that puzzling find: a gash through the shirt into a major artery and almost no blood stains on the fabric surrounding the tear. He said he remembered it very well because he was never able to explain it and also because that day he learned a new forensic term: 'skip finding'. His boss, Tommy Matthews, a good old boy whom I knew too, explained to him what a 'skip finding' was: When one finding does not jibe with the rest, you skip it—because you don't have the time or the budget to pursue the matter and there are other jobs waiting and a deadline to file the report.

"So far, the case was interesting enough for me," the count went on after taking a few more sips of his tea. "I began to play with the idea that perhaps, what Miss Lilly and Mr. Fallow stuffed into the freezer was not a placenta but rather a raccoon or a woodchuck or some small animal of that sort. Or else, if it was indeed the placenta—and they both insisted it was—that attacked Dr. Miller, then it had to be a very unique specimen, one that had undergone some bizarre transformation and had acquired an independent life of its own.

"That idea remained in my head. Some years later, I learned of a professor at the University of Michigan who was recognized as the world's greatest authority on placentology. I called him to request his opinion about this notion of a placenta gone wild.

"Professor Belanger, as you know, is a fine chap, and he was kind enough to share a lot of his knowledge with me. He told me about a scholar in Vietnam who was conducting some research on these chimerical creatures that had been known in his country for centuries. Perhaps the fact that the woman who carried this placenta here also happened to be from Southeast Asia further incensed my curiosity. When Professor Belanger came to give a conference at Emory University, I attended it, and I talked to him at length over lunch.

"The professor from Vietnam—his name was Ta Huynh—was

always very careful to qualify his observations with the 'if it were proven to be true' disclaimer. The beast, to which he referred by the Vietnamese name, 'Con Mēo Tím'—the Cat Purple—he believed was a very primitive form biologically speaking, probably without a bony skeleton, its lungs extremely rudimentary because its oxygen was supplied by the blood it nourished on. He was told it had a suction organ at the end of a short proboscis similar to the ones on the tentacles of an octopus that could attach to another animal. He also mentioned a calcified claw-like structure nearby which, he assumed, could be used to carry out a venipuncture to which the suction cup would then be attached. The professor compared the creature, which was almost entirely composed of blood, to a jellyfish, ninety-nine percent of which is water. Since blood formed most of its body, the heart was also a very elementary two or three-chamber organ that only needed to gently swish the blood around to perfuse every tissue. From the observations of various witnesses, the professor proposed that it propelled itself with long jumps something like a jackrabbit. The creature was said to have long, muscular hind legs and stubby, undeveloped forelegs. He also conjectured that the Cat Purple had no reproductive system, since it was almost certainly a hybrid incapable of reproduction.

"Now, before I continue with Professor Ta Huynh's story," the count said, "let me interject here some other notions very apropos to this subject, which I learned from a young Scottish scientist working in Aberdeen. During a visit to his laboratory, he brought to my attention what obstetricians have known for centuries, what they refer to as placental anomalies. They are known by names exuding scientific affectation, such as 'placenta circumvalata', 'placenta succenturiata' and so on. I am sure you have learned these names during your training, and perhaps you have seen some of them. 'Succenturiate' is what the Scottish chap called 'mom and baby placenta'; it means that one or more cotyledons—the functional unit of a placenta—have separated from the main body and 'set up their own household' as he put it. The 'velamentous placenta', he postulated, was a forma frustra—a form not entirely developed—of some aquatic creature. 'Placenta circumvallata' was the expression of a placenta attempting to develop a shell.

"Actually," the count continued, "the man allowed me to touch a preserved specimen of the placenta circumvallata. I can assure you that the thickness and the consistency of the tissue surrounding the placenta resembled, to the touch at least, far more a shell in the making than the membranes of a conventional placenta.

"The fellow admitted, and so do I, that all these ideas are far-fetched, but he found it very strange that, of the great number of men of science who have studied abnormal placentas, nobody has ever advanced that possibility. True knots in the umbilical cord were attributed to the fetus doing somersaults, as were loops of the cord—sometimes four or five—around the neck of the fetus, without anyone ever considering the possibility that the placenta rather than the fetus was responsible."

If Alfie Santoro had come to see Count Poniatowski in search of support for her wayward hypothesis, what she was hearing was far more than she had bargained for. So much information so diametrically opposed to all her learned notions was not welcome any longer.

The count read the frazzled look on her face. "Pardon this digression," he said. "Back to Professor Ta Huynh. The professor mentioned in one of his letters a game that was often played by the children of the Kha people. The Kha people are part of the Hmong, indigenous mountain people in what it is now Laos. They have been subjugated for centuries by the Lao tribes. Probably Professor Ta Huynh was himself a Kha and had played the game as a child. 'Cat Purple chase' is played in the fields. A player is chosen to be the 'Cat Purple', and he chases the others. The one he catches becomes the next Cat Purple. As the chase takes place, they all sing:

'Cat Purple catches no mice,
Cat Purple feeds on blood.'

What the professor found especially notable was the fact that while the other children ran on hands and knees, the one that stood for the Cat Purple was supposed to run in a crouched position hopping on his flexed legs."

Dr. Santoro's jaw was beginning to drop in sheer amazement. "How did you learn all this, Milord?" she asked at last.

"Professor Ta Huynh was a zoologist educated in Bangkok, a professor of comparative anatomy at the University of Saigon. The professor sent several long letters to biologists in the USA and Germany describing his findings in great detail. He became very involved in the research of this unique biologic entity, the Cat Purple. In his last letter, he revealed that he was planning a fact-finding trip to the mountain where the Kha people lived to obtain more first-hand information about this creature. He referred to the Cat Purple as 'a unique, chimerical creature', probably an amphibian. He always admitted the possibility that it might have never existed except in the minds of simple folk. He also acknowledged that on his trip he ran a risk of being captured by the Khmer Rouge, who controlled most of that area."

"Did you actually see his letters, Milord?" the doctor asked, redirecting her gaze to the count's eyes from the faraway point on which it had been trained while she had been listening.

"The letters were written in Thai. I read copies of the translations. In the last letter, Professor Ta Huynh mentioned that he was mailing separately a very valuable and unique document he thought would be more appreciated and much safer in a medical school in the United States than in his wartorn country. The parcel contained a drawing by an unknown artist of a, quote, 'ferocious, blood-sucking beast as described by two Hmong midwives'. The professor believed that the artist was probably Cambodian or Laotian. You see, the Hmong people did not have a written language until very recently, in the twentieth century; before that, they passed on their knowledge by the 'pa'ndau'—or story cloth. A Hmong artist, possibly based on tales that were related to him, but more likely based on something that he himself had seen, because of the wealth of details, drew a picture of the Cat Purple. Professor Ta Huynh somehow got possession of it and performed an in-depth study of it. Combining his findings with other information to which he was privy, he developed that semi-scientific theory I just related to you."

An uncomfortable silence followed.

"There is something else that further worked to fuel my interest in this matter," the count went on. "In the early sixteenth century, somewhere in Warsaw, not far from my family's place, a very unusual incident took place. A woman and two children were found dead in a cellar where the children had been playing hide-and-go-seek. It was generally accepted that a basilisk killed them. A basilisk is a beast born of the mating of a cockatrice and a toad or some other bizarre interspecies mixing. The most outstanding attribute of the basilisk is its ability to kill with its gaze. At least, that is how the legend goes in Italy and other Western European countries. In the Slavic countries, it is believed—and this seems more logical to me—that the victim goes into some kind of hypnotic state and, while paralyzed, is poisoned by the basilisk's bite. The Warsaw story goes on that a condemned man agreed to face the monster. Dressed in a robe coated with mirrors, he descended to the cellar. The beast died on seeing its own reflection on the mirrors. Another version of the story, the one that circulated in my family, was that the woman who died in the incident sought shelter in the basement to birth a child that was widely known to be the product of sexual relations with her own father. That version of the story also suggested that the monster born of that incestuous mating killed the two children, who were not related to her and whom she probably did not see because they were hiding when she entered the cellar. How the woman herself died is not known, but it may have been due to a heart attack or due to complications from the birth. Now, the bishop did not believe that it would be in the best interest of the townsfolk to divulge this version of the incident, so he supported the story of the basilisk. I have seen some illustrations in old books of basilisks; they were depicted as very different beasts, some of them rather similar to what the Cambodian professor described. At times, they also resembled what in Scotland is called 'Baobhan-Sith', which translates into 'blood-sucking maiden fiend'. In Germany, they call this creature 'blutsauger'—blood sucker. It is my educated guess that all these share the same origin, a placenta gone awry."

"A fine theory," Alfie thought. "It makes my wild assumptions more credible." But her interest was now focused on the picture that the professor had sent to America. "Did the picture ever make it to this country?" she asked.

"It did, indeed. I'm positive."

"Have you seen the picture, Milord?"

The count shook his head.

"Do you know where that Vietnamese professor sent the picture?" insisted the doctor with a hint of impatience.

The count nodded. A mischievous smile flashed on his poker player face for a split second. He delayed the answer to further fuel the doctor's ill-concealed excitement.

"He mailed the picture to Professor Belanger, your friend in Ann Arbor."

An indefinable expression crept onto Alfie's face. Her mind was juggling contradictory thoughts. Was this another one of the count's tricks? Gaston, she remembered, had talked about a Professor Ta Huynh and the letters they exchanged, but he had never mentioned the drawing. Was Gaston willingly keeping this valuable piece of information from her?

"The drawing is now safely kept in the archives of the

University of Michigan and is only accessible to mainline scientists," the count continued. "I asked him many times if he would allow me to examine that unique piece of evidence. The professor always found reasons—excuses, I suppose—to deny my requests. I shall keep insisting until he accedes."

Alfie's mind was in turmoil. She decided that she could not digest much more information. Besides, she had to pack and drive seventy miles to the Atlanta airport. She thanked him profusely for his help and. promised to keep him informed of developments.

The count stood up, kissed her hand most courteously and walked away with a dashing flair. When he was a few feet from the table, he turned about in a theatrical stance and said to Alfie, "By the way, Doctor, do not trouble your busy brain unnecessarily over the pyramid show. The figures are metallicized, and I was holding powerful magnets between my fingers."

She shook her head. "You ought to be ashamed of yourself, Milord," she chided him with feigned indignation.

The count beamed on her a cherubic smile and left the restaurant with the grandiose deportment of a leading man exiting the stage.

Now it was her job to separate the wheat from the chaff.

CHAPTER XXVII

# The First Stage of Labor

etness between her legs awoke Diane from her afternoon nap. Actually, it was a harsh, smarting tightening of her belly that awoke her. Then she found the wetness between her legs. Another new experience—this had not happened in her first pregnancy.

"I'm bleeding," she thought in fear.

She looked under the sheets. It was a clear fluid coming out of her.

"My waters broke," she said aloud.

Quang, asleep in the bed beside her, did not stir.

"Or I peed in the bed," she added chuckling. The old matrons were right after all: Each pregnancy is different.

"This is it, Dào," she said to herself. "The baby is coming." She was a little alarmed because the due date was still three weeks away.

She got up, headed for the bathroom and took a quick shower. The suitcase with the clothes and other womanly stuff she thought she would need in the hospital had been ready for several days.

She placed a folded towel on a little bench to collect the fluid that was still trickling out; she sat on the towel in front of the mirror with her legs wide open to allow the amniotic fluid to flow. She brushed her hair purposefully and vigorously for a few minutes. She tried to keep the thought of the labor out of her mind by engaging in little ritualistic tasks: She wiped dry each of her toes over and over; she massaged her nipples vigorously as she applied the moisturizing cream; she rubbed "Mothers' Friend" on her abdomen with obstinate keenness.

Another contraction returned her mind to the immediate duty; she began to inhale and exhale rhythmically to the tempo her Lamaze instructor had taught her.

When the pain of the uterine contraction subsided, she waddled to the closet and took out the dress she had already selected to wear to the hospital. She rechecked her bag to be sure everything was there. She looked at the clock; it was only a few minutes after four. The schedule that Mai had given her, posted on the closet, read: "Saturday 1:00-3:00 History of Music. Baroque." Mai should be back in her room already.

She called the dorm. The house mother was quite exacting: No incoming calls until after five on Saturdays; could she call in a half-hour? The word "mother" did not move her. "Emergency" was the operative word, according to the woman, but Diane did not want to use it in order not to frighten Mai. The woman relented, though, when she heard the word "labor." She connected her with Mai's room.

"Mai, how are you?" Diane asked.

"Mom!" Mai yelled, surprised to hear her voice. Then she started a non-stop tirade describing in detail the events of the past week and the grades she was getting, the upcoming recital for which she was trying out as second violin, the wedding at which she had played in a trio—and Julian, the composition major she had just made friends with.

Diane listened for a long while. When another contraction commanded her full attention, she decided to interrupt Mai's animated account. "Listen, darling," she said, "I think the baby is coming."

Mai screamed.

"Yes, a little early, but it will be all right. Don't worry. As soon as I get your dad to wake up, we're going to the hospital."

Mai screamed again and passed the news to her roommate, who screamed too. "Love you, Mom," she said. "I think I can get out tomorrow. I think Julian's parents are coming to pick him up, and he said he'd give me a ride, or I'll take the bus. I don't have to be back till Wednesday. I'm going to see the baby."

"I have to go. Be careful, Mai," Diane said and hung up the receiver.

She sat at the side of the bed for a few minutes, looking at her husband and smiling. He enjoyed his Saturday "siesta".

When the next contraction struck, she shook Quang. "Let's go," she said. "The waters broke. Baby will be coming soon."

He protested, in his native language, that babies take a long time to come. "Get up," she said in English. "Let's go. The roads are bad."

He mumbled something and tried to go back to sleep.

"Quang, wake up," she insisted.

"You have plenty of time, Momma," he mumbled.

"Quang!" she screamed in his ear. "I can see the baby's head."

"What?" he said in English, bolting up.

"Come on," she giggled. "True, I can see it. Let's go."

The roads were bad. He tried to get onto the freeway, but the ramp was closed. The fifteen-mile trip, that should have taken twenty minutes, took almost two hours.

When Quang drove into the emergency entrance of Our Lady of Lourdes Hospital, the contractions were coming five minutes apart and were strong enough to make her moan.

The admitting clerk helped her to the wheelchair. "Who is your doctor?" the woman asked.

"Dr. Santoro," Diane said. She hoped that Dr. Santoro was on call that night.

"The Storks," said the admitting clerk.

Diane nodded and smiled.

"Dr. Irving is on call for the group today, and I know he is in the hospital."

CHAPTER XXVIII

# The Tenth Lunar Month

he Division of Histology and Cellular Pathology, which Professor Belanger headed, was inside the Department of Human Pathology at the University of Michigan in Ann Arbor. His office was in the center of a maze of laboratories with animal cages stacked on top of one another; small auditoriums and conference rooms; negative pressure enclosures; laminar flow rooms; corridors flanked by wall-to-wall freezers; and cubicles lined floor to ceiling by file cabinets. Many doors flaunted intimidating signs: "No admission," "Level 5 Isolation," "Super Sterile," "Radioactive Material," "Admission by Dr. B pass only." Many men and women, some in blue lab coats, some in business shirts and ties, and others in scrub suits, scurried in and out of the different quarters carrying test tube trays, microscope slides, glass jars and clipboards, mainly clipboards. Through a small window in one of the doors, one could see figures in space suits in front of computer screens. It was a poorly kept secret that "Cell-path," as the division was known in the medical school, was conducting some classified research for the Department of Defense.

For a place involved in such sensitive research, the security was quite lax. Dr. Santoro, who had never been inside before, had no problems gaining access to the sanctum sanctorum of the unit: Professor Belanger's office. She was viciously angry with her friend, and she had traveled all the way to Ann Arbor to confront him. She had allowed her anger to fester through the Christmas season, punctuated by visits to her mother and other family members, a host of other medical complications and emergencies; and a dreary month of January marked by severe weather. Now, with Diane's delivery date only weeks away, the time had come to act. She could tell herself that she should not act in anger, but that anger showed no signs of abating, and Diane's baby could not wait much longer.

Her first inclination when she saw his name on a brass plate on the door was to march into the office and belch out to his face what she thought of him and his perfidious behavior.

She was about to open the door when she heard voices coming from inside—different tones, some quite muffled, others rather loud, interspersed with a short spot of silence now and again. Although she could not understand what was being said, it sounded as if several people were involved in a somewhat heated argument. The professor was obviously in a meeting; she thought it would be prudent to wait.

She was standing in a small room without windows, the antechamber to the professor's office. It was spartanly furnished with a small desk, a chair where a secretary should be sitting, and two low leather armchairs for visitors. She dropped her heavy body into one of the uncomfortable chairs, seething as she waited.

"How could he do this to me?" she kept repeating to herself. "He knows how involved I am in this and how much it would have helped me to know at least that such a drawing existed."

She remembered that he had volunteered some information—such as, Dr. Santos's ideas and the Vietnamese professor's research—as if to entice her with some tasty morsels but withhold the main course. It was outright cruel to hide from her the most important piece. Then, a thought, a memory rather, sprang forward in her head and recoiled immediately to the habitat of unpleasant memories. "Chancroid Charlotte" uttered the unwanted dweller of the mind's warrens. It stirred her a little, but she ignored it. She kept ruminating on her indignation at her friend's treachery.

"It is not as if it were a minor item that one can easily overlook," she kept repeating to herself. "Judas priest!" She almost said it aloud. "He hid from me, not a mere mention of the thing or an old wives' tale about what has kept me awake for weeks, but a picture! He has a goddamned picture of the thing, and he hides it from me."

She was determined to see that drawing if she had to squeeze his neck to get it; his balls actually came first to her mind.

If he had said, "I have other information, but I am not permitted to share it with you," it would have been different. As it was, there was no excuse. He knew a woman and her baby were at risk. He was a doctor before he was a goddamned highfalutin scientist, and the welfare of a patient should be above anything else.

Yet, in all honesty, she could not believe that he would have done it for selfish reasons. "He is a true friend. I'm sure of it," she rationalized.

"Chancroid Charlotte" sprang up in her mind again. This time the thought climbed into the conscious level. She had to push it back deliberately.

The office door opened. Professor Belanger stood inside the office and shook the hands of two elderly men. There were also two young men and a woman, all carrying large attaché cases. He shook hands perfunctorily with them as well. The quintet did not seem happy as they left.

If the professor had noticed Alfie during the farewell exchange with the group, his face did not acknowledge it, but as soon as the party had walked out of the antechamber, he directed at her a stern look.

"What brings you here unannounced, Sina?" he said.

"May I come in?" she asked, outsterning his look.

"You're already in," he said seriously.

She sat in front of the desk; he sat behind it. They locked glances.

After a short while, he said, "Yes?"

"You know why I'm here," she fired at him.

"If you're coming to visit with me, I'm happy to see you." He looked at his watch. "I might even buy you lunch."

"Why?" she said. She removed her glasses because she knew that the lenses diminished the penetration of her stare. "Why, Gaston, why didn't you tell me about the picture of Professor Ta Huynh? Why? Why?"

He thought for a moment. "The count told you about it?"

"It doesn't matter who told me. You knew all too well how involved I am in this...er...business. As a friend, even as a colleague, you had a moral obligation to tell me about it."

The professor cradled his head on the fingertips of both hands. He was silent for a few seconds. Then he said, "Perhaps it was a mistake, but I did it with your interest in mind."

She believed it. She looked at him, and her severe look slowly turned into the imploring gaze of a puppy about to be punished.

He would not say it, but she could read it on his forehead as if written in red ink: "Chancroid Charlotte."

"It was over ten years ago," she protested.

"What are you talking about?" His face betrayed his pretense of ignorance. He was not a good liar.

"I'm not a baby, Gaston," she affirmed as she had done many times before, but this time she herself was not quite convinced that she really meant it. "I know what was in your mind. I know you did it to protect me. Any other time, I would have appreciated it, but at this particular time it is more than my self-esteem that is at risk."

"You made a mountain out of a molehill. That time it was only an inside embarrassment, but now it could be much worse."

She stopped the quarreling and dropped her poise. "Gaston, please,"—she was conscious that at this moment she was begging—"tell me the truth. This business of the wild placenta, do you think it is all in my head? Do you think I'm going mad?" Her voice was acquiring some pathos.

"Of course not!" he exclaimed.

"Then, why...?"

He interrupted her and began to explain as he would to a preteen daughter. Oddly, this time Alfie welcomed his patronizing tone.

"Of course not," he repeated." Then he looked at his watch. "Wait, wait...Too late for lunch. I have a meeting at two and then a lecture. Meet me in the library at...say, five o'clock. *D'accord?*"

"Thank you, Gaston," she said, grabbing his hand.

"I know," he snickered. "I'll grow up to be a big dog."

They smiled. "God," she thought, her rage spent, "he knows how to pull my strings."

At four-thirty, Alfie was already in the library. Alfie loved books, and she enjoyed the sound of the silence in a library. The musty, mildly acrid smell of thousands of old books filled the large cathedral-like hall. She moved about, in and out of the rows of perfectly ordered volumes, stopping here and there to read some of the titles. She ran her fingers over their spines, every so often pulling one out to examine its cover and then replacing it ever so carefully. She took out an ancient atlas of the world and leafed through it. Finding a map of Canada, she discovered that Newfoundland was named "Terranova," and north of Toronto the map ended just above Moosonee. It was printed in 1890.

The indescribable gratification of toying with books, removing a volume from a shelf, fanning its pages, tarrying at a paragraph here and there, marveling at the quality of an illustration, searching for the first-printing date and place or for the author's bio or the publisher's name—it was all an acquired taste, reserved for hard core bibliophiles. Only the truly addicted would spend time admiring the fonts, examining the intriguing ancient grammar and seeking perversely for a "mackle" here and there that betrayed the wear of the offset cylinder or a "widow," as they called that annoying word standing by itself at the top of a page or a column. Alfie could have spent all afternoon there, all month too, in that scholarly form of loafing.

Professor Belanger arrived a little before five. He shook hands with Alfie and headed for a side door, with her trailing behind. It led into a small room. The woman at the desk welcomed him effusively, and they exchanged some pleasantries. She escorted them into the office of a senior librarian, the curator of special documents. The senior librarian was a lady with the grace and demeanor of a grand dame, which she probably was. She greeted them warmly. He introduced Alfie, and then they became involved in some trivial bantering.

"What kind of mischief are you cooking up now, Gaston?" the lady asked genially.

"This time, the troublemaker is my friend, Dr. Santoro."

"Look out for this man, Doctor," she said smiling.

"Tell me about it," Alfie mumbled.

The lady advised them that the document he had requested had already been pulled out and that Mr. Mahaffy, the assistant curator, would be waiting to take them to see it. She accompanied them through a back exit to the elevator and showed them into the car. She pressed the "Basement 2" button and told them with a smile, "When the door opens, the first thing you'll see will be Mr. Mahaffy. Good luck in your research."

The elevator descended the four levels slowly, noisily and with jerky movements. Mr. Mahaffy, as promised, was the first thing they saw when the door opened. Tall, slim, dressed in a very dark three-piece suit, with gold-rimmed round glasses perched at the end of an aquiline nose, he had the appearance and all the charm of a domesticated vulture. He stretched a cold hand. "I am Mr. Mahaffy, Assistant Curator for Special Documents," he said with the voice of a pubertal boy. "Professor Belanger," he bowed, "and who might this lady be?"

"Allow me to introduce Dr. Santoro, a medical doctor from Grosse Pointe," the professor said with a gravity that seemed put on for the situation. Alfie gave him a reproachful gaze.

"Pleased to meet you, Doctor. I trust that you have some kind of ID? It is required, you know."

She nodded.

"Walk this way, please." He started down a narrow hallway. Mr. Mahaffy walked with a pronounced limp. As they followed him, Gaston began to imitate the gait of Boris, Dr. Frankenstein's hunchbacked assistant. Alfie giggled and nudged him. The winding corridor ended in a long passageway with walls of bricks and mortar. The atmosphere of a catacomb became more noticeable, and the musty odor grew in intensity. The passageway opened into a long and rather narrow hall, very much like the nave of a large cathedral. The high ceiling was vaulted and supported by ornate cement columns. On either side of the hall, like the transepts in a church, there were several recesses six or seven feet deep. Each of these alcoves was furnished with a small table; on either side, a bench attached to the walls ran along the entire length. On the tables there were old library lamps with green shades, a small pile of paper labeled "acid-free," a large magnifying glass chained to the leg of the table, four leather bean-bags with the University of Michigan logo engraved on the top, and two boxes of latex surgical gloves. On the columns that separated the alcoves, plastic boxes displayed thermometers and hygrometers with printed paper strips that registered time, temperature and humidity. Overhead, hanging from the ceiling, was a complex network of sprinklers and fire alarms.

The intensity of the lighting in the hall was midway between that of a romantic lounge and a funeral parlor. Mr. Mahaffy hobbled along as Alfie and the professor followed him to their assigned alcove, which was the last in the hall. By then they were both involuntarily mimicking the man's limp. He motioned them to enter the alcove. A large plastic tube lay on the table. Mr. Mahaffy checked the label on the tube and compared the inventory number with the one on the requisition slip the professor was holding. Then he cross-checked the name of the item and asked for Professor Belanger's ID tag and Alfie's driver's license. He wrote their names and identification numbers in a large logbook that sat on a lectern in the main hall. He asked them to sign the log.

"Take your time," he said as he was leaving. Then he turned suddenly and added, "I'll be just down the corridor. Don't forget to wear the gloves. If you need anything, just press the buzzer."

"Press the buzzer for the buzzard," the professor whispered to Alfie. She giggled.

Before they had time to sit down, Mr. Mahaffy returned with more instructions. "Please, turn on the spot lights only when you really need them. These old documents are extremely photo-sensitive."

Alfie and Gaston smiled and sighed with relief.

But Mr. Mahaffy returned once more. "Remember," he said this time, "no pictures allowed."

They both nodded. When the man was out of hearing range, the professor said, raising his voice two octaves, "And play nice, children."

"Don't make fun of the man," Alfie chided him. "He's been a cave-dweller for decades."

"He looks as if he's been dead for decades."

Alfie sat down. The professor picked up the poster tube and removed the plastic lid. He put on a pair of the rubber gloves and with the utmost care pulled out a roll wrapped in tissue paper. The paper had adhered to the inner roll, the document itself; as he removed the thin layer of tissue paper, it tore many times, and small purple and brown pieces like

confetti fell from the cylinder. A rank smell, like that of de-
cayed flesh, began to saturate the tiny alcove. The professor
finally extricated the inner piece from its wrappings, placed it
on the table and proceeded to unroll it. The scroll measured
about two by three feet. Its borders were very irregular, with
multiple tears and indentations, some of which extended as
thin cracks over half the width of the sheet.

Professor Belanger flattened the document on the surface
of the table and with the same gentle motions placed the
beanbags on each of the comers to prevent it from curling
up. He turned on the four gooseneck lamps and trained their
beams on the document.

Now Alfie could contemplate the fruit of her persever-
ance—a rather thick parchment sheet, apparently a very old
sheepskin or goatskin. There was a single drawing on it that
extended almost to the edges of the sheet. On each of the four
corners there was writing—in Thai, according to the professor.
Parts of the writing were missing where the corners had broken
off, and the top part of the figure had also crumbled away.

The drawing was that of an ovoid-shaped figure. There were
many areas inside it still showing some caked purple coloring
that had peeled away from the rest; some of the purple flakes
floated in the air around the table and eventually settled on
the carpet.

The lines of the drawing and the inscriptions had been
scored into the parchment probably with a burin. The width
and depth of the lines were remarkably even and equal. The
artist, Alfie thought, was obviously a master of the craft.

The drawing, sort of a primitive art form, suggested at
first sight a side view of a fat cat. The long tail had several
knobby outcroppings and ended in ragged fringes. At the
opposite end of the figure, where the mouth should be,
there was a conical snout, the tip of which was the only
feature in the drawing that was not shown in full side view;
it was turned towards the observer and resembled the sucker

cup at the end of an octopus tentacle. Just above this snout, there was a spherical bulge crossed in the middle by a crease, suggestive more of the eye of a frog than that of a cat. The ears, pointed and erect, were the feature most suggestive of a feline.

The top of the figure had corroded away, and the shape of the back of the beast could only be inferred from the rest of the drawing.

"I got it, I got it. A mutant Chinese dragon!" exclaimed Alfie, trying to make light of her excitement.

"Not so, Sina," he replied. "This is it. This is what you have been looking for, the depiction by an unknown Siamese artist, circa 1825, of the infamous Cat Purple."

"There is a Purple Cat after all!" Dr. Santoro thought to herself. She was engrossed in the contemplation of the drawing, trying to make some sense of it.

The professor began to explain that the suction cup at the end of the snout was not really like the ones on an octopus's tentacles but very similar to the mouth of the sea lamprey. The lamprey uses it to attach itself to other fish; then it uses the teeth in its tongue to scrape holes in the victim's skin and feeds on its blood.

"Look here," he pointed to an area towards the rear of the figure. There were several curving lines with straight lines extending from the lower end of them, something like large question marks.

She could not make out what they represented.

"Look here now."

He pointed his finger to some lines at the base of what she thought was the head of the thing.

She shook her head. Still she did not see anything recognizable.

"Close your eyes now," he said, "while I cover part of the picture."

She obeyed. He covered most of the figure with a few

sheets of the white acid-free paper, leaving visible only one of the areas he had pointed out to her before.

"Now you can look," he said.

She opened her eyes. In a moment she exclaimed, "Judas priest! It looks exactly like the bottom half of a rabbit, or a kangaroo!"

He nodded. "Precisely," he said. "Powerful hind legs."

He then moved the sheets to frame the area at the bottom of the drawing towards the front, where the forelegs were.

"See this? You know my friend, Professor Manoogian?"

"The vet."

"A zoologist, young lady. When he saw it, he pointed out that they are identical to the limbs of an amphibian, the so-called mudpuppy or mud-skipper, which is basically a fish that can move on land; it is unique in its form of adaptation because it can breathe through the skin. He claimed that he could see in this drawing a membrane between the toes. I couldn't."

Then he moved the sheets about, to frame a small area by the supposed mouth.

"What does this look like to you?"

She had entirely overlooked this small detail, but when the distracting surroundings were blocked out, it stood unmistakably as a textbook drawing of a lobster claw.

Suddenly, the autopsy report of the laboratory courier came to her mind, as well as the count's comment about the deep puncture wound in the man's shoulder. Now it began to make sense. A shudder ran down her spine as she re-enacted the scene in her mind: the creature crawling out of the cooler in the back of the laboratory van, lunging for the driver's neck, his hands leaving the steering wheel in an instinctive reaction to protect his face, the van careening out of control as the claw ripped the poor devil's subclavian artery. She visualized the suction cup attaching to the skin and the blood being sucked out through the gash that the claw had made.

"That's why there were almost no bloodstains on his shirt!"

(The count had suspected this, she thought.) "Did the count ever see this drawing?" she asked.

"Not since it came to the U of M vaults."

She kept thinking about the perspicacity of the count. Her thoughts were interrupted by the professor.

"Now look at this, Sina," he said.

The artist had meticulously drawn the texture of the tail, and the engravings inside it formed an elegant pattern of lines bending and intertwining capriciously into some tuft towards the end.

"What do you say about that tail?" he asked engagingly.

"A new twist in the tail." She couldn't help it. The more stressed she was, the more she depended on silly jokes. Levity had always been a means to cover up deeper feelings of insecurity.

He ignored her gag. Then he moved the sheets again so as to cover most of the picture, leaving just a small window framing the tail.

"What does it remind you of?" he asked her.

Alfie moved about the table and tilted her head one way and the other, studying the drawing. Then she burst out: "Oh, my God!"

"What do you call that?" he drilled her as if she were a student.

"By George! A true knot on the cord!"

"By George! Quite bright, for someone who is not in academe."

She ignored the ribbing. She was stupefied. The artist had suggested even the semi-transparency of Wharton's gel that makes up the filling of the umbilical cord, and the engorgement of the vessels at the knot.

"It's incredible," she said, "for someone without advanced training in anatomy to picture it so accurately in the details."

The professor thought of Michelangelo and Da Vinci, and he saw another chance to pull her chain. "Of course, you believe that perfectly detailed anatomical drawing is the monopoly of the Italians."

She realized he was out to get her goat, and she would not fall for it. Besides, he was more fun in a jocular mood. Perhaps it was his release as well. The whole affair was serious enough.

"Did you ever have the writings translated?" she asked with unconcealed concern.

"Yes," he said. "Nothing exciting turned up. Two translators agreed on the date, the end of the first quarter of the nineteenth century." He explained that the writings on the corners of the drawing consisted only of a long-winded, subservient dedication of the drawing to some local chieftain, as was customary in those days.

"Sucking up is still in fashion," she interjected.

He smiled and continued. "It referred to the animal in the picture as a 'beast born of sin'—'offensive to the gods', according to another translator—that had caused much suffering to the people and which had been hunted down and destroyed by the artist's tribesmen. See here." He pointed.

"What the heck is it?" She concentrated on an area in the center of the drawing. It looked like an inverted U with one arm longer than the other and hooked to another U facing in the opposite direction. The shadows that the artist had drawn with meticulous precision suggested that this structure bulged on the side of the figure.

"Look carefully," the professor insisted. "Here." He pointed with his finger. There were a series of concentric lines forming incomplete circles around the two Us. "Professor Ta Huynh believed that the U-shaped figure depicted a beating heart, because he said that that was how artists represented motion on a drawing in those days."

They kept observing the area for a long time. Then she raised her eyes to meet his. She shook her head. "Do you believe…?"

He nodded.

"This is creepy," she said. "It can't be a coincidence."

"It could be," he said.

"You just wanted to see if I thought of it too, right?"

"Yes," he nodded. "If we both see it, it's less likely to be a coincidence, but it still could be."

Their thoughts were transported back to the days of Embryology and Comparative Anatomy in medical school. The drawing was a very suggestive depiction of a two or three-chamber heart, typical of reptiles and amphibians.

They looked at the drawing in silence for a while, in a pensive mood.

"This bright light can damage the picture," he said at last, as he turned off the lamps that shone on the sheepskin.

They both sat down in the twilight. The foreboding silence and the musty odor that pervaded the underground vault added to their presentiment that they were on the verge of violating some arcane mystery.

"I'm speechless," she said very softly, as the environs demanded.

"Let's talk it over at my place," he said in the same tone.

～ ～ ～

They rode in Old Faithful in silence the short distance to his house.

They sat down in the living room, and he brought out two Cokes.

Then he talked to her about well-known examples of mass hysteria: the witches of Salem, UFOs, the Loch Ness monster, spiritualist séances.

"Your point being," she interjected, "that just because several independent observers agree on the existence of something, it does not make it necessarily real."

He nodded, still in a pensive mood.

"The way I look at it, Sina," he finally said. "From a practical standpoint, we, you especially, have little to gain and a lot to lose in this game."

"That's correct. But you know, *mon ami*, that if it weren't for the fact that a patient of mine and her baby could be at a grave risk, I wouldn't give a row of pins for a Purple Cat, or a fuchsia ostrich or a burgundy koala bear. You know that." She injected quite a dose of drama into her statement.

"I know," he said under his breath.

"If this"—she searched for the right word—"preposterous conjecture of mine turned out to be true, and Diane or her baby were hurt as a result of it, I would never forgive myself for not having done enough to prevent it, only to avoid the risk of being exposed to ridicule."

In an attempt to encourage her to desist, he pointed out that even in that case, if the killer placenta actually surfaced, in all the stories he had heard, the creature had never attacked the mother or the baby.

"Yes, but as far as we know," she replied, "the creature always managed to break loose and crawl or jump or slither away to hunt for prey to feed on."

"What would it do," she went on, "if it were confined to an eighteen-by-eighteen-foot room? We know for a fact that the…thing wasn't particularly civil to Dr. Miller or to the laboratory courier."

He listened to her quietly.

"We have to accept that there is something odd going on," she said quite seriously now. "You yourself have taught me that if something looked like a duck, walked like a duck and quacked, it probably was a duck. If I had seen the drawing and I had heard Professor Ta Huynh's weird theories before meeting Diane, then you'd be right in suspecting that the power of suggestion had steered me into imagining things."

He kept shaking his head in silence.

"For Pete's sake, Gaston," exclaimed Alfie with obvious irritation now. "I'm not talking about a ghoul or a zombie.

It needn't be more than a low biological life form, a parasite. Think of it as a fungus that grew and grew to humongous size. We have seen it in diabetics or in patients with advanced cancer; when their defenses are low—an unpretentious fungus can spread wildly to line all of a poor devil's membranes." Now she began to gesticulate. "What's so fucking difficult to believe about this piece of live tissue growing wild?!"

There. She had said it. She remembered how a strategically placed expletive could work wonders to shake pig-headed people out of their hidebound ruts.

The professor raised both his arms, palms pointing forward. "Wait, wait, Sina. Bazaar time."

Bazaar time stirred memories in Alfie's mind. It was a sort of game they had played. After a heated discussion, after they both had beaten their side of the argument to death, they agreed to place all their wares on the carpet, and the real haggling would begin. It had worked for them to settle disputes. The only rule was that both parties must put down all their wares. Each item was bartered back and forth until both parties agreed on the value.

She put down the first item: Biologically speaking, the existence of a low form of life as she suggested could not be denied outright. It got her five dollars.

Then she placed Jules Verne on the carpet. "When he envisioned men going to the moon, the notion was preposterous. Today we know it is possible because it has been done." He bought it for $15.

"Take Pasteur, how long it took for science to reject the theory of spontaneous generation." He haggled that one down to $12.

"Pasteur's theory proved to be correct, and that's why you know his name today. But think of the alchemists who spent their lives looking for the philosopher's stone," he said, "the catalyst that turned any metal into gold and would make them rich and famous." The professor's item was very pricey. She agreed to buy it for $35.

"I don't seek fame or fortune in this matter," she clarified.

"That's not what I meant. Sina, one must always weigh in the possibility of failure. Suppose you are wrong. It's possible, isn't it?"

She nodded and looked him in the eye. "I know what you're thinking. You must put that one on the carpet too," she said seriously.

"Forget that. That one is only alive in your head."

"Uh-uh, it's one of the wares, and you must put it down to bargain in good faith."

He hesitated.

"Put it down. Chancroid Charlotte must be on the carpet!" she yelled.

"Very well," he said. He hesitated, searching for the right words to use, "I believed then, and I still believe today, that the whole thing was just a trifle."

"I was very sensitive then, you know."

"It happened a long time ago, and it does not have a high price tag today," he said. "You can have it for five dollars. It hurt you, and you made a mountain out of a molehill."

"This time is different."

"That's right," he agreed. 'It's not going to be the same. Think, Sina. If you blow the horn on this thing, what's going to happen?"

"God," thought Alfie, "he can reason circles around me."

"Let me tell you what will probably happen." This was the hundred-dollar item.

He painted a bleak scenario for her. If she blew the horn, he explained to her, first, she must pass her suspicions to Dr. D'Onofrio. Her wild hypothesis would only add to his concern that she was "different." There was no denying that she marched to a different drummer. He would discuss her concerns with the other members of the group, who would add fuel to his suspicions that she was…a little eccentric. The professor then pointed out that Dr. D'Onofrio was too wise to just brush her off because if something really happened and he had done nothing to prevent it, he would be in hot water. However, if nothing happened, he would keep the fiasco as a bargaining tool for when salary negotiations came up. At any rate, he would pass her theory on to the chief of staff and to the executive committee. Now, they could not take the chance of ignoring it either, not because they would buy the idea of a man-eating monster growing inside a patient's belly, but because if something were actually wrong with the pregnancy, they'd better be prepared for it or else. So, just to cover their asses, they would kick the matter up to the board. Then, Professor Belanger went on to explain, a placenta gone wild would be big news, and they wouldn't be able to prevent it from leaking to the media.

"Oh, boy," she thought. "Did he draw a picture of me standing in the center of all this jam!" That was not what she wanted. God! All she wanted was to gather some help to be prepared to prevent a catastrophe should her suspicions be right.

"I know you are doing it for the patient, but I'm your friend, and I must tell you how things are in real life," Gaston said.

He proceeded slowly now, including details and minutia more suitable for a grade school audience than for a colleague. If her suspicion proved to be correct—and that was far, far less than even odds—she would gain a few minutes of fame. But soon academia—Wayne State, University of Michigan and probably Harvard too—would move in and steal the show and the fame from her. University professors, himself included, would be interviewed by the media, and they would all say that, yes, they knew of some legends from faraway countries about similar incidents and that the phenomenon definitely warranted a serious scientific investigation…blah… blah…blah…Please send money for our research.

"I'm almost six feet tall. I can beat up the average guy." Alfie was mulling things over. "I have a medical degree, and I make a handsome income. I am about as helpless as a US Marine." The morose feeling had fully overtaken her. "And here I am, sitting like a cowering child welcoming guidance." Worse yet, she admitted, it was even possible that subconsciously she had come to Ann Arbor precisely for this kind of face slapping.

He looked at her helplessly. The Chancroid fiasco was indeed in his mind. He couldn't help it, and she read it. "Fuck Chancroid Charlotte," she said as if it were her battle cry. Charlotte's occupation made Alfie's expostulation a bit of pun, but its humor went unnoticed by both.

"Can't anything stop you?" he said dejectedly.

She shook her head.

"At least, think it over for a few days."

"I have procrastinated enough, Gaston. Her due date is less than a month away. If I'm going to do something, I'd better start soon."

"Just promise me that you will wait a couple of days. I'll see how I can help. I'll try to get some of the faculty involved, to try to deflect some of the flack you might take if things go wrong." It was he now who sounded as if he was begging.

She seemed to accept the compromise. "All right, I'll call you tomorrow, but please remember we can't wait too long."

*"Bonne chance*, Sina," he whispered as he squeezed her shoulder.

*"Merci, merci beaucoup!"* she said.

He leaned to kiss her on the cheek. She turned, and they kissed on the lips, puckered though.

"You still have a lot of explaining to do, Monsieur," she said, smiling.

She put on her coat and headed for the door. She stopped in the foyer. "Can I use your telephone?" she said. "I have a thirty-one-weeker with twins threatening to go into labor.

She's on ritodrine. I wonder how she's doing. I might have to stop to see her."

He drew the curtains of the large bay window in the living room. "Look." He pointed to the snow that had already piled above the boxwoods and kept coming down enthusiastically. "You'd better go straight home. That will take you a good while."

She went into the library to make the call. He stayed by the window, broodingly staring at the immaculately white expanse in front of his house. When she came out, her face was as white as the snow.

"She is in labor!" she exclaimed. She fished in her handbag for the car keys and dashed to the front door.

"Be careful, Sina," he said, placing his hand on her shoulder. "It's very slippery."

"Old Faithful can take it. I have fifteen bags of top soil in the trunk." She was already in the car when she finished her sentence.

"Drive slow!" he shouted as the heavy machine rocked back and forth a few times and fishtailed down the driveway and into the deserted street.

After the Checker's taillights were visible no more, Gaston stood at his front door immobile for a while. Then he raised his hand to his head and began to scratch it.

"A friend is the one who stays after everyone else leaves." That quote somehow popped up in his head. He went into the house, put on his heaviest topcoat and walked to the garage. He patted his Mercedes as he passed it by. "This job is not for you, buddy," he said to the roadster.

He got into his 1959 Land Rover. It was a fear-inspiring machine, with one headlight dead, the paint mostly worn away and the body dented and caked in mud. The spare tire on the hood and the brush-guards conjured up images of steep mounds, bogs, ravines, brash and bramble, adventures on the fringes of survival. It was the right vehicle for that kind of night.

It started after some coaxing. Gaston revved it up and shifted into gear. Shivering, he buttoned up the throatlatch of his macintosh. There was a loud clatter as the vehicle rolled over the snow piles in the driveway. It had enough momentum to roll into the icy street. As the Rover noisily lurched into the blinding blizzard, another quote came into his head: "Insanity can be contagious."

## CHAPTER XXIX

# Chancroid Charlotte

wo men, one white, one black, assisted Charlotte De Vries as she walked into the Emergency Room of Detroit Receiving Hospital. They partially dragged her by the armpits because she could not walk alone. She was obviously in pain. An orderly brought out a wheelchair and eased the woman into it. He wheeled her to one of the cubicles. When the registrar attempted to contact the men for information, they had already left the waiting room. She paged, "The relatives or friends of Charlotte De Vries please report to the front desk." No one answered, so, after a while, she approached the patient for the needed information. Miss de Vries gave her name, address and telephone number. When asked about next of kin, she said she had none in this country, which was not true.

"Who are those gentlemen that brought you in?" asked the registrar.

"Friends," whispered Charlotte.

"What are their names?" the registrar went on.

Charlotte shrugged her shoulders. The registrar could see that she was in severe pain, so she stopped the questioning.

Charlotte De Vries was first worked up by an intern. She

was shivering off and on, her temperature was 104.5, and her pain was in the lower abdomen, she told him. The intern told her he needed to do a pelvic examination. When the nurse lifted the blanket and removed the patient's underwear, the intern whistled aloud and exclaimed, "Holy shit!" He motioned to the nurse to cover her again.

"Call the Gyn resident," he said and proceeded to start an intravenous line. He ordered a strong opiate to ease her pain.

The resident came three-quarters of an hour later and brought along a medical student. The nurse led them to the cubicle where Charlotte lay, sleeping now. The resident performed a pelvic examination and pointed something out to the student. "Look," he said. "Pay attention to this. As the fingers touch the cervix, the pain is so severe that the patient pulls away and reaches as if to grab something in the ceiling."

That Charlotte did, and she screamed.

"Sorry, Charlotte," the resident said. "I won't do it again."

Then he said to the student, "That's the 'chandelier sign'. I suppose in the olden days they had chandeliers in the examining rooms." The sign was the hallmark of acute PID, pelvic inflammatory disease.

PID was such a common diagnosis in the ER at Detroit Receiving Hospital that interns routinely took care of it. This woman, however, had other signs that did not fit with the diagnosis of PID. She had multiple bulges in the left groin, some of them crowned by deep ulcerations covered by purulent excretions; some exhibited tracks, like tunnels, that also exuded green pus. That was the unusual finding that had prompted the intern's profanity and his calling for the resident.

The lumps and sores in Charlotte's groin became a cause célèbre at Detroit Receiving Hospital. They healed eventually in the patient but left long-lasting scars on Dr. Santoro's psyche.

Charlotte De Vries spent ten days in the hospital and walked out as good as new, to minister to the homesick sailors at Zug Island. During her ten days in the Staff Ward, poor

Charlotte showed her private parts to dozens of people, including staff physicians, interns, residents, nurses, technicians and curious employees of the hospital.

Fortunately for her, she was neither shy nor modest. Once she said to a timid intern, "It's all right. You can look. I do this for a living. But I usually get paid for it." The intern gazed at her, confused. Then he reached for his wallet. "No, sweetheart," she said, "you can look for free." She was a good sort. She described her occupation as "professional sex supplier," and she did not seem in the least ashamed of her job.

Countless biopsies, smears and cultures were taken of her sores. She did not undergo any major surgery, but she was subjected to a culdocentesis, a barbaric procedure, according to Dr. Santoro. For a culdecentesis, the patient was placed as for a routine gynecologic examination—lithotomy position, it was called. Under local anesthesia—"in cold blood," to quote Dr. Santoro—a needle at the end of a syringe was thrust behind the cervix into the most dependent part of the abdominal cavity, known as "the pouch of Douglas" or "the cul-de-sac". If pus was obtained by aspiration, it was sent to the laboratory to try to identify the germ, which would help in the choice of antibiotics to treat the infection. If red blood was obtained, it usually meant that there was some bleeding inside the abdominal cavity, perhaps due to a pregnancy in a Fallopian tube. (If the syringe filled with brown stuff, oops! The rectum was the next door neighbor.)

In the case of Charlotte De Vries, the diagnosis of PID was all too easy. The reason for the sores—Ahh! That was the question.

Charlotte lived with her mother in a modest but comfortable apartment in the city of Wyandotte, south of Detroit. She owned a nice automobile and a slew of minor amenities she could not have even dreamed of in her native Amsterdam. Her mother, almost sixty years old, every so often contributed to the household by rendering her services to a mostly younger and less affluent clientele.

Alfonsina Santoro was a senior resident when Charlotte De Vries was a patient at Receiving Hospital. She tended to her ulcers with zeal and kindness, and spent hours researching the possible diagnoses of the condition. She developed some kind of relationship with the woman and delayed asking a crucial question because somehow she suspected what the answer would be. One day, when Charlotte mentioned a client, the doctor thought it proper to ask what she did for a living.

"I'm a professional sex supplier," she answered without a hint of humor.

The doctor kept looking at her blankly, searching for an appropriate answer.

"You can say I'm a hooker, I suppose," said the woman, "but I prefer 'professional sex supplier'."

"Where do you...er...practice...your trade?" the doctor stammered.

"At Zug Island," she answered. "My clients are mostly merchant sailors from all over the world. A nice bunch of guys, just homesick."

The doctor sat motionless, staring at the woman, but her eyes were not focused on her; they pierced through her and converged on a point far, far beyond.

"I'm sorry if I shocked you, Doctor," Charlotte said apologetically.

"No, you didn't shock me. It is just that what you told me will help me a great deal to diagnose and treat your condition."

"Good, then." She smiled as the doctor turned and darted out of the ward.

That was when the idea of the possibility of some exotic venereal disease as the cause of Charlotte's ulcers popped up in Alfie's brain, and she started on an ill-fated crusade to diagnose it.

Friday night and all of Saturday Alfie spent in the library researching her working diagnosis. She left no book on infectious and venereal diseases unopened. By nightfall on

Saturday, she cracked a big smile. "By George, you've got it, Alfie."

Sunday night, as she was leaving her mother's house in Windsor after dinner, Alfie said to her, "Mamma, I got a diagnosis that nobody else has thought of. Now that we know what it is, we'll be able to cure her."

*"Brava ragazza!"*—good girl—exclaimed her mother.

She left her mother's house in Windsor, Canada, and headed north for Detroit. She crossed through the tunnel in an unusual state of euphoria.

The next morning, she was on her way to impress the chief resident with her diagnosis. Probably he was going to claim ownership of it, but she would get some of the credit. She ran into one of the junior residents in the parking lot; he was going home after a long weekend on duty. They exchanged some information about problem cases and the operating room schedule. As they were parting, Alfie asked about Charlotte. "Afebrile. The count is coming down," the young man said. "She's doing fine. By the way, Alfie, did you hear that Dr. Mayhew picked the case for the CPC?"

"No kidding?"

"No. What do you think of the ulcers? Got a diagnosis yet?"

"Mmmm…" She hesitated. "I'm working on it," she said finally. Now that the case was going for the CPC, she was not about to share what she had discovered.

"You're not going to tell me, are you?"

"No way. You do your own research," she joked. "Take care, Louie."

The CPC was in two days. She was lucky to have worked on the case already because there was no time to prepare any further.

The CPC, Clinical Pathology Conference, was the closest thing to the Olympic Games in a teaching hospital. It was the arena where the doctors displayed their knowledge and sagacity in public, and there were winners and losers.

The conference usually started with a junior house staff member presenting a clinical history to the audience and another one describing the findings of the physical examination. Then a senior resident would read the laboratory reports, display the radiograph films on the viewers and project on the screen EKGs and other graphics. If there had been a surgical procedure involved in the case, pictures of the operation and the particular specimens were also projected. The primary physician answered questions posed by the audience and supplied more information as it was requested.

At that time, the floor opened for anyone willing to get his/her feet wet. Diagnoses were advanced and evaluated against the clinical picture.

The pathologist had the final word. The slides from the specimens obtained during surgery or, more frequently, at the post-mortem examination were shown, and again the wisdom of the audience was put to the test.

A wrong diagnosis often resulted in mordant ribbing from colleagues. A correct guess could just as well secure a resident position for an intern. A few wrong guesses could also mean the non-renewal of a contract for a resident. The faculty would usually make comments and throw in some pearls but seldom participated in the guessing game. There was little to be gained for them; if the guess was wrong, it meant a major public embarrassment, and if it was correct, there would always be suspicion of inside information.

The CPC when Charlotte's case was discussed was, as these events go, a star-studded show. The chair of the department of Ob/Gyn was there, and many of the senior surgeons happened to be attending as well. Alfie thought it was her lucky day.

After the clinical picture was described and the hospital course reviewed, Dr. Mantega, the third-year resident, as always, stood up to ask for more information: presacral lymph node biopsies, liver function tests, stool cultures and sigmoidoscopy reports.

"Not done," said the presenter.

Dr. Mantega mumbled that without that information all diagnoses were just guesses. Some doctors would never have their fill of laboratory tests.

Dr. Ngamura suggested pelvic tuberculosis. Although it was almost unknown in this country, he had seen his share of it in his native Uganda. The cultures for the acid-fast bacillus had been negative, Dr. Santoro reported, but it was not completely ruled out.

Hydradenitis, an infection of the sweat or scent glands was thrown in by Susan Altman, an intern. She had seen a few of them in the office of her father, a dermatologist. The diagnosis drew quite a bit of support.

The chief resident, Mike Sterras, under pressure from the faculty, ventured a safe guess: "I am convinced that the patient has a thrombophlebitis of the pelvic vessels, and we are treating her accordingly, but I am unsure as to the origin of it." He added, "If I had to make a wager, I'd say it is from a GC infection from one of these new strains imported from Asia." The Vietnam strain of gonorrhea brought back by the troops was making inroads in America.

The formal entries dwindled. There remained some speculations, pronounced *sotto voce* by those not secure enough to make them public.

Dr. Mayhew, the chief pathologist, stood up, picked up his carousel tray with the slides and walked towards the podium.

This was the moment Dr. Santoro had been awaiting impatiently. She stood up and stated, "I would like to make a prediction. I have researched the subject thoroughly, and I'm now convinced that I know what the cultures are going to reveal."

Dr. Mayhew motioned her to go the podium.

"I know that cultures in fresh rabbit blood and in the patient's own serum," she went on, "were taken on specimens removed from the abscesses. *Bubos* would be the correct term for the infected lymph nodes."

There was a soft murmuring as the members of the audience repeated to one another the word "bubo." It was a term seldom used those days. It was applied to a particular form of abscess of the lymph nodes when they became softened by pus and they matted together; it was almost always associated with a sexually transmitted disease that no one in the audience had ever seen. They started to sift backwards through their memories: "What are bubos associated with?"

"I understand that what I'm referring to is an unknown entity in this country today, and so I also found it impossible to believe;" Alfie went on. Now was the time to add a touch of drama, as she had seen done on TV. "Impossible until I learned that the patient works as a prostitute at the Zug Island docks, where, as you know, ships from all nations bring their ore and steel. Our patient has had contacts with sailors from all over the world."

The murmuring increased in intensity. Most faces showed disagreement, and some confusion. Dr. Santoro, who had thought that this would be her triumphal moment, became a little ill at ease at the sight of so many shaking heads. She motioned to the intern at the projector to show the picture of Charlotte's groin.

Some doubt crept into her, but she knew that in that subject she had fresh knowledge, and more of it than all of her colleagues put together. She decided to stay the course, but she thought it prudent to trim her sails regarding the grandeur with which she had planned to deliver her bewildering diagnosis.

"Here you have it"—she aimed the light pointer to the sores—"the shallow, coalescing ulcers surrounded by phagedenic erosions in their ragged edges, the sinuses burrowing into the abscesses with softened centers, the bubos. I believe that right here we have all we need to make a clinical diagnosis.

So, I'm willing to speculate what the cultures grew—a gram negative bacillus, short and slim, stretching out in small chains or clusters."

She stopped for a moment to add some drama to her presentation. Looking at the chief pathologist, she said, "Dr. Mayhew, you grew 'Hemphilus ducreyi' in your cultures, didn't you?" Then she turned to the audience: "Our patient has Chancroid, a very unusual sexually transmitted disease, entirely unheard of in our community."

A soft murmur started in the quiet audience.

"How the hell did she think of that?"

"She must have a friend in the micro lab."

"I still don't buy it."

"I remember that bug was hard to grow."

"Right. It was mostly a clinical diagnosis."

When the hum of the audience began to die out, old Dr. Mayhew walked back to the podium. He stood there silently for a long while.

"Well," he said at last, "who else thinks it is Chancroid?"

Heads continued to swing side to side, the hushed comments surged again in intensity, but not a hand was raised.

Alone against the world, "the sweetest victory," Alfie thought.

Somehow she also began to contemplate the possibility of a king-size embarrassment.

"I believe we all must commend Alfie on her scholarly meticulous search for a diagnosis that would unify and explain all the elements of this very challenging case," said Dr. Mayhew.

Alfie's heart raced, and she reached a level of euphoria she had never experienced before. That blissful state was annihilated by the next word out of Dr. Mayhew's mouth: "Regrettably..."

"Regrettably," the old man repeated, "the final diagnosis is a far more mundane one. We only grew the garden variety of staphylococci, streptococci and Escherichia coli from the abscesses. The cervical cultures were positive for Neisseria gonorrhea. The tracks led to the femoral vein. Anyone want to get his feet wet now?"

Dr. Freddie Martin, an intern, raised his hand. He stood up and said, "Looks like she was mainlining in the femoral vein and got infected."

The residents looked at each other, and then all the eyes converged on Alfie. She stood up and countered, "I don't believe she is a user, at least not a mainliner. She has no needle marks anywhere."

The final diagnosis was "the usual," the commonplace gonorrhea PID plus the just as mundane infected needle punctures of drug addicts.

Alfie took the barbs from her fellow residents as stoically as she could.

At the end of the conference, as Alfie was picking up her papers, Freddy Martin approached her and said, "They looked to me like abscesses over needle pricks."

"She had no other tracks, nowhere. Why would she use the femoral vein if she had so many others available?"

"Some think that if the drug goes straight into the uterus and vagina, it can heighten the sexual pleasure," said the intern.

That was news to Alfie.

"They call it 'express to the shop'," Freddie said. "They don't teach that in med school." He winked at her.

Alfie believed him. Freddie was a reliable source in these matters. He had been a cop in Atlanta and a paramedic in Detroit before getting into medical school.

Before the auditorium was empty, the moniker had already been coined. Alfie heard for the first time what would remain a source of humiliation and grief long after all other memories of her training had dissipated. "Chancroid Charlotte," someone said, and someone else laughed.

Dr. Santoro went directly from the conference room to the inpatient floor. She entered the Gynecology Ward and marched towards Charlotte's bed. Her heels tapping the wooden floors resounded in the large room, causing all heads to turn. When she reached the bed, she pulled the curtain around it for privacy. She stood big and tall in front of the woman and blurted: "Express to the shop, huh?"

Charlotte hesitated for a second. Then she said contritely, "Just a little, and only a few times. Some clients insist on it." The woman was visibly perturbed.

"Why didn't you tell me?" Dr. Santoro said to the woman with a stern look on her face.

"You never asked me. I told you what I do for a living. If you asked, I was not going to lie, but I don't have to volunteer the information. Drugs can put you in prison."

Now, Alfie's shoulders sagged, and she stood crestfallen. Clinical Medicine for Schmucks—she remembered the cute little book that med students used to read: "If the test results don't jibe, take a history."

"You are right, Charlotte," she mumbled and smiled at the woman.

"Keep licking your wounds, Alfonsina," she said under her breath as she scurried out of the ward, noiselessly now.

Young people in general, classmates in particular, can be cruel and unforgiving with each other's mistakes. Alfie, at the end of her training, would still hear somebody call her "Chancroid Charlotte." Even later, at casual encounters, she was tormented by malicious colleagues, perhaps envious of her well-remunerated job, and by others who said it inno-cently, unaware of the pain it revived in her.

CHAPTER XXX

# Ann Arbor to Grosse Pointe on Ice

Sixty-some miles separated Ann Arbor from Grosse Pointe. Interstate 94, a four-lane highway, connected them in a mostly straight line running through the center of Detroit. The freeway—as it was called—had a speed limit of seventy mph; any speed below eighty would almost never spring a police radar trap. So, the trip between the two cities should take about three-quarters of an hour. A few times in the year it did, mostly in the fall and at some particular hour, usually late at night, when the Detroit Tigers, Red Wings and Wolverines were not playing.

In winter, the snow and ice did not permit the maximum speed, and as soon as the last flake of snow melted, the road repair crews moved in to tear up with almost religious zeal whatever portion of pavement had been spared by the ice. Orange cones and barricades sprouted all over the highway, and the road was reduced to two lanes or even one for long stretches. In places, the highway was closed entirely, and the traffic was detoured to the surface streets. Stop-and-go traffic, crawling, merging, exits and detours generated stress-related afflictions such as nervous ticks, ulcers, nail-biting and extreme cases of road rage.

The seasoned traveler of metropolitan Detroit would always allow one-and-a-half hours for the usual journey between the two cities; and that was realistic, weather permitting.

That was the road Alfie had to travel to get to her destination in a hurry. She left the professor's house in Ann Arbor Hills, the elegant enclave within the Angell neighborhood, heading for Our Lady of Lourdes Hospital. Nature was showcasing her most malevolent disposition. There was already a thick coat of fresh snow on Geddes Road, but State Street, the wide road that led to the highway, had already been salted.

"Home, James," Alfie proffered Queen Victoria's order aloud, for its uplifting effect, "and don't spare the horses." With just some skids at the stop signs, she made it to I-94 in a few minutes.

Alfie entered the freeway with the same "full speed ahead" attitude with which she undertook any enterprise. Interstate 94 had not been salted yet. A salt truck in the right lane was moving much slower than she was. In order to avoid it when she merged in, she veered to the middle lane, which was entirely empty. The rear end of her car, however, did not follow the path the front wheels were pointing; it continued in the same direction it was going. Old Faithful began a counterclockwise spin—one, two, two-and-a-quarter turns. She tried to stop the spin by yanking the steering wheel one way and then the other. After the first full turn, she realized that she had no control over the machine. She also noticed that an eighteen-wheeler was moving at a respectable speed in the right lane, precisely where the tail of her automobile was. She shifted into neutral, released the steering wheel and lifted her hands to the rear-view mirror. She gazed over her shoulder at the approaching truck, clutched the beads of her rosary and started to recite: "Hail Mary, Mother of God…"

The mammoth machine tooted its deafening horn and slowed down just enough to allow Old Faithful's tail to spin out of its lane. Alfie's Checker Marathon came to a stop facing the median guardrail, at a right angle to the traffic. But there was no traffic.

She raised her eyes and said, "Thank you, Mother." It was addressed to both.

She had plenty of time to back up, turn the front wheels eastward and start again very slowly until she managed to place her wheels in the tracks made by the previous vehicles. In a few miles, the terrifying near miss was forgotten, and her daring returned. She was again moving faster than the few other vehicles on the road. She began to overtake one and then another and another. To slow down, she threw the lever into neutral and let the weight do the braking. She reached forty-five mph, and it was smooth sailing as long as she did not have to use the brakes. The road was deserted. In the next dozen miles, she overtook only a handful of vehicles, mostly trucks, and was passed only by a fire truck with lights and siren on. There were cars and vans off the road every few yards. Some of them, parked on the shoulder waiting for fair weather, looked like large snow eggs. Others had plunged nose or tail first into the ditch. She saw no major accidents, though.

"You're speeding like a maniac to get to the hospital to protect whom?" she asked herself. The baby probably did not need protection; the Cat Purple, as far as she knew, had never attacked a baby. It made sense, she thought, since the fetus, genetically speaking, was an extension of itself. Of the mother, she was not so sure, although, at least theoretically, she was not at a great risk. Her urgency, she realized, was to avoid harm to the doctor and the nurses—and, she had to admit, to the creature itself.

"All right, Alfie," she went on. "Assume your suspicions prove to be correct. A bloodthirsty monster pops out of Diane's belly right in front of you. How are you going to protect them and yourself? Do you plan to shout at the beast and browbeat it into submission? *Scema!*"

"*Usa il cervello, figlia mia*"—use your brain, my child—her mother would say. Whatever means she had to use to fend off the beast's attack, the last thing she wanted to do was to destroy or even harm it. Her great hope was to capture it alive so it could be studied and thus prevent similar creatures from developing in the future, or, at least, find a way to contain their destructive powers. "Try to preserve the creature at all costs," she decided.

A net or a cage would be the ideal tools.

"For shame, Alfie," she teased herself. "Why don't you carry a cage or a fishing net on top of the dirt bags?"

Two or three adults should be able to contain a sixteen-inch creature, no matter how vicious, she reasoned.

A voice in her head challenged: "Did you ever see a cornered wolverine, Alfie?"

She was able to indulge in these ruminations because she had set Old Faithful in the trail of a heavy truck and she felt in control, mostly, as long as the truck did not slow down suddenly.

She had the nerve to take a hand off the wheel and reach for the glove compartment. It popped open after some struggling, and several objects rolled out of it, mostly candy bars and napkins. But there it was, and it gave Alfie a great deal of security to see her "billy-club-cum-light." She pushed the compartment closed again.

When she raised her sight to the road again, she saw the right turn signals of the truck in front of her begin to blink.

"Oh, shit," she said aloud. "Well, it was good while it lasted." She slowed down to change lanes. As she moved to the side of the truck, she saw, about a half-mile down the road, unfriendly flickering lights. It was a patrol car with its rainbow of strobe lights reflecting off the fresh snow. As she came closer, she saw that it was parked diagonally, pointing to the exit ramp, so as to block all traffic.

After some skidding and fishtailing, Alfie reluctantly brought Old Faithful to a full stop next to the officer, who was standing by the car waving a flashlight. The policeman motioned her towards the exit.

"Pardon me, Officer," she said quite softly, with her best smile. "I'm a doctor. I'm going to Our Lady of Lourdes Hospital in Grosse Pointe. It's a major emergency."

"Sorry, Doctor," the officer replied, brushing icicles off his mustache. "There's a snow emergency in effect, and the freeway is closed to all traffic but police and fire vehicles."

There are times in most people's lives, law-abiding citizens though they may be, when the law will temporarily lose most or all of its intimidating implications and it will be willfully ignored, consequences be damned, even at the risk of loss of life and limb. In the subject's mind, at that moment, the remote desired outcome overrules any other consideration and justifies the wantonness of the action.

Dr. Santoro was at that point.

"I'm sorry, too, Officer," she said as she backed up enough to turn the front of her car into the opening between the patrol car and the median, "but it's a big, big emergency, and it is MY emergency!"

"Stop, stop!" shouted the policeman. "You are disobeying an officer..."

"You should provide me an escort," she shouted back.

She stepped on the accelerator with all the weight of her leg. Old Faithful took off with the grace of an obese hippopotamus. *"Grazie, grazie, Zio Angelo,"* she said under her breath when she felt the machine grab onto the sleek pavement and pass unscathed between the patrol car and the guardrail.

Every fall, Uncle Angelo would load fifteen—not fourteen, not sixteen, but fifteen—forty-pound bags of topsoil into the trunk of Old Faithful. The next spring, he would unload them and spread them on the front and back lawns at her mother's house.

In her rearview mirror, Alfie saw the policeman struggling to get into the patrol car and start the pursuit. The next time she looked, the car, a few dozen feet down the freeway, was spinning wildly. Then she lost sight of it. She supposed that the officer had never been instructed on how to handle this type of situation. By now, he probably was calling the precinct to report her.

Old Faithful bowled along the icy road as poised as a Sherman tank. "Never underestimate the power of six hundred pounds of dirt on top of the traction axle," Zio Angelo had told her many times. "Bless you, bless you, Zio," she answered.

Confident of the dependability of her quarter-ton of ballast, Alfie pressed the gas pedal beyond safe speed. She was a woman on a mission, and the road was all hers. She suspected that the patrolman she had left behind had radioed to the one at the next exit.

Oakland Boulevard, the next exit, came up all too soon, before she had a chance to plan a strategy to elude the cops. But there was no blockade of patrol cars at that exit. Actually, she saw no sign of the police for the next several miles. When she was in downtown Detroit, at the I-75 interchange, a flashing red light appeared in her rearview mirror. It worried her a little, until she recognized it as an ambulance. She pulled to the side of the road to let it through.

The adrenalin rush provoked by these challenges somehow quelled her anxiety for what might be occurring at that moment in the delivery room. Her stake in the existence of the Purple Cat had unquestionably been raised; she was risking her life and had gotten into trouble with the law.

Yet, in her heart, she still hoped that all her suspicions would turn out to be wrong. Truly, she wished that she would run, soaked, scruffy and out of breath, into the maternity ward to be greeted by a healthy baby, a happy Diane and a sarcastic look from her partner—even if it meant for her to become the object of ridicule and merciless taunting. Again.

At the City Airport exit, she saw two patrol cars with lights flashing and drew up a battle plan. She would stop, and when they approached her, she'd gun Old Faithful. She thought she had a good chance of evading them. The encounter turned out to be easier than she had thought. She drove past alongside a salt truck, all but invisible to the cops. She took the pelting from the flying salt pellets for almost a half-mile—unnecessarily, because the patrol cars were tending to a rolled over van.

"Use your brain, my child. I told the cop I was going to Our Lady's Hospital," she suddenly remembered. "First thing he did was to radio the Harper Woods police where the exit to the hospital is. Of course, they'll be waiting for me on Allard Avenue."

She began to empathize with the criminal mind. She could now comprehend how it was possible that the incentive to the crime eventually ceased to be the loot but the sportive achievement of outsmarting the law enforcers. She realized that the game of eluding the cops while practicing controlled skidding with Old Faithful gave her an excitement she had not experienced in a long while.

She understood, however, that if she were stopped before she reached the delivery room, she had lost the game.

## CHAPTER XXXI

# Light at the End of a Tunnel

he's clamping up," said Dr. Irving aloud. He looked at the anesthetist with begging eyes. "Deeper, Sophie, deeper, please."

"But you want her to wake up eventually, don't you?" quipped Sophie.

The doctor's arm was inside Diane up to the elbow. His hand had climbed along the cord to its place of implantation in the placenta. He slid his fingers around it, searching for the cleavage plane that would allow him to separate it from its attachment to the walls of the womb.

"Is there another one?" Sophie asked with obvious apprehension.

"No, no," he said aloud, a little annoyed. "But...what... what the hell..."

"Oh, shit," Sophie shouted at that moment, entirely ignoring his answer. "Her BP is dropping. Leslie, get me some epi right away."

A sudden tightness gripped the doctor's wrist and forced him to release his hold on the placenta. The tightness soon became a painful cramp that extended along his arm. Dr. Irving had learned about that symptom in his cardiology classes in medical school. A troubling thought invaded him at that moment, a memory of his adolescent years. That recollection stood out in his mind more clearly than his cardiology lectures. His father, also an obstetrician, had had his first myocardial infarction in a delivery room, at the age of fifty-four.

"But you're only forty-five," he thought to himself, "you're athletic, and you don't smoke." He laughed in silence. "Shame on you," he chided himself. "The hypochondria of a freshman med student!"

Later on, when a sharp pain in the left shoulder made him tilt his head to that side and doubled him over, his thoughts went back to Dr. Irving Sr. The second myocardial infarction had killed him in the middle of a hysterectomy, at fifty-seven. The thought of calling a Code Blue for himself crossed his mind.

"Sophie, Sophie," he sighed. Sophie and Leslie were talking in the distance. He could not discern their faces, but by the tone of their voices he presumed it was a serious matter they were discussing. A lassitude began to overtake him, his legs lost the strength to support his body, and he slowly dropped to his knees, pulling at the drapes as he slid down. He saw the lights in the room dim, except for the overhead surgical lamp. He saw the delivery table turn sideways first, then topsy-turvy. The brass crucifix and the large clock on the wall in front of him began to spin, and the overhead light receded at a great speed until it was no more than a brilliant spot at the end of a very dark tube, far, far away. He teetered for some time in the liminal world between life and else. Eventually the distant blinding light also faded into darkness, and everything around him was no more.

## CHAPTER XXXII

# The Third Stage of Labor

Sergeant Browne of the Harper Woods Police Department walked into the Emergency Room staff lounge. He poured himself a cup of coffee from the hot urn and took a half of a glazed doughnut from the open box. Lisa, the head nurse, hurried to greet him.

"Hi, Constable," she said. "Don't tell me there's an inebriated teenager driving around tonight."

There had been, traditionally, a warm relationship between docs, cops and nurses in any hospital. It was particularly so with the Emergency Room staff because they saw each other often under stressful circumstances and mutual cooperation could make each other's lives a lot easier.

"No, not the usual drunk tonight," he answered, his mouth still crowded with the doughnut. "Tell me. Is there a major emergency going on in the hospital tonight?"

"No. We just had one DOA, we admitted a kidney stone, we sent a croup to Peds, and we took two possible MIs to ICU," the young woman answered. MIs, myocardial infarcts, were very common in Our Lady's Emergency Ward because it was located in an area with a high concentration of older people. "Maybe they have an emergency in the OR, but I don't think so. Why?"

"Someone who claimed to be a doctor coming to Our Lady for a major emergency ran a road block on I-94, in Allen Park."

"Allen Park—where the hell is that?" Lisa asked.

"A small town on the west side. The officer reported her, and I'm supposed to find her and get a statement from her," said the sergeant. He seemed more interested in Lisa's anatomy than in his assignment.

"A she?" Lisa sounded surprised. She, too, was busy, assessing the sergeant's masculine attributes. "We only have a few female docs here."

"Then, maybe you can help me."

"What would one of our docs be doing in Allard Pike? Are they sure she was coming to Our Lady? What kind of car was she driving?"

"That's what they said. Hell, I don't know. It's Allen Park, though."

"How 'bout a cookie, sergeant?" she asked with a naughty smile.

"Can't now," he replied. "I'm on duty."

"A chocolate-chip cookie, you pervert."

"That kind of cookie is fine. Thank you." He picked up two cookies from the tray she was offering. Then he added, "Wait, wait. I got it here in the report. The car was an old...light-colored...heavy sedan; the guy could not tell the make."

"I think that Dr. Santoro has a car like that," Lisa said as she was leaving the room. "My break is over. I got to get back. She is the kind that would run a roadblock if she was in a hurry, but what would she be doing in Allard Park on a night like this?"

"It's Allen Park," the sergeant repeated. "What's the doctor's name?"

"San-to–ro," she said, "but you didn't hear it from me."

"Are you working tomorrow?" he asked with his most genial smile as he jotted down the name: "Saint-te-low."

"Not tomorrow. Monday," Lisa yelled from the hallway.

"Buy you coffee, Monday," he said. His eyes were glued to Lisa's hips, which she purposely wiggled in a seductive way. She knew he'd be watching.

"Your treat," she said, waving at him.

Fred walked into the staff room. It was his break. "Hi, Sarge," he said and added, pointing to the sergeant's dripping jacket, "Still coming down, huh?"

"Fast and furious. How's it going, Fred?" the Sergeant responded.

Fred walked up to the cupboard. He took out a mug adorned with a large NRA emblem and a piece of adhesive tape with "Big Fred's. Keep your hands off" scribbled on it. He filled up the mug with coffee and sat down at the counter. The sergeant pushed the sugar bowl and the Cremora jar towards Fred.

Fred raised his hand as if to stop him. "Real men take their coffee black," he said smiling.

"Say, Fred," asked the officer, "do you know a doctor by the name of...."—he looked at his notebook—"Saint-te-low?"

"Uh-uh. I can tell you there's no doctor by that name at Our Lady."

"Are you sure?"

"You bet," the man replied. Fred was a nurse's aid, big and muscular like a bouncer—and a bouncer was sometimes needed in an emergency room. His passions were bodybuilding—he was a California Gold Gym grad, he bragged—and guns. Fred moved his stool closer to the sergeant and hurried to shift the conversation to his favorite subject. "You hear about the new nine mil Beretta is coming out with?"

"Yeah,"—the officer was also quite willing to change the conversation to the new subject—"but I don't think it's going to be all it's cracked up to be. The barrel's too short."

They went on on that topic. The sergeant loved guns too.

~ ~ ~

Dr. Santoro had just passed the Detroit City Airport exit. On top of her primary anxiety about the wayward placenta, a more immediate concern invaded her mind. How would she elude the police? If she were stopped, her chances of arriving on time for the delivery would be shot.

All the way from Ann Arbor, Dr. Santoro had had only a modicum of control over Old Faithful. A few times she had had to let it skid onto the shoulder to bring it to a stop. When she had been learning how drive with Zio Vito, he had taught her one of his secrets for driving on slippery roads. "A soon as you feel you're losing control," he had told her, "release the gas pedal and shift to neutral. That takes the traction off the wheels. Then you steer and brake very gingerly." It had worked for her before. That night, especially, it had helped her coax "the pregnant hippo"—that was another name she used for Old Faithful, because of the grace with which it moved—to go more or less where she pointed it.

Without any previous experience on the subject of law-breaking, Dr. Santoro had overestimated the magnitude of her infraction. She was really expecting a multitude of patrol cars filled with detectives and other officers ready to snap handcuffs on her. She was convinced that since they knew that she was going to Our Lady of Lourdes, they would be waiting for her in full force at the Allard Avenue exit, so she decided to leave the freeway at Moross Road, the seven mile exit, the one before Allard.

The service roads were in worse condition, if that was possible, than the freeway. She could feel mounds of snow and ice scraping the bottom of her car. She slid onto the right and then onto the left shoulder of the exit ramp. She deliberately did not stop at the Moross traffic light because she knew she would have trouble starting again. The next light, Mack Av-enue, was blinking yellow. She went through the intersection with a little fishtailing. There were no other vehicles on the road. This was indeed the blizzard the TV had been forecasting all week. The streets had been cleared of parked cars for the snow emergency, and that at least saved her from running into other vehicles.

Half a mile down Moross, she turned north into Chalfonte. Old Faithful settled into the deep tracks, its wheels spun wildly, and she had to rock it a few times to convince it to move on. Chalfonte was a narrow road that wound about the Country Club of Detroit. She had chosen it because she thought she would be less likely to run into the police there and also because that road was usually one of the first ones to have the snow removed. Next, with a certain amount of effort, she enticed Old Faithful to turn east onto Cook Road. Driving along the grounds of the Grosse Pointe Hunt Club, she saw that the stables were dark and lifeless but the parking lot was almost full and the clubhouse was aglow; the members would not hear of mother nature interfering with their Saturday night partying.

Her mother's repeated advice came to Alfie's mind, how many times she had told her, "You should join the Hunt Club." "I don't like horses," Alfie had replied every time. "You just have to get on one, and look pitifully helpless," Mother had insisted. "A gentleman will soon come to the rescue—and, you know, mostly rich people own horses." Poor Mamma, Alfie thought; she did not understand that the image of a damsel in distress did not apply to a two-hundred-pound, six-foot-tall woman.

Her driving, all the way from Ann Arbor, had been mainly instinctive because her mind was in the delivery room, still tormented by her fear that she had not adequately alerted the staff. "Be very, very careful," she kept repeating to herself. "Is that all one can say to forewarn somebody about a possible attack by a vicious creature?"

If she made it for the delivery, she was confident that she could fend off the creature and prevent it from harming any-one. This time she did not qualify her statement with "if I am correct in my suspicions" as she usually did. That uncertainty had dissipated almost entirely after her recent conversation with Gaston Belanger. Now she had little doubt that some strange and hostile entity would emerge from Diane's belly after the baby was delivered.

That disturbing thought still hovering in her head, she passed the main entrance to the Hunt Club where Morn-ingside Road met Cook Road. She made the turn without slowing down, but still she did not have enough momentum to break through the snow piled at the intersection. The car settled comfortably in the waist-high mounds and refused to move on. Her anxiety made her feed it more gas than neces-sary, and the wheels burrowed deeper into the slush. As she rocked the car back and forth, the transmission whined, and Old Faithful trembled.

From where she was, she could see in the distance the Promised Land: the massive metal cross perched on the roof of Our Lady of Lourdes Hospital illuminated by four enormous converging floodlights. If push came to shove, she judged that she could always walk to the hospital from there, but it would take her over a half-hour. That and the memories of frostbitten fingers and noses she had seen in her early years in the ER gave her motivation to persevere in her attempts to get Old Faithful going. She shifted into first gear, touched the rosary beads on the rearview mirror with her fingers and crossed herself. Then she bent her head down like a charging bull and floored the accelerator. Old Faithful clattered, groaned and whimpered. It shook as in an epileptic fit and eventually started to advance along Morningside Road, sideswiping and fishtailing.

If her automobile ever deserved to be called "the pregnant hippo," it was then, because that was the image it projected, large and boxy, as it crawled out of the rut hesitantly and noisily, bobbing and pitching. Alfie, fearful of hurting its feelings, addressed it by its more genteel name. "Love you, Old Faithful," she said aloud. "You're the mightiest."

When the engine whirred in anger at the high revolutions, she eased it into second. Once it had picked up some momentum, propelled by the fifteen bags of dirt in its trunk, it became a formidable machine that sailed straight through the ice and the sludge smoothly and proudly, like a mother swan gliding across a serene lake. It was second gear all the way, although the motor sounded less than happy.

When Alfie looked up again, the steel cross was almost above her head. She released the gas pedal, and her heart did a quick somersault.

~ ~ ~

Any anesthesiologist would tell her that their practice consists of ninety-nine percent sheer boredom laced with one percent pure, unadulterated panic. And no amount of training or experience could ever prepare the practitioner for those unforeseeable and unpreventable ordeals that only occur once or twice in a lifetime.

Diane's blood pressure began to drop, from one-ten over seventy down to ninety over fifty, then to sixty over forty. The powerful intravenous injection of epinephrine that was expected to raise the blood pressure and improve its flow through the tissues had not worked.

"Get another line going," shouted Sophie.

They did not know that the epinephrine was not exerting its intended effect because it had never gone into the patient's circulation system but was lying in a puddle on the tile floor underneath her elbow. Diane's arms were comfortably covered by a warm, thick blanket. Under the blanket, unnoticed by the anesthetist or the nurse or the doctor, when she had had that spastic contraction; when her legs had closed on the doctor, she had also bent her forearm. The tip of the needle in the vein had pierced through the skin. Out of it the fluids and the medications that the anesthetist was injecting flowed freely onto the floor, and the puddle grew faster and faster as the rate of the infusion was increased.

"Leslie," commanded Sophie. "Get on the horn and get some help."

"I did already," she answered. "Nobody's coming. They have an abruptio bleeding out of control in the Section Room."

"Call the fucking OR. Then call the ER, Housekeeping, I don't care. We need help here, now!" Sophie's plea had acquired a pathetic tone.

"If I go out to call for help, I can't start the new line," Leslie said, looking up, irritated at the anesthetist. She stopped her attempt to start the intravenous line and looked Sophie square in the face. "Which one d'you want me to do first?" she said poignantly.

"Oh, shit!" Sophie blurted out, ignoring Leslie's remark. She turned off the halothane flow. "Sorry, Doc," she said. "I can't keep her down any longer. She's going into shock."

There was no answer. Sophie would rather he did not answer, but she did not greatly care what he would say. She really had no other options. She began to bag pure oxygen and checked on Leslie's chore. The line was running already, dripping at full speed.

Then, as if missing the doctor's reaction and feeling she should face it, Sophie looked between Diane's wide-spread legs. She saw Dr. Irving in a grotesque pose, his face barely above Diane's belly, his shoulder at the level of the vaginal introitus, his right hand clamped on Diane's left knee. The small portion of his face that was visible between the mask and the cap had a ghostly pallor, as white as his conjunctiva, which fully filled the opening of his eyelids. The gray pupils, those stunning gray pearls that had charmed Sophie to distraction, had vanished, rolled up under the upper lids. The furtive look that Sophie had stolen to beg forgiveness for her inability to keep the patient in a deep plane of unconsciousness, lingered on his terrifying countenance.

"Doctor, what's the matter?" she screamed.

At that very moment, the doctor's hand released its grip on Diane's knee and slid down her thigh. His head bent backwards like a puppet's whose strings had snapped. His widely-opened pupil-less eyes pointed at the overhead lamp. His flaccid body slumped downwards, then to one side, pulling down the drapes on the Mayo stand and knocking down the placenta basin and the bucket at the foot of the table. His left hand remained in Diane's birth canal.

~ ~ ~

Fred and the sergeant had kept a spirited conversation going as they exchanged technical information on Berettas, Kalishnikoffs and M7s, and the new developments in the Vietnam War. During a lull in the conversation, Fred snapped, "Hey, Sarge, what kind of car was that doctor driving?"

The sergeant was taken aback. At first he did not understand what Fred was referring to. In his mind, the doctor business had gone to rest. He was not very at ease with the idea of confronting a doctor for a questionable offense in a distant town. "Wait," he said finally, pulling the notebook from his side pocket. "The car was…er…a light-colored heavy sedan, it says here. Make not identified."

"What did you say the name of the doctor was?"

"Saint–te-low," the officer read slowly.

Fred tapped his forehead excitedly, "You mean Dr. Santoro. She has an old powder blue car. A Checker Marathon. Those taxicabs."

"You know her?" asked the officer, much less excited than Fred.

"Sure, she's a weirdo," he answered. "Actually, she might be here right now."

Fred bolted up out of his chair. "C'mon, Sarge. Let's go see." He started towards the hallway and waved to the sergeant to follow him.

He led the policeman to the glass windows that made up all of the front side of the corridor above waist level. Fred rubbed the condensation off one of the panes with his bare hands and tapped it to dislodge the snow and ice that clung to it on the outside. A small circle in the center of the pane became transparent enough for him to see through.

Fred shaded the sides of his face with his hands and looked into the doctors' parking lot, which was the closest one to the entrance and sheltered somewhat from the falling snow. "The white Lincoln is Dr. Irving's," he said, "the Caddy is Dr. Barnett's, the ER doc, and the red Cutlass is Dr. Puig's, the anesthesiologist. He turned towards the sergeant. "I don't think Dr. Santoro is in," he added wretchedly.

Sergeant Browne was not disappointed at all. "Thanks all the same, Fred," he said. "At least, we tried."

They walked back to the ER staff lounge. Fred refilled his mug, and the officer grabbed the remaining glazed doughnut. They were the only ones in the lounge now. They sat down in silence.

~ ~ ~

Dr. Santoro drove into the hospital's back parking lot much faster than would have been prudent. No cops were to be seen, and she breathed easier. "They are waiting for me at the Emergency Room entrance," she thought to herself. "Smart move to use the back entrance."

Old Faithful careened on the fresh snow and came to a stop against a bank of snow as high as its hood. It settled down askew under a lamppost. There were snow mounds strewn all over the lot; under them, all kinds of vehicles rested in peace, idly awaiting the resurrection after the storm.

Alfie opened the glove compartment after some struggling with the latch. She pulled out a flashlight with five size-D batteries housed in a steel tube with a little light bulb at one end; a friend had named it the "billy-club-cum-light." Swung by the muscular arm of a two-hundred-pound human being, it could become a formidable weapon.

She buttoned up her coat and jumped out of the car. She waded through the thick snow with big strides, head down to protect her nose under the lapels of her coat, arms outstretched to keep her balance. The wind kept blowing the wet snow onto her face.

After slipping and sliding for a few yards, she stopped abruptly, turned around and retraced her steps to the car. She struggled to open the passenger door sealed by the wet snow, which had melted and refrozen as ice. When it finally yielded, she bent down, one knee on the ground, and reached under the seat, fumbling for a while in that precarious stance. She finally withdrew her hand clutching a six-inch wooden handle.

When it was given to her, she had been reluctant to accept it.

"You drive alone, at night, in the tough side of town," Zio Vito had said. "It may come in handy some day."

Alfie had turned to her mother for approval. Mother had nodded: *"Che Dio ce ne libere"*—God forbid, you might need it some time.

That night, she thought she might need it and was a little surprised that it was still there after more than five years. She only had to apply a little pressure on a button at the side of the wooden handle and a six-inch pointed steel blade would spring out. Alfie had never opened it before. The light of the lamppost shone on it, giving the knife the look of a murderous weapon. She had to tweak it for a moment to release the lock; it folded at last, and she dropped it into her jacket pocket.

Now, intensely concentrating on keeping her balance, she headed again towards the building, at a faster pace to make up for the delay. She entered it through a door next to a ramp for delivering supplies. She ran upstairs to the second floor and accessed the Labor and Delivery Suite through the Newborn Nursery in the east wing. The lights were on in the Newborn Nursery, but the curtains were drawn on the newborn viewing window, which was normal for this time of the night. She experienced a mixed feeling of relief and embarrassment at finding everything normal.

Normal, except for the silence.

She walked into the women's locker room and grabbed an extra large scrub suit from the shelves. There was nothing unusual going on in there either.

Except for the silence.

She hurried into the OB call room. There was no one in it. All was in order, but she was surprised by the silence. The TV was off, and so was the radio; she missed the dissonant, ear-splitting sounds of the music that the young residents kept on all day.

Silence, one of the commodities she longed for most of the time, was beginning to exasperate her.

She threw her street clothes onto a bed, slipped into the white scrub outfit and put on her blood-stained OR shoes. She then tucked the bulky flashlight under the waist string of her pants and put the switchblade into the back pocket. Finally, she grabbed a surgical cap from her locker and went into the long corridor that led to the delivery rooms. Her footsteps echoed on the tiled walls.

Her heart was pounding.

It was indeed the wee hours of the morning, but this silence…

~ ~ ~

No sooner had they sat down again in the staff lounge than Fred cried out, "Wait, now that I think about it, sometimes she parks in the back. Let's go."

Sergeant Browne placed on a dish what was left of his doughnut and stood up rather reluctantly. Fred led him along the hallway, then around the Pathology Department and the Research Laboratory. They cut through the empty cafeteria heading for the back of the building. Fred was quite excited; to be an eyewitness to an event of this kind would make him the center of the conversation at The Crow Bar for weeks.

"They're going to lock her up?" he asked.

"I doubt it very much," replied the officer. "The guy in Allen Park did not even get her license number, he wasn't quite sure of the color or the make of the car, and he hasn't filed a formal report yet; he just radioed us. I think I'm just going to ask her for a statement."

"Well," mumbled Fred. "She ran a police block; that's a felony."

The officer ignored the remark. When they reached the Central Supply Room, Fred said, "There's a door to the back parking lot." They crossed the room between rows of trolleys stacked with surgical trays all wrapped in blue sterile sheets. There was not a soul in the Central Supply Room. They walked quickly and determinedly towards the back wall, the loud tapping of their footsteps muffled by the fabric that covered the sterile trays.

When they reached the door, Fred pushed it open with the heels of his hands.

"You look," he said. "I'll hold it open for you. If it closes, we're SOL. It's locked outside."

Sergeant Browne stepped out. The blustering, frigid wind hit him full force on the face. He was not very pleased with what he saw; probably he would have ignored it had it not been so conspicuous. Under the lamppost just a few yards from him, at the end of fresh tracks in the snow, stood the powder blue Checker, its checkered strip at the waist barely visible under crusted mud and ice.

"There she is," yelled Fred excitedly. "She just got here, you can tell. See the steam coming off the hood?"

"I see," said the sergeant. "You'll make a good detective."

Fred flashed an appreciative smile for the compliment. "She's probably upstairs in Delivery," he added.

"Thanks, Fred," said Sergeant Browne without any enthusiasm. "Can you take me there?"

"Sorry, Sarge, I can't go upstairs," said Fred, visibly disappointed, "but I'll show you how to get there by the west wing. She'll never expect you coming from that side."

The officer followed the burly nurse's aid, whose gait resembled that of a circus bear, to the rear stairway that, according to him, led to the second floor by the Laboratory. That was the west end of the corridor that led to the Labor and Delivery Suite. As the sergeant started to climb up, Fred said aloud, "Hey, Sarge, you know Lisa has the hots for you."

"She's a cute one," said the officer.

"You lucky dog," shouted Fred and cupped his hands on his chest as if grabbing very large imaginary bosoms.

~ ~ ~

"What's wrong, Dr. Irving?" shouted Leslie, stopping her chore. It was, of course, a rhetorical question. The doctor's stance left no doubt that there was a lot wrong.

Seldom does such a dramatic choice between duty and personal sentiment present itself to a human being. When it does, any prediction of the response becomes worthless. What would you do if a child you've been entrusted to watch over and one of your own children were both drowning and you could only save one? What would you do if your dying mother was calling you when your battalion gets its marching orders? What would you do if...?

Legend has it that, many years ago, a wise old guru presented to three of his acolytes a parable. He told them: "Suppose you are strolling in the woods and in your path you find a purse containing 10,000 rupees. What would you do?" The first disciple hastened to answer. "Master," he said, "I should run to the closest constabulary, and I should return it." The learned man struck the novice across the face. "You fool!" he said. "Shun this man." The second one answered by saying, "I should keep the rupees, Pukka Sahib, and distribute them among the poor." The sage slapped him across the face too, chiding him, "It is not your money, you thief! Shun this man." The third disciple remained quiet. "What would you do, my child?" the master entreated him. "I do not know, O Holy One," the last man responded. "I have never found 10,000 rupees." The guru pointed to him and said to the other novices, "He is a wise man. Follow him."

At the crossroads of duty and personal feelings pointing in opposite directions, all predictions are null and void, all bets are off.

Leslie noticed that the doctor, a co-worker, almost a friend, seemed in distress, but she felt that the patient in her charge was her first priority. She remained at Diane's side, searching for a vein into which to instill the fluids that would drive her out of the shock. When she finally succeeded in placing the needle in a vein in Diane's arm and saw the Ringer's Lactate solution run freely, she stopped to reassess the situation. "We can't handle this alone. I'd better go for help," she muttered under her breath and boomed out of the room.

Sophie looked at the situation from a different angle: A co-worker in major distress was as high a priority as her patient. The fact that the co-worker happened to be her lover did not enter into the decision; she honestly believed that. She increased the oxygen flow to the maximum, set the anesthetic gas to a minimum and turned on the breathing machine that freed her from the chore of manually squeezing the bag. She rushed to the foot of the table where Dr. Irving was lying. She knelt down and reached for his wrist. There was no palpable pulse.

She screamed, "Oh, my God!" then shouted to Leslie, "Get an IV going on the doc, right away."

Leslie was already running towards the Caesarean Section Room to beg for help.

"Doctor, Doctor, what's the matter?" shouted Sophie straight in his face.

She opened his eye; the conjunctiva was as white as the skin, and the pupil was widely dilated and fixed. Of course, she knew what that meant, but the meaning did not register because it was unacceptable. She yanked his mask off with one violent motion and began mouth-to-mouth resuscitation.

"Jon, darling, please talk to me," she said between the bouts of breathing. She did not care who heard it. "Darling, please don't die on me. Please."

Minutes before, when the doctor had advanced his arm into Diane's uterus along the umbilical cord, the placenta had wrapped around it and a sharp claw had dug deeply into it. That was when he thought about the heart attack. The suction cup at the end of the beast's snout had attached itself to the skin opening. The blood, propelled by the doctor's strong heart contractions, flowed freely from his large humeral artery into the beast's body. It sucked and sucked the vital fluid. When there was not enough blood left to supply the needed oxygen to its muscle, the heart stopped the pumping, and the parasite sucked the remainder of Dr. Irving's blood by its own power.

The residues of the beast's impromptu feast were eliminated as a gelatinous dark brown substance that adhered to the walls of Diane's birth canal, where it was still lodged. The creature's excrement eventually filled the cavity entirely and began to drip onto the floor between the doctor's feet. The doctor did not notice it, of course, because, earlier, when his heart had begun to lose strength, his brain had gone into hibernation, and his awareness, narrowed and dull by then, could only focus on the dark tunnel with the brilliant light at the end.

When the doctor's legs buckled and his knees touched the floor, the unctuous blood that had dripped from Diane's vagina began to cling to the doctor's white scrubs. Punctilious as he was about his appearance, the hideous stain—which was beginning to give off a nauseating acrid odor—would have been certain to have caused major consternation and wrath in the man, had he been capable of noticing it. As it was, by the time his knees hit the ground, the doctor was in what in his business would be referred to as the irreversible stage of hemorrhagic shock.

In fact, by the time Sophie made up her mind to abandon her post at the head of the table and rush to assist him, he was certifiably dead. Any nurse, especially a nurse anesthetist, should have been able to ascertain that fact; but emotions are notorious for obscuring critical judgment.

Sophie knelt next to the doctor; her scrub pants wallowing in the smelly puddle of the fresh blood and the beast's excrement, and she began to pound on his chest. One, two, three, four vigorous thumps and a hefty puff into his mouth. One, two, three, four thumps on the chest and another breath into his mouth. One, two, three, four...

Large, ponderous tears were flowing out of Sophie's eyes as she crouched on the floor next to her lover, engrossed in her futile resuscitation efforts.

Sophie was still concentrating on these efforts when the beast's proboscis emerged between the lips of Diane's opening. It slid along the doctor's hand that was then forcefully, with the strength of rigor mortis, clasping the drapes that surrounded Diane's perineum. As the creature slid down the doctor's arm, it still had the flat cake shape of a conventional placenta, although on its fetal side—the shiny surface that had faced the cavity where the baby developed—there were raised contours that a sagacious observer could have identified as rudimentary anatomical parts.

As the placenta started to separate from the arm on which it perched, the two edges of the lower surface—the maternal side, the side that had been attached to the uterine wall—dropped down and moved toward each other, as if it were folding along an imaginary longitudinal line. By the time the placenta had detached itself entirely from the doctor's lifeless arm on its descent to Sophie's shoulder, the metamorphosis had been completed. The dropping edges of the membranes came together, coalescing in a line where the belly was expected to be, thus forming a watertight body with one opening at the tip of the snout and one at the posterior end, which excreted the digested waste. The umbilical cord was still attached to the rest of the membranes inside the canal.

Had Dr. Santoro been in the room, she would have readily noticed that the creature had assumed an appearance very similar to the drawing that she had seen in the vaults of the library at the University of Michigan.

A violent convulsive motion of the rear of the beast tore off part of the umbilical cord, which then became its tail. Most of the secundines, the membranes that formed the sac inside of which the fetus grew, remained hidden in the birth canal; some ragged strips protruded outside incongruously like the fringes of a ripped sack. Blood, some fresh red, some a lifeless brown, flowed along the flimsy tendrils.

Unpredictable is human behavior under extreme stress.

When the Cat Purple made contact with Sophie's shoulder, she did not notice it; she continued her frantic pounding on the doctor's chest as her lips, sealed to his, blew air into his obliterated lungs. Every so often, she would shout aloud, "Help, somebody, help!" or "Please don't die on me, Jon."

When the Cat Purple sank its sharp claw into the soft flesh above Sophie's left collarbone, her only reaction to the assault was a swipe with her hand as if to shoo away a pestering fly.

The warm excretion of the digested blood streaked out of the rear of the beast onto Sophie's shirt and ran down to her pants. Her white outfit was gradually turning a muddy brown. As her life was being sucked away, her hands lost their strength, and she stopped the heart massage; she blew several more times into the now cold body of her lover, oblivious to her own pain and her increasing weakness. Eventually, her heart ran out of blood to pump. Her lithe body collapsed, and her lips separated from his as she slumped gradually on the floor next to the doctor. She lay on her back enveloped by the same stench of the rotting blood.

The automatic breathing machine to which Diane was connected kept inflating her lungs at an optimal seventeen-per-minute rate, and her blood remained optimally oxygenated. The light anesthetic was enough to keep her asleep now that there was no major stimulus.

~ ~ ~

The sound of her own heels hitting the tiles was all Alfie could hear, and, unconsciously perhaps, she tapped them harder and harder. It was comforting, like whistling by a graveyard. The delivery rooms were in the middle of a long corridor that ran east-to-west the length of the whole hospital. At one end was the Nursery, and at the other end the Laboratory.

She passed in front of the Labor and Delivery desk; it was deserted too. That was unusual, but definitely not alarming, because when they were very busy, the desk clerk was mobilized to fetch supplies or to take samples to the Laboratory.

Alfie glanced at the "board" as she rushed past it. The first patient logged was Dr. Youssef's. "CSR 1," it said, short for "Caesarean Section Room One." She did not read the patient's name, but "4 units + 2" was scribbled next to it—four units of blood ordered on top of the two already in the room. That spelled big trouble.

The next name she recognized: "Diane Truong, Dr. Irving." In the column where the status was recorded "DR 5" was chalked in.

"Dammit," she muttered and broke into a brisk jog.

She was passing in front of Delivery Room Two when she heard "God."

~ ~ ~

Leslie returned to Delivery Room Five from her fruitless efforts to gather some help; she was still alone and now very frightened.

The paper strip that flowed out of the EKG machine connected to Diane displayed a dull tracing: an ominous flat line.

"Oh, my God," Leslie shouted and repeated time and again Dr. Santoro's warning: "Be very, very careful." The words kept resounding in her head, and her conscience ignited a lifelong feeling of remorse for having neglected the advice.

There was blood on the floor, and there was blood on the walls, splatters of blood on the patient's blanket and on the sides of the bassinet. A few stands had remained upright as impassive witnesses to a macabre orgy. Blood was clinging to their rigid chrome tubes in long stylized streaks as the legs of a strong wine cling to the sides of a glass. The tables that had held the instruments were lying on their sides on the floor. The sheets that had been spread out to repel fluids were soaked in a dark brown fluid. Now and again, a drop of blood would slide out of Diane's birth canal and plink in the bucket on the floor between her legs. The smell of the dried essential tissue, sweet and pungent, permeated the room.

Leslie turned at once towards the Ohio Warmer. The baby seemed pink and content, breathing easily on his own, oblivious to the tragedy that was playing out around him.

Yet, Leslie had not captured the whole scene. The discovery

of the doctor and the nurse anesthetist on the floor topped the nightmarish picture.

The silvery gray hue of their skins was enough testimony to their status. Leslie stood at the side of the table paralyzed. A thunderous shrill sound began to build inside her, but halted in her throat. The terror generated by the sight of the lifeless bodies in the room of which she was in charge was soon replaced by an even more powerful feeling.

Only the instinct of self-preservation could upstage her horror at seeing such a scene of devastation, and a shadow had triggered it. The surgical lamp projected onto the far wall of the room the shadow of a nightmarish creature that was perched on Diane's belly.

~ ~ ~

Sergeant Browne was climbing very slowly the stairs to the second floor. He still did not know what he was supposed to do with the doctor. Without the license plate number, if she denied being there, the charge would not stick, and probably it would get his ass in trouble, he thought. Perhaps the best thing to do would be to tell her that a complaint had been filed against her and to report to the police station as soon as possible. Yes! That was what he would do.

He pushed open the heavy fireproof door of the second floor and walked in with trepidation. "Hell, a delivery room is just like an operating room," he thought. "What's the right thing to wear into a maternity area?"

"Police!" he shouted. ("Dammit," he thought. "This is Grosse Pointe. I'm actually out of my jurisdiction.") "Police," he repeated loudly. His voice bounced off the naked walls. There was no sign or sound of life. The vaults of a cemetery came to his mind; it was like looking into a long condemned building. A couple of carts parked by the walls and a hamper overflowing with surgical gowns suggested that he was indeed in a hospital, but the feeling everything else conveyed to him was that of an extinct infirmary in a ghost town.

He stood by the door for a while. On the wall in front of him. an unfriendly sign read, "Scrub suit, shoe covers and headwear required."

"Shit," he said aloud. "This is not covered in the procedural manual." He turned around. 'I'd better check with the lieutenant."

That's when he heard "God."

~ ~ ~

The shadow Leslie saw was that of an incongruous, yet definitely alive and evidently hostile, entity.

That shadow was the first thing Leslie saw when she raised her eyes from the bodies that lay next to each other on the floor in the viscous puddle of drying blood.

Leslie turned her eyes at once to the large, feline-like creature that cast the formidable shadow.

She saw its body under the spotlight; it was primarily aligned along the axis of Diane's body. Its snout was sweeping side to side in small arcs. When it sensed her presence, it moved so as to face her. The movements of its snout narrowed and focused on her. The tip of the stout proboscis did not seem to point to her face, though, but rather somewhere on her shoulder. The base of the beast's head, because it had no noticeable neck, began to swell and flare to the sides. As a result, the fearsome protruding eyes, which sat on either side of the head pointing laterally, were pushed into a frontal plane, and their gaze also seemed to converge somewhere on Leslie's shoulder or neck. The side-to-side motion of the snout suddenly turned into a paroxysmal up and down sort of vibration; the hind legs flexed even further, and the animal assumed the typical stance of a feline ready to spring for its prey.

Leslie realized that the cat's intended prey was her. If any-

thing can quickly clear a confused mind, it is the perception
of imminent personal doom. Without moving, she surveyed
her surroundings in search of any object that might help her
against the beast's looming onslaught. The Mayo stand, its
drapes on the floor where the doctor had dragged them in
his fall, stood bare near her. The removable stainless steel
tray was still sitting on top of the stand, and it was within
her reach. She grabbed it in a swift motion and placed it
as a combat shield between the attacker and her torso. The
powerful beam of the other surgical lamp at the head of the
table reflected on the shiny metal of the tray. She aimed the
reflected light at the beast's eyes. The creature, blinded by it,
shook its head violently and retreated from Diane's belly to
her upper torso.

Leslie soon noticed the effect that the light had. She realized that the mirror-like tray of the Mayo table was her
powerful—and only—weapon against the beast. She kept
the reflection aimed at its head. Now she could see it well.
Its skin, hairless, was the most striking feature; it was a deep
hue of purple, varying from ruddy to bluish as the light
reflected on it. The silhouette of the creature was that of a
very fat cat or an opossum. Feline-like ears stood on top of
the head and moved constantly. The eyes protruded and had
a reptilian slit for pupils, resembling more those of a toad
than a cat. The face ended in a trunk-like nose with a suction cup at its tip. She could see no mouth, but a claw-like
structure projected from under the snout.

Obviously impaired by the strong light, the cat protected
itself by pointing its eyes at the ceiling. Keeping its sight away
from its prey, however, reduced its ability to attack.

The woman and the cat stalked each other in silence. The
only sound in Delivery Room Five was the rhythmic draft of
air and the tap of the valves that the breathing machine generated as it blew oxygen and anesthetic gas into Diane's lungs.

Of course, Leslie never understood what the animal was,

how it had gained entrance to the delivery area or how Dr. Santoro could have known about it. She guessed that, somehow,
it had something to do with the two victims and she had no
doubts that she would be the next one. She kept the reflected
light aimed at the animal's face as she moved with small steps
towards the door that imprisoned her in close proximity with
that infernal creature. Her feet bumped a metal object. She stole
a quick look at it; it was a blade of a Piper forceps. The Piper
forceps was an instrument used in breech deliveries. Designed
to help extract the so-called "aftercoming head" when it did not
yield to traction, it consisted of two separate blades that locked
after being applied on the head of the baby. Each blade was
about two feet long with a long shank that flared at the business
end into a spoon-like shape intended to hug the fetal head.

One of these blades was lying among other instruments
strewn on the floor by the upturned tables. Leslie bent down
and swiftly picked it up without turning her sight away from
the creature. "Weapon number two," she thought to herself.
"A two-foot metal bar can be a very persuasive tool for a
twenty-inch creature."

She kept inching her way towards the gate to freedom.

The creature, propelled by its powerful hind legs, leaped
from the table to the top of the Ohio warmer. In the bassinet
underneath, the newborn would coo and whimper from time
to time.

Leslie gained a couple of feet towards the door as the creature jumped, but that changed her angle relative to the light
beam, and she could not aim it at the cat any longer.

Unencumbered now by the blinding reflection, the cat
jumped back onto the delivery table and landed on Diane's
chest. Its bulging, toady eyes converged on Leslie's face. A
spine-chilling sensation invaded the nurse, and she realized
in horror that she was either unwilling or unable to move.
Instinctively, she raised the tray to her eye level, to be in the
path of the beast's line of sight.

Below the tray Leslie could see the cat's hind legs shifting side to side, readying for the jump. As soon as the cat saw its reflection on the mirror-like surface, it froze, then recoiled a few inches. Below the tray, Leslie watched its belly swell up and engorge out of all proportion to the size of the creature. The next moment, a flood of fresh liquid hit the tray, and the parts of Leslie's face and chest that were not covered by the tray were bathed in the humor. The liquid felt thick, cold and oily; Leslie sensed it soaking her chest and dripping down over her eyes and cheeks. She dropped the tray. It hit the tile and bounced several times with a strident clatter, which seemed to go unnoticed by the creature.

Leslie immediately realized she could move her legs again; she was not paralyzed any longer, but she had lost her prime weapon. At the sight of the cat ready to attack, Leslie let out the scream that had been building up in her.

"G-O-O-O-O-D!"

The blood-congealing sound ricocheted a hundred times off the hard walls of Delivery Room Five and spilled into the corridors of the second floor, from the Newborn Nursery to the Laboratory.

Dr. Santoro at one end and Sergeant Browne at the other end of the long corridor heard "God" simultaneously.

Yet, the "God," as they heard it, did not sound like an invocation to a paternal god who tends his wayward sheep with infinite mercy. The "God" that Leslie's shriek evoked was the thundering Jehovah, the judge, of just but unforgiving retribution.

The beast's eyes locked on Leslie's, and she became unable, or unwilling perhaps, to look away again. The blade of the forceps that she had been wielding in the direction of the attacker seemed incongruous in her hand; her grip loosened, and her last weapon slipped away.

Her petrifying terror began to dissipate, and she thought it quite natural. Her instinct of self-preservation seemed to her out of place now, and it began to melt down. Soothing visions of endless cornfields gently waving in a breeze, or a calm sea perhaps, filled her senses. An inexpressible lassitude overcame her. Her arms fell to her sides, and she stood motionless against the wall by the double doors. She was not lifeless. She felt that she could resist and repel the onslaught; she just did not want to do it. She noticed ecstatically that she could project herself outside of her material body. It was an exhilarating feeling. She saw herself as the propitiatory victim. She relived in her mind the atavistic experience of the virgin awaiting the sacrifice of her own body in joyous anticipation. Her senses overflowed with visions of a high priest standing by a sacrificial pyre on a mountaintop, the aromas of the primal dirt and wild flowers, the archangels sounding the trumpets of her final liberation.

"There is a time to fight, and there is a time to surrender," she kept repeating to herself.

~ ~ ~

Dr. Santoro headed for Delivery Room Five with the same determination with which she normally approached any target, considerably increased this time by her heightened anxiety.

The heavy double doors—the ones with the "PUSH—DON'T PUSH" sign—swung halfway open from her vigorous shove.

The scene registered instantaneously in Dr. Santoro's mind. At the foot of the delivery table, she saw the immobile, rigid legs of Dr. Irving and Sophie. Flowing out of the EKG machine at the head of the table, the paper strip showed a flat line, and perched on Diane's chest was the creature of her nightmares.

Alfie pulled her "billy-club-cum-light" from her waist at once and began to swing it wildly between herself and the cat.

After the doors slammed shut behind her, her mind grasped the rest of the horrendous scene. Very close to her, on her right side, the doctor saw Leslie leaning against the angle formed by the side of the supplies cabinet and the wall, her right hand grasping the cabinet handle, her eyes half-open, gazing into empty space.

As if the noise made by the doors closing had been the cue Leslie's limp body was awaiting, it slid slowly down along the wall and collapsed on the ground quietly, rather gracefully.

The doctor looked at her. She seemed unhurt but incapable of moving. With a start, Alfie remembered the count's description of the hypnotic powers of the basilisk. Could those stories be true? She said, "It's all right, Leslie. I can handle this alone."

Still brandishing the sturdy flashlight in her left hand, Alfie moved forward towards the cat on the delivery table. As she did so, her hand slid against the switch, and the light came on. The cat suddenly retreated. It jumped down to the floor on the other side of the table. Its squat proboscis was sweeping violently side to side, and its eyes struggled to remain fixed on the doctor's while avoiding the swinging light. The cat backed up slowly and with calculated steps, retreating into the large open cabinet on the other side of the room. It stopped when its tail made contact with the back wall of the cabinet.

Alfie advanced swiftly towards the head of the table, "If I can shut the cabinet door on the cat, we'll have it alive," she thought. As she moved, her hand brushed Diane's face.

*"Dio benedetto!"* she uttered—"God be blessed!" The skin was warm.

Without stopping the swinging of the flashlight, she opened Diane's eye with her right hand. The light invaded the woman's retina, and the pupil contracted. Alfie lifted her eyes to see the wires of the EKG machine disconnected from the electrodes. That explained the flat line.

~ ~ ~

Sergeant Browne had followed his eyes and his ears to the site—the only room on that floor that seemed to contain life. He approached Delivery Room Five stealthily, walking up to the side door which opened next to the scrub sinks, the door the doctors habitually used to enter the room after scrubbing.

Sergeant Browne's concern was mainly with his being in a delivery room in the first place. He hoped that the cry of distress he unquestionably had heard, would be sufficient justification for his presence in this sterile, almost holy site.

The side door had a small glass pane at eye level. The sergeant peeked into the room. Diane's private parts, her legs widely spread apart on the stirrups, stared back at him.

"Full beaver," crossed his mind. "I don't think a male police officer should be seeing this." Frightened by the thought that he might have some explaining to do to the lieutenant, he backed off.

Catching a glimpse of blood on the walls as he moved his head back made him reconsider. He had heard his mother say that childbirth was a bloody affair and that his grandmother had bled to death after a delivery—but blood all over the walls? He looked in again, this time pressing his nose against the glass. Now the sergeant saw the upset tables, the instruments scattered all over the floor, two lifeless bodies lying in front of the delivery table and another one lying by the wall. Then he saw a large human form, all in white, madly swinging a club.

What a relief! Three corpses on the floor and the perpetrator still holding the lethal weapon. Now that was a police situation all right. Not only would that justify his presence in the delivery room, if he handled the situation properly—and it wouldn't be easy to botch it—it might very well mean a promotion. Sergeant Browne unfastened his gun holster, drew his pistol and released the safety. A clean arrest at gunpoint of a murderer caught in flagrante delicto, no violence, no fuss—the dreams of suburban police officers were made of this kind of stuff.

He stretched his right arm holding the weapon, rested the

barrel on his left arm and cocked the hammer. He crouched a little to reduce his target size, kicked the door in with all his might and stormed into the room screaming, "Freeze! Police!"

Alfie turned about to face the mouth of the pistol pointing at her eyes. Without slowing down the swinging motion of the flashlight, she pointed it at the creature. "Tell it to freeze, you moron," she shouted unapologetically.

The officer saw a dark object moving inside the cabinet. The situation was turning out to be more complex than he had anticipated. "Who killed these people?" he asked in an authoritarian tone.

"The kitty-cat did it," Alfie said, "but this one is still alive." She pointed at Leslie. "Keep the damn cat at bay while I shut off the anesthetic."

She stopped swinging the stick while she turned towards the anesthesia machine and turned off the halothane gas. The beast left the closet and began to jump over tables and stands, bouncing from corner to corner of the room. The image of a cornered wolverine returned to her mind.

"That's no cat," yelled Sergeant Browne. He was still holding his gun, pointing at the ceiling now.

"I don't know what the hell it is, but don't shoot it. We need it alive," she said. "Don't look at it either. If you have a flashlight, aim it at the eyes. Seems to be afraid of the light."

"Why not? And who are you?"

"I'm Dr. Santoro," Alfie said. "You can look at it if you don't mind being knocked out like this one." She pointed at Leslie still sprawled on the floor.

"And you can look at it?"

"I think it's the glasses. If we can get it back into the closet, we can lock it in."

At that moment, Diane moved her head and tried to lift her left arm.

"Don't move, Diane," Alfie shouted.

"My baby is all right?" Diane slurred.

"Your baby is fine. Don't move."

Leslie began to fidget.

"She is alive," said the officer, pointing at Leslie.

"She'll be fine," mumbled Alfie as she bent over Diane's face to release the gas mask, "but why the hell is no one coming to help?"

"Watch out!" shouted the sergeant. The cat surged up from the floor, aiming towards Alfie's neck. As it made contact with her shoulder, she turned and threw a full-strength punch at it. She missed the target, her feet slipped on the bloody floor, and she lost her balance. As she staggered, her eyeglasses slipped off, and she dropped the flashlight. The creature landed on the floor by the head of the table. It sat on its hind legs, facing the doctor. The doctor looked down at the beast, and their gazes locked.

They had been hard weeks for Alfie—sleepless nights, the fear of not doing enough, the fear of doing the wrong thing. An insidious notion struck her that, against all odds, her wild, outrageous premonition had turned out to be right. The result had been two deaths that should have been prevented.

There is just so much one can do.

For the first time in weeks, she felt at ease. Her anxiety began to yield to a pervasive feeling of primal comfort. At long last, she felt a lethargy that she welcomed. She experienced the soldier's relief at the end of a fierce battle, a passive serenity indifferent to which side had prevailed. Peace at last had prevailed over Alfie's obstinacy. She deserved it; she opened herself to it; she welcomed it. She felt the force of those penetrating eyes invading her restless soul, promising a path to a kingdom of bliss. To attempt to struggle against it seemed absurd. Peace was permeating her body and her soul, not an active peace, purchased, negotiated, strained by constant give and take, but a passive, effortless peace. Alfie's arms fell to her sides. Her hands, palms up, jutted forward a little as if reaching for a hand to lead her to that kingdom.

Peace.

Shalom.

Requiescat in pace.

~ ~ ~

The Cat Purple narrowed its aim. Its stout trunk pointed at the doctor's neck. The sergeant observed the situation with concern and confusion. The beast was definitely targeting the doctor's neck, and she was ignoring it. When the beast propelled itself towards the doctor, Sergeant Browne lifted his pistol. When the beast made contact with her neck, the officer yelled, "Stop, stop!" as he advanced towards it. When the beast attached itself to the doctor's neck, Sergeant Browne took aim; the mouth of the pistol was not quite a foot away from it. When he saw a red spot on the doctor's shirt, he squeezed the trigger.

The report reverberated in the room; it echoed forever.

The sound seemed to wake Dr. Santoro from her weird dream. Her eyes, without her glasses, tried in vain to set things in focus. She mumbled and blabbered for a while. Eventually she began to comprehend the situation. She realized that the incongruous mass on the floor, in the middle of a puddle of dried blood, was the remains of the fiendish, runaway placenta. Her anger crested at the sight of the elusive monster that she had longed to conquer and suppress, reduced to an amorphous heap of decomposing flesh.

She turned towards the sergeant. "You destroyed it, you moron," she yelled at him.

Sergeant Browne stared at her for a few seconds. He had had as much abuse as he could take from her. With the utmost disgust and contempt he said, "I saved your life, you ungrateful fat cow."

Dr. Santoro had at this time regained enough consciousness to fully realize what had happened. She looked at her scrub shirt and saw the bloodstained tear at the level of her collarbone. She turned her eyes to the sergeant and said with a contrite expression, "I am sorry. I do thank you."

~ ~ ~

"Are you Mr. Truong?" Alfie asked, pointing at him—although there were only two men in the "Heirport" and there was no doubt about which Diane's husband was.

Quang nodded and hurried up to her.

"Congratulations. You have a lovely little baby boy," she said with feigned alacrity.

"Diane all right?" Quang asked.

Alfie wound down. Her facade of excitement crumbled. "Yes, Diane's fine," she said. Her mind began to wander.

"You had troubles?" he asked.

"No, not really," she said unconvincingly. "We had just a few...small...technical problems. Diane will need some minor surgery, a small tear that we couldn't fix tonight. We'll do it tomorrow."

"You had troubles?" he repeated. This time it sounded more like a statement than a question.

Alfie's appearance bespoke trouble, anxiety, exhaustion.

"Tell him now, Alfonsina." It rang in her head like an order.

"Very difficult delivery," she said. "I don't think Diane should have any more babies." This was as close as she could get to revealing what she knew.

"No more!" he exclaimed. "One girl, one boy. Enough."

"Good idea," she said.

Alfie looked Quang in the eyes. Even under the subdued light of the "Heirport" she could discern the little punch-out defect at the edge of his right pupil. An iris coloboma, small and subtle, but unquestionably there, at the seven o'clock position, the same as Diane's.

Iris coloboma was the medical term for a round-shaped

defect in the pupil, as if a piece on the edge of the iris had been punched out. Dr. Santoro remembered that colobomas were transmitted as a recessive trait. That meant that the chances of two defects in the same place occurring in unrelated persons were statistically close to nonexistent.

"There'll be no better time. Tell him now, Alfonsina." Her pesky conscience again.

She could not hide her perturbation.

"You all right, Doctor?" He could sense her restlessness.

"He should know. It's the truth. I must tell him."

Big decision, little time, no help.

Words she had learned long ago pounded in her head: "Seek the truth. The truth will set you free," said the voice.

The very essence of her creed as a doctor, that she be open and frank with her patients, was put to the test at this moment.

"The truth will set you free all right, Alfonsina, but what will it do to Quang, and to Diane, and to Mai and the baby?" said another voice.

"Tomorrow you can consult with Monsignor Collucci or with Sister Redempta or with an ethicist or the chaplain. But in the end it will be your decision, Alfonsina."

"The truth will set you free."

"The truth can be a cop out."

Her face betrayed her. As this turmoil was playing out in Dr. Santoro's conscience, she froze in her stance, she turned sickly pale, and her eyes, looking above Quang's head, converged on the infinite.

"You all right, Doctor?" Quang asked again. "Sit down, Doctor."

"I'm all right, just a little tired."

"Big trouble with delivery?"

She did not answer.

"Con Mèo Tím?" he said.

She looked at him, surprised. She had heard those words. Professor Belanger had said them. They were Vietnamese for...

"Cat Purple?" Quang repeated in English.

Her father's words came to the rescue at the right time. What Gelsumino Santoro had said to her brother, those words that as a child she had thought were so wise, the quote she had translated and written on the back of Rebecca of Sunnybrook Farm, came back to her with the force of a divine revelation.

"When only you know the truth and the truth is too *'cativa'*—wicked—it is all right to keep it to yourself and do what must be done."

*"Grazie, Babbo"*—Thanks, Dad—she muttered, almost aloud.

The color came back to her cheeks, and she resumed her professional demeanor. She smiled and stretched her hand to him as if she had not heard his last words. "You'll see the baby very soon, Mr. Truong. Excuse me. They need me in the back."

She rushed out of the waiting room. Mr. Truong went back to his chair; he picked up a pink satchel with tassels and sequins that was lying on it. He sat down and held the sack with both hands on his lap.

"He's too smart not to have suspected it," she thought. She had not dispelled his doubt—but a doubt can never be as hurtful as a cativa truth.

"If he really wants to know," she reasoned, "if ever he feels ready to trade the suspicion for the truth, he'll manage to find out."

~ ~ ~

The switchboard operator called Sister Mary Redempta at the convent which was attached to the hospital to inform her of the happenings in the Labor and Delivery Suite. Within minutes, Sister Redempta entered Delivery Room Five in full religious attire: crown band, coif, scapular, veil, quimpe and tunic. Who knows? Perhaps it was true. Perhaps nuns slept in their habits.

The bodies were still there, untouched as the policeman had instructed. The nun did not ask what had happened. She stood silently by the corpses looking down at them. She crossed herself and said a short prayer for the deceased. Then she helped move Diane to a stretcher and gave instructions to transfer her to the Recovery Room on the third floor, in the Surgery Suite.

Sister Redempta, like all clerics of all religions—the people who deal in the business of eternity—had been trained to rein in her emotions as they related to secular affairs to the point of callousness.

Besides the prayers she articulated in front of the bodies, she said nothing.

Later, she called Leslie, the sergeant and Dr. Santoro one at a time to one of the other delivery rooms and asked them for details of the incident.

She told them that she herself would notify the next of kin.

Dr. Santoro seemed somehow to be involved in most of the unusual incidents that took place at Our Lady of Lourdes; so Sister Redempta was not surprised when she learned that Dr. Santoro was at the very center of "the incident in Delivery Room Five," the euphemism she concocted to refer to the tragedy.

When the nun asked Dr. Santoro if she had suspected anything during Mrs. Truong's pregnancy, the doctor said that she was just beginning to put together the pieces of the puzzle. "I know I should have done more," Alfie said. When the nun saw the tears welling up in Alfie's eyes, she looked away. It is very likely that the nun liked Dr. Santoro in spite of the doctor's propensity to create trouble, probably because she had often seen her in the chapel praying in earnest.

"You mustn't blame yourself, Doctor," Sister Redempta said. "There are things that we humans cannot understand, let alone prevent."

Sister asked the sergeant to wait for the Grosse Pointe police before allowing the bodies to be moved to the morgue, and she told him that she would talk to the police chief. When the nun was convinced that the situation was more or less under control, she left the Labor and Delivery Suite.

Sister Redempta walked to the chapel and knelt in front of the statue of Our Lady of Lourdes. She prayed for the souls of Dr. Irving and Sophie, for Dr. Santoro, who looked to her as if she needed prayers, and for herself too, for divine assistance in handling the aftermath of the calamity.

After she had finished the prayers, she called Monsignor Wyszynski at The Michigan Catholic, Pat Quinlan at the Detroit Free Press and Mr. Bernard Goldberg, the hospital lawyer. She got advice from each one of them. Basically they told her to "play up the positive" ("Mother and baby are fine") and "play down the negative" ("Suggest factors out of your control—a heart attack or placenta previa—explain each one, and state that a full investigation has started.") She jotted down some points, and in a few hours, after some more praying, she decided she was ready to face the media in the morning.

As it turned out, she never had to.

~ ~ ~

When Dr. Santoro left the room after her conference with Sister Redempta, she wandered aimlessly along the hallways of the maternity unit rehashing her remorse. She finally sat on the steps of the dark fire escape staircase to collect her thoughts. She kept holding back her tears with all the force she could still muster.

A heavy metal door with a small glass pane separated the stairs from the corridor of the Labor and Delivery Suite. Through that little window she saw the gurney that an orderly was pushing. On it was the body of Dr. Irving, or of Sophie perhaps. She could not tell which because it was entirely covered by a white sheet.

It was then that the floodgates opened. The tears that had been building for all those years since her father's death, the tears she had held at bay for hours that night, poured forth freely. Big, ponderous tears, as could be expected from a big woman, ran down profusely. Dr. Santoro, uninitiated in the womanly art of weeping—she did not even carry a handkerchief—was not able to control their flow. The tears rolled down her cheeks, smearing whatever of her makeup had survived the wild ride on the freeway and the tumult in Delivery Room Five.

For some time she fought to rein in the sobbing, but at last she yielded to that urge too. She sobbed aloud, in spastic fits, and when she thought all the tears had dried, she started again.

Just as it hadn't when she was eight years old, crying did not make her feel any better.

There were still tears and sobs when a coarse, heavy hand descended gently on her shoulder. Although she had not expected it, it did not elicit any self-protective reflex. A familiar voice then whispered in her ear, "There will always be things in the world that humans will not be able to prevent."

Alfie turned her head around. He planted a warm kiss on her wet forehead and said apologetically, "I'm sorry I'm late. The Rover broke down."

"Old Faithful didn't," she couldn't help quipping.

"Let's go," he said as he helped her up.

As they emerged into the white world outside, he pointed to the reddish glow insinuating itself over the distant Canadian coastline. Dawn was breaking.

"After all, Sina," he said with an ironic smile, "it is already another day."

# Epilogue

The ancient F4H touched down at Selfridge Air National Guard Base in Mt. Clemens, Michigan, before dawn. It bounced off the runway a few times before it settled down. The pilot applied the reverse thrust full force to bring it to a halt close to where he saw the car lights. Colonel Brian Ardmore, in full aviator costume, was the first to step out of the plane. He had been pulled from a peaceful sleep and flown from Denver to Michigan in this tin can that shook so hard he could not sleep a wink. His disposition was far from congenial.

"Welcome to Selfridge, sir," said the young woman.

"Where the hell is the C-133 with the toys?" he growled back at the dispatcher, who was the only one who had come to welcome him.

"They were over Grand Rapids last time I heard; they should be here soon," she answered. "Some hot coffee?"

She drove him in a canvas-topped Jeep to the officers' clubhouse. They were both shivering when they walked in.

"Where the hell is this goddamned hospital?"

"It's about thirty miles from here," she said. "If you want, I can put you in a chopper, but with all the stuff you're carrying and this weather, you'll be better off in a truck."

"You know this is all classified; we've never been here."

"I know," she said. Her beeper went off. "The C-133 must be asking for a wheel-up check. Excuse me."

Colonel Ardmore was left alone in an easy chair holding a lukewarm cup of coffee. He woke up when the dispatcher walked back in with the group from the cargo plane that was bringing the sophisticated equipment they needed.

"Hi, Brian. How's it going?" said Major Di Mario. "What is it this time?"

"Same one as in Lahore. But this one killed two." He added, "Do you have all the stuff?"

"Ralph is putting it in the truck."

"How's Molly doing?"

"Not too good. She has some spine metastasis."

"What a shame. I miss her. I still remember she saved our asses in Roswell."

"How can one forget? She was good."

"Is Ralph all right?"

"He's still got a lot to learn."

"But he knows how to get the stuff, right? And he's got Cosmic Clearance, right?"

"Sure."

"Listen. You talk to Sister Whatever. You're a Catholic. You speak her language."

"What's there to say?"

"Not much, really. Just tell her not to talk to the press under any circumstances, to give them our PR local number; they can handle it."

They both slept as they traveled along the snow-covered Jefferson Road.

They marched into the Emergency Room of Our Lady of Lourdes Hospital wielding their badges.

"US Army, PPRB," said the colonel to the ER doctor. "We're going to the delivery room."

The PPRB, Paranormal Phenomena Research Bureau, dealt

mainly with UFOs and other extraterrestrial claims. Colonel Ardmore was the chief of one of its branches, the BET, the Bestiary Encounter Team. The BET had recently been made a "Division" of the Bureau. It was not much of a "Division"; in fact, not counting the clerical staff, the whole "Division" was made up of nine people—five medical doctors, two veterinarians and two biologists. When some bizarre occurrence took place involving inexplicable animal behavior, they were summoned on short notice, and those available were flown to mostly exotic places. Recently they had been in Lahore, Pakistan; Lake Titicaca, Bolivia; Taiwan; the Amazon; a holler in West Virginia; and a kibutz in Israel. They did not seem to mind the travel; perhaps they even enjoyed it. The team had remained intact for twelve years, except for Dr. Maureen Lichmann, Molly, who had not gone out in over a year; she had breast cancer and was still getting chemotherapy.

When the group entered Delivery Room Five, they were pleased to see that the officer had set a perimeter and that the "object" had been covered with wet sponges, just as they had told him. They shook hands with Sergeant Browne, who was still in the room.

Technicians dressed in spacesuits moved in and scooped up the unrecognizable remnants of the wild placenta.

"Looks like shit," said the major.

"FUBAR. The yahoo shot it," whispered the colonel to the major while smiling at the police officer.

When they had finished their job of removing samples, Colonel Ardmore said aloud, "This is top secret. If you disseminate any information related to this incident, you will— and I don't mean "may"; I mean WILL—be prosecuted."

"Did you know that the woman is Vietnamese?" the sergeant whispered to the colonel. The colonel stared at the sergeant.

"Do you think the communists are behind this?" Sergeant Browne asked.

"You bet," the colonel answered, "but that's just between you and me."

The sergeant felt quite important to be included in a top secret piece of international intrigue.

As they were leaving the room, the colonel said to Major Di Mario, "The yahoo thinks the communists are behind this."

They both chuckled.

# About the Author

J C Di Musto obtained his MD degree at the age of twenty-two from the University of Buenos Aires, Argentina. He specialized in Obstetrics and Gynecology at Wayne State University and worked as a "delivery boy" in the metropolitan Detroit area for twenty years, delivering over five thousand bundles of joy. He chaired the Department of Obstetrics and Gynecology at St. Joseph's Mercy Macomb Hospital in Clinton Township and was President of the Macomb County Medical Society.

On his extensive travels in Europe and South America, J C D became fascinated by local legends of paranormal occurrences surrounding childbirth. Folk stories related to him by Laotian and Vietnamese patients and acquaintances further fueled his interest in the subject.

J C D has authored many articles on technical subjects in his specialty and on the practice of medicine in general. He also penned "The True Making of a Doctor" as a guest essayist for *MD Magazine* and "Reunion," an award-winning short thriller.

After finding babies quite inconsiderate about their arrival time, J C D restricted his practice to gynecologic surgery. He lives in Grosse Pointe, Michigan, with his wife Renée, and with HRC (His Royal Catness) Duxter I.

*Cat Purple in Grosse Pointe* is his first novel.